THE CIRCLE IS CLOSING IN.

I made my way out of the sun and back into the boat's cabin, and I heard Stellan's voice.

"Why don't you tell her anything? You can only keep her in a bubble for so long."

I stopped, holding the door so it wouldn't slam and give me away.

Something banged on the counter. "I'm keeping her safe." It was Jack. "You know what the Circle can do to people."

"I do. That's why you shouldn't keep things from her. Let her make her own decisions."

"I don't recall asking for your opinion."

"You used to." Stellan's voice was mock wistful. "Remember those days when we were in things together?"

"No." I heard the refrigerator close and footsteps recede.

"I'm just saying," Stellan called. "If you're not careful, she's going to realize she has other options. You see how they all look at her. It's not even just the eyes. She's so *little* and *pretty*. It's like blood in the water."

A cabinet door banged shut so loudly, I jumped.

"I said *they*," said Stellan, but it was obvious he was goading Jack on purpose. "This is just business for me. A business transaction with historically wide-reaching political, moral, and personal implications. The usual."

"Would you please stop talking?"

"Only saying you don't have to worry. Wide-eyed innocent isn't my type. I wouldn't touch your not-girlfriend." Stellan paused, and I could hear a grin in his voice when he said, "Unless she asked me to."

OTHER BOOKS YOU MAY ENJOY

MAP *of* FATES

MAGGIE HALL

speak

SPEAK

An imprint of Penguin Random House LLC

375 Hudson Street

New York, New York 10014

First published in the United States of America by G. P. Putnam's Sons,
an imprint of Penguin Random House LLC, 2016
Published by Speak, an imprint of Penguin Random House LLC, 2017

THE LIBRARY OF CONGRESS HAS CATALOGED THE G. P. PUTNAM'S SONS EDITION AS FOLLOWS:

Names: Hall, Maggie, 1982– author.

Title: Map of fates / Maggie Hall.

Description: New York, NY : G.P. Putnam's Sons Books for Young Readers, 2016.

Summary: "Heiress to the powerful secret society known as the Circle, Avery West crosses continents following a trail of clues she hopes will lead to Alexander the Great's Tomb—and the earth shattering secret it holds—before it's too late"—Provided by publisher.

Identifiers: LCCN 2015032476 | ISBN 9780399166518 (hardback)

Subjects: | CYAC: Adventure and adventurers—Fiction. | Secret societies—Fiction. | Kidnapping—Fiction. | Love—Fiction. | Voyages and travels—Fiction. | Mystery and detective stories. | BISAC: JUVENILE FICTION / Love & Romance. | JUVENILE FICTION / Historical / Europe. | JUVENILE FICTION / Mysteries & Detective Stories.

Classification: LCC PZ7.H14616 Map 2016 | DDC [Fic]—dc23

LC record available at http://lccn.loc.gov/2015032476

Speak ISBN 9780147510464

Printed in the United States of America

1 3 5 7 9 10 8 6 4 2

For Dahlia.
I feel sorry for people who have to navigate
publishing—and life—without you. Lucky for me, I don't.

And for Sofia,
for overthinking everything right alongside me,
then fixing it all with good advice and wine.

CHAPTER 1

Tourists streamed up the steep staircase toward the wedding-cake contours of the Sacré-Coeur Basilica, and I pressed myself against the railing, out of their way. "Are we sure this is where he said to meet him?"

"First landing on the stairs to the west of the carousel," Jack said. "That's here."

Jolly accordion music started up nearby, like we were in an old-timey Charlie Chaplin movie.

"He's late," I said.

"You can't expect criminals to keep regular hours." Jack boosted himself onto the low wall lining the landing, and I paced in front of him, searching faces for the heavyset man we'd given our photos to a week ago. All I found was the regular Montmartre Sunday-afternoon crowds.

The accordion in the courtyard down the street stopped, and there was a smattering of applause. At any time of the day here, street performers could be found playing instruments or doing over-the-top mime shows or painting portraits of tourists. This neighborhood had been a haven for authors and artists since groups of expats claimed it in the early 1900s—Montmartre had been home to Hemingway, Picasso, F. Scott Fitzgerald.

And now us.

It had been two weeks since Jack and I had escaped the wedding where I was supposed to marry Luc Dauphin, after which the Order kidnapped my mother and killed my friend and Jack's mentor, Mr. Emerson. Overall, not a great day.

Two weeks since the chase across Europe that left us with this bracelet I kept on my wrist all the time now, even while I was sleeping. I held up my arm, and it glinted dully in the warm afternoon sun. The wide band of tarnished gold had belonged to Napoleon Bonaparte, and it was part of a string of clues he'd left that led to the tomb of Alexander the Great.

The tomb and the weapon against the Order allegedly inside it—which the Order would do anything to keep the Circle from procuring—were our only bargaining chips for my mom's release. The bracelet had an inscription on it that referred to *my twin and I*, indicating that it was part of a matching set. To find the tomb, we had to find the other bracelet.

And so it had been two agonizing weeks of holing up in a tiny apartment and spending the days searching the Internet and scouring museums online and around Paris for the bracelet's twin.

Two weeks of my heart racing every time the phone rang, wondering if it was the Order calling to say they'd killed my mother because we weren't fast enough. I hoped that as long as we were actively searching, they wouldn't do that—why would they want to lose their leverage? But Jack was worried that they might do it on a whim, and then kill or kidnap me. That'd be just as good for them—then *no one* would find Alexander's tomb.

They were already working on making sure the *Circle* would

never be able to find it. At first the attacks had seemed random: A Saudi Circle member. Liam Blackstone, an American actor. An attack on the Dauphin family, which killed one of the twins Madame Dauphin was carrying. But it *wasn't* random. The baby girl would have been the first girl in the Circle with purple eyes . . . besides me. The rest of the assassinations targeted boys who might be the One, so they couldn't marry me and fulfill the mandate, which was meant to reveal the way to the tomb.

So it had been two weeks of looking over my shoulder for the Order *and* for the Circle, who still wanted me for their own and still thought Jack was a traitor.

I rubbed my eyes and scanned the area. Like the rest of Paris, Montmartre straddled the line between dirty big city and fairy tale. At the bottom of these steps was an apartment building that would have been considered a castle anywhere else. It had wide wrought iron balconies and dark stone turrets, which contrasted starkly with the dirty ground-level tourist shops that sold postcards and scarves and fake Dior sunglasses, like the huge pair I was wearing right now as a disguise.

This neighborhood was also the highest point in Paris. One day I'd spent a good half hour looking for Notre-Dame. I found it immediately now, even though its twin spires were barely visible among the rest of the cream and gray buildings.

"You didn't see anything when you did recon, did you?" I said.

Jack shook his head.

I knew he was good at watching out for us, but I couldn't stop being extra cautious. We never went outside without sunglasses and hats, and tried to stay away from places like Metro stations—which we knew had cameras. "I just keep thinking someone's going to see us."

Jack rocked forward on his palms, and the compass tattoo bulged on his forearm. "I know. But they probably think we're halfway across the world by now. Eating dim sum in Shanghai. Hiding out on a beach in Brazil. We'd never be dumb enough to stay in the Dauphins' backyard, right?"

That was true, but it was also the problem, and the reason we were waiting here now. As of this week, we'd exhausted every bit of research we could do in Paris, and at the worst possible time.

Scarface, one of the Order's minions, called to check on our progress every few days. Yesterday, though, he'd sounded agitated. The Commander, his boss, was getting antsy. They'd already given us two weeks to follow these clues, he'd said. Two more seemed sufficient.

So now we had two more weeks to deliver Alexander the Great's tomb, and that was it. *Two weeks* to find something archaeologists and treasure hunters had been searching for unsuccessfully for centuries. If we didn't find it, they'd kill my mother.

Two more weeks.

We had to get out of Paris. We had to figure out where Napoleon might have planted the twin bracelet, and search there. Museums and art collections and historical sites . . . There was a whole world to consider.

The problem was, I had *no* documents, Jack's were under tight surveillance, and unless you happened to be on a jet chartered by the Circle, you needed a passport to leave the country. Jack was used to getting what he needed through the Circle, but after a bit of searching, we'd found this seedy dealer of fake passports right in our neighborhood.

Off the landing was a narrow street lined with cafes, their rickety tables spilling onto the cobblestones, and finally, between them, lumbered a familiar stocky guy in a stained gray T-shirt and khakis.

Jack hopped down from the wall, brushing dust off his dark jeans. "There he is."

I readjusted my wide-brimmed hat over my face, and we made our way down the steps to a bench next to the carousel. The music stopped, and a round of kids got off while another hopped on.

"Have you got them?" Jack said.

The guy wheezed, pushing greasy red hair back from his face. "It is taking longer than I anticipated," he said in a heavy French accent. "Complications."

"You told us it would be this week," I said, my voice rising. "How much longer?"

"One week longer." He wiped his nose. "Perhaps two."

I gritted my teeth. Over Jack's shoulder, an opera singer had replaced the accordion player.

"That's too long," I said. "Is there any way to rush it? We'll pay more." I was trying to make my voice sound annoyed, but it came out somewhere between defeated and panicked.

"*Non*," he said. "There is no way."

I felt like cursing, and throwing things, and crying. Instead, I said, "Forget it, then." We walked away from the guy's protests, and I took the flight after flight of steep steps into the hills of Montmartre two at a time. I think I'd almost been expecting this. It couldn't be that easy.

"Hey," Jack said, catching up to me. "It'll be okay, yeah? We'll figure something out."

I nodded silently, but didn't slow down. I felt Jack watching me. There was one other way to get around Europe, and he hadn't been subtle about the fact that he thought it was the best idea.

The Saxons could help us. My newfound family.

It had also been two weeks since we'd seen them.

If I was being honest with myself, I was practically obsessed with the idea of my father, and the brother and sister I'd just learned about. It wasn't that I didn't *want* to get to know them, and to give them the chance to help. But with so much on the line, I couldn't take any chances. Could I trust these strangers when my mother's life hung in the balance?

Jack stopped me at the top landing and pulled off his sunglasses. I tensed, not ready to have this conversation again right now. But he just said, "There have got to be other delinquents in this city who can get us fake passports on short notice. We'll just pop in to every dodgy bar we pass until we find them. All right?"

A desperate laugh escaped my throat, but I nodded, and actually did relax a bit. Maybe there was another way. He took my hand, dragging a thumb across my palm. Goose bumps rose on my arms, like they always did when he touched me like that.

Jack noticed and dropped my hand so abruptly, it fell to my side. He pushed the sunglasses back over his face and turned away from the stairs, down a side street. "We should go to the market on the way home. We're out of coffee."

I rubbed my arms to banish the chills and caught up with him. I wasn't allowed to feel like that.

Despite everything that had happened, Jack and I were not together. Not dating. *Certainly* not boyfriend and girlfriend.

Early on, we'd talked. It would be too distracting. He didn't want to put me in an uncomfortable position. No matter what we felt for each other, it would be best to put our relationship on the back burner until we were no longer in a life-or-death situation.

I knew he was right. Besides, it was bad enough that he was helping me hide from the Saxons. If they found out that something inappropriate was going on . . .

Yes, we'd slipped up sometimes. Just last week, we were sitting on the couch, flipping through Napoleon history books, and we thought we'd made a breakthrough about a museum in Austria. Without thinking about it, I'd kissed him. He'd kissed me back like he'd never wanted to do anything more in his life, which only made it more awkward minutes later, when he'd let go of me like he'd just committed a crime. The Austrian museum turned out to be nothing, anyway.

So Jack and I were friends now. Teammates. People who lived together—slept in the same *room* in our tiny apartment—but in separate beds. People who tried really hard not to remember how it felt to wake up with my head on his chest.

Or maybe that was just me.

I looked up at him, heavy brows over gray eyes like storm clouds, the square line of his jaw, a knit beanie that disguised his dark hair.

We were the definition of *it's complicated*.

"Yeah." I adjusted my own dark glasses. "Coffee. And more Parisian document forgers. It'll be fine."

We were almost back to the apartment when my phone rang. Out of the corner of my eye, I could see Jack sigh.

It had also been two weeks of Stellan. He was across Paris, at the Dauphins', but ever since we learned he was part of the lost thirteenth bloodline of the Circle of Twelve, he might as well have been living in our little apartment with us. And though no one besides us knew it, he was also the One. The heir of Alexander the Great. And the person who I, according to the Circle's ancient mandate, was meant to marry in order to find Alexander's tomb. Of course, I didn't believe that part for a second.

I answered the phone. "Do you need something?"

"Only wondering what you're doing today," he said casually. A car horn sounded up the street from us just as one honked in the background on the phone, and I could picture Stellan weaving between little black Vespas near the Louvre, out on an errand for the Dauphins.

"Nothing important," I answered. Jack and I paused on the curb as a red Fiat sped by, then continued across the cobblestones and around the overgrown garden on our corner.

Jack pulled off his hat and ran a hand through his hair. He pretended he thought the whole thing was as ridiculous as I did. That me marrying Stellan wouldn't do anything. But he'd grown up in the Circle. The *union* in the mandate, between the One and the girl with the purple eyes, meant *marriage* to him, like it did to the rest of the Circle. I knew it bothered him more than he'd say.

"Where are you?" Stellan asked. Over the past few weeks, his light Russian accent had become as familiar to me as Jack's British one.

"Why?" I answered suspiciously. "Where are *you*?"

We stepped onto our street, and there was Stellan, leaning against the wall in front of our apartment, his tall, slim frame clad in his usual uniform of skinny jeans, a close-fitting T-shirt, and boots. He flipped his blond hair out of his eyes and grinned. I sighed and put my phone back in my bag.

"Does he realize he doesn't have a standing invitation?" Jack grumbled.

"I can hear you," Stellan called.

Jack pushed past him without a hello and punched in the door code to our building. The now-familiar scent of old wood followed me up the stairs. Jack held the apartment door open for me, then frowned. "We forgot the coffee."

"I can go out later—"

"I'll just go. You all right?" His eyes cut to Stellan, who stepped inside the apartment. I nodded. "I'll be back in a minute," Jack said, closing the door behind him.

"This *playing house* you two are doing is adorable." Stellan flopped onto the couch, stretching his arms along the back. The apartment had only two rooms—a closet-sized bedroom and this one, which contained an efficiency kitchen, one small table, and a couch that backed up to windows overlooking a sunny courtyard.

I tossed my hat and sunglasses on the table and glanced at our wall of clues, where we'd pinned Xeroxes of pages from Napoleon's diary—which we'd also found from Mr. Emerson's clues—the wording of the inscription on the bracelet, photos of the gargoyle that had pointed us to the diary, and a map of the world. I'd marked the cities we might want to visit with colorful pins, and tacked up museum brochures and notes. All in all, it looked like crazy conspiracy theorists lived here. I guess that wasn't far from the truth.

"Do you actually need something, or are you just here to bother us?" I said over my shoulder.

"Have you actually made any progress, or did your fake passport idea not go as intended?" he retorted.

My chest squeezed painfully. "I guess I missed the part where you had a better idea. Or where you were willing to search the continent for the second bracelet on your own."

Stellan drummed his fingers on the back of the couch. "You know very well that I *do* have a better idea . . ."

I shook my head and retrieved a newspaper article we'd found earlier from my bag. Another item for the crazy clue wall.

"Just tell me one thing," Stellan said after a minute. I could feel him watching me as I tacked up the article. "Is it because of him?"

"What?" I knew exactly what he was talking about.

"I mean, *kuklachka*, do you refuse to fulfill the mandate because of your feelings for someone you've only just met?"

I rubbed my face. "I think the real question is, why do *you* want to marry *me*? The tomb of Alexander the Great has been lost for centuries. I'm not denying that us getting married might mean something in the world of the Circle, but a church and a white dress isn't magic." He started to protest, but I cut him off. "'Union' *could* mean something besides marriage—something that would actually help us find the tomb—but until we figure out if that's true and what it is, we have a better chance of finding it by following actual clues left by someone who's been there than by pledging our eternal love. And we *have* those clues. There's a second bracelet out there that we need to find. And then we'll find the password, and it'll tell us how to get to the tomb. I hope," I finished under my breath.

That was another thing. It wasn't just the twin bracelet we had to find. I slipped a thumb between the bracelet and my wrist. The outside of it just had the inscription and decorations. But once we'd inspected it more, we'd realized the *inside* was a whole separate layer. Its width was divided into five equal bands I could spin around my wrist independently, each with a long string of letters etched into it. We assumed it would work like a combination lock: if we rotated the rings so the letters were arranged in the correct password along the indicated line, something would happen. We hoped the rest of the letters might line up to form more words—like, for instance, the location of the tomb.

Stellan sat forward, fingers steepled under his chin. The backlight from the window made him look like he was glowing at the edges. "First off, let me remind you that I've got fireproof skin."

His hand drifted to the translucent scars that showed above his collar. It was true. When he'd held a lighter to his skin in the

Dauphins' basement, his skin hadn't even singed. *The One who walks through fire and does not burn*, the mandate said. The Circle didn't realize it was so literal.

"I'm not going to say the word *magic*, because if it is a trait in my bloodline, there must be a scientific explanation," he went on, "but there's more going on here than we understand."

I pressed my lips together and turned back to the clue wall.

"And second," he went on, "if anyone in the Circle finds out about the thirteenth bloodline—which *you* uncovered, by the way, so thank you for that—and you don't back me, I'm dead. They'll assume I'm planning a coup. If I did manage to get away, I'd be running my whole life, and so would my sister."

Stellan's accent got a little thicker on the last words. I pictured the little blond girl he'd showed me a picture of. Anya. Just after we'd escaped the wedding, he arranged for someone in Russia to hide her away, just in case, but I knew he still worried.

"But if I did have you on my side," he continued, "if I was bound to the girl they believe to be their savior? The Circle might not have a single leader, but the closest to it is *you*. And if we were together, *us*. Then I could sleep at night no more worried someone was going to kill me than I am right now. *That's* why I want to do it."

Somehow, through all of this, I hadn't thought of it that way. The *leader* of the Circle? I twisted a pushpin deeper into the wall. "You think someone's planning to kill you?"

Stellan sank back into the stiff green couch, and it creaked in the quiet. "In this world, there's always someone planning to kill you."

At that, we both glanced out the window, then at the door. "And besides," he said, "how do you know the union is *not* marriage?"

"Napoleon's diary—"

"Didn't say specifically that it's not."

"I know what the Circle believes, but why would Napoleon have left clues if marrying two people created some kind of North Star that pointed the way?" I repeated, gesturing to the wall.

"I am only saying." Stellan stood up from the couch. "You claim you'll do anything to help your mother, but even with this new *very* short time line, you're not willing to consider the union. Or going to the Saxons, for that matter."

I stiffened. "You too? They're *my* family. I should be the one to decide what I want to do or not do with them."

He raised a finger to stop me. "They're your *blood*. They don't have to be your *family* unless you want them to be. Maybe you don't."

I shivered. It was warm outside, but these old stone buildings retained the cold. "What does that even mean? Of course I want them to be my family." I only wished it was as easy as that; that wanting made things true. My fingers tightened around my locket, which contained the only picture I had of the person who had always been my family. The person who had to be my first priority now.

If my mom were here, what would she do? Would she trust the Saxons? Would she try to find another way? My mom had never been the pro-and-con-list type. Whenever I was trying to make a decision, she'd tell me my heart knew what it wanted, and if I followed it, I wouldn't go wrong. And then I'd remind her that my heart would probably never want to take three AP classes in one semester, but that my college applications would. And it wasn't like that helped me now. All my heart wanted was to save her, but I didn't know how.

Stellan raised his eyebrows.

"I just think I should be the one to choose who I want to marry and when. And for all I know, the Saxons could marry me off to someone who might—maybe—be even worse than you," I said flippantly.

"Now, that is just rude." Stellan crossed the room and pulled aside the heavy front drapes that we usually kept closed and peered into the street, letting in the soft glow of sunset.

I brushed a stray bread crumb off the counter. "If I went to the Saxons, they might help . . . or they might lock me up in their basement and force me to marry the highest bidder. Which means the safest thing for me to do is find the tomb on my own."

"*If* you find it."

I huffed out a breath. "Don't the Dauphins need you for . . . something? Anything?"

"That's code for she doesn't want you here." Jack came inside, tossing a bag of espresso beans on the counter.

"Fine." Stellan let the curtains fall, and the light in the room dimmed. "Lovely to see you both, as always. Talk tomorrow."

He left, but everything he'd said had brought my worries rushing back even stronger. My plan—to figure out and follow these clues on our own—wasn't working. Something was going to have to change.

After dinner, I sat on the couch and Jack stood in front of the clue wall, reading over the new article I'd pinned up earlier. It was about a cache of Napoleon artifacts found at a site near New Delhi, India.

"So what this means is that Napoleon's been everywhere," he said.

I shrugged. We knew we had to search places other than Paris—if we could ever get passports—but the list of *where* to search just kept growing.

I buried my face in my hands, and after a second, I felt the couch dip as Jack sat beside me.

"Yes, there are lots of possibilities," he said. "But we've already determined that he'd likely have left the second bracelet, or any other clues, in places important to him or the Circle or Alexander, right?"

I nodded. If he wanted someone to find the clues, he wouldn't bury them in a random field somewhere.

"So we'll figure out how to get out of here, then we'll do a methodical search of Circle headquarters cities, Alexander monuments . . . every place we can in the time we have," he said.

He always sounded so calm. So logical. He stood up and put a hand on my shoulder, then pulled back and hovered awkwardly. "I'm going to bed."

Don't, I almost said. *I don't want to be alone in my own head right now. I need somebody. I need you.*

"Good night," I said instead. At least pretending not to care—*forcing* myself not to care—was something I had plenty of practice with.

"It's like I said before," Jack said after a second. "It'll be all right, yeah? We'll figure it out."

I nodded and tried to believe him.

He disappeared into the bedroom, kicking off his shoes as he went. I sighed and pulled a history book from the stack on the coffee table. I read about Napoleon's campaign through France for the thousandth time. Alexander's time in Egypt. Napoleon's outposts in northern France. Alexander's conquests in India.

I grabbed my phone. India. Elephants. Bright colors. Bright colors painted *onto* elephants. The Napoleon treasure they found recently was in Delhi, not Kolkata, where the Circle family based in India lived. I looked up important monuments in Kolkata. Temples. The Indian Museum, which supposedly had both Alexander artifacts and European art and jewelry. It was a pretty building, but too new-looking. Built—hmm. Built in 1814. The year Napoleon was exiled from France.

I scribbled a note about it on a piece of paper and tacked it to the board. Maybe India could be our first stop, if we ever figured out how to get out of Paris.

For just a second, I pictured allowing myself to trust the Saxons. With their resources, we could go anywhere. And, whispered a little voice in the back of my head, I'd really be part of their family. *My* family. I'd been trying not to think about how badly I wanted that, but it was like any craving—the more I denied it, the worse it got.

No matter what, it wasn't worth risking my mom's life, said my logical side. But would it really be *that* much of a risk?

I scrubbed my hands over my face. I couldn't do this anymore today. I had to at least try to sleep.

I took out the brown contacts disguising my purple eyes and snuck into the dark bedroom.

Jack had made up my slim, hard bed this morning, tucking the blankets in to form precise corners, the pillow fluffed and centered. Just as perfectly as he made our beds every day, like he washed every dish, like he patrolled the neighborhood for anything out of the ordinary on a down-to-the-minute schedule. Everything was tidy and in its place, including him, a dark lump under the covers in a sliver of moonlight, sleeping. Just like he was supposed to be, just like he was every night while I lay awake, staring at the ceiling. Thinking, worrying, trying to shut off my brain long enough to close my eyes without seeing terrible things behind my eyelids.

I was mentally preparing myself for another long, restless night when Jack stirred. In the dim light, the whites of his eyes glowed as he blinked once, twice. His covers lifted, and he moved to the edge of the mattress, leaving a me-sized space next to him on the bed that was barely big enough for one person.

I hesitated only a second before bypassing my own bed and crawling gratefully into his, my head on his chest and his arm tight around me. That night, I didn't have to stare at the ceiling long at all.

The next morning, on the first day of the third week, I woke up still in Jack's arms. He opened his eyes when I sat up. "G'morning," he said sleepily, his hair matted down on one side. I fought the urge to pull my fingers through it.

"Good morning." I don't know whether it was finally getting a little sleep or being reminded that, even if we weren't technically in a relationship, Jack really did care about me and would never suggest anything he thought was dangerous, but all of a sudden, I knew what I had to do. There was only one thing that made sense. "We have to go to the Saxons," I said.

CHAPTER 2

My father must have had a jet on standby. By early afternoon, just hours after I'd called him, Jack and I were at Heathrow Airport, and my stomach was churning from more than the plane ride. We disembarked to find a sleek black helicopter waiting for us on the tarmac.

"Miss West, I presume. And Jack Bishop." The pilot gave Jack a quick once-over, and I could see in his eyes that it wasn't just the Saxons who disapproved of Jack running off with me. Everyone who worked for them was so loyal—what Jack had done was unthinkable.

I glanced at Jack, who, for the first time, looked a little uncertain about this plan.

A Keeper—which was what Jack and Stellan were to the Saxons and the Dauphins respectively—were more than employees. A Keeper was a combination of security director, adviser, and personal assistant. As close to a family member as an employee could get. There were only two Keepers per family—one older and established, and one second-in-command, an apprentice who was preparing to take over when the older Keeper could do longer do his job . . . or if anything happened to him. That was Jack and Stellan. Both Keepers did the jobs the family didn't trust to anyone else. When a family's Keeper suddenly disappeared with one of those jobs—in this case, *me*—it wasn't taken lightly.

Not to mention the fact that anything romantic between employees and family members was taboo enough to warrant termination—the Circle's euphemism for killing rule breakers. Even though Jack and I should be safe on that front now, the pilot's glare made me fidget.

But his gaze slid to me. "There's been a last-minute change of plans. You'll be meeting Miss Lydia in the city before returning to the estate." He handed me huge yellow earphones. "Please, Miss West, make yourself comfortable."

A moment later, I was gripping the arms of the seat as I watched the ground shrink away below. We rose quickly over fields of green and yellow toward the city of London, which grew closer by the minute. Though it had a river running through its center like Paris, London looked newer and more metropolitan. More gleaming skyscrapers, wider streets, bigger boats sailing down the wide river. The city stretched away as far as I could see.

We zipped over squares of bright green parks, a white Ferris wheel that looked small enough to scoop up with my ring finger—"*That's the London Eye,*" came Jack's voice through my headset—then a bridge straight out of a Dickens novel—"*Tower Bridge,*" Jack said as it hinged open from the center to let a cruise ship pass beneath.

Paris had come to feel so familiar that being in this new city was more of a shock to my senses than I expected. We passed over Big Ben, Parliament, the British Museum, all names I'd heard a thousand times. My mom would have loved this. One of her favorite things was touring each new city we lived in. And then I remembered with a start that she'd lived in London, too. This was where she'd met my dad.

After what seemed like no time, we dropped onto a rooftop in the city's center. The rotors were still spinning when Jack swung open the door and helped me down, and I clung to him a little longer than I should have while I got my shaky legs underneath me.

He let go of me abruptly, and I turned to see why. Lydia Saxon was walking across the landing pad. My sister.

I'd only met Lydia once, at the Eiffel Tower ball, where I first realized the Saxons were my family. In the past two weeks, though, I'd taken every opportunity to look her up online. The Saxons' cover story for being so rich and well connected was that they were minor British royalty, and the tabloids reported on their exploits as such. Lydia dragging her twin brother, Cole, away from a fight at a bar. The two of them, him in a proper waistcoat and her in a hat, attending the christening of a new royal baby. Every time I saw a picture of her, it seemed more and more surreal. Seeing her in person was stranger still.

Lydia was wearing a classic khaki trench over a blue summer dress, her dark hair in a bun. Her eyes were like mine, minus the color. A little too big, a little too wide set under dark brows. Where I was so pale I was almost translucent, she had olive skin, and when she got close, I saw that without her towering heels we'd be just the same height.

Lydia stopped in front of us. "Hi," she said, twirling a long pendant necklace around her fingers.

"Lydia." I realized I was twisting my own necklace, and forced myself to stop. Was I supposed to hug her? Shake her hand? I did neither. "Hi. Thanks for picking me up. Is everything okay? I thought we were going to your house." I was rambling, one doomsday scenario after another running through my mind. She had security waiting to toss me in a cell. They had a wedding ceremony already set up at a nearby church, and I wouldn't have time to run.

But she shook her head. "Father's meeting at Parliament ran over. He was going to come get you, but now I'm meant to show you around until he's finished and then we'll meet at home." Her eyes got wide. "Are you okay with the helicopter? I wasn't sure since you might not be used to them, but Father said it would be fastest, and—"

"It's fine," I said, the tension draining out of me. A helicopter was the least of my worries.

Lydia was shifting back and forth on her heels. Could she possibly be acting so weird because she was nervous, too?

As if in answer to my unasked question, she looked up. "When we first met, I didn't even realize you were my sister," she said. "I'm so happy you're here now."

My heart exploded into a thousand relieved, ecstatic pieces. I had to force myself not to throw my arms around her. This feeling—happiness?—was foreign after the past few weeks.

"Me too," I said. "I'm really happy to be here." Lydia grinned, and the tension finally broke. I had a sister. I had a family. And they'd *have* to help me. That was what family did, right?

Lydia giggled at Jack, who had retreated a few feet and was looking off into the distance. "Oh, quit it," she said, and crossed to plant a kiss on his cheek. Just like I remembered from the ball, Jack didn't seem anywhere near as comfortable with her as Stellan did with his charge, Luc Dauphin.

"Lydia." Jack bowed his head formally.

"Father's not here. You don't have to be so bloody proper," she said, and I relaxed even more. Lydia certainly didn't seem to harbor any ill will toward Jack. "I want to hear all about the adventures you two have been having."

She took my arm and pulled Jack after us to an elevator that let us out in a dark wood lobby off a bustling street. Jack kept up conversation with her, feeding her our lines about how we hadn't come to them earlier because I was scared, and about what he'd done to keep me safe.

"Were you in Paris this whole time?" Lydia said, and I watched a red double-decker bus drive by on the wrong side of the road, followed by a whole row of black cabs that looked like bowler hats.

"Yes," I answered, tearing myself away from London's charms. "Like I told your father—our—Alistair—" What was I supposed to call him? "Like I told him on the phone, the Order has my mom, and I've been trying to help her. Paris seemed like the best place to do it, but I'm not sure that's true anymore."

Lydia nodded. "You said the Order wants you to find the tomb? And swap it for your mum?"

Jack met my eyes quickly. We'd talked about this. We were going to tell the Saxons *almost* everything. "That's their demand," Jack said. "Of course, we hope to stop them directly."

A frown flashed across Lydia's face, but was gone just as quickly. "Of course," she said.

I touched the bracelet on my arm, currently hidden under a cardigan.

We walked in silence for a few minutes. I couldn't help but gawk at the city. The stone turrets and gleaming skyscrapers. Bright red phone booths and crisp new street signs. The clean and modern contrasting with the charming, comfortably worn-in look of the rest of the city, like the buildings just wanted to sit down with you and have a cup of tea.

The people, though, were like people in any big city: crowded, rushed, pushing. I wasn't sure I'd ever seen so many different *kinds* of people in one place, either. You always heard London was a melting pot, but I hadn't quite realized. We passed a group of Asian business-men in expensive suits, sitting on a bench next to a few kids whose accents sounded Eastern European maybe, and who were younger than me, but whose mullets and acid-wash jeans were from a time before I was born. And running between them, a whole swarm of preschool kids, one little Indian girl screeching to a pale redhead in the cutest tiny British accent that she wanted to *have the next go* with the jump rope.

I'd forgotten what it was like to understand conversations on the street. I paused for a second, listening to a couple argue about where to eat dinner, marveling at how *foreign* my native language sounded.

Out of everywhere I'd ever lived, this was where I technically belonged. My family lived here. London would have been my home if things had been different. My sister looked perfectly at ease on these wide, clean streets. I think I'd been expecting to feel some kind of connection to the city.

But there was nothing more than the usual feel of a new place. When you moved as much as my mom and I did, everywhere was home and nowhere was. You got as used to washing your hair at the Days Inn off the highway as you did to learning the quirks of a new kitchen. It was the same with people, I guess. Would I really feel like the Saxons were who I belonged to more than anyone else?

As if on cue, Lydia answered a phone call and told the person on the other end we'd be there shortly. "Father's ready," she said. "Let's take you home."

CHAPTER 3

"Home" was a gated estate on the outskirts of London, with a wide walkway leading from the front drive up to the house. We had touched down on a rooftop landing pad, and were now looking over grounds that stretched away into a sparkling pool, a stable complex, and what appeared to be a racetrack with a single car circling it. Keeping the estate from looking too formal were beds of wildflowers that swayed in the late-afternoon breeze.

The second Jack had helped us down from the helicopter, he'd disappeared with nothing more than a nod in my direction, leaving me and my sister alone. Lydia began giving me the full tour immediately and stopped talking only to change for dinner. She'd offered me a change of clothes, too, but I wasn't sure we were at the clothes-sharing point yet, and when we left Paris this morning, I'd dressed nicely on purpose, in a plain black dress. While I waited for her in a sitting room, my phone chimed with a text. I hoped it was Jack telling me where he was, and that everything was okay.

It wasn't. It was Scarface. *13 days,* the text said.

I tossed the phone back in my bag like it was on fire. Another reminder that not only was my mom's life on the line, but that I'd be going behind the Saxons' backs. Up until now, I hadn't felt bad about that, but after meeting Lydia, I was starting to.

Lydia reemerged in a black dress with a lacy bodice and a flowing A-line skirt, and we made our way toward the dining room. The inside of the house matched what I'd seen of the outside—old and elegant, but understated in a way that made the Dauphins' décor in the Louvre seem showy.

Around every corner on the home tour, I expected to find my father waiting for us, but by the time we got to the formal dining room, we were still alone except for two girls in black uniforms who stood along the back wall. The dining room was wallpapered in a subtle damask and trimmed in dark wood, with heavy velvet drapes covering the windows. The light in the room came from a tinkling crystal chandelier above a long table, which was set with four places at one end, candles flickering down the center. Lydia sat on one side and pointed me to the seat across from her. "And you grew up in . . . Minnesota, was it?"

I nodded. "Minnesota, and before that Oregon, New York, Texas, Florida . . ."

Lydia set down her glass of sparkling water and wrinkled her nose. "That sounds ghastly."

"It wasn't ideal." I gestured around the room. "Not like living somewhere like this."

"You *could* have grown up here." Lydia leaned her elbows on the table and cocked her head to one side. "It's so *odd* your mother never told you about us. She kept so much from you . . . You could have had so much more in your life."

I leaned back against the padded back of the chair, surprised. "I—" Of course I'd wondered what it would have been like to grow up as part of the Circle. I'd been so angry when I'd found out how long my mom had been lying. But still . . . "She had her reasons."

"I'm sure. Sorry. I don't mean to pry." Lydia smiled, and it looked genuine, but I could see questions that I wasn't sure I wanted to answer churning behind her eyes. I changed the subject. "Is *your* mom coming to dinner?"

Lydia ran a finger along the gold fork next to her plate. "My mother is still getting used to the idea of you. She won't be joining us."

Right. Even if this wasn't the Circle, finding out that your husband had an illegitimate child would be awkward.

I gestured to the fourth place setting. "And your brother——"

The hardwood floor creaked, and I spun to see my father in the doorway.

My father.

What a strange thing to be able to say. I'd only met him that once, at the ball, but he was just how I remembered him. The awe I felt was reflected right back at me from eyes so much like mine, it was as if I were looking into a mirror.

He took a step inside, and I snapped out of it. Was I supposed to stand? I pushed halfway out of my chair, but fell back to sitting when I saw Lydia leaning back casually. My father came around the table, and I stood again, awkwardly. He was handsome, with dark hair and heavy brows like mine and Lydia's, and he wasn't tall, for a guy—probably only six inches taller than me. I had my mom's complexion, and her little nose, but it was obvious that I'd gotten a lot from the Saxons.

My father kissed me on the cheek. "Avery," he said, and I flashed back to the memory box under my bed back in Minnesota, where I'd stashed all the research I'd done on my father over the years. As much as I'd wished and hoped and daydreamed, I don't think I'd ever really believed he'd be part of my life one day.

"I'm so glad you're here," he went on, and squeezed both my hands in his. "I wish it could have been sooner, but it's good to have you now."

He made his way to the head of the table, and for the first time, I noticed Jack. He must have come in with my father. He stood with his hands behind his back, blending into the wall like all the other servants. He didn't look hurt or upset, so maybe he'd been forgiven.

My father looked to Lydia as a butler pulled out his chair. "Where's Cole?"

Lydia shrugged, and just then, Cole Saxon strode into the room in a red and white jumpsuit, gripping a helmet, his hair sweaty.

My father pressed his lips together and waited for Cole to make his way around the table.

My half brother was just taller than my father, and the jumpsuit made his slight frame look a little bigger, but I could tell the whole family was small. Cole threw himself into the chair next to his sister and plucked a roll from the untouched breadbasket. There was a rip at the shoulder of the jumpsuit, and Lydia poked at it, raising her brows.

"Crashed the Ferrari," Cole mumbled around a bite of bread.

Lydia's mouth dropped open. "Cole! The '64?"

Cole nodded. He had the same olive skin and dark hair as his sister, but there was none of Lydia's warmth in his violet eyes.

"That was the one car I actually liked." Lydia crossed her arms over her chest. "Did you just leave it sitting there?"

"It's off the track. Somebody'll deal with it." He glanced up at Jack, standing in the corner. "The Keeper's back. Send him."

Lydia braced her small hands on the ivory tablecloth. "Jack doesn't work on cars, idiot."

"Since he's taken it upon himself to be personal bodyguard to the sister who doesn't even want to be part of our family, I thought other things might have changed, too."

I had stopped trying to pretend I wasn't listening. Jack didn't react. Lydia just sighed.

"Cole, please be civil at the dinner table." My father's chair, at the head of the table, was bigger than the others, with a carved back like a small throne. He gestured to me. "We're here to *welcome* your sister."

"Half sister," Cole muttered. Until now, it was as though he hadn't noticed me sitting there, but now he stared, unblinking. "I was going to come into the city with Lydia to show her around, but then I realized I didn't want to."

Flustered, I looked down at my hands, which were twisting the napkin in my lap. I should be back in the US right now, I reminded myself. We would have just moved to Maine, and I'd be starting at an unfamiliar school at the end of the year, once again the new girl in a place where nobody had any use for a new girl. In a way, this wasn't that different. And honestly, part of me didn't mind Cole's hostility. At least I knew it was real. If they were just pretending to be nice to me until they could use me, he wouldn't be allowed to act like this. I let myself hope that Lydia's and my father's happiness to have me here was real, too.

My father cleared his throat and raised his wineglass. "A toast. Avery, you've belonged with us all along, and we enjoy nothing more than you being here with us now. Welcome to our family."

I raised my glass of sparkling water, and so did Lydia. Even Cole picked his up grudgingly, after a pointed look from his sister. "Thank you. I'm glad to be here," I said truthfully.

Once we all had dainty plates of salad in front of us, my father sat forward. "I assume there's a reason you've chosen to join us now."

I took a deep breath. We'd already told Lydia some of the story, but my father knew only the bare bones we'd told him on the phone. I glanced at Jack, still standing against the wall like a good Keeper, pretending he wasn't listening to our conversation.

"As I mentioned earlier," I said, "the Order kidnapped my mother."

I paused to gauge my father's reaction. He must have cared about my mom once, after all. For just a second, I tried to see him through her eyes, a young leader of the Circle, and wondered for the millionth time how their relationship had come to be. I had so much to talk to her about.

My father sipped his wine. "Again, I'm very sorry to hear this. Go on."

"They want us—me—" I corrected myself. Jack wasn't part of this now. "They want me to find Alexander's tomb and exchange its contents for my mom, to keep the Circle from having a weapon against them." That part was all true. The next part, on the other hand . . . "What *I* want is to find the tomb—with your help—and use it to stop them," I said. It was *close* to the truth. As much as I wanted the Order taken down, I wanted my mom safe more and would happily do whatever it took for her freedom. But the Saxons didn't have to know that.

My father shook out his napkin and set it in his lap. "And how do you expect us to help?"

"Before I knew who you were, and exactly who I was, I found some clues Emerson Fitzpatrick had left, before the Order killed him, too." I swallowed. It was still hard to say. "The clues suggested that Napoleon found Alexander's tomb during his campaign."

All three Saxons paused. Lydia had a bite of salad halfway to her mouth, and my father carefully set down a saltshaker.

"Does that mean you already know where the tomb is?" Cole demanded, planting his elbows on the table with a bang.

I shook my head. "Napoleon found it, then hid it again. He thought whatever was in there was dangerous. But he left his own set of clues I'm following now, including this."

I pulled up the sleeve of my cardigan and slid the bracelet off my arm. I ran a finger over the engraved lettering as I explained what it meant, and what we were looking for. "I was hoping to use your resources to search for the second bracelet and the password," I finished.

I handed the bracelet across the table to Lydia. Cole looked at it over her shoulder; then she passed it to my father.

He slipped reading glasses out of his jacket pocket and inspected it, squinting at the rings on the inside. "Are you sure this is genuine?"

I glanced at Jack. We'd never questioned the bracelet's authenticity. "I think so. Mr. Emerson—Fitz—thought so."

My father took off his glasses and pinched the bridge of his nose. "I can have my intelligence people take a look, but . . . Fitzpatrick was a tutor, correct? I remember him going on about history and theories. The children liked him." My father looked at Jack. "I know this is an exciting possibility, but we must look at the facts. No one has ever seen this before. What he left you could be a miracle . . . or it could be the ramblings of an incoherent old man."

"He wasn't—" I bristled. He didn't know Mr. Emerson like I did. Like Jack did. He never would have left these clues and put us in danger if he wasn't sure he was right. The clues being *real* wasn't the issue here. "The Order believes in it, too. They tried to *kill* us to get this information. They did kill Fitz. They took my mom."

My father tapped the bracelet on his place mat. "The Order is desperate."

I held out my hand to take the bracelet back, suddenly wary.

"I can keep it for you, if you'd like," my father said. "Have it examined."

"No!" I said. Across the table, Lydia coughed and raised her eyebrows, but I didn't care. "I'll take it back, please." When the bracelet was safely returned to my arm, I said, "Whatever's in the tomb would be good for *you*, too. Don't you want to do everything you can to find it?"

"Of course." My father sat back in his chair. He *looked* like a king now, about to make a pronouncement. "Avery, as new as this is for you, you're one of us. Family. And I want you to feel like family, but that means being realistic. It would be wonderful if your clues did lead to the tomb. Miraculous. But there's more for us to consider."

My stomach knotted. The family reunion I thought was going so well had suddenly taken a turn I didn't like at all. "I still find it hard to believe my marrying someone would do anything," I said.

Lydia held up a hand. "We know marrying you into another family won't open a portal to an Order-killing death ray in Alexander the Great's tomb."

"She's right." My father signaled for a refill of his wineglass. "But the union has been a cornerstone of Circle philosophy for centuries. *Logically* we know nothing magical will happen when a marriage occurs, but there's more to it. As much as the mandate is about finding the tomb, it's also about politics. And power. It's about a united Circle, defeating all its enemies, including the Order."

"But finding the tomb would be at least as good," I argued again.

"Maybe." My father leaned back in his chair. He suddenly looked taller. "But I assume you know about the Order's attacks on Circle members. Thanks to Dauphin's little stunt, the Circle knows you exist. We would appear both weak and cruel if we didn't try to stop the assassination campaign now that the girl we've been all waiting for has turned up."

A server set a plate of some fancy-looking chicken dish in front of me, and I pushed it away. I had to admit I understood his points: to the Circle, fulfilling the mandate was absolutely the right thing to do, and of course I didn't want anyone else to die. But asking for me to get *married* wasn't a small favor.

And then there was the fact that I knew perfectly well who was destined to fulfill the mandate with me, and it was *not* a son of the twelve. That was the second thing we weren't telling them.

Lydia and my father were watching me intently, but Cole had procured a pen and started sketching on his cloth napkin.

I shifted, suddenly uncomfortable in the hard chair. Next they'd forbid me to leave the house. I thought of the Order's text. *13 days.* "It's a lot to think about," I said. Even if they did actually care about me, to them, this wasn't strange or wrong. Was coming here a huge mistake after all?

My father must have seen my hesitation, because for just a second, the *business* look dropped off his face, and his small, sympathetic smile was very *father.* I tried my best not to let it sway me. "I have a proposition," he said gently. "I know this is odd for you, and I don't want you to feel forced into a union with someone you don't care for. But there are loads of good candidates. I'm confident you could find one you wouldn't be opposed to."

Spoken from a place where forcing your daughter to marry someone she doesn't know is normal.

"There are ten heirs, from ten families," my father continued.

That made me look up from my plate. "Only ten?"

"The Dauphins had their chance, and they've proven they're not worthy of our trust."

Oh. Right.

"Order-killing death ray," Cole interjected, holding up his napkin like it was a canvas in a fine museum. I had to admit, he had talent. The sheer number of dismembered bodies he'd drawn in the past few minutes was impressive.

Lydia batted the napkin down, and Cole smirked. I felt a little bad thinking of my brother as creepy, but there it was.

My father ignored him and went on. The more he talked, the more I realized this was not a plan he'd made up on the spot. "We'll try to meet one family every day, but some of the traveling will take longer."

"Traveling? So we'll go to each family's city?" That was the first spark of good news I'd heard. I glanced up at Jack and remembered the conversation we'd had last night. *Napoleon would have hidden clues in places important to the Circle.*

My father nodded. "If we start tomorrow, visiting all ten families should take somewhere around—"

"Two weeks," I said. The same amount of time the Order had given us.

"Around two weeks," my father agreed. He'd been ignoring his dinner, but now he dug in. "That sounds about right. During that time, you're welcome to keep researching your bracelet. I would be thrilled if your theory were true, so feel free to use our databases, our history books, whatever you need." Like an afterthought, he added, "And I'll assign troops to search any leads you have in the field."

"Wait," I said. "No. I have to look myself—"

He stopped me. "The Order may claim they're leaving you to find the tomb, but I will never believe they're not dangerous to any Circle member, let alone a very important one."

I looked down at my untouched food. That was inconvenient. I wondered whether he cared about my safety because I was his daughter or because I was a new possession. The thought stung more than I wanted it to.

"While you're under our protection," my father went on, "you'll stay under guard, and we'll do the searching. If we find the tomb before we've decided on a family to unite with, we can reevaluate the union. But in the absence of that, you'll agree that it makes the most sense for our family, for the Circle, *and* for your mother, for you to marry."

I pressed my lips together. It did make sense, as much as I didn't want to admit it, but I was sure it wouldn't come to that. "Okay. But you have to promise me you'll make saving my mom a first priority."

My father inclined his head in agreement.

"She has demands." Lydia smiled at me, almost proudly. "Sister's learning to be one of us."

I glanced up at Jack, who studiously avoided my eyes. "Where are we going first?" I said, like it was a vacation and not an arranged marriage.

My father looked pleased. "How would you like to visit India?"

Now Jack did look up, catching my eye ever so briefly. "I've always wanted to go there," I said, and the smile that spread across my father's face was so genuine, I felt guilty again.

After dinner, my father had Jack escort me to my room. No doubt the family wanted to be alone to discuss my future. Jack walked a little farther than a respectable distance ahead of me as we padded down the hall. He glanced up at a camera on the ceiling, its little red light following our progress. We continued past it, and suddenly, Jack grabbed my hand and squeezed.

"Are you really going to let them do all the work while you're wined and dined by a bunch of Circle suitors?" he whispered.

I looked back down the hall toward the dining room, where the door was firmly shut. "Of course not," I whispered back.

The camera down the hall was swinging toward us. We sprang apart and continued walking, like we'd never stopped.

CHAPTER 4

The next afternoon, I was in another massive house, on the other side of the world.

The Rajesh family lived near the center of Kolkata. Their compound's high walls sheltered a secret garden of palms and orange trees and overgrown ivy and moss-covered fountains that looked like they'd been running for centuries. The home itself was white marble, with columns all across its front, grand enough that I would call it more palace than house. We'd been ushered straight to our suites, and I was perched on a tall stool, with Lydia and two Rajesh servant girls flitting around me.

"There," Lydia said, putting the finishing touches on my eyes. My sister had done my makeup while telling me about the Rajesh family—the names and ages of all their kids, even how far their territory stretched, making it seem like us sitting here in a bedroom in India was the most normal thing in the world.

She had hardly left my side since the moment I woke up this morning back in London. I'd thought there might be a little tension after I didn't immediately agree to their plans last night, but Lydia just seemed excited for the adventure, and it was making me feel a little better about it, too.

One of the servant girls hovered in front of me, squinted at my face, and frowned. She took the eyeliner out of Lydia's hand and nudged her out of the way—the girls didn't seem to speak English, and neither of us spoke Bengali, so the girl gestured for me to look up and went at my eyes with small strokes of the pencil. Lydia gave a bemused smile and sat on the edge of the bed. "Like I was saying—"

There was a knock at the door, and she got up to answer it. I looked past the girl's hands to see Cole peering inside. I waved, but he said something to Lydia and left without giving me a glance, so I let the hand fall back to my lap.

"He doesn't mean any harm." Lydia helped the second girl finish braiding thin strands of my hair. The one with the eyeliner gestured for me to close my eyes. "He's just a little hurt by . . ." I could tell she was trying to phrase it diplomatically. "*I* get that you're worried about your mum and that all this is overwhelming. If I were in your position, I might've sat in my closet and cried for a week. But Cole doesn't understand anything other than doing what's right for the family. He'll come around. Especially when you fulfill the mandate."

"Okay," said the girl in front of me in heavily accented English, and I opened my eyes.

Lydia leaned around to peer at my face. "Ooh! Pretty!" She gestured at her face. "Me too, please!"

"If," I corrected her as she sat on the bed and the girl began drawing lines of heavy kohl around her eyes, too. "*If* I fulfill the mandate. Marriage is still a last resort."

She glanced up at me, one eye partially rimmed in black. "You know all Circle marriages are arranged, right?"

"*All?*"

"All in the direct line. Even when they don't change the *entire fate* of the Circle." She watched the other girl prepare what must be the sari they were about to dress me in. Lydia told me that I'd be wearing her clothes during some of the visits, but in some cases, it was a sign of goodwill to wear the traditional dress provided by the family. "Purple," she said. "Fitting. I like it."

I blinked. The sari was a deep plum color, with a pattern of red and gold metallic vines around the edges. The girl gestured for me to get undressed. "So when you get married," I said to Lydia, "that'll be arranged, too?"

Lydia nodded.

"Does that bother you?"

She shrugged. "I'm used to the idea."

"Wait. Does that mean you'll marry one of the guys we're meeting on these trips?" The only thing more awkward than being paraded around in front of ten guys I didn't care about would be if one of them had already been promised to my sister.

She stood up and inspected her makeup in the mirror, which I hadn't been allowed to do yet. If it looked anything like hers, it was very dramatic. "No. Circle unions don't usually cross families in that way. That's one reason *you* are such an occasion."

I'd been trying not to be nervous, but this wasn't helping. I held my arms out to the side as the girls wrapped the sari around me, and the beaded tassels running along the edges swayed and clicked in the breeze from the overhead fan.

After a few seconds of silence, Lydia came in front of me and smoothed a stray strand of hair back from my face. "I'm sorry," she said quietly. "I keep forgetting how little you know, and how traumatic it all must be. If I'm being an insensitive arse, just smack me, all right?"

I let out a breathless laugh.

"I'm serious. And we should have a secret signal in case you need anything. Like—" She scratched her eyebrow with her pinky finger. "Yeah? Do that, and I'll know to come help." She paused. "I'll try not to bother you too much about it, but it *is* fascinating to me. My marriage will never matter much. Cole's the heir—or he was until you showed up. He's twelve minutes older than me, you know." Her confident smile looked momentarily brittle. "And now it's you."

I watched Lydia's fingers—unmanicured, with bitten nails—pull at a thread at the hem of her skirt. All I'd been thinking about was how unfair this was to *me*. But what if you had to watch someone get all this attention you'd never have—and they didn't even want it?

"I couldn't do this without you, you know," I said quietly. It was all I could think to say, and it was true. "So thank you."

Lydia smiled.

There was another knock on the door. "Ten minutes," Jack called, and I started but was careful to not react. I'd convinced my father to let him come with us to India, but it was getting harder and harder to pretend I didn't care about him more than any member of the Circle cared about the help. Watching him in his element was fascinating. He was laser focused, intense, stern. It was the Jack I knew, magnified. And it didn't help that I hadn't been able to so much as talk to him since that moment in the hall last night.

I smoothed my sari. I couldn't get distracted now, especially not by a guy I wasn't supposed to be thinking about that way, especially not just before meeting somebody who thought they might marry me. I put up walls in my brain. "Anything else I need to know?" I said.

The girls were dressing Lydia in a ruby-red sari, and when they finished, they adorned us both with heavy necklaces, bracelets, and earrings. "Even if you're nervous, try to have a good time," Lydia said. "Dev is actually . . . It could be a fun night."

"What do you mean?"

"Last year he attended a UN summit on agriculture dressed as a banana. As in, wearing a full-body banana suit."

I laughed. "He did not."

"Time to go," came a voice at the door, and I got final prods and pins and then one of the girls set a sparkling golden chain on my head. Finally, they let me see myself in the mirror.

The silk of the sari shimmered, dark purple set off against my pale skin, and gold and jewels shone on my hands, at my throat, in my hair. The eyes *were* dramatic, but with the outfit, they worked. Lydia came up beside me, just as elegant and glittering.

I watched our reflections and was surprised when she took my hand. Hers was small and cool, and our bangle bracelets clinked together prettily. Her mouth curved up at the corners, like we were in on a secret together. "You look like a princess," she said.

I'd expected my first meeting with another family of the Circle to be like meeting the Dauphins, complete with either thinly veiled scorn or obsequious praise, but the Rajesh family wasn't like that at all. Lydia and I joined them, plus my father and Cole and Jack, in a room filled with dancing candlelight and brightly colored wall hangings and a human-sized statue of Ganesh, the elephant god.

Dev's mother, Indra Rajesh, had a soft smile. She clasped my hand warmly in hers and asked me about my life and my family, assuring me how easily I'd fit into theirs. His father, Arjun, had a thick mustache and a thicker midsection, and must have had a dozen cups of coffee before dinner because he talked a mile a minute, about everything from the art in their home to the weather, all in a posh British accent.

Dev himself had dark purple eyes that crinkled when he smiled in a way that made me want to smile back. He'd poured me a steaming, fragrant cup of tea when we'd first entered the sitting room, and now he sat next to me as we listened to his father.

"And of course, we've implemented new security measures since the attacks began," Mr. Rajesh went on. "Horrible. I spoke with George Frederick yesterday. They are, understandably, having a hard time recovering from Liam's death . . ." They were talking about Liam Blackstone, who was a famous actor and member of the American Circle family, and Colette LeGrand's late boyfriend. I'd hung out with both of them just before he was killed.

The conversation faded as my father and Mr. Rajesh moved toward the dining room. I stood to follow, and Dev offered me his arm. I took it.

"Well then," Dev said, his voice low and smooth, "we've made the conversational jump from awkward to depressing, so I'd say the evening is on track so far, wouldn't you?"

"Oh." I tried to rearrange my face into a smile. "No. Everything's great. I—"

Dev chuckled. I looked up, and his eyes were sparkling. He really was attractive—was anyone in the Circle *not*?—with longish, wavy dark hair, a smattering of stubble across his cheeks, and an easy smile.

"It's all right. You don't have to pretend the whole thing's not wildly uncomfortable." Dev gestured ahead of us. On the floor of the dining room, there was a tile mosaic in the shape of a wheel with twelve spokes. It must be the Rajesh symbol. "My parents are not usually like this. They're nervous. About the attacks and about . . . well . . . you."

I watched Mrs. Rajesh hover anxiously at the dinner table, her eyes darting over the place settings as if a mismatched napkin could ruin their chances at the union.

"They're nice," I said, actually relaxing for the first time. "I appreciate your family going to all this trouble for me."

"We appreciate your visit, and I hope *you'll* appreciate the paneer makhani masala we're having with supper." He guided me to a chair near the head of the table. "The tandoori lamb is meant to be the main dish, but the paneer is my favorite. It's a recipe my mother made as a girl. She insisted on the best for you."

I caught Mrs. Rajesh staring at us, then making a show of pretending she hadn't been. I hid a smile.

By the third course, I was stuffed, but there was no way I was going to stop. The lamb had more flavor than I realized meat could have. The paneer—which looked like chunks of tofu, but was actually cheese—was savory and sweet and buttery and spicy all at once.

"What's in this?" I said to Dev as I wiped up every last bit of the sauce with a piece of soft flat bread called naan. "How can it possibly taste this good?"

"It's a secret." He winked. "And that secret is a massive spice cupboard and hours of simmering. But let's pretend it's magic."

"It *is* magic." I watched the candlelight play on the embroidered tablecloth, the china. Then I glanced at Dev, who still wore a hint of a mischievous smile. I had to ask: "Did you actually wear a banana costume to a UN summit?"

He shrugged. "I had to sneak it in. It sounds silly, but it made people actually pay attention to what I had to say." He leaned closer and whispered in my ear, "Besides, it was either a banana or a bunch of grapes, and I figured there's got to be a meeting on the wine industry at some point. I'm saving my grapes. Don't tell my father."

I laughed loud enough that half the table turned to look at us. A radiant smile spread across Mrs. Rajesh's face to see us getting along, and my father seemed to relax a little.

"Our fathers have been friends since childhood," Dev said. He sat back to let a server take away his empty paneer plate. "But I don't really know your brother and sister."

He glanced down the table, where Lydia and Cole were chatting with the younger Rajesh children.

"I did know Oliver when we were children," Dev continued. He bowed his head. "Such a tragedy."

Oliver?

A voice chimed in from my other elbow before I could ask Dev what he meant. "How is it that we've met your lovely siblings, but we're only just meeting you now?" Mrs. Rajesh asked.

"I grew up away from the Circle," I said, giving the polite but vague answer to that inevitable question that we'd practiced, and then moving the conversation in a different direction as quickly as I could.

After a dessert of cinnamon cake and sweet, milky chai, I let myself glance up at Jack again. He stood stoically inside the door, like he had all through dinner. This whole night had felt like an odd, though pleasant-enough dream, but his presence reminded me it was time to get back to the real world.

I got ready to say my thank-yous and good nights. Besides the fact that Jack and I had somewhere to be, I actually liked Dev—I'd want to be friends with him. But I didn't want to *marry* him, and because I did like him, I didn't want to lead him on more than I already had just by being here.

But before I could excuse myself, Mr. Rajesh stood up and clapped his hands. "Now it is time for the party."

I set down my cup with the last dregs of chai. "Party?"

"Dinner's only the beginning." Dev offered a hand, which I took tentatively.

"I didn't realize." I met Lydia's eyes, and my father's. Neither seemed surprised by the party news. Jack, however, met my eyes briefly and frowned.

Everyone rose from the table, chatting, and I glanced at my watch. "Can you tell me where the restroom is?" I asked Indra Rajesh quietly, and she called a servant to walk me down the hall.

I locked the door and pulled my phone from my little beaded clutch. *We'll be later than we thought,* I texted, and adjusted the jeweled hairpiece over my forehead before the servant girl escorted me back out to the dining room, which had cleared out except for Dev.

"We're to make a grand entrance," he said, and with no other choice, I took his arm once more.

I should have known there would be a ballroom *in* the Rajesh home. Two men in white opened the tall, carved doors, and a hush fell over the room as Dev and I walked inside.

I stopped still. There were *hundreds* of people here under a ceiling dripping with jewels and flowers. From the bottom of the steps, Arjun Rajesh raised his arms, a distinctively Indian dance beat came from the speakers, and a cheer swelled from the crowd, so loud it reverberated from my chest down through my toes.

"Are they all Circle?" I asked Dev over the commotion.

"At least distantly," he yelled. "They all want to see you." He laughed as a dozen men ran up the stairs and, without so much as a hint of warning, swept me and Dev onto their shoulders. Dev grinned, and I yelped and held up my precariously pinned sari as the men bounced us into the crowd.

We were moving so fast, I could only catch flashes of the beaming faces staring up at me, but I could tell their expressions were magnified versions of what Mr. and Mrs. Rajesh's had been all night. This shining, open look of . . . what? Admiration? Yes, but that wasn't all. Optimism. Trust.

Hope.

I'd known what I was signing up for when I agreed to my father's plan. But it was only there, on the shoulders of two men I didn't know, being twirled to the rhythm of a Bollywood dance track, confetti being thrown at me from every side, catching like snowflakes in my hair, that I realized what I was really doing. I'd been viewing it as politics. But until this moment, I hadn't realized that I'd also agreed to be the symbol of the hopes and dreams of the most powerful people in the world.

Women surrounded us, wearing every color I could imagine, gleaming with strings of sequins and waving white scarves around their heads. When the men finally set Dev and me down, I clung to his arm, dizzy, and the women draped garlands of white, yellow, and orange marigolds around our necks until the pile threatened to suffocate me.

Dev took my hand, spinning me into the center of the dance floor again before I had a chance to catch my breath. The music and laughter pulled me in, and, even though I knew I could never *really* be what they wanted, right now there was no way I could do anything but go along with it. Soon, I was laughing too, and I dragged Lydia into a dance with me. Even Cole wasn't scowling.

After a time, though, my feet ached from dancing and my cheeks from smiling, both real smiles and the ones I knew I should give. I was nearly too tired to stand, anyway, and Jack and I had somewhere to be, so I caught Lydia's eye and ran my pinky across my eyebrow.

She nodded, and minutes later, my father was next to me, thanking

Dev and his parents for the evening, begging off the rest of the party because of jet lag.

They looked disappointed—it was still early—but Dev kissed my hand, I smiled and waved from the top of the steps, and we finally emerged into the quiet of the hallway.

My father walked me back to my room. The silk of my sari swishing was the only sound in the residential wing of the mansion, but my head still echoed with the drums and flutes and cheers of the ballroom. I pulled off the top few flower garlands until my shoulders felt lighter.

My father cleared his throat. I hadn't spoken with him much since dinner last night, and even though Lydia seemed to accept and even understand my grudging compliance with their terms, I wasn't sure he did. I was expecting a lecture on following the customs of these families, and how I couldn't just leave when I was tired, so I was surprised when he said, "You're doing a good job."

I looked up. My father was wearing a tunic similar to Mr. Rajesh's, and it was charmingly askew after a night of dancing.

"I know this isn't easy for you," he said. "Your mother—Claire always hated Circle politics."

Claire. I kept forgetting that Carol wasn't my mother's real name. Neither was West. She must have made both up after she found out she was pregnant with me and ran away from the Circle.

My father—I still couldn't think of him as *Dad*, a word that conjured up images of plaid shirts and summer barbecues—must have taken my silence as agreement, because he said, "It means a lot to us, and to the Circle, that you're willing to work with us on this. They adored you tonight."

Guilt flashed through me again. I wasn't cooperating quite as much as he thought.

A heavy velvet curtain led to the hall of bedrooms, and my father held it aside for me to walk through. "I'm not sure if it would help you to know this, but what you're doing here—being courted by these young men and their families—is very traditional. All our marriages are arranged."

I studied my hands, covered in bracelets and rings, delicate chains connecting them. "Lydia told me."

I felt my father watching me. "You can learn to love someone."

I couldn't stop myself. "So you and my mother—"

"Could never have had a future." It was gentle, but final. "Now it's obvious. But we were young then. Idealistic."

We passed beneath a gilded archway, where two lanterns flickered against the gold-threaded tapestries on the walls. Yes, tonight had been fine—more than fine—and all the dinners and parties and traveling to come might be fun in their own way. And I *was* glad I could help my family—it made me feel like I was actually one of them, for however long it lasted. But how was any of this different from that almost-wedding to Luc Dauphin? Different families, different countries, different cages.

At least the door to this cage was still propped open.

"Have your people made any headway with the clues or my mom?" I asked, my voice squeaking. My throat was parched and raw from talking over the music all night.

My father shook his head. "We're working on it."

We stopped at an ornately carved door off the long tile hallway. Overhead, a ceiling fan spun lazily, stirring my curls.

"I'll see you in the morning, then," my father said. "We have a farewell tea with the Rajesh family at ten, and we leave for Germany at noon."

"I'll be ready," I said. There was an awkward pause where I

thought he might hug me, but he just patted me on the shoulder and headed back down the hall.

I pushed into the bedroom and slumped against the door. Alone in the dark, I wanted nothing more than to curl up and close my eyes and decompress.

I didn't have time to rest, though. We were supposed to be out of here by nine, and it was already ten. I undid my sari and folded it on a dressing table. I replaced it with my jeans and a flowing top from the closet, and draped a scarf around my head.

There was a set of double doors leading from my room to a wide balcony, and while I was downstairs, someone had opened them and turned on low flute music that blended with the sound of the tinkling fountain in the courtyard below. The courtyard was lush and overgrown and perfect for hiding, and luckily, as much security as there was outside the palace, there weren't many guards patrolling *in*side. I switched off the overhead light and peered over the balcony's edge, hoping to catch a glimpse of the one guard I knew was there.

The air in India, at least as I'd experienced it so far, was heavy and oppressively hot and fragrant. Right now it still smelled like dinner—butter and spices and meat cooking. The streetlights in the distance were hazy.

I heard a crunch of gravel below me. The guard was passing beneath my room. He moved at a slow stroll—nothing here seemed to move faster than that. I wiped a bead of sweat that trickled down my neck. It had topped a hundred degrees today, and even after sunset, the air had barely cooled. I had to wear this scarf, though—Western faces attracted attention here, and attention was something we didn't need.

The guard was humming to himself as he rounded a corner. I hesitated for only a second before climbing over the carved marble balcony.

CHAPTER 5

I had mostly gotten rid of my fear of heights—maybe too many other fears had crowded it out. Still, I held my breath as I inched along the balcony to a trellis that ran down into the courtyard. Jack had scouted earlier and told me this was the best way to get out of my room. The trellis was splintered but sturdy, and I was on the ground and ducking behind a fern as the flute music from above changed to string instruments.

I picked a sliver of wood from my palm and watched the guard's shadow cross the exit from the courtyard, which led to a delivery entrance off the kitchen. As soon as he was out of sight, I skirted the edge of the courtyard and stuck to the shadows as I snuck by the brightly lit kitchen door.

I was so keyed up, I almost screamed when I felt a hand on my elbow.

"Shh."

I wondered briefly when I'd come to recognize Jack from just this tiny noise. He looked as handsome and serious as he had all day, but when I met his eyes, his face broke into a smile and he squeezed my arm. I could tell he was as glad to see me as I was to see him—we'd gotten so used to being together all the time that today had felt wrong. I almost threw my arms around him but stopped myself, and we stole off the property onto a bustling Kolkata street.

Jack pulled up the hood of his sweatshirt to hide his face. "Did you have any trouble getting out?"

I shook my head and glanced behind me. I didn't think I'd been followed by anyone from the palace, but I couldn't be sure. Plus, I had to assume the Order knew I was in India. I still didn't think they'd come after me, but my father's paranoia—and Jack's—were rubbing off.

I touched the little knife in the side pocket of my purse. I'd kept it in there since Elodie, the Dauphins' maid-slash-assistant-slash-secret-assassin, had given it to me at the failed wedding. I still wondered why she'd done it. Whatever her reason, the knife now felt like a good-luck charm in addition to being a weapon, and I kept it on me all the time, even though I'd never had to actually use it.

No one seemed to be following us, though, and I wasn't sure they'd have been able to keep us in their sights if they had. There were just so many people. People lounging in doorways of closed shops, watching us walk by. A group of men bathing at a faucet off the side of the road, soaping up and using a bucket to pour water over their heads, the cloths wrapped around their waists getting wet along with the rest of them.

Jack flagged down a bright yellow three-wheeled rickshaw with a fringe of tinsel around its canopy, and we squeezed inside.

I collapsed back into the seat, finally letting myself relax, and rubbed at my face before realizing that the black eyeliner was coming off on my hands. I'd had time to change back into my brown contacts, but not to wash off the heavy kohl.

Jack pushed his hood back. We were pressed close in the tiny rickshaw. "Did Lydia do your makeup?"

I told him about getting ready.

Jack smiled. "I think Lydia rather likes having a sister."

So did I. I wondered if there'd ever be a time when it would be me and Lydia sneaking out, hiding it from our dad like normal people.

"You don't think they're suspicious, do you?" I said.

Jack shook his head. "You're playing your part perfectly. As long as we don't get caught out here, we should be fine."

The rickshaw was stuck in a chaotic snarl of traffic alongside a motorbike with an entire family piled on top, and a cart being pulled by what I could swear were water buffalo, horns painted orange and blue and jingling bells on their collars.

Streetlights showed that there were almost as many colors on these streets as there were people. A salmon doorway in a turquoise wall. Blue buses with a yellow stripe, matching the yellow taxis. One bus had a display of birds painted across its side, and the words *Please honk* were scrawled across the backs of any large automobiles. The drivers behind them took the request to heart.

"I feel like I'm hallucinating," I whispered.

"This country can do that." Jack was staring out his side, too, where a wizened old man cooked up chunks of potato by flashlight in a metal wok as wide as the sidewalk, then handed them out to customers in makeshift newspaper bowls.

We were already late and the traffic was bad, so Jack asked the driver to stop. Just like at the palace, the air here had a scent, but this one wasn't so nice. We rounded a corner and found three goats eating from a pile of garbage, one wearing a My Little Pony T-shirt around its scrawny rib cage. It butted its head against my bag gently as we walked by, and I shrank against the opposite wall, but they let us pass, and we hurried on. Stellan would be wondering where we were.

The square where we were meeting him was wide and open, and we had to dodge a nighttime flower market to get there. Sari-clad ladies with gold hoops sparkling in their ears squatted on their haunches and strung heaps of bright orange and yellow marigolds into garlands like the ones I'd worn earlier, calling to us as we passed and holding up their wares. Behind them, toddlers climbed on a pile of abandoned cardboard boxes. One little boy looked up at us, and I did a double take. "Is that baby wearing makeup?" I said. He couldn't have been more than two, and he had kohl liner thicker than mine rimming his eyes.

"It's common here," Jack said. "Superstition."

I took a deep breath. "Where are we meeting Stellan?"

Jack pointed across the square, and I saw him immediately. Unlike us, Stellan was making no effort to disguise himself.

He was leaning against a light post and studying his phone, his worn leather jacket open to expose a black T-shirt, his blond hair glowing in the streetlight above. If pale skin drew looks here, blond hair caused downright gawking. Sure enough, a crowd had gathered a few yards from Stellan, but he appeared unconcerned. When he saw us, he stashed the phone in a pocket. "You didn't leave me to fend for myself after all."

"Couldn't you have put on a hat?" Jack said. The men were now staring at all three of us, whispering to one another. Great.

Stellan smirked and waved to the crowd. "You mean I'm not allowed to enjoy the hundred-percent humidity in my own clothes?"

"No." I grabbed his arm and pulled him out of the circle of admirers and toward the street.

"If you'll remember, some of us don't have the luxury of traipsing about without a care," Jack said shortly.

"No, some of us have to invent excuses to follow you two around the world." After the Circle learned about the Saxons' plan to marry me off to any family but the Dauphins, Stellan told his employers that he would follow us and report back. "Monsieur Dauphin was happy to let me go if it meant spying on you, but it's not going to be easy to lie to Elodie and Luc."

Luc and Stellan and Elodie had a strange relationship—it was as if they were a combination of siblings and best friends. Not what you'd expect to see between Circle family and staff. "You'll figure something out," I said.

We made our way across the street to the Indian Museum. It was dark and quiet, with a few stray dogs sleeping on its front stoop.

"So you think the other bracelet could be here?" Stellan said, looking up at the looming facade.

"This museum was built in 1814," I said. "The right time for Napoleon to slip something into their collection. Plus, it's in a Circle city, and it looks like there are Alexander artifacts in this collection."

Stellan lit a cigarette. "Have either of you been to this museum?" Jack shook his head, and obviously *I* hadn't.

"I *have* been here. This collection is curated, but it's a very haphazard job. If the bracelet was ever here, it might be in the same spot as it was in the eighteen hundreds, or it might have gotten tossed in a cardboard box in the basement, or walked right out of the museum on someone's arm . . ."

I frowned at him. "Well, it's the best chance we've had for a long time, and I had to trick a very nice family into thinking I might marry their son to get here," I said, "so *I'm* going to give it my best shot. Now what's the plan? Is there an unlocked door?"

The group of Indian men had followed us across the street and were edging closer. Stellan grinned at them. He called out something in what must be Bengali, and a few of them responded, then did those side-to-side head shakes I'd seen everyone here doing. Stellan pulled a wad of money from his pocket, peeled off some bills, and pressed them into the hand of one man, who counted it and hurried off, while the rest of them continued to gawk at us.

I raised my eyebrows.

"He's letting us in," Stellan said simply.

"I thought you said you had a *plan* to get us access," Jack said witheringly.

"This is the plan." We followed Stellan through a propped-open iron gate into a wide courtyard. "Everyone here has a cousin or a brother-in-law or a barber who can make things happen. Trust me."

I shook my head and looked around. The inner courtyard was impressive, with double rows of arches surrounding an immaculately manicured lawn and hedges. "Yeah, this place looks like a complete mess," I said sarcastically.

"Just wait." Stellan stubbed out his cigarette and held up a hand to wave at a different man, who'd just opened a door at the far end of the complex. "After you," he said.

The guy let us in, and Stellan asked him something. He shrugged and answered, pointing down the hall, then left and shut the door behind him, plunging us into a dark, damp quiet.

"That was sudden," Stellan said. "He said he has no idea if there are any Napoleon artifacts here, but that if there were, they'd probably be this way. He also said we shouldn't get caught, because he'll pretend he doesn't know how we got in and then we'll go to jail for breaking and entering."

"Wonderful." Jack clicked on a flashlight he must have stashed in his pocket and handed me another, and we made our way up a set of dingy steps. We emerged into an impressive gallery formed by arched wooden beams that loomed high overhead. Down the middle of the gallery marched—"Elephant skeletons?" I said.

They were bathed in moonlight from the windows above, and it wasn't just elephants. Deer, giraffes, and smaller animals whose bones I couldn't identify, all in a macabre parade. "I don't think this is the gallery we're looking for," I whispered.

Just then, a door slammed shut at the opposite end of the gallery. I scrambled one way, pulling Jack after me, and Stellan ducked behind a cabinet in the other direction. Unfortunately, Jack and I had nothing to hide behind but the elephants themselves.

A flashlight beam swept toward us. Jack hit the floor flat on his stomach behind the elephant skeleton's platform, and I started to do the same but it was too late. The guard was looking this way. I froze just behind the elephant's rear leg.

The flashlight beam hovered for a moment. Then the sound of footsteps receded.

I let out a breath as Jack jumped up, and we tiptoed across the room. Stellan was already heading down a connecting hall, gesturing for us to follow. "Apparently there are night guards on patrol," he whispered.

"Thanks," I said sarcastically.

We made our way into a long gallery with dim security lighting, and for the next hour, we scoured rows of glass cases, first in this room, then in a second, and I grudgingly admitted that Stellan had been right about the mess. It reminded me of the thrift store in Lakehaven where my friend Lara and I pawed through the cases for old jewelry. This was less fun—and took forever, especially since each of us only had one little flashlight. Even so, it felt amazing to finally be doing *something* after weeks of feeling powerless.

As far as I could tell, though, nothing we'd seen so far was connected to Napoleon. And none of the jewelry looked even a little like the bracelet we had.

Jack joined me at the end of the rows we were searching, and shook his head.

"Let's try the next gallery—" I whispered, but stopped.

Over his shoulder, there was movement at the far end of the gallery. "Stellan," I hissed under my breath, and yanked on Jack's sleeve. We crouched behind a display case and I had to bite my lip to stay quiet when an unidentifiable insect scurried across my foot. But after a few seconds, no footsteps came into the gallery and there was no flashlight beam, so it couldn't have been a security guard.

I stood up, shaking off thoughts of cockroaches, and Stellan emerged from behind a cabinet a few feet away. "I guess I'm seeing things," I whispered. "Sorry. Do you know where the Alexander artifacts are?"

Stellan led us down another hall.

The next gallery was less crowded and easier to search. We split up again, and I made it through most of the art on my side of the room pretty quickly—it was all paintings of landscapes and statues of animals. I shone my flashlight on a vertical case containing some jewelry, but it was full of crowns and necklaces, pieces far older than our bracelet.

And then I shone the light on the art next to the case, and for a second, I was too startled to do anything but stare. There on the wall, above a bas-relief of three women with their heads bent together, was a carving of the thirteen-loop knotted symbol from the locket

I wore around my neck: the same symbol that had led us on Mr. Emerson's trail of clues. It wasn't what we'd been looking for, but it wasn't a coincidence, either. And just below it was an inscription in French. "Guys," I whispered.

Jack reached me first and looked as surprised as I was. "Do you see the bracelet?" He looked at the surrounding artwork.

"No," I whispered, and pointed to the inscription. "But look. What does it say?"

Stellan pushed past us, muttering to himself. "*La Serenissima. One step closer to unlocking the secret through a union forged in blood,*" he translated.

I grabbed Jack's sleeve excitedly. The language was so similar to our current clues, we *had* to be on the right track.

"Unlocking. Maybe it's about the password." Jack snapped a picture of the inscription with his phone.

Stellan was squinting at the words. "The Serene One. That part's not in French, it's in Italian. *La Serenissima,* like it's a name."

"A statue? A painting?" I looked around for where it might be pointing.

A slam echoed through the museum, and all three of us jumped. Heavy footsteps sounded on the wood floor, and we scrambled behind the nearest statue's base in a jumble of arms and legs.

The footsteps continued on.

"We should go. We can't afford to be caught in here," Jack whispered. I was half sitting on his leg, and I could feel Stellan's pulse pounding where his back pressed into mine. "Even if *La Serenissima* is another piece of artwork, it's probably not in this museum."

We waited until the footsteps had faded to nothing, and then Jack hauled me to my feet and we hurried down the steps, out the door, and back out into the soupy air of Kolkata.

CHAPTER 6

The next morning—even though I'd crawled back onto my balcony after midnight and hadn't fallen asleep for hours after that—I was up with the sun. I thought I might sleep better than usual knowing we were making progress, but I'd been wrong. I rubbed my shoulders, tired and stiff from the dancing and the lack of sleep, and sat down cross-legged on one of the low couches on the balcony, where the morning air was a little cooler than the temperature inside.

When I pulled out my phone to look at the photo of the carving Jack had sent me, I was surprised to see a text from just a few minutes ago.

Venice's nickname is La Serenissima, it said. Stellan.

Why are you awake? I wrote back. He'd stayed elsewhere in the city, and had been up as late as I was. *Does that mean the bracelet's in Venice?*

Maybe. Lots of Napoleonic history there. Would make sense.

The Mikado family would be visiting Venice in a few days. My father had mentioned that we'd probably meet them while they were there.

Venice is already on my itinerary, but not for a few days, I texted. *Maybe by then we can figure out what "a union forged in blood" means.*

By the afternoon, we were on a plane to the next family visit in Germany, and I was decidedly less apprehensive than I'd been on the way to India. Knowing that we were on the right track was a huge relief, and I'd even asked Lydia if we could add some museums to the schedule so I wouldn't have to go behind the Saxons' backs quite as much. We'd had a family meeting earlier to debrief the Rajesh visit, and sitting around with my dad and Lydia—and even Cole, though he was playing on his phone the whole time—was weird, but nice. All those fantasies I'd had about family over the years didn't involve planning my arranged marriage, but minus that part, laughing and chatting with my father and sister was kind of a dream come true. And if all the families we'd be meeting the next few days were like the Rajeshes, even that part wouldn't be too bad.

Unfortunately, they weren't all like the Rajeshes.

First was the Hersch family, in Frankfurt. We arrived ahead of schedule and took a tour. I loved the city—it was huge and bustling and a little gritty, with surprise pockets of old-world charm. I could picture myself living there if I had to. The family themselves were another story. Their only son, Jakob, was twenty-eight years old and already married. Lydia had prepared me for it—apparently a union with me would be advantageous enough that his wife would be okay giving him up. Which wasn't awkward at all.

So after a day of museums that yielded nothing Napoleon-connected, Jakob's wife and daughter sat at the dinner table with us as Jakob and Mr. Hersch attempted to sell themselves to my father. Jakob kept staring at me—well, not at me, at my *eyes*—the way I imagined a vampire would look at a girl he was about to have for dinner. At least Lydia had told me on the plane earlier that Jakob wasn't a serious contender—my father just had to be fair. When I asked her which of them *was* a real possibility, she said that was still to be determined. Not that it mattered, I reminded myself. We still had eleven days to find the tomb and get me out of this.

Then the Melech family, in Jerusalem. Daniel had a mop of thick dark hair and a slim, handsome face. I could tell from the way Lydia had talked about him that she liked him, so I was surprised when we met him and he looked me up and down so clinically I wasn't sure whether to be offended or relieved when he nodded and shook my hand.

They, like many other families, adhered to certain local customs. There were candles, songs, blessings I didn't understand. A sweet, soft bread shared between us, wine, more food than I could have eaten in a month. And then another hard sell. The Melechs could offer a population base the Saxons couldn't reach from London. Historical significance. Military might unrivaled in any other small territory. They even outlined exactly what the ceremony would entail if we got married. It was so businesslike, they may as well have used a PowerPoint presentation.

We hadn't had time to make it to any cultural sites during the day, so Jack and I snuck out that night, hopeful. Alexander the Great had visited Jerusalem. The two of us met Stellan and searched a few museums, but came up empty. Stellan was probably right when he said the area's centuries of political unrest may have scattered any pieces Napoleon left here.

10 days, the Order texted that night. The optimism I'd been feeling before Germany was fading fast.

Next the Emir family, Saudi Arabia. I'd been sleeping worse and worse as the days wore on, and was so tired by that time that the whole visit felt like a series of hallucinations. Standing in the scorching heat, staring up at their Riyadh skyrise, a gleaming glass building in the desert sun. The terrible look on Samarah Emir's face when they talked about their oldest son Malik, killed by the Order just before I found out the Circle existed. A Saudi prince killed by a car bomb, the news had said, back when I thought the news told the truth.

They had a full-grown Bengal tiger in a penthouse petting zoo. Cole pushed its fur the wrong way, earning a snap of teeth that were as long as my little finger. That meant one of Jack's hands on his gun and the other on me—the only time he'd so much as acknowledged my presence in front of the Saxons during the visits. The tiger got a squirt with a spray bottle like it was a house cat scratching the sofa. The animals had been Malik's, Lydia said. Maybe they'd turn them out on the street to entertain themselves now that he was dead, Cole whispered when no one was listening.

Earlier, we'd seen the Emirs' oldest daughter, who was around my age, with big, sad eyes. I remembered Jack telling me she'd been caught having a relationship with a Keeper, and been forced to terminate him herself. I decided Cole might not be kidding about the animals.

At dinner, a parading of their younger son, the one who was supposed to marry me, even though he was twelve years old. The look in his eyes was too grown-up when he took my hand and pledged his eternal love and protection for me if we chose him.

I could never live here. Or with the Melechs. Or the Hersch family. I'd rather marry *Stellan*. During dessert, as I picked at sweet tea and sticky dates and thought about how days ten and nine had just been wasted and we weren't even certain our next clue was right, I felt the door of this pretty cage closing faster and faster.

In the middle of the night, I woke up gasping for breath.

I'd been dreaming about falling from a high-rise building, my mom holding me by the hand. It took me a second to remember where I was, and when I did, I sank back against the pillow and stared up at the tapestry hanging over my head. The air-conditioning stirred the mustard-yellow tassels surrounding it, and I clutched a pillow to my chest. During the day, I was holding it together, but nighttime conspires against a person's brain.

Eight days, a voice echoed in my head.

I switched on the lamp beside the bed. At least my insomnia gave me plenty of time for research, because over the past couple days, I'd been clinging to Venice like a life preserver. We had to be right about that clue. Right before I'd fallen asleep, I'd found a site that mentioned a conspiracy theory about San Marco Basilica in Venice and the bones of Alexander the Great. It was farfetched, but it at least gave us somewhere to start. Suddenly, I remembered when we'd been searching for Napoleon's diaries in the library at the Dauphins.

Stellan would be leaving to meet us in Venice later today. I texted him, *I think there's a book in the Dauphins' library about the secrets of San Marco or something like that. Bring it?*

I was surprised when my phone buzzed a second later. *Am I your errand boy now?*

Don't you sleep? I texted back.

Says the girl who just texted me at 4 a.m. her time. Dinner with the Emirs not go so well?

I made a face at the phone. *Just bring the book.*

After a couple minutes, the phone buzzed again. *Admit it. The more potential husbands you meet, the more appealing I look.*

You are even more obnoxious at 4 a.m., I responded, trying to forget that I'd already had that exact thought. Not that it mattered. It wouldn't come to that. It *wouldn't.*

I settled back against the pillows and waited for the sun to peek through the curtains before I texted Jack.

Want to train when you wake up?

Jack had been teaching me self-defense and a few fighting techniques while we were in Paris. We hadn't had any lessons since we'd been on the road, but we'd mentioned it to the Saxons, and the tour of the Emirs' home yesterday included a huge gym facility they'd encouraged me to use while I was here.

Jack texted back a few minutes later. *Pick you up in ten.*

The Emirs' gym took up an entire floor, with a sparkling pool and steam room on one end and a set of mats on the other. All four walls were floor-to-ceiling windows, and I watched the sunrise glint off the city skyline while I tied my sneakers and took off my necklace and Napoleon's bracelet and piled them on top of my sweatshirt in a corner.

"Ready?" Jack said.

"Whenever you are." I pulled my hair into a ponytail, knowing what was coming, but not when. A few seconds later, Jack grabbed me hard around the waist.

I hooked a foot around his ankle and tried to knock him over, but he stepped away easily. It made him loosen his grip, though, and I snagged his arm and bent his wrist backward. Just as quickly, he wrenched my other arm behind me hard enough that I cried out and let go.

The second I made a noise, he released me, and I rested my hands on my knees, breathing hard. Being exhausted was not helping my stamina. For the next half hour, Jack taught me how to break someone's fingers and exactly where on the shin to kick so it'd hurt the most.

And then he pulled out a knife. I reached into the pocket of the sweatshirt I'd left lying on the floor and pulled out my own.

"Like we talked about last lesson, the knife should be your last resort," Jack said. "It's a risk."

"A tactical risk," I remembered. "Only do it if I have to, because bringing out a weapon escalates a fight."

Jack nodded. "And it would be best for you to err on the side of caution."

I looked down at the knife and nodded.

"Where did we leave off?" Jack said.

I held out my blade like he'd taught me and rotated my wrist inward.

"Good," Jack said. "Now strike like I'm attacking you."

When he came at me with his knife, I jumped back and my knife fell to the mat. "Sorry," I said as I bent to pick it up. "Sorry. Again."

Jack came at me again, and I held on to the knife this time, but still flinched.

"Everything okay?" he said. He reached for me, but paused, glancing up at a small glass dome in the ceiling that was probably a camera. His hand dropped to his side.

"It's like I forgot how to do anything," I said crossly. "Go again."

We kept sparring, but my heart wasn't in it anymore. "Can we do something else?"

His eyes softened. "You really are doing well."

"No I'm not. I never do well with the knife. If someone was *actually* trying to kill me, I'd be screwed."

"No, you are." He glanced up again, subtly, at the camera overhead. "It's just . . . you could use a little help with your grip."

He came behind me and wrapped both arms around me, taking my hand in his. "Like this," he said, drawing me closer so I could feel the heat of his chest on my back, and I leaned into him, relaxing a little. I knew I was worried about more than the training, and so did he. "Your fingers go just here, like this. See, you've got it. It really is going fine, I promise." He squeezed my hands, subtly enough for the cameras to miss. "All of it."

I took one more deep breath. I hoped he was right.

Then I tightened my grip on the knife, and without any preamble, I twisted away and pointed the tip at Jack's chest.

The surprise took a second to drop from his face, but when it did, he raised his hands in surrender. "You win."

I dropped the knife to my side, and Jack's eyes glowed with a look so affectionate, I wished more than anything I could at least hug him. Instead, I said, "Let's go to Venice."

CHAPTER 7

The moment the plane landed in Venice, everyone's phones were buzzing. My father frowned and started making calls. Lydia was on her phone, too.

Once we were on the tarmac, I took advantage of their distraction to catch up to Jack. He, too, was staring at his screen. "What's going on?"

His face was a terrible mix of shock and sadness. "It's Dev Rajesh," Jack said. "He was found dead early this morning. They think he was poisoned."

My body went hot, then cold. "Oh no. No no no." Not only was I failing my mom, I was failing the Circle. "It's my fault."

"It isn't your fault. It isn't our fault. It's their fault. They're *terrorists*," Jack said, but he looked just as gutted as I felt.

I wrapped my necklace around my fingers and followed Jack to a waiting car, the knots of security around me noticeably tighter than they were yesterday. With all the Saxons on their phones, Jack and I ended up alone in a car together, and he draped his jacket in such a way that we could pretend to ignore each other and the driver couldn't see us clinging to each other's hands.

· · ·

There were no cars in Venice. Starting at the edge of the city all transportation was by boat, down the wide, rippling Grand Canal running through the middle of the city or one of the small side canals that led to residential areas. Once we got to our hotel, I took a quick shower, and Lydia was waiting with her entire hair and makeup arsenal when I got out. Tonight, though, I didn't feel much like getting ready for a party.

"Dev wouldn't want you to be deterred by this," Lydia said. She was dragging a brush through my hair, expertly pinning it into an elaborate updo. "He'd want you to get married and stop the Order. All the boys who have been killed—they'd want their sacrifice to make the Circle stronger."

I raised my eyebrows at her in the mirror. I somehow doubted that anyone's response to being attacked would be to hope I'd marry someone else. I guess I still had a lot to understand about the Circle. "It's weird," I said. "The Circle is so strong in every other way, but . . ." I didn't know if I should say it. If she'd be offended. "If the only thing they can do about the assassinations is hope that some girl getting married to one of them stops it . . . Doesn't that seem strange? It's like the Order makes them weak."

To my surprise, Lydia's mouth curled into a smile. "It's interesting that you see it that way. I disagree. You may not be able to tell yet, but the Circle is headed toward being stronger than we've been in a long time."

"What do you mean?"

"The Order hasn't always been this powerful." She pinned two braids together at the back of my head, and I watched to make sure she gathered up the section of hair that had been cut short at the wedding. I hated looking at it. "We've haven't faced obstacles to our rule for centuries. It's made us complacent. Do you know what first brought the Order into our consciousness again?"

I shook my head.

"My grandfather and my uncle. Just before I—" She glanced down at me. "Just before *we* were born, they were murdered by the Order. That's how Father became the head of our family."

I remembered Jack mentioning Alistair's brother being killed, but he'd never mentioned that the Order had done it.

"Fighting the Order gives us a reason to come together," Lydia went on. She crossed to a closet, where clothes that were obviously hers had been arranged. She pulled out a white dress with long sleeves and laid it on the bed.

I hadn't thought about it that way. "You can't mean you're *glad* the Order is doing this, though."

"No! But it's our destiny to defeat the Order, just like it's your destiny to be part of this fight, with our family."

Last year in history class we'd learned about Manifest Destiny. It was the belief that it was inevitable—*fated*—for the United States to expand across North America, no matter who or what got in the way. It was an appealing thing—a powerful thing—knowing you had fate on your side.

And for the Circle, that fate was me. *Their fates mapped together become the fate of the Circle*—that was what the mandate said about the union between the girl with the purple eyes and the One. Destiny.

I pulled on the white dress while Lydia did touch-ups to her own hair and makeup and got a red dress from the closet. As she changed into it, I noticed a tattoo on her rib cage.

"I thought you didn't get the tattoos until your seventeenth birthday," I said.

Lydia ran her fingers over the inked skin. "This isn't the Saxon symbol."

She turned and showed me the tattoo—a flower, with only a few petals filled in, like someone had been playing *he loves me, he loves me not* with the rest. It looked fresh. She pulled her dress on, covering it.

"What does it mean?" I said.

She smiled at herself in the mirror. "I'll tell you someday."

I looked at us side by side in the mirror, me, pale and in all white, like a ghost of my fiery sister, with her olive skin and bright lipstick and red dress. She took my arm. "Ready to meet suitor number five?" she said. "This one's hot."

The boat pulled up to the landing outside the Mikados' hotel, and a man in a pressed suit and top hat held out his hand to help me onto solid ground. The Saxons' guards surrounded me immediately, Jack sticking closest.

I glanced over my shoulder at the sun setting over the Grand Canal. It had been a gray day, with rain pockmarking the canals on and off throughout the afternoon. Just as we'd left the hotel, though, the sun had broken through, and now the whole city glowed rosy, the building facades stacked like multicolored dominoes.

Reflections of the San Marco Basilica and the surrounding buildings shimmered on the canal's surface, making watercolor paintings in the misty light, until a *vaporetto*—a water bus—cut through it, the ripples glowing bright orange in its wake. I wished I could enjoy the view, and the party. I was supposed to go there and smile and have fun. The last time that had happened, I'd been in India, and now Dev was dead. It felt wrong, and on top of everything else, I was starting to get really nervous that we wouldn't find anything when we tried to follow the *La Serenissima* clue tonight.

"Is everything all right?" my father asked, and I jumped.

"Yeah," I said. "Yes. Fine."

"I know it's frightening," he said. "But we'll keep you safe."

I nodded again, though my own safety was the least of my worries. I took one more look over my shoulder and followed him inside.

The Mikados were ostensibly in Venice for a fund-raiser—the kind of vague charity rich people used as an excuse for a social event. But I doubt they would have made the trip if they didn't want to meet me, especially because they were actually the first family of Japan. Most of the Circle families had lower-ranking family members doing the public jobs, but Ryo Mikado was prime minister.

Of course, attendance had swelled once the Mikados announced that I'd be coming. My father said they had to cap the guest list, and enough celebrities had joined up that the event was going to be taped, with parts of it broadcast live. I thought people might back out after the latest assassination, but the news seemed to have the opposite effect. It did make for a massive security detail, though. Jack stood with a small army of guards who spoke quietly into their lapels and watched the velvet-draped windows that looked out on the Grand Canal.

I was seated with my father and Lydia and Cole at the head table, under a faded but intricate ceiling mural of scenes from Greek mythology. Straight across from us and past some smaller tables was a stage, where a jazz trio had been playing since we came in, and where the main attraction—Sunday Six, the most popular boy band in the past few years—would be performing between the appetizer and dinner courses.

And between me and the stage were dozens of Circle members.

In India, the guests' interest in me had been overt, but here I was the object of subtle glances, whispers, and a steady stream of well-wishers who couldn't stop staring at my eyes. I understood for the first time what it would be like to be famous and have the whole world think you belonged to them.

I wished I could make them stop. I wasn't so sure I was going to be a good Circle princess tonight.

Soon, the crowd hushed and Lydia reached around my father's chair to squeeze my shoulder as the doors opened and the Mikados made their grand entrance.

I pasted on a fake smile. Lydia hadn't let on whether the Mikados would be an "advantageous match," but I suppose it didn't matter—it wasn't like I had to impress them. They'd want me no matter what. The family made their way to the head table, and Takumi bowed before sitting next to me. "It's a pleasure to meet you," he said quietly.

I don't know what I'd expected Takumi to be like, but it wasn't this. He was tall and slim and wore black-rimmed glasses. His hair was undercut and swept rakishly to the side, and while his father wore a traditional tuxedo, he had on slim pants and a long, asymmetrical jacket that belonged on a runway.

Even though he *looked* more like a high-fashion mannequin than a real person, Takumi was pleasant and polite, and all through the appetizer course we talked about how lovely Venice was and what I'd seen in London. He told me about his favorite restaurant in Tokyo and offered to take me there one day and teach me how to order real Japanese ramen—which he promised me was much different from the crunchy packets you get in the grocery store—out of a vending machine, of all things. He was shocked that I'd never had sushi, and I told him that if he ever came to the US and wanted a good American hamburger, he had to try In-N-Out. We talked about everything but the important stuff, and it helped me forget that the rest of the room was watching, no doubt analyzing my every move.

I realized that I hadn't even looked at my watch since Takumi sat down, and his parents hadn't done anything weird, either, which was a nice change. The past few families we'd met had been so terrible that imagining a future with them had made me feel sick. The thought of Dev had been okay, but now . . . did this mean, if it came down to it, that Takumi was my best option?

Him or Stellan, I guess. There was always Stellan. The more I thought about being married to somebody, the more I was forced to think about being married to *him*. At least I wouldn't have to worry about a creepy family or a surprise first wife with him. And I knew him way better than any of the Circle guys, so I'd know what I was getting into. On the other hand . . . I *knew* him. So I knew what I'd be getting into.

I was glad when the static of the microphone hissed from the speakers onstage.

I may have been getting used to the Circle, but there were still moments when I was struck by how strange it was. My friend Lara back in Lakehaven—or anyone else I knew—would have had a heart attack if they got to be in the same room as Eli, Alexsi, and Noah. Sunday Six usually played to sold-out stadiums of screaming girls, and they were about to perform on a tiny stage ten feet away from me. If someone I knew hadn't been killed earlier today, this whole evening would actually be pretty fun.

Lydia told me that all three band members were Circle. Noah Day was a Saxon cousin, Alexsi Popov was related to the Vasilyevs, and Eli Abraham, the lead singer, was a Melech. With three families' worth of Circle support, it was no wonder they were so popular.

The TV cameras that had been idly roaming the crowd focused on the stage, and the lights went down. The three boys strolled out to polite applause. Alexsi tuned his guitar and Noah tapped his drumstick experimentally on a cymbal, but Eli swung the micro-phone stand between his hands and peered out into the crowd. He had chin-length, wavy black hair, held back today with a wide head-band. None of them had purple eyes, but they all had the swagger that came with being part of the Circle. And with being rock stars, I guess.

Eli's eyes landed on our table, then found me. His lips curled into something that couldn't quite be called a smile, and then he went back to adjusting the mic. I wasn't a Sunday Six superfan, so I could be wrong, but Eli was different than I would have imagined. He seemed more distant than he was on TV. Maybe an event like this wasn't as exciting as playing to screaming thirteen-year-olds. "One, two, three, four!" he counted off, and they broke into one of their first hits, "After Midnight."

Despite the somber mood hanging over the party, the wine and the music had loosened people up. Around the room, a few heads bopped to the music, and next to me, Lydia was mouthing the words to the chorus. Even Takumi was tapping his foot.

When the song finished, Eli wiped his face with the hem of his plaid shirt, then leaned close to the mic. "This next one," he said with another of those weird, sad smiles, "is for a very special young lady. Hi, Avery West. You're going to change the world, you know."

I sat up straight, startled. The Circle didn't usually say things like that in public. The cameras panned to me, and I tried not to look like a deer in the headlights. For just a second, I pictured Lara watching at home and wondered if she'd even recognize me. If she did, she would be so confused. Then the band started playing again, and the camera swung away.

Lydia poked my arm behind my father's back and raised a sugges-tive eyebrow in Eli's direction. "Yeah right," I mouthed. Not being in the direct line made him ineligible for the mandate, and he was also *Eli Abraham*. But then again, *he* was the one who kept smiling at and talking to *me*. My eyes made people like Eli Abraham interested in me. This was all so, so strange.

I had to admit Sunday Six were actually good live, even though Eli seemed distracted. I still wasn't feeling cheerful enough to dance in my seat like Lydia, but I did teach Takumi the words to some of the choruses.

To finish the set, they played my favorite song of theirs. As it built to the end, Eli jumped off the stage, mic in hand. He crooned to a few tables before making his way back to ours.

"In the name of loooooove!" As he hit the highest note, punctuated with a bang on the bass drum, the crowd burst into applause. With another of those sad smiles right at me, he bowed to our table. Whistles and cheers sounded across the room.

Eli took a few seconds to stand. When he did, I flashed him a grin, a genuine one this time, but he didn't smile back. In fact, his expression was oddly tortured.

"I'm so sorry," he said, and set the microphone on the table next to him.

I sat forward, confused, and felt the rest of the room do the same.

And then Eli Abraham pulled a gun out of the waistband of his skinny jeans. He raised it at our table. And he shot Takumi Mikado in the chest.

CHAPTER 8

There was a moment of complete silence before the room burst into screams. People stampeded toward the doors, chairs were knocked over, well-dressed guests were shoved to the floor.

I was still sitting, stock-still, not least because Takumi had collapsed onto me. He made a gurgling noise in his throat, and behind his glasses, his eyes were glassy, blinking.

Guards rushed Eli from both sides. Jack was the first to knock him to the ground.

Eli raised his gun. "Jack!" I screamed. But Eli pointed it at his own head and pulled the trigger.

And then Jack was pinning down the dead lead singer of the world's most famous pop group and I had a guy I'd just met dying in my arms.

Takumi sagged across my lap, his flop of hair fallen over his eyes. I clapped a hand over the wound on his chest. There was so much blood, I couldn't see where the bullet had actually hit. "It's okay," I said blindly, my voice thin, reedy, desperate. "It'll be okay. You'll be okay."

He wouldn't be okay. He blinked twice more, staring up at me, and then his eyes slipped closed and his rasping breaths stopped.

Hands were lifting him off me, and then I was being bundled outside and into a boat. Only when we were zipping away down the Grand Canal did I realize that my hands and my white dress were caked in blood.

Eli acted alone, they were saying. The other band members realized something had been bothering him for a few days, but had no idea what was going to happen. How the Order had managed to coerce Eli no one knew, but it was clear they'd killed two birds with one stone. Literally. A boy who could be the One and another important Circle member, both in spectacular fashion.

Back at our hotel, security stashed me in the suite of rooms they'd secured for us. As soon as I'd showered and put on clean clothes, I started working on a way out. Maybe we should have canceled our plans after what had just happened, but Takumi Mikado's blood still felt like it was all over me. Eli Abraham's apology, and his odd assertion that *I* could change things, had been burned into my mind.

Following the clues felt more important than ever.

But now there were even more guards outside my door and new ones posted at either end of the hallway. My original plan to sneak off once they left me here wouldn't work. I crossed to the window and pushed aside the heavy silk curtains. No way. It was four stories to the canal below.

For a few minutes, I wore a path in front of the door. On top of everything else, they'd spirited me away before I could be sure Jack wasn't hurt, and he hadn't responded to my texts. I tapped my phone with my fingernails, faster and faster. And then I heard Jack's voice in the hall. I stopped. He wasn't supposed to be here. But it was definitely him, chatting like everything was normal. Relief flooded through me.

And then, from down the hall, a loud *boom*. A flurry of exclamations and running footsteps, then Jack saying, "Go. I'll watch her door." A few seconds later, two knocks, a pause, two more. The signal we'd agreed on.

I grabbed my bag and opened the door a crack.

Jack stood, his back to me, looking down the hall. Plausible deniability. If this was caught on camera, he could pretend he hadn't seen me sneak out.

"Three doors down on the left," he murmured, not turning around. "Emergency exit. I turned off the alarm."

"Okay," I whispered, easing the door shut behind me and padding down the plushly carpeted hallway. I pushed open the door to the emergency stairs and hurried down, emerging into a narrow alley between buildings. I listened for a moment, then let the door shut behind me and shrank back into the shadows halfway down the block.

The door opened a few minutes later. I went as still as I could, just in case—and Jack stuck his head out and looked around. I waited to make sure he was alone, then ran to him.

Before I could say a word, he swept me up in his arms, and I let my guard down for the first time since dinner, the shock I'd been holding back finally washing over me in waves.

Jack hugged me tighter.

I disentangled myself just enough to pull him down and kiss him. He broke away. "I—"

I just shook my head and kissed him again, and then we were kissing so fiercely, nothing else mattered.

That last time we'd slipped up, Jack had stopped it as quickly as it had started.

Not this time.

We pulled each other so close, I could feel the hard ropes of muscle in his arms as he wrapped them around me. Everywhere his skin touched mine felt like it was melting, in the best way.

This was so much better than I'd remembered. How had we possibly been able to *not* do this all the time? Kissing him felt safe. Kissing him made me forget.

It was only when we ran roughly into the damp stone wall of the next building over that we pulled away, gasping. I hadn't even realized I had his shirt half off, my palms pressed to his ribs, just under those mysterious round scars.

Jack pushed my hair back from my face. "You were so close. He could have shot you."

"He didn't." I slipped my hands out from under his shirt and around his back. "He could have, and he didn't. That's what I've been saying—the Order doesn't actually want to kill *me*. But he could have shot *you*."

"He didn't."

Another violent shudder ran through me. Jack pulled me to his chest again.

"We have to stop this." It wasn't just for my mom anymore. Dev Rajesh, then Eli and Takumi . . . I'd realized intellectually that the Order was killing people, but I didn't *know* them.

If I did marry somebody, though, would that stop it? The Saxons thought so, but I'd never been sure. Maybe if it proved that the union didn't lead to the tomb after all, they'd have no reason to kill any more boys . . . but that wouldn't help my mom. Finding the tomb was the only thing that would solve both problems. After tonight, seven days. "We have to find it," I said. "There has to be something here."

"I know."

I took a deep breath, and felt Jack's chest expand with one of his own. Finally, I pulled away and smoothed my hair back from my face. "We should go."

Jack's hair was wild, his shirt askew. I saw his arm move, almost reach for my hand. Stop. Notice me notice the hesitation. Both of us frozen, waiting for the other to make a move. To acknowledge that the worse everything got, the more difficult it became not to have each other to fall back on.

"I—" Jack said. He stuffed both hands into his pockets.

I nodded, smoothed my skirt, and we ran out of the narrow alley without a word.

The fog that had settled since dinner made it impossible to see more than ten feet in any direction, but it seemed to amplify sounds echoing off the narrow alleys that served as streets for anyone not moving around by boat. I flinched at every slamming door or boat motor, and glanced over my shoulder at every set of footsteps.

Jack walked quietly beside me, lost in his own thoughts. I wondered suddenly what would happen if—*when*—I did get my mom back. If I stayed with the Circle, I might not have to be married off, but unless I had enough power to change the rules, Jack and I would never work, anyway. Maybe we'd leave, but then I'd be abandoning the family I'd just met, and he'd be leaving the only family he'd ever had. Maybe, maybe, maybe.

The only certainty was that we had to find this bracelet.

Finally, after ten minutes of weaving quietly through the maze, a glimmer of light shone up ahead and the alley opened up onto a wide square. "Oh," I breathed. Despite everything, the square ahead looked like magic.

The fog wasn't as dense here—it must have had more space to dissipate. But the driver had told us earlier today about the *acqua alta*. "Just be glad it's not August," he'd said in broken English. "If the *acqua alta* comes in August, you can smell Venice from anywhere in Italia."

Now I saw what he meant.

The Piazza San Marco was underwater. Tourists strolled along wooden walkways that stretched across it, but it looked like they were walking on the water's surface. The lights from the basilica and the surrounding buildings shimmered in the ripples, creating gleaming pinstripes in the settling dusk. Around the edges of the square, locals went about their business as usual, ducking into stores and sitting at half-submerged cafe tables in knee-high galoshes.

I licked my lips. The air in Venice tasted a little like stagnant ocean and fish, but with an overtone of fresh breeze that made it not unpleasant.

I looked around and got my bearings. We'd emerged at the corner of the piazza nearest the San Marco Basilica, with a small cafe on one side of us and a row of shuttered shops and outdoor bistros on the other. "*La Serenissima* doesn't refer to any specific part of Venice, so that doesn't give us a lot of direction," I said, "but there's this conspiracy theory about Alexander the Great's bones being hidden at San Marco Basilica." Stellan had found the book I'd asked for from the Dauphins' library and told me the details.

"Napoleon might have heard that rumor, too. He was really interested in the church. And that over there"—I pointed across the piazza—"is called the *Ala Napoleonica*. The Napoleonic Wing.

Though it seems to have only Venetian history these days, which is why I want to check the basilica first."

Jack was nodding along. "Sounds like as good an idea as any."

"Actually," said a girl's voice from behind us, in a light French accent, "I've got a better idea, but by all means continue to waste more time."

We both spun around toward the cafe. There, leaning against a column, hundreds of miles away from Paris where she should be, was the Dauphins' maid, Elodie.

CHAPTER 9

Jack pulled me behind his back, and I reached into my purse for my knife, like it would do much good against the throng of guards the Dauphins had probably sent to bring me back to the cell in their basement.

"Where are they?" I said, looking behind her. "Where are your guards?"

Elodie pushed off the wall, strolling a few feet out to nudge the water's edge with her boot. The platinum highlights in her blond hair glinted in the dark. "I was beginning to think the earlier unpleasantness kept you inside for the night."

"*Unpleasantness*?" I snapped. "Two people died."

"How did you know we were here?" Jack said.

She rolled her eyes. "Can you really not guess?"

Jack tensed. "I'm going to kill Stellan—"

"He didn't *tell* me. I just happened to remember the little threesome thing you all had going on, and what with his extended absences to *spy on the Saxons* lately, it wasn't hard to put two and two together. Found the hidden phone he's been using to communicate with you, and here I am. You know," she said, glancing appraisingly at the bracelet gleaming on my wrist, "you should really be more careful."

In a second, Jack was behind her, his gun to her back. "What do you want, Elodie?"

"Jack!" I started, but before I could say any more, Elodie wheeled around and kneed him in the crotch. He stumbled backward.

She retreated a few feet. "Don't touch me—"

She went quiet when Jack pointed his gun at her again. Luckily, the small cafe we stood at the edge of was empty enough that no one was watching us.

"I didn't realize things were quite so murderous around here." Elodie raised her hands to waist-height.

"Did you not notice what happened tonight?" I nearly shrieked, and made myself quiet down. "I don't care if you *are* telling the truth. You picked the worst possible time to sneak up on us."

"I'm not here to hurt you," she said, her palms still out, placating.

"Put the gun away," I said to Jack.

"She could sound the alarm to the Dauphins at any second." Jack's eyes still roamed the piazza, but no one had approached us. "I don't even know what they think they'd be able to do with you, but I guarantee she's not just here to chat."

"Just put the gun down," I said. "Nobody else is getting shot tonight."

He lowered it slowly, and I reached into my bag and swapped my knife for pepper spray. "It's just mace," I said to Elodie. "But you can't expect us to trust you."

"There," Jack said, pointing to the cafe's spindly bistro tables. "Sit." While I held her at mace-point, he took a pair of handcuffs from an inside pocket of his jacket and cuffed her wrist to the chair.

"Are you serious?" Elodie huffed, flopping back dramatically.

"It's just a precaution." Once she was strapped in, I dropped the mace.

"I have to admit that after I helped you escape the wedding"—Elodie's almond-shaped eyes got artificially wide, innocent—"I thought you'd be a little happier to see me."

So it *was* on purpose. "Why did you do that, anyway?"

Elodie drummed her fingers—the only part of her able to move freely—on the arm of the chair. "I was bored. Thought I'd stir up some drama."

"Be serious."

"You seriously want to know why I'm here?" she said in her haughty French accent. "You could have asked *before* handcuffing me. As I said, I've been monitoring your conversations with Stellan. And I think I know things about your clues that you don't."

We left Elodie cuffed to the chair, her long, slim legs crossed casually like she was just out for an espresso on a foggy evening. I'd texted Stellan and changed our meeting place, and now I raked my free hand through my hair. I hadn't had time to dry it after I showered earlier, and it was tangling in the breeze as it dried. Soon, I turned around to heavy footfalls on the wooden pathway.

"I heard what happened with Eli Abraham," Stellan said. "Are you all right?" He looked over my shoulder and stopped short when he saw Elodie.

"If it isn't the third wheel," Elodie said, waving her fingers at him.

Stellan turned back to Jack and me. "I'm assuming the light bondage isn't recreational, so who's going to fill me in?"

I told him as much as we knew over the strains of a string quartet that had started playing at a nearby bistro. Stellan chewed his lower lip, then pulled up another chair and sat knee-to-knee with Elodie.

"The Dauphins didn't send you? You haven't told them what we're doing? If we untie you, are you going to hurt us or run?"

"No, no, and no." Elodie rolled her eyes. "I wouldn't have shown up here alone and relatively unarmed if I wanted to hurt you or your precious purple-eyed girl, okay?"

"*Relatively* unarmed?" I said, but Stellan leaned forward, elbows on his knees, and locked eyes with Elodie.

"Are you telling the truth, El?"

She didn't flinch. "Yes." Then she looked up at Jack with the same flat determination. "Jackie, you know I am. You have always been able to tell when I'm lying. And after tonight, I'd think you'd want as much help as you can get to stop the Order for good."

Jackie?

Jack took the keys to the handcuffs out of his pocket. Elodie batted her eyelashes at him sarcastically, and I was struck by the feeling of being an outsider. I knew Jack and Stellan had history, but hadn't really thought about how Jack would have known Elodie for half his life, too. And try as I might, I couldn't picture him as ever having been a "Jackie."

"Okay," I said. "But what's in this for you?"

Elodie flicked the bangs out of her eyes, and I wondered, stupidly, how she kept her hair so perfect. She was part Asian, and I didn't think there was any way the platinum blond was natural, but it always looked freshly done.

"What's in it for me is that they'll go after Luc eventually," she said. "They're hitting every other person who could be the One, in every Circle family. Maybe they've given Luc a reprieve since they already killed the Dauphins' baby girl, but I don't know. I'd rather stop them before they try."

I didn't think she was lying.

"And, of course," Elodie went on, "everything that would come with finding the tomb, which I'm sure these two care about, too. Fame, fortune, acclaim . . ."The sarcastic note in her voice was back.

Jack palmed the back of his neck and shrugged at me. He was willing to trust her.

"Fine,"I said. It was later than we'd realized, though, and it'd be a lot easier to search for clues while the basilica and the museum were open rather than sneaking in, so we put whatever Elodie had to say on hold for a few minutes. I wasn't about to give up this chance just because she thought she had a better idea.

Inside San Marco Basilica, Elodie was pointing out something on a fresco to Jack, so I said, "Split up; meet back here in ten?" and grabbed Stellan's arm, pulling him down the center aisle.

"Yes, I trust her," he said before I could open my mouth.

I sucked in an indignant breath.

"You are blindingly obvious,"he said, cutting me off again. "That's how I know exactly what you wanted to ask."

I frowned and made my way toward the first few pieces of artwork down one side of the church. He inspected the ones higher on the wall. I thought of Elodie smiling at him earlier and flashed back to the club in Istanbul I'd visited with them, which seemed like a lifetime ago. I remembered the look on her face while she watched some girl hit on him. *Everyone's interested in him in that way*, she'd said.

I glanced over my shoulder, searching Stellan's fine-boned profile for any hint that he might be lying to me. "Is something going on between you two?"

Stellan regarded a statue of Jesus and the Virgin Mary. "Is that relevant?"

"I don't know, is it?"

His mouth curved up at the corners. We moved toward the altar.

"You believed her *immediately* when she said she wasn't trying to hurt us," I said. "And maybe she's not, but I think I have the right to know if it's more than rational deduction that makes you want to hand her all our secrets."

Stellan turned from a gilded cross. "Jealous, wifey?"

I bristled. "I'm just saying that you two obviously have a history of . . . something. At least friendship."

Stellan's grin grew. "Oh, more than friendship."

"See!"

"Let me give you a life lesson. Just because two people have a history doesn't mean they've pledged their eternal love and loyalty." He raised an eyebrow. "Sometimes a hookup is just a hookup."

"You've known each other forever. I don't believe anything is *just* anything."

"I believe Elodie *because* I've known her for that long. Trust me, *kuklachka*," he said when I tried to interrupt. "I know what I'm doing. I'm smart enough not to put faith in a girl just because she's pretty. I still question half of what *you* tell me, after all."

I ignored the flirting. At least none of the potential Circle husbands had actually tried to hit on me. On the contrary, they were fairly businesslike about the whole arrangement, unlike Stellan. "I haven't lied to you. At least not since the time I lied to you. But I didn't know I could trust you then. I'd like to think I can trust you now." Yes, it was trust with a healthy side of suspicion, but still.

He bumped my shoulder lightly with his. "If you can't trust your future husband, who can you trust?" he said in my ear, and dodged my elbow to his ribs.

When it became clear we weren't going to find anything here, we met back up with Jack and Elodie to do a quick recon of the front of the church together. While we finished looking, I started to interrogate Elodie.

"Before I tell you my thoughts," she said, "let me make sure I have this straight. You have a bracelet that may lead to the location of Alexander's tomb. You're searching for a matching bracelet that would complete that clue. You're looking for the tomb because the Circle wants the weapon against the Order, obviously, to stop the assassinations and get rid of them for good."

I nodded.

"And something else?" she prodded, glancing between the three of us.

I scowled. Elodie had been sure I had a thing for Stellan since I first met her. "It's not anything like *that*," I said. "Stellan's just helping."

Elodie smirked. "I did not *actually* think you all were in some kind of three-way relationship, but nice to know that's the first place your mind goes. I mean, I noticed that you mentioned your mother."

I met Jack's eye, and he shrugged. I guess we were telling her everything.

"The Order kidnapped my mom," I said. "I want her back." Close enough to the truth.

"And they killed Emerson Fitzpatrick," Stellan said.

"What?" Elodie stopped dead, and Jack nearly ran into her. "Fitz is *dead*?"

"The Order killed him," I repeated.

"How—when?"

"A couple weeks ago. Right after the wedding thing with Luc."

Elodie started walking again, but she looked shell-shocked.

"I'm sorry," I said. "I didn't know you knew him that well."

"Neither did I," Stellan said.

Elodie pushed her hair behind her ears. "I . . . didn't. I just didn't realize that had happened."

Someday I might be able to think about Mr. Emerson beyond a quick mention without this ache that made it hard to think, but today wasn't that day. I had to change the subject. "And besides all that, I don't want to be forced to marry somebody to fulfill the mandate when I seriously doubt it'll work."

We headed out of the basilica and back into the night air. A silence had fallen over us as heavy as the fog. Our shoes made hollow clunks across the wooden pathways, and I shivered, wrapping my arms around myself. I wished I'd thought to grab a jacket.

Jack came up beside me and, without even asking if I needed it, shrugged out of his and put it around my shoulders.

"Thanks," I mouthed. The jacket smelled like him—that combination of earthy and warm and a little sweet that brought back memories of things I shouldn't be thinking about.

Behind us, the San Marco Basilica rose gleaming white against the dark night. Its facade was an endlessly intricate amalgamation of arches and frescoes and soaring pillars, layered like the architects couldn't decide when to stop, and behind that, domes that reminded me a little of the Hagia Sophia.

Elodie lit a cigarette and flicked a burning bit of ash into the dark water we were walking over. The little orange ember winked out, and she seemed to compose herself. "So I was saying, I'm here because I saw your texts about the clue you found. 'A union forged in blood.'"

I still couldn't believe she'd been spying on us for weeks. I nodded.

"I'd already been working on the other clues, trying to see angles you hadn't. When you got that clue, I thought of something. Do you remember when I told you about the idea of fate mapping, in the biological sense?"

I nodded. We'd talked about it while she was getting me ready for the wedding to Luc. I'd assumed it was her way of cluing me in to the fact that she was helping me escape. "What does it mean again?"

We stopped to let a line of tourists pass on an intersecting wooden walkway. "A fate map is the developmental history of a cell. Which is important to *us* first because of the line in the mandate: 'Their fates mapped together.'"

I glanced at Stellan.

"And second, because Olympias—"

From ahead of me, Stellan sighed.

"Who's Olympias?" The name sounded familiar, but I couldn't place it.

"Alexander the Great's mother," Stellan answered. "Elodie could tell you an encyclopedia's worth of facts about her."

"She's only one of the most fascinating women in history," Elodie retorted. "People said she was a witch, but really she was just very advanced for her time, scientifically. She and Aristotle. They're the reason the Circle has purple eyes, you know. She linked them together genetically in a way that's unheard of even now." She took a long drag of her cigarette. "Genetics have always been important to the Circle, from the start. And genetics have a lot to do with blood."

I raised my eyebrows. Of course blood was important to the Circle. *Rule by blood.* I'd never really thought to consider, though, whether that meant blood as in violence, or blood as in bloodline. I assumed both. "So?"

"So, 'a union forged in blood.' That doesn't sound like a social construct like marriage, does it?"

It didn't—that was what I'd been saying all along. Marriage as the end-all of the mandate didn't make sense. And Napoleon had written in his diary that *they're wrong about the mandate.* "What else do you think it might mean?"

"My prevailing theory," Elodie dragged it out, like she was enjoying having an audience, "and one I know some of the Circle share, is that the union has nothing to do with the actual marriage, and more to do with what the marriage can produce. As in," she said, turning to look over her shoulder at me, "a child."

A strangled noise came from my throat. Stellan paused in the middle of a step, and I was careful to avert my eyes before he looked my direction. If I couldn't stop obsessing about having to marry him now, what would the idea that we were supposed to *make a baby* do?

I swallowed. "I thought you said you had ideas about our clues. Getting me pregnant wouldn't help us find the second bracelet, or the tomb."

Elodie stubbed out her cigarette with her boot as we stepped off the wooden walkway at the other end of the Piazza San Marco. "You're right—a child likely has more to do with uniting two bloodlines than it does with Napoleon's quest. But you've also been looking for ways to *unlock* the bracelets, right? What I'm proposing is that maybe your clues, in addition to sending you on the hunt for the second bracelet, have to do with that, too. Like if a word related to blood, or DNA, or a child could be the password?"

I slipped the bracelet off my arm, rotating the rows of letters. *One step closer to unlocking the secret through a union forged in blood,* the clue had read. "How do you say blood in French?" I asked.

"*Sang,*" Jack answered. "Four letters."

The password had five. The rest of the way to the museum, we listed off various words related to Elodie's theory. Baby. Child. Fate. Union. Most of them didn't have five-letter translations, and the few that did didn't work.

"It's a good idea, though," Stellan admitted. "One we should look into more."

"See?" Elodie said. "You're lucky I thought to watch your phone." Stellan snorted.

"For now," Jack reminded us as we approached the entrance to the Museo Correr, in the Napoleonic Wing, "we still have a second bracelet to search for."

The museum staff was already closing up and didn't want to let us in. Stellan leaned in close to the window and said something beseeching, and I was about to tell him his charms probably wouldn't work on the burly museum guard sitting there when he passed a handful of euros across the counter. *That* worked.

We hurried inside. "He's only giving us ten minutes, but there aren't many rooms here," Stellan said. "Split up."

Jack and Elodie took off in one direction, and Stellan and I took a room with gleaming marble floors and a soaring ceiling covered in frescoes. I walked through quickly, scanning the walls.

"Do you trust her now?" Stellan said from the other side of the room.

"I don't know if trust is the right word, but I'm willing to listen to her theories." I skirted a painting of wood nymphs, then finished looking through the room. Nothing. I stopped, hands on my hips. "What if *La Serenissima* didn't even mean Venice?" I said, voicing the worry that had started to creep in even before we came out tonight. "We could be at a dead end."

"Let's at least finish searching this place before we jump to any conclusions."

We made our way into the next room. "What do we do if it's not here?" I said.

"We—" Stellan stopped, looking over my shoulder.

"What?"

He pointed. "The symbol from your necklace."

I wheeled around. Sure enough, the symbol was carved into the wall above my head, and above it was a bas-relief of three women. Between them was an inscription in French.

I ran out into the next room and called for Jack and Elodie. We gathered around Stellan, who was standing, hands in his pockets, reading the inscription. Jack and Elodie joined him.

"Can someone please translate for the girl who doesn't speak French?" I asked.

"It says, *Where Alexander once sought counsel, the spirits of the priestesses guard one twin, but only through the union shall it open,*" Stellan said. "Yet another clue, leading somewhere else."

"But it says 'one twin,'" I said hopefully. "Maybe this one is actually pointing to the next bracelet."

Elodie was staring at the carving with narrowed eyes. "'Only through the union' . . . ," she said to herself. "'Union forged in blood.'" The three of us looked at her, but she just bit her lip and paced across the room, muttering to herself. "Fate mapping. Fates mapped together. Fates." She looked up, her eyes wide. "*Fates.*"

I snapped a quick photo of the carving with my phone. "What about fates?"

"You said the clue in India was near a carving of the Moirai, right? The Greek Fates?" she said.

I nodded. I hadn't realized who the three women in the bas-relief were at first, but we'd seen it later while looking at the photo Jack had taken.

"And this one is, too." Elodie smiled triumphantly. "The bracelet will be in a place that's important to Alexander that also has to do with the Greek Fates. This clue says 'spirits of the priestesses.' It's obvious. It's at the world's most famous oracle—Delphi."

CHAPTER 10

"How are we going to convince the Saxons to let me go to Greece?" I said to Jack. We stopped under the portico surrounding the Piazza San Marco. A cheerful, brightly lit cafe called to us, the smell of the slabs of pizza in the window wafting through the open doors. "We can't wait until after all these visits are over. We have less than eight days left." And when the visits were over, I'd be expected to choose someone.

"Tell them you need a break," Elodie said. "Tell them you're going to a resort. Colette's there right now, on her yacht. We can stay with her."

Colette LeGrand. She was a Dauphin cousin and also one of the world's most famous actresses. It was her boyfriend, Liam, who had been one of the Order's first victims.

"I don't think telling them I'm going to a resort will work," I said.

Elodie wrinkled her nose. "You're not thinking of telling them the *truth*, are you?"

I looked at Jack. "We haven't exactly told them everything."

"Because you'd give it all to the Order in exchange for your mother." Elodie leaned against one of the arches, surveying the square. The tourist traffic had thinned out for the night, so it was even easier to see the reflections of the buildings in the mirror surface of the water. Elodie turned to Jack. "And you're okay with that?"

He didn't answer, but his mouth pressed into a hard line. He had never liked the idea much, but he knew it was what I had to do.

"I guess we should go," I said, changing the subject.

"Sneaking back into the hotel will be harder than getting out was," Jack said. I'd just been thinking the same thing.

"The Dauphins have a staff apartment here," Stellan said. He handed me the bracelet with a small shake of his head. He'd been twisting it absently, trying new passwords.

"How nice for you," Jack muttered.

"Obviously what I meant was that you can stay there with us," Stellan said patiently. "There are plenty of beds at the apartment."

"And plenty of cameras." I slipped the bracelet on my arm as we headed back into the labyrinth of narrow streets. "That'd be really smart to let the Dauphins see us, with you." I turned to Elodie. "How are you even here, anyway? They think Stellan's spying on the Saxons—"

"And so am I," Elodie said. "In case you hadn't noticed, you're the most important thing going on in the Circle at the moment."

The light dimmed as we walked deeper between tall buildings and the sidewalk narrowed. Our feet, damp now, squished on the cobblestones.

"The only cameras at the apartment are at the door," Stellan continued. "So you'll hide your face until we get inside. If they care enough to be watching right now, which they don't, they'll just think . . . well, let's just say I've brought girls back there before."

Of course he had.

"So you can sneak me in," I continued. "But—" I shot a look at Jack.

Stellan followed my gaze. "Elodie's staying there, too. Or maybe they'll think I'm having an especially wild night." He gave an exaggerated wink. "The Dauphins have more important things to worry about right now, I promise. I was just trying to be nice, but by all means, have fun sneaking back into your gilded cage."

It only took a quick consultation with Jack to decide on the Dauphins' apartment. It would be much easier to get back in in the morning in the rush of tourists checking out. We stopped in front of a four-story building, its facade a crumbling but colorful fresco, and Stellan punched in a door code.

I pulled the collar of Jack's coat up and hunched my face down into it, and Jack ducked his head, and we followed Stellan and Elodie into a hallway that was well lit but still so damp that I wondered if anything in this city ever really dried.

We got to a door on the third floor, and Elodie paused outside. "There's one more thing I probably should have told you—"

Before she could finish, the door flew open. Luc Dauphin stood in the doorway, with messy hair and red-rimmed eyes.

Stellan cursed. "Elodie, what is wrong with you—"

Luc cut him off with a stream of chatter in French that, as far as I could tell from the looks passing between Stellan and Elodie, was something along the lines of *it was my idea to come and she couldn't stop me.*

"Okay, everybody inside." Jack bundled us in and locked the door.

"It's horrible." Luc scrubbed a hand through his hair. "Eli Abraham and Takumi Mikado both. It's—oh, *cherie.*" He cut off and swept me up in a hug so tight he pulled me right off the ground. He set me back down and planted a loud kiss on each of my cheeks.

"You had to be there. I'm so sorry. I was going to—" He gestured behind him to where a sumptuous buffet of desserts was set up. "I wanted to apologize, and I know you like pistachio ice cream"—he nodded to Jack—"and I thought I might be able to say *I'm sorry my family tried to arrange our marriage against your will* with dessert, but then *this* happened. And now . . ." He sighed dramatically and led me into the living room. "And now my party is a wake."

He stepped out of the way, and I stopped dead. In the center of the darkened living room was what I could only call a shrine.

Between when he heard the news and now, Luc must have raided every newsstand in Venice, and half the religious paraphernalia shops. He'd arranged Virgin Mary statues, crosses, and flickering candles with unidentifiable saints painted on the front in an elaborate diorama around a collage of magazine photos of Eli and Takumi. Eli kissing a Brazilian supermodel. Takumi shirtless on a beach. In the center was the cover of Sunday Six's most recent album.

Luc fell into a chair set in front of the shrine and made an awkward sign of the cross over his chest. We all stared. Somehow all that came out of my mouth was, "Are you even Catholic?"

"No." Luc sighed again. "But it seemed appropriate, *non*? And it was all I could find on short notice. When in Rome."

"When in Venice, actually," Elodie murmured.

My mouth was still hanging open. "I'm sorry," Jack said low in my ear. "He doesn't mean to be disrespectful—"

"And this is the only jacket I have with me dark enough to be appropriate for mourning." Luc plucked at the shoulder of his blazer, purple velvet with a subtle floral pattern, if you could really call anything about it subtle. "But I think they both would have liked it. I only met Eli once, and Takumi a few times, but I felt like we had a connection."

Luc picked up a bottle of wine he already had open on the shrine and took a swig, then passed it back to us. Elodie shrugged and took a drink.

I rubbed my forehead. I'd seen them both die. It was horrible for everyone. But still, it felt weird. "Even if the Order coerced him, Eli *murdered* somebody," I said. "Isn't it strange to look at him as if he were as much of a victim as Takumi?"

They all looked at me, a grim set to each of their mouths. "You don't understand the Order," Stellan said. "They do terrible things. Eli had younger siblings. Maybe the Order threatened them. He obviously felt like he had no choice."

"But to *kill* someone—"

"Aren't *you* planning to give up the thing that could stop these murders to save your mom?" Elodie cut in. "How is it so different?"

"I—" I suddenly felt sick. I studied the shrine again, the happy, smiling faces of two people I'd seen die just hours ago. The lump in my throat that maybe should have been there all night was rising.

I pulled out my phone. In a few seconds, I had pulled up a photo of Dev Rajesh. I leaned the phone against a candle on the shrine. "He was a victim, too."

Elodie set down the bottle of wine and found a picture of Liam Blackstone to go next to Dev. On Jack's phone, Malik Emir. Stellan rested a hand on Luc's shoulder, and I knew they were thinking about Luc's baby sister.

"And to the rest of them, all our brothers killed by the Order," Luc said quietly.

Jack took out his wallet and pulled out the photo of him and Mr. Emerson on Mont Blanc, the photo Mr. Emerson had left as a clue. He set it in the shrine, too, then squeezed my hand.

"There's a tradition I know of," Elodie said. "You open a window to let the spirits of the dead out, like smoke."

I released a shaky breath.

"You're not forgetting them, but you're allowing them—and yourself—to move on."

I felt my nails digging into my palms. We were still in the middle of this. I wasn't sure any moving on could happen right now.

But Luc ran across the room and opened the balcony door. He grabbed a package of incense and lit one of the sticks in a candle flame and waved the smoke back and forth across the shrine. The smoke thickened as we passed the bottle of wine between the five of us. It was sweet, syrupy. I kept one eye on the smoke, but none of it was drifting out the open door at all.

An hour later, we were down almost two bottles of wine. A few of the candles had burned out, but the rest flickered over the photos. Cream rugs covered the hardwood floors in the apartment, and there was a small kitchen and two overstuffed leather couches that all five of us lounged on now. I stayed a careful distance from Jack on one couch, while Elodie's legs sprawled across Stellan's lap on the other.

Luc sat on the furry rug at Stellan and Elodie's feet, and he set to opening another bottle of wine, clumsily. I got the feeling he'd already had a little to drink before we arrived. "Is it horrible to say this is fun?" he said. "It's like a—what is the American word? Slumber party? A very tragic slumber party."

We should have been using the time to plan our trip to Greece, but I realized I was glad we weren't. "Fun" might not have been the right word, but it really *was* like a slumber party in the cozy apartment, and after the exhaustion and frustration about the clue that wasn't a clue and all the literal and figurative blood on my hands, I needed that right now. I think we all did.

Elodie leaned over to grab the wine from Luc, and Stellan pushed off the couch and went into the other room.

I stretched and got up, too, and made my way across the room to the small balcony. Jack followed. He stopped me at the French doors and peered outside. "Seems safe."

I looked out over the piazza below, where a steady rain was now falling, making the cobblestones shiny in the lone streetlight. The piazza was a rectangle, enclosed on three sides by buildings with barred windows and planter boxes, and bordered by a canal on the fourth. It was chilly out, and I shivered even though I was still wearing Jack's coat.

"You okay?" Jack said.

I hugged my arms around myself and nodded.

"Do you really think Greece is a good idea?" he said.

I looked up sharply. "Of course. Eight days, remember? Do you *not* think it's a good idea?"

"I don't like being so far away from Saxon security. Especially after the attack today." Jack paused. "The Saxons want the tomb as much as we do. If we told them the truth, they could at least send guards."

I was shaking my head before he'd even finished speaking. "You know why we can't tell them. They'd never let me give what we find to the Order."

I leaned on the railing. We were sheltered from the rain by the building's overhang, but the occasional breeze sent a drop or two our way. My shoulders stiffened when Jack leaned beside me.

"I know. I understand." He took a deep breath. "It's just—you've got to understand my point of view, too. The way you feel about doing everything you can to keep your mom safe? That's how I feel about you. I know I'm not supposed to," he continued. "I know we're not . . . But you can't imagine what it felt like today to see him raise that gun in your direction."

I swallowed. "I really don't think they're going to hurt *me*—"

"And I think you need to take into account the opinions of people who don't have an emotional stake in this like you do."

I pushed back from the railing. "You just admitted you *do* have an emotional stake in it."

Jack turned. Earlier I had been so relieved for us to be back to-gether, and needed the comfort of *us* so much, that I couldn't not kiss him. I knew he felt it too—he'd just *admitted* he still felt it as much as I did. But this—this suddenly not being on the same page when I had thought we were—was a different kind of tension entirely, and one I wasn't used to.

"Avery—" he said.

"You can't *always* be perfectly cautious. We can figure out ways to be safer, but we're going to Greece. And we're not telling the Saxons."

He gripped the railing hard, very controlled as always, then nodded.

We stood in silence for a few minutes. Under the streetlight across from us, on an expanse of crumbling brick, was a smattering of graffiti. The only words that stood out well enough to read were *Ti amo!*

"What does that mean?" I pointed.

"Um." He paused. "It means *I love you*. In Italian."

"Oh." Even though it was in this context, *those* words, coming out of Jack's mouth, in his accent—I was suddenly too conscious of my heart hammering against my ribs. "That's the sweetest graffiti I've ever seen."

I could feel him looking at me. "I don't want us to be angry at each other," he said.

I leaned beside him at the rain-slicked railing again. "I'm not angry. It's just—you get why I have to do this, right?"

"I do," he said. "You'll do whatever it takes for someone you love. I get it."

I reached my hand out, and he took it. We let our fingers intertwine for a second.

"What are you doing out there?" Elodie yelled. "Hurry up and come inside."

We let go, and I balled the cuffs of Jack's coat in my palms as we headed back in.

"I didn't realize we were on a schedule." I flopped back down on the soft leather couch, still feeling unsettled.

"We're not." Elodie was lying on her back on the white fur rug, staring up at the beams crisscrossing the ceiling, holding the wine bottle. "Luc has an idea."

Luc was grinning too big, considering the circumstances. I eyed him warily. "What?"

"We have finished our sadness for the night. Let's do something fun. Let's play a game."

Jack, perched on the arm of the couch next to me, raised an eyebrow. "A game?"

Elodie sat up and finished the last sip from the bottle, then put it on the floor, sending it into a shaky twirl. "Spin the bottle."

CHAPTER 11

I crossed my arms and settled further back into the couch. "You're kidding, right?"

"Come on," Elodie said. "We're teenagers without adult supervision. Aren't we obligated to get drunk and play kissing games?"

"First of all, this might be the most inappropriate night ever to do something like that. And second, we're not exactly normal teenagers," I said. "I'd probably be the closest, and I'm far from normal."

Which was an odd thing to think. I was the world's most normal teenager until recently, and now I was—to quote Stellan—the closest thing the most powerful group in the world had to a leader.

"That is why we will do it. Celebrate life rather than being sad about death," Luc said dreamily. Obviously more than a little tipsy.

"And who cares if we're normal?" Elodie sat up. "Spin the bottle is what all the American teenagers do in the movies. Ooh, or truth or dare. Want to play truth or dare instead?"

I frowned at her. "I have never once played spin the bottle *or* truth or dare. The movies lie to you."

"Well then." Elodie handed the bottle to Stellan, who shrugged and put it on the ground. He gave it a twirl. "This'll be everyone's first time."

The bottle spun wildly, then slowed, wobbled a bit . . . and came to a stop, pointing right at me.

Stellan looked up with a slow smile.

"Oh my God. Okay. We'll play truth or dare. I choose truth," I said.

"Ouch," said Stellan.

Elodie smiled triumphantly, plucking the bottle off the ground. "Truth. Never have I ever . . ."

"You're mixing your games," I interrupted. "Never have I ever is like group truth. You say what you've never done, and whoever *has* done it has to drink."

"Well, that sounds perfect." Elodie opened another bottle of wine and refilled our glasses.

Jack looked at me. "Are we really—"

"Apparently."

Elodie settled back against the couch, twirling ends of her hair between her thumb and forefinger. "Never have I ever kissed somebody in this room," she said, and merrily took a drink of her wine. Beside her, Stellan drank, too.

I looked at Jack.

We could lie, I told him with my eyes. *We might not want Elodie knowing everything.*

Elodie rolled her eyes. "I'm not stupid. You were caught *in her room* at our house."

Stellan held up a mocking finger. "But they're not *together.* Ask them why."

I glared at him. "This is more important. We don't want to be distracted, and—"

Elodie snorted. "Is it exhausting to be so upstanding and self-righteous all the time?"

"Some of us take life-or-death matters seriously—" Jack started.

Elodie turned to Stellan. "You've been having to deal with this? I'm sorry for you." She gestured at me with her wineglass, nearly spilling the contents out on the carpet. She didn't notice. She'd had more to drink than I'd realized. I was surprised—she was usually so controlled. "You have at least kissed. So drink. That's the game."

I bit back a retort, and Jack and I sipped our wine.

"I feel left out," Luc said. "All of you have kissed each other."

"Aw, Lucien," Elodie said, reaching out to him. "I will kiss you anytime."

Luc blew an air kiss in her direction. "*Merci*, El, but you're not exactly my type."

There was a beat of silence, then Stellan sat forward. "If you want—"

Luc's cheeks went bright pink, and he threw a piece of baguette at Stellan. Grinning, Stellan caught it and whipped it back.

"Okay, okay," Elodie said, holding up her glass. "Never have I ever kissed *more than one* person in this room."

She cocked an eyebrow, and I cocked mine back, watching her gaze flit between Stellan, Jack, and me. "Really?" I said flatly. "I told you—"

She shrugged innocently. "Why else are they *both* putting their lives on the line to follow you around the world? Jackie's being the noble knight, keeping her safe, but . . ."

She looked at Stellan. I knew he wouldn't tell her about the thirteenth thing.

"Fine," Elodie said, but her face broke into a slow smile. "But I know there are people who will drink to it." She raised her glass and took a drink, then looked pointedly around, eyes landing on Jack.

He cleared his throat. "This game is ridiculous," he said, and took a sip.

I don't think my mouth actually fell open, but it might have. Jack wouldn't meet my gaze, but Elodie smiled smugly.

But that meant—Jack. And Elodie.

"Yes," she said in her pretty French accent. "Exactly what you're thinking."

It was like there was this whole version of Jack I didn't know existed. It wasn't my place to be annoyed about it, for lots of reasons, but . . . "Getting off the subject of kissing," I said.

"Aw, why?"

"Never have I ever lied to the people I cared about to get my way," I continued pointedly. I still wasn't sure I trusted Elodie's intentions for being here.

Something flashed across her face, but she took a drink, with a hint of an eye roll at me like, *I get what you're doing.* "If any of you say you have not done that, you're lying *now.* You are not getting into the spirit of this game."

The room was suddenly subdued. It had started raining harder, and it pattered onto the balcony outside. My head was spinning. I wasn't sure whether it was the wine or the conversation or the long day or the fact that I'd barely slept last night, as usual. "Maybe it's time for bed," I said.

"Boring," Luc said, but he rubbed his eyes sleepily and stood up. Stellan blew out the candles on the shrine and Elodie let me borrow a pair of leggings and a T-shirt.

The bedroom was large, with four sets of bunk beds. Jack and I took two lower bunks across from each other, and the rest of them sprawled across various other beds in the room.

"Good night," I whispered.

"Good night," Jack answered.

"Good night," Elodie called teasingly from across the room, then switched off the light.

Of course, the minute the light went off, my eyes wouldn't close. Illumination from the street outside made shadows on the wall, and I watched them for a while. There had to come a time, biologically, when I was exhausted enough to fall asleep no matter what, right?

But not exhausted enough that you won't wake up with nightmares, a little voice whispered. Especially after today.

From across the room, someone was snoring lightly. I was okay just an hour ago. Did drinking wine always give you this kind of emotional whiplash? I flopped onto my side again, kicking the blankets restlessly.

We had just over a week to find the bracelet, the tomb, save my mom. Stop the Circle suitor countdown and the assassinations. Decide what I was going to do after that. Assuming what was in the tomb really would stop the Order, my duty to the Circle would be done.

But would I leave? Leave Lydia, and my father?

Jack?

In the bed across from me, he stirred, then settled with a sigh. Would he come with me if I left? Did I . . . Would . . . If . . .

In my dream, I was in seventh grade, but in Venice. Poppy Levine, the richest girl in our grade, was throwing the bat mitzvah I wasn't invited to in real seventh grade at San Marco Basilica, and just as she blew out candles on a giant birthday cake, everyone at the party fell down dead.

My eyes shot open, and it took me a second to remember where I was. Watery early morning light was filtering through the windows, and it was hot and stuffy and a little damp in the room.

Every part of me, on the other hand, felt dried out: my eyelids stuck together with every blink, my contacts had dried to my eyeballs, and my mouth was sticky and parched.

I slipped out of bed, put some drops in my eyes, and popped a mint from my bag. Jack was turned toward the wall. Luc was fast asleep, too, his pajama-clad leg hanging off a top bunk. Below him, Elodie's hair flopped across her face, and she looked remarkably peaceful. Stellan's bed was empty.

I opened the bedroom door as quietly as I could, and wandered into the empty living room. Maybe Stellan had gone out to get coffee or something. An atlas someone must have pulled off a shelf last night lay on the couch, open to a map of Greece. I picked it up and headed toward the balcony. When I got there, though, the smell of cigarette smoke was drifting into the room.

Stellan stood with his back to me. He was wearing the same T-shirt and gray jeans he'd had on yesterday.

I paused, but before I could decide whether I wanted to turn around, he glanced over his shoulder.

"Cigarettes are disgusting," I said, coming to stand beside him, leaning the atlas on the railing.

"I *so* value your opinion." He took a slow drag and blew smoke out of the corner of his mouth, then stubbed out the cigarette in the small ashtray. The smoke curled away in the first rays of sunlight.

"Sleep well?" he said.

"Fine." In the courtyard below, vendors were setting up for what looked like a vegetable market. A middle-aged woman in a leather jacket and heavy black eyeliner unloaded box after box of bright red and yellow tomatoes.

Stellan gestured to the atlas. "Map to the bracelet?"

"Map to Delphi, at least." Off the other end of the wrought-iron balcony, two old men greeted each other from passing boats in the tiny canal.

Stellan took the atlas and flipped through it, to India, then Venice. He laughed. "Have you realized that Napoleon left his own literal *map of fates,* and we're following it?"

"'Their fates mapped together,'" I said. "Do you think he did that on purpose?"

"He certainly seemed to think the rest of it out pretty thoroughly."

I looked at the *Ti amo!* graffiti across the piazza.

"Do you actually believe in it?" I said. "Fate. Destiny. Whatever."

Stellan leaned over the railing, watching the vendors below us. "Do you think all those people believe in fate? Or do you think they're just living their lives the best they can with whatever's thrown at them?" An older man tossing a bucket of fish onto ice looked up and waved at us. I waved back.

"I believe certain people are set on a certain path," Stellan went on. "But I also think we *always* have a choice. It just depends how much you want to fight. If you're meant to sell fish at a street market in Italy, you could spend your whole life trying to change that, but selling fish isn't so bad, is it?"

I blinked into the rising sun. "When you make it sound so appealing . . ."

I heard movement inside, then voices. Time to get the day started. Stellan closed the atlas and gestured inside. "Destiny awaits," he said.

CHAPTER 12

We managed to get back into the hotel without anyone noticing. I changed into a flowered sundress and met Lydia and Cole and my father in the lobby like we'd planned the night before. My father led us to the hotel's outdoor cafe overlooking the Grand Canal, where rows of gondolas were tied to posts, their sleek silhouettes bobbing lazily with the breeze. My foot wouldn't stop tapping under the table.

Lydia settled into the wicker chair next to me and put on her sunglasses as a waiter poured us tiny cups of thick espresso. I stirred two sugar cubes into mine. "We'd better eat quickly if we plan to be in Beijing by tomorrow," Lydia said, scanning her menu.

"Beijing?" I squinted at my father through the morning sun. "I thought Johannesburg was next. The Konings." That was who I'd hoped to postpone for a few days. Until after Greece.

"Yes." My father shifted. Across the table, Cole downed his espresso in one gulp. "There's been a change of plans."

I looked at Lydia, but she was staring intently at her menu. "What kind of change of plans?" I said.

My father cleared his throat. "In light of recent events, our time line needs to change. The Wang family in Beijing. The Fredericks in Washington. And that will be all."

I put my cup back down in its saucer with a clatter. "What about the other families?" He couldn't mean what I thought he meant.

"We won't be visiting the others. After meeting these final two, we'll take a day to consider the options, and then you'll choose one."

The coffee turned bitter in my throat. "You said I had two *weeks*. It's only been five days."

My father reached into his briefcase and pulled out a newspaper. He set it on the table in front of me. *Murders Around the Globe: Coincidence or Conspiracy?* said the headline. "This is getting out of hand. There isn't time to consider families who aren't real options."

I tried to pick up my espresso cup again, but my hands were shaking too hard. "But what about my clues? Finding the tomb? Saving my *mom*?" I looked around for Jack, but he was posted at the entrance to the restaurant, too far away to hear.

Lydia was still avoiding my gaze. I tried not to be hurt that she hadn't warned me about this.

My father refolded the newspaper. "I *do* hope we'll be able to get your mother back once the mandate is fulfilled. Since your clues haven't produced anything concrete, this appears to be the only way."

The clues *were* producing something concrete. I just couldn't tell them about it—at least not until my mom was safe. A *vaporetto* passed with a low hum and the quiet splashing of propellers. "I'm not coming, then," I said.

My father took off his sunglasses. "Avery."

"No." If they were really going to do this, I had to get to Greece as soon as possible. "If I don't want to get married, and you're not even going to let me meet all the candidates, why bother pretending you care who or what I choose?"

Lydia finally spoke up. "You'll like Alex Frederick," she pleaded. At least I could hear the guilt in her voice. "He's really nice. And—"

I shook my head. Maybe he was, but that wasn't the point. And I could no longer afford to take the Saxons' feelings into consideration.

"You can go to Beijing and Washington alone." I injected a little extra venom into the words so they wouldn't question my motives. "Colette LeGrand's invited me to spend some time on her yacht, and I'm going. I'll be there until you get back."

"No," Lydia said. "Even if you don't come with us, you being alone is too dangerous—"

"Jack will come with me." I pushed back from the table, and my father started to get up, too. I held out one hand. "Just stop. You're getting exactly what you want. I won't even be there to argue while you decide what to do with my life."

I stalked out of the restaurant and didn't look back, not wanting to see the hurt on my sister's face or the disappointment on my father's. We'd better be right about Delphi. It was my last chance.

A few hours later, Jack and I were on Colette's private plane. The second we touched down, three missed calls pinged on my phone, the number showing up only as UNAVAILABLE. The Order. As we taxied to a stop, I put the phone on speaker and called back, Jack tense in the seat beside me.

"I was beginning to think you were ignoring my calls." Scarface. I hadn't heard his voice for a while. They hadn't called since we were in Paris—it had just been those texts.

Jack leaned forward, elbows on his knees.

"I'm not ignoring anything. We've found some clues," I said. "We're looking into the next one right now."

"Where are you?"

I met Jack's eyes. They probably had ways of finding out where we were even if we didn't tell them. I didn't want to lie and give them any reason to take it out on my mom. "Greece," I said.

"Hmm. You'd better hope it's lucky for you. The Commander is getting restless."

I huffed out a breath. "I need to talk to my mom," I said. "That was part of the deal."

There was some shuffling, and then a voice. "Avery?"

My breath caught, and I clawed for Jack's hand. "Mom. I love you. I—"

"That's enough," Scarface said, and a door slammed on the other end of the phone.

I gulped back a tightness in my throat. She was okay. "I'm not going to marry anyone," I said suddenly. "Killing those boys is just making the Circle more determined to find you. It's not helping."

Scarface chuckled. "You have seven days." With that, he hung up.

Last chance, my brain kept repeating as we walked through the Athens airport. *Last chance.* My mom was alive and okay, for now. According to the Order we had seven days, but I only had four until I was expected to do my Circle duty.

Elodie and Stellan and Luc had arrived minutes after we did. Walking out of the airport, we passed a magazine stand, and I realized exactly why Colette had been hiding. *Colette LeGrand's Pain,* said one of the headlines in English. All the magazines had paparazzi photos of her coming out of an apartment building, her heart-shaped face drawn and sad and framed by her famous tumble of auburn curls, looking straight into the camera like the photographer was the one who had killed her boyfriend.

"Are you sure she's okay with us being here?" I felt bad having to bring her into our schemes so soon after her boyfriend's death.

"I think she wants the distraction," Luc said. "She's been all alone, hiding out before she has to make an appearance at Cannes."

I nodded. It wasn't like we had much of a choice, anyway.

The Mediterranean was a color of aqua I didn't realize water could be in real life. Colette's yacht was in a marina near Athens, where dozens of white boats bobbed on the sparkling water, backed by whitewashed cliffs.

Colette greeted us from under a wide-brimmed hat and sunglasses, her hair as wild as ever, but her smile noticeably dimmed. She ushered us up the gangplank and onto the boat, where she'd arranged a spread of cheese and fruit and bread and olives that covered every surface in the yacht's small, well-appointed kitchen. She must have had every grocery store in Greece on speed dial.

Luc sat down at the booth table, digging in like he hadn't eaten for weeks. I blinked, letting my eyes adjust, and Colette grabbed my hand.

"Come in, *cherie*," she said, wrapping me in a hug. I was surprised again, even though I'd met her before, to realize she wasn't any taller than me. And just like I'd thought when we'd met in Istanbul, despite being one of the world's biggest movie stars and on the top of every men's magazine's Hottest List year after year, she was soft and warm and welcoming and almost momlike in a way that nearly brought tears to my eyes, not least because *she* was the one *we* should be comforting. It was only then I realized I was expecting to see blame in her eyes, or at least that horrible hope. But she just pulled away and looked me up and down. "Eat. You look thin. What have these ruffians been feeding you?"

She thrust a plate in my hands—she must have also bought out the Anthropologie kitchen department—and perched on a bar stool, watching us all anxiously. Last time I'd seen her, she'd been so relaxed, joking around with her boyfriend Liam even though the Order was attacking Circle members all over the globe.

Later that night, they'd gotten to Liam, too. And Colette hadn't escaped unscathed. When their car's brakes had gone out and the gas tank exploded, she'd gotten out alive, but the lace tunic she wore exposed the angry red scar on her neck and shoulder.

"Thanks," I said, filling the plate with fruit. Jack, Stellan, and Elodie gradually wandered over, too, picking at the spread.

"Lucien told me a little, but what exactly are you all doing in Greece?" Colette said in her soft accent.

Elodie glanced at Jack and me, and I shrugged. Just by coming here, we'd obviously decided to trust her.

Jack told our story, and Stellan added details until we got to the part about Delphi.

Colette had taken it all in surprisingly easily. "What's the plan?" she asked. "What can I do?"

"Get us to Delphi," Jack said.

"The captain of the boat is just up in the village. I'll make a call." Colette disappeared and was back a few minutes later. "Done. We'll be outside Delphi by morning. Now what?"

Elodie unzipped her bag and pulled out a bathing suit. "Now come sit out on the deck and let's enjoy Greece."

A few hours later, I set my knife on a lounge chair on the upper deck and angrily flicked back the strands of hair that had come loose from my ponytail. Jack and I had decided to take the free afternoon to train. I had a scrape on my arm that was smarting from sweat, and I'd narrowly missed giving Jack a black eye with my elbow.

As usual, the knife training was not going well. It was like my hands weren't meant to hold it. The second I tried a move, I'd drop it, or fumble, or forget everything I'd learned about blocking and leave myself open to attack.

I leaned on the railing, watching the wake behind the boat as we chugged toward Delphi. Elodie, Colette, and Luc were sunbathing on the next deck down. Elodie looked even taller and thinner than usual in her sleek black one-piece, and Colette was her opposite, a modern-day Marilyn Monroe, curvy and soft in a white crochet bikini, her hair pulled back in a boho headband and topped with sunglasses big enough to cover her entire face. She looked more relaxed already, and I was glad we were at least able to do that for her. But it wasn't them that made me laugh out loud. Luc lounged on a chair between the girls, gesturing animatedly with a cigarette. I had forgotten how many European men wore Speedos instead of swim trunks, and Luc was wearing a tiny one, turquoise with white flowers. If I was seeing correctly, the earpieces of his mirrored sunglasses matched.

"Oh wow," I said.

Colette heard me, and waved. "Come down! We only have a few more minutes of good sun."

"I don't have a bathing suit," I called, and then turned to Jack. "Do you?"

He shook his head and gestured to Luc. "And I would not be able to compete with *that* if I did."

I'd seen Jack with no shirt on, and flowered Speedo or no, Luc had nothing on him. But I didn't say that.

"We should go in," I said instead. I shoved my knife back into the makeshift sheath I'd made of cardboard and stuck it in my bag. "I have to call Alistair and Lydia back." My father and sister had both left me messages earlier. I couldn't tell whether they genuinely felt bad about our fight, or were worried about me, or were just trying to make sure I hadn't run away. I tried not to care, but I couldn't help hoping they hadn't given up on me. If we found the tomb—*when* we found it—everything could be different.

That made me remember something I'd been meaning to ask Jack for days. More important stuff had kept crowding it out. "Dev Rajesh—" I bit my lip. If talking about every dead person we knew was going to be this difficult, I was in for a hard time. "Dev said something, at dinner the other day. About an *Oliver* Saxon."

Jack, who was picking his jacket up off the railing, stiffened. "What did he say?"

"He just mentioned the name, and I didn't get a chance to ask any more."

Jack's face had gone blank as a mask. "It doesn't matter. It's not something you need to worry about." His words were clipped.

"But—"

"I'm going inside. I think Elodie wanted to do dinner soon."

The cabin door swung shut behind him before I could respond, and I was left trying to talk to empty air. What was that?

I made my way out of the sun and back into the boat's cabin, and I heard Stellan's voice.

"Why don't you tell her anything? You can only keep her in a bubble for so long."

I stopped, holding the door so it wouldn't slam and give me away.

Something banged on the counter. "I'm keeping her safe." It was Jack. "You know what the Circle can do to people."

"I do. That's why you shouldn't keep things from her. Let her make her own decisions."

"I don't recall asking for your opinion."

"You used to." Stellan's voice was mock wistful. "Remember those days when we were in things together?"

"No." I heard the refrigerator close and footsteps recede.

"I'm just saying," Stellan called, "If you're not careful, she's going to realize she has other options. You see how they all look at her. It's not even just the eyes. She's so *little* and *pretty*. It's like blood in the water."

A cabinet door banged shut so loudly, I jumped.

"I said *they*," said Stellan, but it was obvious he was goading Jack on purpose. "This is just business for me. A business transaction with historically wide-reaching political, moral, and personal implications. The usual."

"Would you please stop talking?"

"Only saying you don't have to worry. Wide-eyed innocent isn't my type. I wouldn't touch your not-girlfriend." Stellan paused, and I could hear a grin in his voice when he said, "Unless she asked me to."

Okay, enough.

I made a show of slamming the door and clomping loudly down the stairs, and not a moment too soon. Jack looked ready to punch him. "Elodie was talking earlier about getting dressed up for dinner," I said, so cheerful I'm sure I sounded fake. "Are we stopping somewhere?"

Jack shot one more glare at Stellan, who sat at the dining table, his legs stretched out along the booth on one side, a laptop open in front of him.

"I assume Elodie wants to do a formal dinner on the boat. She loves family dinners," Stellan said. "We don't get to do it that often."

The sun was starting to set, and as I watched, the strings of white lights flickered to life out on the deck. Elodie appeared, still in her bathing suit, holding an armload of flowers and candles that she plunked down on the long table in the outdoor dining room. Colette flitted in after her, with napkins and silverware.

I squeezed Jack's arm. "Let's go help," I said, and pulled him outside. I wondered what Stellan had been talking about.

"Wait." Jack stopped me in the breezeway. He chewed his lower lip. "Oliver Saxon was Lydia and Cole's older brother. He was killed in an accident two years ago."

I froze. "What?"

Jack tugged on the sleeve of his T-shirt, obviously uncomfortable.

"The oldest son of the Saxon family was killed?" I repeated. "Does that not sound exactly like what's going on now?"

"It was a freak accident. I don't think it has anything to do with the current attacks, which is why I didn't tell you. No need for extra worries." An unconvincing smile touched his lips. "Shall we go help Elodie with dinner?"

I nodded and followed him slowly, trying to picture the half brother I'd never know.

CHAPTER 13

The next morning, we woke up docked outside Delphi. The cries of seagulls and the light metallic ting of ropes hanging off the sailboats bobbing alongside our yacht normally would have been calming, but I was too tense to even eat breakfast. The bracelet *had* to be here, or we were finished.

We headed inland, where the air was arid and hot. I'd imagined Greece green and tropical, but the part of the country near Delphi wasn't like that at all. Gnarled shrubbery and rocky outcroppings gave way to spring grass dotted with modestly sized pines and olive trees, with sage green leaves and twisted trunks straight out of a fairy tale. Towns dotted the hillsides, all whitewashed walls and red roofs.

At the Oracle site, I thought there'd be a single temple, but built into the dramatic hillside were ruins of several temples and a large amphitheater. We had a way bigger area to search than I'd anticipated.

When we got out of the cab, Stellan touched my arm. "There's a car that looked like it was tailing us," he murmured. "Stay close."

I cursed under my breath. It wouldn't be my father's people, so if someone was following us now, it was the Order. "Luc?" I said. He was ahead of us, standing in the shade of an olive tree with Jack.

"I told him, too. He'll be careful."

I glanced over my shoulder, but all I saw was a tour bus with a stream of elderly people climbing on. "Let's go, then."

Colette and Elodie had already gone one way, toward a circular temple with just a few columns still standing that seemed to be on all the tourist brochures. The rest of us spread out around the main temples. Stellan stuck close to Luc, and they headed up the hill to an amphitheater, while Jack and I scrambled down a fall of white stones gone gray with age and onto the foundation of a mostly destroyed structure.

The temple was fenced off with a single rope running along the edge of the path. Since there was no one else around, we stepped over it. Spears of bright green grass pierced the stone, like the earth thought the temple was part of it now, after all these years. It was eerily quiet. I glanced back toward the parking lot before kneeling down and inspecting one of the columns. "Where would he have hidden a bracelet? This place is huge."

"I would assume one of two possibilities," Jack said. "He could have buried it, in which case we're looking for a marker or the entrance to a tunnel. Or he could have hidden it inside something. A secret space in one of these columns, maybe?"

We combed every inch of the temple. I crawled between stones, dirtying the knees of my jeans, looking with my hands as much as my eyes for anything that seemed out of place. The whole time, I watched for anyone coming too close. A couple with a baby walked by once, and another time I thought a couple guys in touristy Greece T-shirts may have been watching us from a nearby path, but they stayed a good distance away. Maybe Stellan had been wrong about the car.

Finally, I sat back on my heels and wiped the back of my hand across my forehead. "I haven't seen anywhere it looks like we should dig."

Jack sat on part of the stone wall. "Agreed."

"Hello!" came a voice from above. I shielded my eyes against the scorching midday sun to see Luc at the next level up, waving happily. "Any luck?"

"No," I called. I peered off across the site, at another temple just past a wide stone amphitheater, and saw movement. One of the guys in the tourist T-shirts had just ducked behind a scrubby tree, closer now.

"Did you see that?" I said.

Jack stood up, on automatic alert. "What?"

"Some guys have been watching us. One of them just hid when I looked at him."

Jack's brow crinkled, and he stepped in front of me protectively.

I looked behind us. "Luc!" I gestured for him to get down. He was about as exposed as possible, standing on that ledge.

"Come up here and look before we go," Luc called back. "I see baby goats in a field!"

"Luc!" I repeated, gesturing frantically. Jack clambered up the rocks toward him, and I followed, but Stellan must have heard the fear in my voice, because he suddenly appeared, bundling Luc away. Jack climbed over the cliff ahead of me and reached back to pull me up, but I hesitated, peering at where the guy had gone. I didn't see him anymore.

"Avery!" Jack said, and I let him help me up the rocks and behind some columns.

"What did you see?" Stellan said quietly.

"These two guys. I swear they've been watching us." I peered out again, but besides a tour group led by an older lady carrying a yellow flag, I didn't see anybody. "Maybe I'm just going crazy. Did *you* see anything?"

Jack shook his head, and Stellan did, too.

I sat back against a broken column and realized I'd ripped the knee of my jeans scrambling up the hill. "Let's move on, then. Just be careful."

But ever since Stellan had mentioned the car following us, something besides fear of the Order had been building in the back of my mind. What if we *didn't* find anything here, or it wasn't enough? I'd be back to either marrying someone or going on the run, neither of which was conducive to helping my mom. I knew the Order were dangerous, but if I confronted one of them face-to-face, there was a chance I could get information out of them. And if that was my only option? I'd do it in a second.

Just then, all our phones buzzed with a text from Elodie. *We found something. Round temple.*

Unlike where we'd just been, the temple Colette and Elodie were waiting at was full of people, so the six of us huddled at its edge, waiting for the crowd to thin. "It's that symbol from your necklace," Colette said. "It's there, on a brick."

It was all I could do not to shove a bunch of little kids out of the way and run straight for it. When the temple area emptied out, we gathered around a partial wall off the main circular pedestal. Sure enough, the symbol was carved into a weathered stone.

"And this," Elodie said, pointing two bricks up. It was more eroded than the symbol, but it looked like writing, in French.

Jack translated, "*To learn the secrets my twin and I hold, look where he looks. Those who gave all hold the key.*"

"That sounds like the clue on the first bracelet." I looked down at my arm. I had its inscription memorized. *He watches over our lady, above the sacred site. Where he looks, it will be found. When it is found, my twin and I will reveal all, only to the true.* "This one says 'where he looks,' too. That was the clue we used to find the diary."

"It makes sense the clues would have parallels," Elodie said.

"Wait," Stellan interrupted. "It says 'my twin and I,' like it's from the perspective of the other bracelet. It could be around here somewhere."

I kneeled in the dirt. "Like maybe buried?"

"Or behind one of these bricks." Luc tapped on the edge of the one with the inscription.

Elodie glanced behind us and, seeing no one paying attention, pulled a chisel and a small hammer out of her bag. While she chipped away at the mortar surrounding the brick, Jack joined me in brushing dirt from the base of the wall, looking for anything out of place.

After a few minutes, Luc said, "*Merde.* Someone's seen us."

I peered over the wall to see a middle-aged site employee in a black uniform striding purposefully toward us.

"Everyone get away from here," Elodie said, putting her tools in her bag as she stood up. "*Casually.*"

I grabbed Jack's hand, and we wandered away down the hill, pointing into the distance and chatting like ordinary tourists. I glanced back to see Luc and Stellan going the other way. And Colette and Elodie stayed put, heading off the park employee with flirtatious smiles and a barrage of questions. I saw him try to put them off and keep the rest of us in his sights, but after a second of indecision and a glance around the area to see that things looked okay, he let Colette lead him back toward the main temples.

I stopped Jack and waited until Colette and the guy were out of sight. Up the hill, Elodie was doing the same thing. Then she made her way back to the symbol. Jack and I followed, and I could see Stellan and Luc heading back from up the rocky hillside, weaving between another screaming group of kids.

"I don't know that there's anything behind here," Elodie said. "If the brick had been taken out and replaced, I probably would have broken through the mortar by now."

"What about the other bricks?" I said. "Like the one with the symbol?"

Elodie set to chiseling—and almost immediately, there was a cracking noise. She looked up, excited, and tapped at the other three sides. As Luc and Stellan got back to our spot, she was prying the mortar out of the wall with dirt-crusted fingernails.

Finally, I grabbed one side of the brick, and Elodie held the other. I held my breath, and we pulled.

The brick came tumbling out of the wall. We dropped it on the ground, and I fell to my knees, brushing away bits of dried grass and dirt. Behind the brick was a slim, dark hollow. I hesitated for a second, but pushed aside thoughts of spiders and thrust my hand inside.

It was cool and dry—and empty.

I sat back on my heels, brushing dirt from my hands. "There's nothing in here."

Elodie felt inside, too, and shook her head.

I felt like screaming. "It *had* to be there," I said. I yanked the chisel away from Elodie and tried to chip at another brick, but my sweaty fingers slipped on the metal and I nicked the side of my hand instead. I threw the tools to the ground with a curse and sucked on my bleeding finger.

"Wait," Jack said. "There's a museum here. What if they found it and moved it there?"

I pushed back the strands of hair clinging to my face. "There's a *museum?*"

Moments later, we were making our way back down the mountain. I was trying to force myself to calm down. And then I stopped, and Jack came to a halt, too. "That's them again," I said, staring at the backs of two white T-shirts, one of which had a map of the Delphi site printed on it. "The guys I saw earlier."

"They're probably just tourists," Jack said, but I saw his hand drift to his waistband, where I knew he had a gun hidden.

"Did you see how the one just turned around when I saw him so I couldn't get a look at his face?" It was crazy, but—"What if they're Order?"

"Then we should all get to the car." Jack put a protective hand on my arm.

I shook it off. "You should get *Luc* to the car. They've already had the chance to kill me, and they haven't. If they want to kidnap me, they wouldn't be able to do it from a public place." The idea wouldn't get out of my head. "If they are Order . . . what if they know something? What if they know where my *mom* is?"

"Avery . . ." Jack's voice was a warning.

I felt around in my bag. I had my knife. I thought I was being calm and collected about this, but after hearing my mom's voice yesterday, and knowing that I now only had *three days* to save her . . .

I watched the guy's blue baseball cap bob through the crowd and remembered all the times the Order had tried to kill me and Jack. Shooting at us on Mr. Emerson's balcony. Cornering us at a market in Istanbul. Chasing us through the Louvre.

My hand tightened around my knife. I knew I wasn't any good at fighting with it. Trying to chase a trained killer probably wouldn't end well. And if I was wrong, and they did want to hurt me—

At the temple just below, both the guys had stopped. Next to them were two families. Two women and some little kids. Delphi T-shirt guy ruffled the blond curls on one of their heads.

I let out a breath through pursed lips. "Tourists," I said under my breath. "Just tourists."

Subdued, we kept going toward the museum.

Colette had beaten us there. "It's a small collection," she said. "I've already looked. There's nothing like the bracelet there."

"We should ask someone," Stellan said, and flagged down a docent, describing what we were looking for.

"Actually," said the woman, "we did have an item like that, years back, when I first started work here. A gold bracelet."

My heart leaped, and I grabbed Jack's hand. The woman glanced my way, and suddenly, I remembered the matching gold bracelet on my own arm. I surreptitiously slipped it off and into my bag, and luckily, the docent didn't see.

"It was very mysterious," she continued. "It wasn't an ancient piece, so it must have been placed here at Delphi more recently. Then one of our archaeologists associated it with Napoleon Bonaparte, of all people. And almost immediately, it was taken from us back to France and is now in a private collection."

We all glanced at each other. "Do you have a photo of the bracelet?" Stellan asked. The docent disappeared into a back office and came back minutes later with a file folder. She handed us a snapshot, and our collective intake of breath was almost comical.

"What is your interest in it?" the docent asked.

"We're scholars of Napoleon history," Elodie said, squinting at the photo. I looked over her shoulder. There was an inscription visible on it, just like there was on mine. Elodie read it out loud, in French, then translated. *"Only through the union will my twin and I reveal the dark secret we keep in our hearts,"* she said, and to the docent, "Do you mind if I take a photo of this picture?"

Back at the boat, we all leaned over Jack's phone, which was on speaker in the middle of the table. Elodie had angled the photo she took to capture the file folder the docent was holding as well, and on the paperwork, there was the name and phone number of the collector who now owned the bracelet. The number was ringing. And ringing. Finally, an answering machine picked up. During the long message in French, everyone's faces fell. "The collector passed away," Jack translated after he hung up. "The items have been willed to museums or are being sold off to other private collections."

I leaned my head back against the bench seat. "There has to be some way to find out where the bracelet ended up."

"I doubt his estate would give out that information," Colette said.

"What did the new inscription say again?" I said to the faux wood ceiling.

Elodie repeated it. "'Only through the union will my twin and I reveal the dark secret we keep in our hearts.'"

I sat up and ran a finger over the matching bracelet on my arm. It had gotten dusty. "'In our hearts.' It sounds like there's something *inside* the bracelets. Not just that we'll get another clue when the letters line up." I couldn't imagine what would fit inside, but everyone else nodded. "Which means we have to physically have the other one, too. Seeing this clue on it isn't enough." I looked at Luc, who was perched on a bar stool, his shirt smudged with dirt. "The collector was French. Can't you force whoever's taking care of the collection to tell you where the bracelet is?"

He cocked his head to one side. "Probably, yes. I might have to go back to France and make some calls."

"Okay," I said. "Good. I was thinking you should leave, anyway, after that false alarm today. If anything happened to you while you were helping me . . ."

"I agree." Elodie smoothed her hair behind her ears with both hands, then let it fall forward again. I wouldn't have thought someone like Elodie would have a nervous tic, but her hair was definitely it. "But the problem is that this clue mentions the union. 'Only through the union will my twin and I reveal the dark secret we keep in our hearts.' Luc's the only one here capable of fulfilling the union with Avery if it comes to that. And this seems to imply that somebody's going to have to get married after all. Or just skip ahead to the baby making?" Elodie elbowed Luc.

I watched Stellan's fingers tap out a suddenly quicker rhythm on the tabletop. Jack's mouth was set in a straight line.

"What?" Elodie said. Of course she'd caught that little look. Now she stood up, so abruptly the table shook and rattled the untouched tray of pastries Colette had set out. "I knew it. I *knew* you weren't telling us everything. If there's more, we deserve to know."

Beside me, Jack shifted in his seat. I put a silencing hand on his knee. It wasn't his secret to tell, or mine.

Stellan dragged a hand through his hair, pulling it back from his face. "All right," he said. "Yes, we know more than we've told you about the identity of the One."

Elodie huffed out a frustrated breath. "Well? What? Is it not just whichever Circle boy Avery marries?"

Stellan shook his head and touched the scars on the back of his neck. "It's someone specific. It's not Luc. It's not any of the others, either."

Elodie, Luc, and Colette all frowned in unison. "What does that mean?" Elodie demanded.

"It's not a member of the twelve families at all," Stellan continued. His eyes met mine before he continued, "It's me."

CHAPTER 14

Elodie was the most skeptical at first, but now she grinned, then fixed me, Jack, and Stellan with pointed looks. "So you two," she said, looking from me to Jack, "are . . . whatever you are. And you two"—her gaze flicked back to me and to Stellan—"are supposed to be getting *married*?"

"Yes," I said shortly.

"Ooh, and that's why you acted so strange when I mentioned a baby," Elodie went on. "Now *this* is fun."

"Don't be mean, El," Luc said distractedly. He scrubbed a hand through his already-wild brown hair. "So there's no way *I'm* . . ."

"Assuming we're right," Jack answered, "no."

Luc paced the galley kitchen and flicked the bamboo blinds over the sink. "That's a relief," he said. "Thank God. What a relief, right?"

I realized for the first time that the idea of the power appealed to Luc as much as it did to everyone else.

"At least you know you won't have to marry me," I said, trying to lighten the mood.

"That would have been *terrible*," Luc quipped. He ran a distracted hand over my hair, and I squeezed his fingers.

"Well then. There's no reason for Luc to stay here." Elodie stood up, already pulling out her phone. Luc tried to protest, but she cut him off.

"You can get back to Paris and contact the museum. It makes the most sense. You're on a plane back to France as soon as they can send one."

Later, I stood on the upper deck watching the sun go down in spectacular fashion, all oranges and cotton candy pinks over the water. The sea breeze was fresh and cool and smelled like salt, and the hot tub behind me bubbled happily. Stellan had taken Luc to a plane, and the rest of us had been looking over the clue again. I'd had to take a breather after we got another text from the Order. *Six days.* But that hardly mattered since, according to the Saxons, I didn't even have that much time. My sister had texted earlier that they were in Beijing. Apparently she and Cole had accompanied my father to try to smooth over how rude I was being by not showing up myself. But even without me there, the visits were progressing as planned, with my fate growing closer by the hour.

The doors behind me slid open, and Jack came out. "Doing okay?"

I nodded.

He shifted, staring out at the water. "That person you thought you saw earlier . . . I know it turned out to be nothing, but if it had been, and you'd gone after them . . ."

I frowned at the sunset.

"I know you don't think the Order will disrupt your search," he went on, "but what if they've heard the union is happening sooner than they thought, and they want to stop it?"

I hadn't thought of that.

Jack rubbed at the compass tattoo on his forearm. "Maybe we should reconsider letting the Saxons' people go out in the field instead of you."

I huffed out a frustrated breath. "We're *not* doing that."

"There might come a point where I don't think it should be entirely your choice," he said.

I stared at him. "Excuse me?"

"I don't mean—I only mean to say your judgment is clouded. For good reason. But—"

"Don't."

"Avery—"

"No. I have been very clear about how I feel, and if you can't respect that, we're just not going to talk about it anymore." I turned away from him and hugged my arms around my chest. The last couple times he'd said things like this, I'd tried to make excuses. He was worried. He didn't really mean it. But it was getting harder to deny that he *did* mean what he was saying.

I felt him watching me for a second, and he finally said, "I'm going for a walk."

He disappeared into the cabin. When I was sure he was gone, I made my way inside, too. I heard Elodie and Colette talking in the other room, and I paced the three steps from the bedroom area to the kitchen. I grabbed a handful of dark red cherries from a bowl and sat at the breakfast bar, plucking the stems off them and rolling them around on the counter in little agitated circles. Across the deck, I watched the turquoise water of the Mediterranean turn orange from the setting sun.

"What did that fruit do to you?"

I frowned up at Stellan and then cursed when a cherry squished under my fingers, spraying bloodred juice across the marble and onto the front of my dress.

"Or maybe the better question is, What did Bishop do to you? What was that little fight about?"

It wasn't a fight, I started to say, wiping at the cherry juice. "I don't know," I found myself saying instead, and then added quickly, "It wasn't a fight. It's none of your business."

"Let me guess." Stellan took one of my cherries and popped it in his mouth. "He's worried about your safety, etcetera, etcetera."

I wrinkled my nose. "We weren't *fighting*," I said again. I wanted it to be true. Jack was the one person I was sure I could trust. And if we disagreed so strongly about this, it meant one of two things I didn't want it to mean. Either I couldn't trust him as much as I thought—or he was right and I was going about this all wrong.

Stellan leaned on the counter across from me. "He wants to keep you safe. It's sort of his thing, if you hadn't noticed."

I didn't even bother looking up from my cherries.

"It's valid," he continued. "There could be people trying to kill you. And I've seen your sparring sessions. You're not very good."

I pushed my stool back and stalked across the room for a napkin. "Do you spy on *everything* I do?"

"You were training on this boat. Anyone with eyes was 'spying' on you." Stellan sat at the table, resting one long arm across the back of the bench.

"I—" I didn't know what to say in response, because he was right. "Just shut up."

"If you ever need somebody else to train with," Stellan said after a minute. "For whatever reason . . ."

"Thanks but no thanks," I said.

"You know," he said, "it's remarkable to me that you are willing to train so much, to come up with all these dangerous, difficult schemes, but you're not willing to even *consider* the way the Circle has interpreted the union for centuries."

I tossed the napkin onto the mutilated fruit. "We've actually gotten really far with the clues, if you hadn't noticed. Either way, I'm not marrying you."

"Turned down before I could even propose," Stellan sighed. "You're going to give a guy a complex."

"Do we have to go over this again?" But I couldn't deny that the little voice in the back of my mind was wondering how much longer I could go before seriously considering it. This new clue left little doubt the union actually was important. Us getting *married* still made no sense in the context of unlocking the bracelets, but if nothing else worked . . . And what if it could get lots of people behind us, searching for my mom? What if it helped in finding the tomb after all? I knew marrying any other Circle members would do nothing, but with Stellan, there was a chance. An insane, far-fetched chance, but still a chance.

"If we did it—" It was the first time I'd ever said it out loud. "Not that we *are*, but if we did, it would mean outing yourself. Which we *think* they might accept if we came out together, but could also be dangerous."

"I know. Trust me, I know."

"And, you know, pledging your eternal love to me." I opened a cupboard, surveying the huge amount of food Colette had.

"You do yourself a disservice if you think that's as repulsive as you're implying." The boat rocked suddenly in what must have been the wake of another boat speeding by. "Plus, there's the happy fact that the Circle's wedding ceremony requires the marriage to be consummated immediately for it to be valid."

I pulled out a jar of Nutella and a spoon and rolled my eyes. "No it doesn't."

"It does. It's part of the ceremony—a holdover from medieval times. The priest and the families and a few special guests watch. To make sure it happens."

I paused with the spoon halfway to my mouth. "Are you serious?"

"Serious as you can be about live pornography."

"So if the wedding with Luc had happened . . ."

Stellan nodded. I sat down heavily in the chair across from him. "Have you ever seen . . . ?"

"Sadly, no," he said. "Luc's the only Dauphin child—well, he was until recently—and so there's been no occasion for it."

I rested my elbows on the table. "That doesn't matter. We're not getting married, so we won't have to actually—" I waved one hand.

"I think that might be more offensive than saying no to the marriage part," Stellan mused.

I didn't give him the satisfaction of a reply. After a few seconds, I said, "What if, hypothetically, we were to . . . pretend. Would they believe us if we *said* we'd gotten married?"

He shrugged. "I don't know. It'd be our word against any doubters. But if it was only pretend, we wouldn't get the benefit of the union for finding the tomb. Or unlocking the bracelets."

"If 'union' actually does mean 'marriage.'" I drew my feet up onto the seat and wrapped my arms around my knees. As usual, this argument was going nowhere.

"Will someone throw me the white top drying by the door?" a voice called from the bedrooms. Colette stuck her head around the corner, arms crossed over her more-than-ample chest. She wore only a pink polka-dotted bra and a flowing skirt.

I turned around quickly, averting my eyes. Stellan didn't. He gave her a teasing smile. "No," he said. "We won't."

Colette gave him a look of mock outrage and teased back in French. I grabbed the shirt and tossed it toward her.

"Thank you, *cherie*," she said, shooting an eye roll in Stellan's direction before disappearing back into the room.

When the door closed behind her, I turned to Stellan. "Her boyfriend just died."

"Yes."

"You're *flirting* with her." He'd been doing it since we got to Greece. She'd cozy up to his side; he'd whisper something that made her giggle.

"Hmm. I take issue with that categorization. Technically, she's flirting with *me*. I'm just following her lead." The sun had just started to dip below the horizon, and Stellan made his way outside.

I followed. "Don't you dare take advantage of Colette. I like her."

He looked back inside and lowered his voice. "I like her, too. That's the point. People grieve in different ways. Lettie wants a distraction, so I'm being nice."

"Does *she* know that?"

He cocked his head to one side, and the sea breeze rippled his white button-down shirt. "Yes. How can I make you understand this? Lettie . . . she's been in the spotlight for so long that she hates being alone. Being adored is her safe place. But everyone who usually fawns over her just treats her like a sad war widow now." He paused, and I let it sink in. I'd never really thought about Colette that way. Stellan continued, "Harmless flirting happens to serve both our interests. And yours, really."

"*My* interests?"

"If she's happy, she's more likely to help us with whatever insane plan you think up next."

I paced down the stairs to the lower deck, Stellan on my heels.

"Do you always use sex to get your way?" I said, swirling a finger on a water mark on the top of the bar.

He scowled. "I'm not sleeping with her. As you so judgingly pointed out, her boyfriend just died. Her boyfriend who was a friend of mine, I might add, just like Colette is. I have *some* morals, you know." He paused. "And anyway, girls do it all the time."

I started to protest, but he went on. "Listen. I said I'd train you. Here's a lesson that doesn't have to do with fighting. Being *nice* doesn't get you far in the world of the Circle. You have to use whatever tools you have to get ahead."

He sounded surprisingly bitter. And the conversation sounded over.

"Just . . . don't take advantage of her," I said.

Stellan held up his hands in surrender or exasperation or both and settled down on a lounge chair two down from mine. After a few minutes, he gestured to the bracelet on my arm. I handed it over, and he spun it to a new word, paused when nothing happened, then tried a few more before handing it back to me.

I slipped it on my arm. "Three days," I said under my breath.

Stellan looked out at the water. "That bracelet is somewhere. We'll find it."

"Maybe," I said bitterly. "If I'm still allowed to, between the Saxons and Jack." I didn't really mean to, but I found myself telling Stellan about Jack wanting to bring my family into our search. "Being able to follow these clues myself is the only thing I still had a choice in, and if it were up to Jack, even that wouldn't be my decision anymore."

Stellan hauled himself to sitting. "You always have a choice."

I fiddled with the hem of my dress. "I don't think you've been paying very close attention. I'm so important in every aspect of what we're doing, but it's becoming obvious that *none* of it is my choice. I have literally three days until the Saxons marry me off. I'm just a particularly valuable puppet."

Stellan swung his legs around and perched on the edge of the chaise, facing me. "Lots of people in your shoes would already be on the beach in Indonesia. Refusing to run away *is* a choice. It's a brave one."

Suddenly, I couldn't sit still. "Why do you say stuff like that?" I paced the deck, my bare feet slapping the smooth, cool wood, remembering what Jack said had first attracted him to me. He saw me at school, looking like I didn't care. Doing what I wanted, even if it wasn't what everyone normally did. He didn't realize I was doing it because I didn't have another option.

"I'm only here because I have to be. It's not exactly something to be proud of."

I could feel Stellan's eyes on me. "So you care about people and get stronger in response to difficult circumstances," he said. "Those are good things."

The ropes anchoring the boat next to us—the *Konstantinos*, according to the name emblazoned on its side—creaked against the dock.

Then a strange sound came from outside. A kind of a gruff growl. Stellan jumped up and hurried into the cabin. Just as quickly, he reemerged. "Hide," he mouthed at the same time I heard a strange voice call out, "*Astynomía.* Police."

Stellan dragged me behind the bar. We crouched side by side under the bar top.

"Why would the police be here?" I whispered.

"I don't think they would," he said, confirming my fears. What if Jack was right, and the Order had come to kidnap me?

The voices were closer now. I heard Colette speaking in French, then Elodie chimed in using English, obviously for my benefit.

"I think you have the wrong boat," she said sweetly.

"We have orders. We must make a search," the man said. A low bark accompanied the statement. *Dogs.* Even if the men didn't find us, dogs would in seconds.

I leaned close to Stellan. "The water," I breathed. Stellan nodded, then pointed at the bracelet on my arm. I slipped it off, and he stashed it inside an empty ice bucket, covering it with cocktail napkins and stuffing it under the bar.

While Colette and Elodie led the men around inside—stalling, thank God—I stayed low and slipped over the boat's dive deck, clinging to the metal ladder.

The water was *freezing.* I bit back a gasp as my sundress billowed around my waist. I was about to remind Stellan *he* didn't need to hide, but he'd already lowered himself after me and flicked his fingers toward the dinghy tied to the side of the yacht.

There wasn't much sunlight left, and down here it felt even darker than on the deck. We approached the dinghy, making for the narrow crevice between the smaller boat and the larger one—this was as hidden as we were going to get. I pushed myself back into it. Stellan glided silently behind me.

I realized immediately this wasn't the best hiding place. The "police" only had to lean over the edge behind the bar to see us. The *Konstantinos* wasn't more than ten feet away. Maybe we should get around the other side of it. It'd involve being exposed for a few seconds, but—

The water around us went from dusky to fully lit. Someone had flipped the floodlights on the deck. We were still in relative shadow, but the ripples from our swim fanned out, crystal clear in the reflections.

We both went very still, me pressed back into the nook between the barnacle-covered hull of the yacht and the slick surface of the dinghy, and Stellan with his back to me, my face on level with his sunburst tattoo. I could see both it and his sword tattoo perfectly through his soaked white shirt.

I tried to hold on to the side of the boat, but my fingers kept slipping. Stellan was gripping a rope from the dinghy I couldn't quite grasp, so he reached behind him and grabbed a handful of my dress, pulling me against him and locking me there. I pushed away for a second, automatically, until I realized I was being stupid. This was much easier. And he was *warm*. I let my arms snake around his waist.

The voices came closer. Stellan put one of his hands over mine.

"Can I interest you in a drink?" Colette's sugary voice echoed off the hull of the next boat over. I marveled for a second at how quickly she'd taken to scheming with us. We'd arrived just yesterday, upended her whole world, and now she was playing the perfect distraction. "We have a bar with a *magnifique* view on the upper deck."

Stellan's hand tightened. Oh no. Colette must have assumed we were hidden on the lower deck and was giving us time to get away. But on the lower deck, at least they'd have to maneuver around a pile of life jackets to see us. On the upper deck, all they had to do was stand by the railing.

One of the men grunted, the dogs snuffled, and I heard a clear "Yes."

Their boots clomped up the stairs, and I let go of Stellan, who took the opportunity to turn silently to face me. The tips of his blond hair were wet, darkened. The scars on his shoulders almost glowed. "Around the other side," I mouthed, pointing, but it was too late. A hollow thump of boots, and I looked up to see a shadow heading straight toward the railing overhead.

I heard Colette follow, asking about the city farther down the shore. One of the guards reached the railing and leaned over, and I froze. He looked down—then his dog gave a gruff yap and he turned back. I let out a breath.

"Show us what is kept down there," one of the "police" said. He leaned over the railing again.

I looked around frantically for a hiding place that didn't exist— and Stellan pulled on my hand and pointed down. With no time to think of anything else, I took the deepest breath I could and slipped under the dark water.

We may not have been able to see much, but we could still hear Colette laughing, and the low rumble of men's voices. *Go get that drink,* I urged her silently. *Show them your movie poster. Do something.* Pressure was already building in my chest. I was starting to twitch, to feel the carbon dioxide building up behind my eyeballs. Stellan didn't seem distressed at all. Of course—Keepers probably had Navy SEAL–level water training. I let the air out of my lungs in a string of tiny bubbles, like you're supposed to do to hold your breath longer, but just seconds later, my body, on its own, was straining toward the surface. I pushed against Stellan, forcing myself farther under the water. I could hold on for maybe another thirty seconds.

But they were *still* talking, still directly above us. *Move!* I screamed in my head. In front of me, I felt Stellan rising a little. I wasn't used to opening my eyes underwater while I had contacts in, but I couldn't help it. The salt stung, but my contacts seemed to stay in place, and after a couple blinks, I could see Stellan's outline. He rose enough to stick just his face out of the water, take a breath, and come back down into the murky dark.

Yes. Why hadn't I thought of that?

My body gasped for breath, and I had to force my mouth not to open yet. I rose just like he did—but stopped. I tried again.

Something was pulling on the back of my dress. I yanked on it, but it wouldn't budge. It took me a second to process what was happening. I'd pressed far enough back into this crevice that I'd run into the ropes or the hooks or something. My dress was stuck.

I was trapped underwater. And I was out of air.

CHAPTER 15

I looked up frantically to see Stellan's face right above me. I yanked on the dress again, harder. Stellan's eyes went wide. Sparkles danced in front of my eyes.

The men were above us, still talking, sounding fainter now as my head fuzzed. I pushed out the last tiny bit of air as I yanked harder on my dress, then Stellan was pulling at it, too.

Air.

I felt Stellan move away—maybe, I wasn't sure. Air air air *air* any second now my mouth was going to pop open and I was going to inhale water it was physiological you couldn't stop it that was how you drowned *air* it was like my mouth was being forced open *air* if I died no one else would save my mom the Order would kill her *air*—no no no *no* said the last wisps of thought in my mind—but I was breathing in and I couldn't stop it—

Air. I was breathing in air. Clarity came rushing back to my mind. I grabbed on to Stellan, whose mouth was suctioned over mine, giving me all the air from his lungs.

He detached carefully, holding up one finger. I flailed, shaking my head frantically, definitely not enough oxygen in me yet. I let out bubbles, so I had empty lungs again as he rose once more, then came back, holding my face between his hands, and I drank in the air greedily, unable to stop myself from clutching his head to me, pulling him as close as I could. This time, I realized water was leaking into my mouth, too, a briny taste on my tongue.

I was still dizzy, not quite there. I remembered somewhere in the back of my mind a lifeguarding class I took when we were living on the coast. This kind of rescue breathing was not advised because the victim always panics and takes too many breaths. But the lifeguard had said she'd seen it work where the two people breathed back and forth for a few seconds to get the victim's lungs working normally again.

Stellan tried to pull away, but I pulled his head back to mine. At first he resisted the air going back into his chest, but then he got it. There was so little light down here a couple feet below the surface, but I could see his eyes staring straight into mine until mine fluttered closed at the euphoria of *breathing*, in and out, in and out. I almost forgot Stellan's mouth was on mine until he gently closed off our lips and detached my hands from where they'd clawed into his hair. The air we were passing probably didn't have any oxygen left. He held up a finger again.

This time, I was alert enough to think about what was happening as he slid back down beside me, his hands pushing back the hair swirling around my face. I felt a ridiculous flash of guilt for just a second. But I wasn't *kissing* him. This was clammy and salty and terrifying and entirely unsexy. He was literally breathing life into me, and I pulled him close hungrily again, emptying my lungs to make room for more before I brought his lips to mine. Unlike the last two times, I was aware of his chest contracting against me as he emptied his lungs into mine and let me breathe back and forth with him for a second.

As I took the last of this breath, I realized the voices above had stopped. Stellan looked up, too, his blond hair floating out around his head like a halo. He let go of my face and rose to the surface again, slowly peering out of the water. He must have decided they were gone, because he popped the rest of the way out, swimming quickly away. I didn't know what he was doing, but I knew he'd come back. And sure enough, a second later, he was shooting toward me underwater, something in his hand. My lungs ached again, out of air so much faster now that they'd been traumatized.

He gave me one more lungful of his breath, and I could feel heat at the corners of my eyes. Even surrounded by water, I could tell I was crying as the dreamy panic lifted and the reality of what was happening set in. Stellan pulled away and swam behind me. He plunged whatever was in his hand into the material of my dress, and I felt a pull, then a sudden lightness.

I shot to the surface. My head broke into the cold dry dark, and I took gasp after sobbing, coughing gasp of air air air air.

Hot tears streamed down my cold cheeks and my whole body quaked. Stellan popped up beside me, and there was finally enough light for me to see he looked terrified. He took my face between his hands, examining me.

"Are you okay? Can you breathe?" he whispered.

My throat was raw. My eyes burned. My lungs felt like they couldn't possibly expand enough to hold all the oxygen I wanted. I nodded.

Stellan muttered what I could tell was a string of curses in Russian, and I wanted to apologize, for whatever I'd done that had gotten me stuck down there, for being who I was that made it necessary for us to hide. For putting him in danger, too. But I couldn't form the words, and before I could, he planted a hard, clammy kiss on my forehead.

The curses weren't anger, I realized. They were relief. He pulled away quickly, like he was expecting me to shove him off the way I usually would if he did that.

Instead, I threw my arms around his neck.

He didn't hesitate for a second before he pulled me to his chest, like he'd been waiting for it.

I wasn't sure if it was how grateful I was or if I needed to rest or if I just needed a hug that badly, but I wrapped myself around him like I'd never let go. I was shaking hard enough to make waves in the water. My tears rolled over his shoulder, and he held me tight, murmuring into my ear in Russian. I couldn't understand a word, but it was the most soothing sound in the world. After a second, I felt him release the side of the boat and wrap his other arm around me. He was treading water to support both of us so he could hold me tighter, and all I could do was press my face into his neck with a silent *alive alive alive thank you I'm alive.*

Elodie's voice echoed out over the water. "Stellan!" Then, more quietly to Colette, "Where *are* they? I swear, if they're not even here and we had to flirt with those disgusting men for no reason . . ."

"Here," Stellan croaked. I unwrapped my legs from his waist, realizing what we'd look like, soaking wet and clinging to each other in the shadows. He didn't loosen his grip on me at all.

Two heads peered over the deck, silhouetted by the deck light. Elodie sniffed, and I could feel her raised eyebrows of scorn from here.

"Can you swim?" Stellan said quietly. I nodded, even though I didn't really want to let go. He kept an arm around me as we made our way back to the ladder.

Before we climbed up, I turned around one more time. Stellan's hair was slicked back, throwing the angles of his face into even higher relief. His T-shirt was ripped at the shoulder. I had to restrain myself from throwing my arms around him again, and he opened his mouth like he was about to say something.

Heavy footsteps sounded on the deck. I groped for Stellan again, ready to hide, but Jack's voice boomed out. "What's going on? Where's Avery?"

Stellan let me go like I was burning his hands, and Jack ran across the deck to pull me the rest of the way up.

I'd been in the plush terry-cloth robe for ten minutes, but I hadn't stopped shivering.

"At first they just said they had to search the boat," Elodie was explaining. "It wasn't until we'd talked to them for a while that they told us there had been a vandalism incident at the temple and they'd gotten reports of the suspects being in this area."

"They were actually police?" My fingernails were a sickly blue, and I tucked my hands under my legs. "It was all because of that brick?"

"It looks that way," Elodie said. "But we thought they were—"

"So did we," Stellan said. "And we almost drowned while you asked them which town has the best shellfish." After they'd gotten us towels and robes, we'd settled in the lower cabin, where we couldn't be seen through the windows, just in case.

"What happened?" Colette leaned forward, her rosebud mouth a perfect circle of shock. She'd been flitting around the boat like an agitated bird, tucking extra blankets around my legs, trying to get me to eat, making a pot of tea, then another when I said I didn't like peppermint, even though I really didn't want anything at all. Now she was sitting next to Stellan, bandaging the scrape on his shoulder.

Stellan met my eyes across the table. I'd felt nothing but numb since we got out of the water, but I suddenly, fiercely wanted to keep what happened between us. I didn't want Elodie declaring that we'd finally found an excuse to make out. I didn't want Jack to be jealous and have to pretend he wasn't. I didn't want to try to describe what it was like to really, not-exaggerating almost die and have Stellan save my life in a manner so intimate, I actually felt embarrassed looking at him now.

Stellan's lips parted, and he looked away. "We didn't drown after all," he said simply. He took the bandage from Colette and stood up. Her hands dropped to her lap and she started to get up after him, but he turned away without noticing. "And now I'm going to go take a really hot shower. Turns out the Mediterranean is still *vraiment* cold in June."

Colette sat back down awkwardly, and I leaned back, only to realize I'd been tucked under Jack's warm arm the whole time. He wrapped me up in the blanket, pulling me to his chest, and I watched over his shoulder as Stellan disappeared down the hallway.

CHAPTER 16

Elodie and Colette were still sleeping when I woke up the next morning. The last thing I remembered was Colette making me eat soup while I sat in a nest of blankets on her bed. I must have passed out, because I woke up to find the covers tucked around me and Colette and Elodie sharing the next bed over. *Two more days*, was my first thought. The Saxons had left Beijing yesterday, were passing through London today, then headed to DC. I had two more days until the Circle marriage countdown clock ran out.

I pulled on a sweatshirt and slipped out of the room. Stellan was sitting on one of the bar stools.

He looked up when I came onto the deck, and set a little cup of espresso on the bar. A violent wave of unexpected emotion crashed over me, so strong I stopped still.

I was drowning last night. I was drowning and he saved my life, but all I could think of now was what had happened right after.

We could just have easily have swum straight to the swim ladder. I would have thanked Stellan, then cried on *Jack's* shoulder. Stellan would have joked about having to save me and ribbed Elodie and Colette for almost killing the purple-eyed girl.

That would have been what I'd expected. What actually happened wasn't.

Stellan broke the eye contact I wasn't able to break and took a sip of his coffee. "I was surprised to see Bishop all alone in his bed. I expected a *glad you're not dead* make-out session keeping me awake all night."

The spell holding me in place broke.

"Good morning to you, too," I said, my voice still scratchy and throat aching. I leaned on the end of the bar. Obviously any awkwardness was coming from me, and he thought nothing of it. That was a relief.

I gazed out over the bay. It looked so unthreatening this morning, the pinks and yellows of the sunrise glinting off the water.

"The training thing," I said, but stopped myself. I didn't realize I was going to say that. It made sense, though. *Two days.* If we couldn't solve the clues, maybe I really would have to confront the Order directly. Despite any doubts I might have had yesterday, I wasn't wrong. No matter how much Jack disapproved, I knew I'd do whatever it took to save my mom, even if it was dangerous. We were getting into last-resort territory.

Stellan's face shifted into an infuriatingly triumphant smile. "What happened to the *thanks but no thanks* of twenty-four hours ago?"

I felt my face blaze with annoyance, and maybe a little embarrassment. I turned to go. "Never mind. I'll practice by myself."

"Hey." Stellan reached out, his hand on my upper arm. "I didn't say no."

I looked down at his hand, and he removed it. "It's *not* that Jack is a bad teacher." I looked over my shoulder toward the bedrooms, trying not to feel guilty.

Stellan shrugged and looked down at his own bare feet. "Give me a second."

I barely had time to put on shoes and retrieve my knife before he reappeared. I tucked the knife into the front pocket of my sweatshirt, and Stellan rooted through the fridge.

"Bringing breakfast?" I asked.

He pulled out a paper-wrapped package. "No," he said simply, cocking his head toward the end of the docks. "There's a hidden cove down on the beach. Come on."

At this time of morning, the only people we saw were a couple swimmers far out at sea, bright yellow and white swim caps bobbing along in the turquoise water, and a few early risers having breakfast on their boats' sundecks. I pulled a baseball cap low over my eyes, anyway.

The cove was tucked away on the far end of the beach, white sand stretching to the foot of a rocky, brush-covered cliff. We had to take our shoes off and wade through the shallow water to slip past a fall of dark boulders, and when we got there, Stellan was right—we were completely hidden from the walkway and the rest of the shoreline. The gentle lapping of the waves echoed off the rocks all around, completing the illusion that we were shut off from the world.

Stellan put his shoes back on, but I squished my toes in the sand. "This place is beautiful."

Stellan looked down at my bare feet and then up over my leggings and sweatshirt. The knife tucked into my pocket burned into the skin of my stomach, and I shifted self-consciously.

"Well?" he said. "I need to know what I'm working with. What have you learned?"

I took a deep breath and took my knife out, tossing its sheath on a rock.

Stellan laughed. "Oh, definitely not. I didn't come down here to die." He picked up the sheath and slipped it over the knife, taking the whole thing carefully out of my hand.

"This is better to practice with." He picked up a piece of driftwood as big around as my wrist and snapped it in half. He handed me a piece about six inches long and kept the other half for himself. "Well?"

I wondered if he was being more careful with me because of last night. He was probably thinking I couldn't handle this.

I cleared my throat. The piece of wood felt different in my hand than my knife. "Jack taught me how to stand. And hold the knife. Mostly self-defense stuff. He thinks I shouldn't count on fighting with the knife, so he hasn't taught me much about it, but I looked up some tutorials online . . ."

"You've been watching YouTube videos about knife fighting?" he said incredulously. "No wonder you've been having a hard time."

I frowned. "What do you want me to do?"

He shrugged. "Stab me."

I adjusted the stick in my hand, planted my feet, and—

Stellan threw his elbow into my "knife" and knocked it six feet away. He lifted his chin in the direction it had gone. "Try again."

This time, I made a point not to prepare much so he wouldn't know which way I was going. I stabbed at his side, but he sidestepped effortlessly. "Again."

I lashed out at his shoulder. Sidestepped again. At his side. Straight on, like I was trying to stab him in the heart. He grabbed my wrist with one hand. He was so much stronger than me, he pushed my hand back until it was against my own chest. I jerked away.

"So the baseline's nothing," he said.

"You knew I wasn't good at this," I grumbled. I hated being bad at things.

"All right." Stellan shrugged out of his gray hoodie so he was just in a thin white tank that showed the tops of his scars creeping over his shoulders. "Let's look at this differently. *Tell* me what you've learned."

I tore my eyes from him and described the stance I was supposed to take.

"Show me." I did, and he corrected me, nudging my bare feet a little farther apart with his boots and pushing down on my shoulders. "You've got to loosen up. At least half of fighting is being ready to dodge, defend, or attack. That can't happen if you're tense." He put his hands on my shoulders and shook them. "Relax. More."

The second he let go, I felt my shoulders rise back up to my ears. Stellan sighed. "Next?"

He corrected my grip and my striking posture. "You're not entirely terrible," he conceded. "At least you remember a lot of what you learn. What else?"

Besides what Jack had taught me and the videos I'd watched, I'd read a lot on the Internet. "I learned about where the best places are to—if you want to, you know. Hurt somebody."

"Or kill somebody," Stellan corrected.

I felt myself hesitate, but nodded silently. He gestured for me to go on.

"The arteries," I said. "I read that they, um, they bleed a lot."

The sun had just popped over the cliff, and Stellan squinted into it before directing us into a shady spot. "All right, arteries. Like where?"

"The, um, the carotid artery? In the neck." I looked at Stellan's and could just make out the throb of his pulse.

He nodded. "Come here. Put down your stick."

I did, warily.

"You're right. You so much as nick the carotid artery and it'll bleed everywhere. Stab it good, and the person will be unconscious in fifteen seconds, dead in a minute. But . . . Give me your hand." He pressed the tips of my fingers to the side of my own throat, pressing hard enough I could feel my pulse speed up. He moved my hand around, exploring the area. I felt my hard swallow. "Feel that? This is where the carotid artery is, but it's under a lot of muscle, even on someone as small as you. On someone bigger . . ." He moved my fingers to his own neck. It was harder, much less pliable than mine. "That artery is buried deep. And that's if you can even get a person in the position necessary to reach it." He lowered his chin to his chest and brought my hand to his neck again. I could barely reach past his jawline. I pulled away, and there were red marks on his neck from my fingertips.

"If you have the element of surprise *and* are strong enough *and* have a big enough knife, you could take off somebody's head. You will probably have none of these things, so the carotid artery's going to be hard for you. Next?"

I tried not to think about Prada, about Luc *actually* taking off someone's head, followed by Stellan stabbing someone else in the chest. It seemed like so long ago now. "Um," I said. "The heart. The heart is pretty much *the* place to stab someone, right?"

This time, he took my hand without asking and pressed my fingers to his chest. "Show me exactly where the knife would go."

"I . . ." I felt awkwardly around the left side of his chest for just a second. "I don't know. Somewhere around here."

He moved my hand lower than I'd had it and pressed down hard.

"Pretty small area," he said, pushing up and down so I could feel between two ribs. "Through the back is easier." He pulled my hand behind him so it probably looked from afar like we were embracing. His back wasn't quite as muscular as his chest, and I could feel the ribs more clearly. "But it's still a space barely big enough for a blade, and you'd need a lot of practice to get that kind of precision."

He let go and I backed up a step, two.

"What else?" he said.

I shoved my hands in my sweatshirt pockets. "The femoral artery. On the Internet, it said you'd bleed out really quickly from there."

A smile flashed across Stellan's face. "Very quickly," he agreed.

"It's in the upper thigh," I offered.

"The *very* upper thigh," he said, his grin growing. Before I could stop myself, I was staring at his *very upper thigh*. He shifted his weight purposefully.

"I won't make you touch that one," he said. "But suffice it to say, similar problems apply. Though there won't be as much muscle protecting it, it's usually covered by clothes, which are actually quite difficult to stab through. And besides that, men tend to have very good reflexes against attacks to that area."

My eyes flicked involuntarily back to *that area*. He might as well have a glowing neon sign on his crotch. "Right," I said quickly. "I guess I should have realized that."

Stellan was still grinning. "You Americans are so puritanical. I'm teaching you how to *kill* somebody and you're being a tough little soldier about it, but I mention a man's crotch in a completely nonsexual way and you can't look me in the eye."

"I don't think you've ever said anything in a completely nonsexual way," I retorted.

"Innuendo is all in the interpretation, *kuklachka*. So that says rather more about your mind than mine, doesn't it?" He cocked an eyebrow.

I was not going to let him goad me. "So when are you actually going to teach me something? All you've told me so far is that nothing I know will work."

Stellan plucked his wooden knife out of the sand, then tossed mine to me. "That's the most important thing there is to learn," he said. "It's hard to kill or gravely injure with a knife when you don't know what you're doing and can't physically overpower your opponent. That's both a bad thing and a good thing."

I remembered the club in Istanbul. I'd asked him why he used a knife. *It takes more effort to kill with a dagger,* he'd said. *Guns make it too easy.*

"So why even learn?" I said.

"You know more than you did an hour ago, don't you? Now you might not make the mistake of trying to stab someone in the groin."

I stabbed out with my stick and knocked him on the arm.

"Good," he said. "The joints are a fine place to strike. A good hit to the elbow will throw your attacker off-balance."

He held out his arm, showing me the vulnerable space inside his arm. For the next half hour, he tutored me, and by the time the sun had risen fully over the bluff, I was dripping with sweat.

"You're making progress," he said when we stopped for breath. "Better than when you were practicing with Jack."

I bristled, but it didn't seem like he was accusing, or taunting.

Stellan picked up the package he'd taken from the boat, and when he peeled back the white paper from one edge, I was definitely not expecting to see a rack of raw ribs.

"Toughening me up by feeding me raw meat?" I asked warily.

"It's not for eating." Stellan set the ribs on a large, flat rock. "Stab it."

"Excuse me?"

Stellan picked up my knife, slipped off the sheath, and handed it to me. "Stab the meat."

"Why—"

Stellan took my hands, the knife clutched in them, in his. "Do you remember stabbing me at Notre-Dame?"

I nodded hard. We were escaping the wedding. We had to make it look like Stellan hadn't just let us get away, and I remembered it *too* well. The initial cut where I broke his skin myself, like pricking a water balloon until it burst. Then when he grabbed my hand and stabbed the knife farther into his shoulder, and I could feel the muscle ripping under my hand. I shuddered.

"That's what I thought," Stellan said. "This will help."

He led me to the slab of meat. "Remember what you know about the grip," he said. "Try to loosen up. Let your shoulders go. And then . . ."

He stabbed into the meat and then pulled my hand back, and the knife came out sticky.

I swallowed. "Isn't the actual stabbing the easy part? I don't have to practice this."

"Okay, show me," he said.

I stabbed out at the meat, and even I could see all my form go out the window. I did it again, defiantly, and the knife barely glanced off. I sniffed.

"Have you never cut meat before?" Stellan said. "Are you a vegetarian?"

I shook my head.

"Pretend it's a steak you're making for dinner. Start by slicing off a piece. Whatever you need to do to get comfortable with it."

I scowled up at him, but he shrugged. He was serious. I faced the hunk of meat. "Okay," I whispered. "Okay." I stabbed at the meat.

I hit a rib.

"That's why stabbing in the heart is so difficult," Stellan said. "Now try again with better form. Don't rush."

I frowned and stabbed the meat again. This time my blade sank deep into the muscle, and I thought for a second that I might throw up.

"Do it again," Stellan said.

I did.

"Again."

I did it again. Just meat. I could be cooking this for dinner. Don't think of it as a person. Don't even think of the animal it came from. It's something in your kitchen. I stabbed it again. And again, and again. I was hitting muscle consistently now. The revulsion pulsing through me was cut in half, then half again, and then I could barely remember feeling like the meat was anything else, and I was able to really think about holding the knife correctly, and how to stand.

I pushed back a sweaty strand of hair and dropped the knife to my side.

Stellan was watching me, his arms folded across his chest. "Is it starting to feel better?"

My fingers tightened around the bloodied knife, and I nodded.

"You cringe every time you talk about training. Or fighting. Or if you so much as look at a knife."

"No I don't." A single fly buzzed along the surface of the mangled rack of ribs, settling on one end.

"You do. It's perfectly normal," Stellan said. He flicked the fly away with the tip of the stick he still held in one hand. "You don't have to be ashamed about being afraid to stab somebody. Or of getting hurt."

"I'm not afraid—" I started to say, but stopped myself. If fear wasn't my problem, would this little therapy session really have worked so well? I took my knife to the edge of the water, where I knelt and let the waves lap at the blade.

When a more powerful wave soaked the bottoms of my leggings, I jumped up. I wasn't surprised to find Stellan standing quietly next to me, his boots making hard indents in the wet sand. "When I first came to the Circle, the Dauphins sent me straight into training with the older kids," he said. "I had no idea what I was doing. My childhood was . . . sheltered. Easy. I had never so much as gotten in a fistfight. And here I was, twelve years old, straight from the hospital, most of my family dead, and they had me learning to kill people. There was no pretense of it being self-defense. It was a declaration that you would be doing jobs for the Circle, and some of those jobs would involve killing."

We both watched a seagull skim the water, then dive and come up with a fish flopping in its mouth. "What happened?" I asked.

"The first time I—" He paused and scratched at one eyebrow. "I had a full-on panic attack. I almost compromised the whole mission. I was in danger of being terminated if I couldn't pull it together."

"What?" A wave lapped at my toes. "They'd terminate a *kid?*"

"I was a liability. It's how it is." Stellan turned the stick over and over in his fingers. "I'd just started my tutoring with Fitz. He was the one who brought me to the Circle, so it was his responsibility if I turned out bad. And he did this with me." He gestured to the slab of meat. "Classic desensitization therapy. After that, I didn't panic anymore."

I thought again about the Order's attack at Prada. Stellan had driven that knife through the guy's heart like it was nothing. "Are you sure detaching is a good thing?"

He looked down at me now. His expression was unreadable, searching. "You shouldn't forget that question."

I shook the last drops of salt water off my knife. "Why didn't Jack ever have me do this?" I said, casually bringing him back into the conversation. Back into our consciousnesses.

We headed back up the beach, and Stellan wrapped the paper around the meat. "Fitz probably never had to give *him* remedial lessons." There was an unexpected note of bitterness in his voice, but when he saw the question in my eyes as I pulled my sneakers back on, he continued. "Jack grew up in the Circle. He didn't have to learn to be okay with it."

I would have laughed at the thought of *Jack* being more acclimated to violence than Stellan, but I could see that he was telling the truth. I realized that Stellan would probably tell me the truth about anything I asked. He had this mysterious air about him, but his secrets sat close to the surface.

"I've never shot a gun, either." I looked at the bulge at the back of Stellan's waistband.

He raised an eyebrow. "I'm not teaching you to shoot on a beach. We'll get arrested."

"Obviously," I said. But I was feeling brave now. Curious. "Can I just hold it for a second? Show me how to do that? Just in case."

"You've never even *held* one? Jack didn't do that with you?"

I shook my head.

Stellan looked up and down the beach and, seeing that we were still alone, pulled the gun from his waistband. I held out one hand.

"This is the safety," he said, flicking a switch back and forth. "This is on; this is off. I'm leaving the safety *on*. You don't turn it off, ever, unless you're going to shoot the gun."

"I'm not stupid," I said, and he set the gun in my hand.

It was heavy, warm. Stellan showed me how to wrap my hand around it and where my fingers rested when I wasn't about to shoot. Told me this particular gun was too big for my hands, and that it would feel better if it was the right size.

It felt okay.

"Jack hopes you'll never be forced to defend yourself. That's why he tries to keep you so sheltered. But if you had to—" Stellan leaned over to show me where to sight the target. "I'm sure he thinks you'd be a natural. That's why he didn't see you flinching with the knife."

I lowered the gun from my line of vision. It suddenly felt heavy.

"He has you on such a pedestal," Stellan continued. My thumb skimmed the handle of the gun as he took it away. "It's . . ." He trailed off.

"He believes in me." I scratched my nose. My fingers smelled like metal. "That's not a bad thing."

Something flitted across Stellan's face; then his expression went blank and he turned away. "Or maybe he thinks you're bad at fighting and doesn't want you to kill yourself. He's probably right. We shouldn't do this again."

Stellan stashed the gun and pulled his sweatshirt back on as I watched, taken aback at the abrupt change of tone. He tossed the mutilated slab of meat onto the rocks at the edge of the cliff, and a cluster of scrawny cats appeared.

"You coming, or are you going to stand there feeling sorry for yourself?" he said over his shoulder.

For once, I had nothing to say. I just frowned at his back and followed him around the rocks and up to the boardwalk.

CHAPTER 17

Once we'd gotten to the dock, I'd told Stellan I wanted to stop and get pastries, and he just shrugged and left me alone. Back at the boat, Elodie was lounging on the deck. She opened one eye. "There you are, and without either of your boyfriends. I'm sure at least one of them is looking for you."

I glanced behind her, hoping neither of them was listening. "That's not fair."

"It's true, though." Elodie stood and crossed the deck to lean out over the railing. "I understand why they're so fascinated with you, what with the whole savior of the Circle thing, but you're right—it's not *fair* to mess with them both, and it's not *fair* to the rest of us for the three of you to be doing . . . whatever you're doing, when you should be clearheaded and concentrating on not getting us killed."

"We're not—" I snapped my mouth shut. Elodie *wanted* an argument. "We're on the trail of maybe the most important discovery in world history and *this* is what you want to talk about? I'm already bored with this conversation," I said, stepping around her and ignoring the obnoxious smirk on her face.

"You should find Jackie, though," she called after me. "He has that worried look on his face. I hate that look."

Jack was pacing back and forth on the front deck of the boat, and came into the kitchen when he saw me. Through an upper window I saw Stellan sitting on the top deck, alone.

Jack didn't ask where we'd been all morning, but the quick narrowing of his eyes said everything he didn't.

I held out the bag. "We woke up early," I said awkwardly. After I'd almost drowned last night, Jack and I hadn't talked about the fight we'd had, but now it was hanging in the air. "We were taking a walk, then Stellan wanted to come back, but I wanted to get food and—" Why was I lying? "Breakfast," I said, shoving the bag of pastries in his hands.

Jack looked over his shoulder at the giant bowl of fruit on the table, at the fridge stuffed with food.

"Colette doesn't have fresh *bougatsa*." He opened the bag, and the smell wafted through the room. "It's phyllo dough and custard. I thought you might like it."

The boat swayed just a little bit in the morning breeze.

After a second, Jack tossed the pastries on the table, pulled a chair out, and pulled me down into his lap. I hugged him tight.

"How are you feeling?" he said into the top of my head.

"I'm actually fine." Surprisingly. My chest and throat were still a little sore, but running around and training didn't seem to have aggravated it.

Over his shoulder, I saw Elodie emerge onto the upper deck and glance in at us before talking to Stellan. I got off Jack's lap and spread the *bougatsa* on a plate. In a few minutes, Stellan and Elodie joined us, followed by Colette.

"I hate to break up this party, but I may have to," Colette said, tying shut a rose-colored silk robe before taking a seat at the booth next to Stellan. "I have a film festival to attend." Stellan rested his arm across her shoulders. I pretended not to notice. I wasn't sure why I *did* notice.

"There's nothing else to find here, anyway," Jack said. "Is there?"

"And there's no more *time*," I said.

They all exchanged glances, and I knew they were thinking about my Saxon-imposed deadline. Even *I* wasn't sure what I'd do when the clock ran out, but the more I thought about it, the more certain I was that marrying Daniel Melech or Jakob Hersch or any of the others wasn't an option.

"I talked to Luc earlier," Elodie said. "He's been looking into the twin bracelet. He doesn't have anything yet, but he thinks he will soon."

"I hope 'soon' means in the next few hours," I said under my breath. I grabbed the bracelet from the top of the fridge, where it had been sitting since we'd retrieved it from the ice bucket the night before, and spun the rings of letters, willing it to give up its secrets.

"I have to leave tonight," Colette said. "Until then, we hope for a miracle."

For the next few hours, the five of us sprawled around the yacht, on lounge chairs, on the floor, in the sparkling midday sunlight out on the deck, all deep in thought. Elodie was muttering to herself about the scientific implications of what a blood union could mean. Jack had written all the clues down and was trying slightly different translations. I had a thesaurus, a translation dictionary, and regular old Google search up on my phone. The bracelet was next to me, and every once in a while, I'd try a new password. By lunchtime, though, I could barely put a sentence together, much less think about synonyms and riddles and how I wished I knew French idioms. I was about to throw the bracelet across the room.

"Where will we go?" Jack said quietly from the deck chair next to me. "Paris?"

I buried my face in my hands. "I guess." The bracelet being in France made as much sense as anything.

Jack nodded. "I'll tell everybody."

I glared at the bracelet through my spread fingers. We had to be missing something.

Look where he looks. Those who gave all hold the key. Then there was the bracelet we already had: *Only to the true.* True. Accurate. Authentic. Legitimate. Genuine. The words were still scrolling through my mind, like my subconscious was trying to tell me something I was missing. *True.* Factual. Trustworthy. Morally right. Like Jack's compass, true north.

But it wasn't like Napoleon had anything to do with the Saxons' compass. He was a Dauphin relative. I'd tried the word *north* earlier, anyway, even though it wasn't in French, just in case. I rubbed my eyes hard. It did seem like Napoleon liked the physical in his riddles at least as much as he liked wordplay. We'd had to actually *go* to the gargoyle at the top of Notre-Dame to discover where he was looking. And that was where we found the diary Mr. Emerson had hidden inside the sarcophagus at the Louvre.

Suddenly, the fog cleared.

Look where he looks. That was what the clue had said. And on the first bracelet: *Where he looks, it will be found. When it is found, my twin and I will reveal all.*

I sat up straight. Oh my God. That was it. This was what had been at the tip of my tongue for days. We'd been ignoring the "where he looks" clue that kept popping up because we'd already found the diary by using it, but *Mr. Emerson* had hidden the diary.

Not Napoleon.

We were such idiots.

Mr. Emerson had figured out Napoleon's clues and knew where the gargoyle was looking, so he hid something in that line of sight—at the Louvre.

But the "where he looks, it will be found" clue Napoleon left on the bracelet *couldn't* refer to the diary we found at the Louvre. It had to refer to something that was there in *Napoleon's* time. At the Louvre or anywhere else the gargoyle might be pointing. *Look where he looks. Where he looks, it will be found. Those who gave all hold the key.*

The password was somewhere in the gargoyle's sight line.

I was so keyed up, I had to type *the louvre paris* into my phone four times before I spelled it right. Finally, I brought up pictures. It was unlikely we were looking for something inside the museum. The collection would have changed too much since Napoleon's time. Maybe there was a really obvious inscription on the building that unlocked the bracelets.

But I got frustrated quickly. Most of the photos weren't good enough to tell if there was anything there at all. I called everyone into the kitchen.

"This isn't a bad idea," Jack said, his eyes lighting up. "Or maybe it's not at the Louvre. That was the right direction for the gargoyle, but there are an infinite number of other buildings in the same direction."

"'Those who gave all,'" I thought out loud. "It sounds like someone who's dead. Like a martyr. Or a saint? Could it be a church?"

"It could be any number of things," Stellan said.

He pulled up a map of Paris on his phone, but it was too hard to continue the gargoyle's sight line on the small screen.

"We need a map," I said.

Elodie shook her head. "What we need is to go to Paris."

CHAPTER *18*

A few hours later, we were on the ground, back in the city that felt more like home than anywhere had in a long time.

Since we couldn't let the Saxons know we were with Stellan and Elodie, Colette left me and Jack in Paris before continuing to Cannes, while Stellan and Elodie had taken a separate plane. During the flight, Jack and I studied one of the paper maps of Paris we'd picked up in an Athens bookstore. We'd isolated the area that could be in the gargoyle's line of sight, and now we were making a list of landmarks that fell within it. Churches, small museums. Anything that may have been important to Napoleon.

I got out my phone in the cab on the way from the airport. Six missed calls from my father. I listened to the first voice mail just as Jack's phone rang.

"Elodie?" he said, then sat forward in his seat. "What? Is he— thank God."

In my ear, my father's voice said, "Avery, there's been another attack, in Paris. They tried to get to Luc Dauphin. Call me as soon as you can."

I gasped out loud. Jack put down his phone.

"He's fine," he said. "An attacker came at him in the Louvre courtyard, right in plain sight. Dauphin security fought him off and got Luc to safety. They're interrogating the attacker, but he's not talking. Elodie and Stellan wanted to go back immediately, but the Dauphins already have Luc secured. They're still meeting us."

We got out of the cab, and I kept looking over my shoulder, expecting to see somebody coming at us with a gun at any moment, and if they did, I swear I was ready to kill them with my bare hands. I could have sworn a couple times I even saw somebody watching us, but whenever I looked twice, it was nothing.

A cab pulled up, and Elodie leaped out and started running to us before it came to a complete stop. "I just talked to Luc. The reason he was out alone was that he was coming to meet us. He figured out where the bracelet is."

She thrust her phone into my hands.

It was zoomed in on what looked like the itinerary of the Cannes Film Festival. I looked up, confused, and Elodie pointed to one sentence. *Priceless antiques from around the globe will be on display at the opening gala of the Festival. 6–10 p.m., Main Lobby.*

I looked up. "Does this mean . . ."

Elodie smiled triumphantly. "Luc talked to the collector's estate manager. The bracelet will be displayed in Cannes in two days."

The bracelet on my arm gleamed in the sunlight, and my heart sped to a gallop. "We're going to have to steal it," I breathed.

"Correction," Elodie said, taking her phone back. "We're going to have to *heist* it. From the Cannes Film Festival."

Jack wanted to go immediately, but Elodie disagreed. "First of all, even if we manage to get the other bracelet, we still need the password.

Secondly, right now, the bracelet is in transit on its way to the exhibition space."

"But the festival will be crawling with security," I said. We were sitting on the edge of a fountain in the Place de la Concorde. "What if we went after it while it was in a warehouse or something?"

Stellan nodded his assent. "Could I just jump a guard in a back alley?"

Elodie ran her fingers through the water. "At the party, there will be distractions. Drunk people leaning on the cases, celebrities wanting closer looks, beautiful women in evening gowns. Plus, everyone will be wondering if the Order is going to try to kill them. And also, we have no idea where the bracelet is right now. Trust me, the party is the best opportunity for a heist."

Stellan looked up at the obelisk in the center of the square. "So we head down before the opening ceremony. Avery and Jack can't come on our plane, so maybe we'll take the overnight train tonight?"

We all nodded.

"Which means we have time to look around Paris today, then check on Lucien before we leave the city again," said Elodie.

We pulled out our maps with renewed energy.

There was nothing at the Place de la Concorde. I'd started to get excited, since the obelisk at the center of the plaza was Egyptian, and so maybe had some connection to Alexander, but I felt like an idiot when we realized it hadn't been put in until after Napoleon's death. The surrounding buildings were old enough, but there was nothing to indicate an important inscription or anything to do with Napoleon.

I shielded my eyes from the sun and looked around. "Moving on?"

A person in a blue hat disappeared behind a crepe stand, and I stopped talking.

"What?" Jack said, looking over his shoulder.

"I could swear someone's been following us," I said quietly. "Did you see that?"

He shook his head.

I'm sure everyone thought I was crazy after my previous false accusations. I guess I *was* tired enough to hallucinate. I dropped it. "What's next?"

We had all flagged landmarks to check, and we made our way to the next ones. Unfortunately, nothing seemed to be right. It didn't help that every monument in France wanted to tout their connection to Napoleon, so most of the connections were quite slim.

At the third small church on one of the map lines, I was looking at plaques on statues of saints at the entrance and Jack was crouched, inspecting the bases of another, when I realized he wasn't looking at the statue at all. He was looking past me, chewing his lip. He noticed me watching him and turned his attention to the floor, but his shoulders were drawn up to his ears.

"What is it?" I glanced behind me, immediately on guard.

"Nothing." He stood and moved down the line of statues.

All I could see where he'd been looking were Stellan and Elodie, searching the other side of the church. "Did you see something?"

"No." Jack moved farther away. "It's nothing."

"Okay . . ." I took a photo on my phone of each plaque, just in case I thought of something later. Jack was standing halfway to the altar now, and my footsteps echoed on the worn hardwood as I caught up with him. "No, seriously, what's going on?"

Jack had been tracing a raised metal plaque with one finger, but let his hand drop to his side. "I'm—this isn't the right time for this conversation." He glanced over his shoulder again, to where Stellan and Elodie were whispering in a pew. "It's just that—I have to know—is there something going on between you and Stellan?"

My nerves, already frayed, started firing overtime. I had to sit on the edge of the pew behind me. "What?" I said stupidly.

Jack's face dropped. He thought my reaction meant more than it did. But I was just surprised. And annoyed that he'd ask something like that. No, I didn't hate Stellan anymore. Yes, things were a little different between us now. But that was all.

Jack turned back to the plaque and rubbed his neck. "I know you and I aren't *together*, and I know this is bigger than that, but . . ."

I checked to make sure Elodie and Stellan weren't listening and lowered my voice. "Then why ask? Because the answer is obviously no, besides the supposed-to-get-married thing. I think you know that."

"I thought I did."

The words hit like he'd slapped me. "And what could possibly make you think otherwise?"

Jack glanced toward the front of the church again, then headed out the doors and pulled out the map. "You've been closer lately."

I followed him and leaned over the map without really seeing it. "We've *all* been closer lately." I sounded so defensive. I took a deep breath and slowed down. "We've been living on a boat. And in small apartments. And seeing each other every day. You don't see me asking if there's anything going on between you and Elodie."

"I saw him coming out of the room you were in on the boat last night," Jack said quietly.

My finger paused on the map. "No, I can guarantee you didn't."

"I did. I was wide awake."

"Then he was probably *visiting* one of the other two people sleeping in that same room."

"Lettie and Elodie were out taking a walk," Jack said. "I think . . . I saw him leave our room. Go to yours. Come back a couple minutes later. He was either hoping for something else, or checking on you." Jack didn't sound angry. He just sounded . . . resigned.

"He was probably getting a sleeping pill from Elodie's bag," I said. "I was asleep. Whatever you saw was nothing. Less than nothing."

"You're probably right," Jack said.

"Yeah. I am." I leaned against one of the metal poles lining the sidewalk and held my hand out for the map. Part of me wondered why I was quite so bothered, and all of me really didn't want to think about it. I yanked the map out of Jack's hand a little more forcefully than necessary.

"You're considering it, though," Jack said quietly. "Considering him, I mean."

"If the bracelet doesn't come through, I'll have to do something. And yeah, Stellan's a better option than whoever Alistair chooses." I was running a finger up the map when I suddenly heard the words that had just come out of my mouth. Really? When had I decided that?

"But right now I'm doing my best to figure out this next clue," I said quickly, "and this is a distraction I don't need."

Jack shoved his hands in his pockets. "I just can't not think about it when I see how he looks at you."

I glanced back at the church. The heavy wooden doors were still closed, Elodie and Stellan still inside. "He looks at me like I'm a gold-plated statue to put on his mantel. The same way everyone in the Circle looks at me."

And that was true, usually. Except for last night, when he realized I wasn't dead. Except this morning, when he apparently wanted nothing to do with me.

Jack touched the back of my hand. "Forget I said anything, okay? It's just—it's everything, you know?"

I stared down at our hands. "Yeah." I was getting tired of it all, too.

I pulled away and traced over the lines I'd made on the map. We'd been sticking inside the triangle formed by the outermost ones, but now I traced a little farther out with two fingers.

"Are we sure these angles are exactly right?" I said, changing the subject.

"No," Jack said. "This is everything *approximately* within the gargoyle's sight line."

I squinted at the map. "I wonder if the key word is *approximately*. I'm sure Napoleon was careful about the clues he planted, but maybe when the gargoyle was installed, he got moved a few millimeters. That could change the angle as you get farther away from Notre-Dame."

"And to Fitz, the Louvre was the best bet, so he planted *his* clue there—"

"But it doesn't necessarily mean Napoleon's was on that same line," I finished. We leaned over the map excitedly. "Maybe we could go a little outside this triangle."

"You know what is really close . . ." Jack pointed.

The Arc de Triomphe. "Napoleon put it up, right?" I said.

"He commissioned it. It wasn't finished before his death, but it was on its way. He would certainly have been able to inscribe anything he wanted there."

The church doors opened, and Stellan and Elodie came out. We explained our thoughts.

"And the other monument Napoleon used was a big one," I finished. "He chose Notre-Dame, not one of these tiny churches. Maybe he assumed his own monument would achieve just as much fame." And he was right. Besides the Eiffel Tower, which was put in well after Napoleon's death, the Arc de Triomphe was probably the most famous monument in Paris.

Elodie suddenly looked up with a sharp intake of breath. "The Arc de Triomphe is a monument to soldiers who fought in the French Revolution and the Napoleonic Wars."

Jack and Stellan both looked confused for a second, then their faces lit up, too, and finally, I got it.

"'Those who gave all hold the key,'" I said. "Let's go."

CHAPTER 19

The car let us off in the center of a bustling traffic circle. The Arc de Triomphe loomed overhead, an embodiment of Paris itself: statuesque, historic, incredibly detailed. Surrounded by the modern Paris of stylish ladies on Vespas and tourists and slinking vendors selling Eiffel Tower key chains.

All around the grand arch were intricate carvings of battles and angels and soldiers. Jack split off to the opposite side without waiting for me, and Elodie followed, throwing me a curious look. I leaned against the carved stone and closed my eyes with a sigh.

Someone leaned beside me, and I wasn't surprised to hear Stellan's voice. "So your kind-of-but-not-really boyfriend thinks you and I are doing a little *something* on the side?"

"How do you know—never mind." It didn't matter. I opened my eyes. Stellan's arms were tight, shoulders hunched to his ears, and his eyes darted over the throngs of tourists under the monument. He was trying to act normal, but the attack on Luc had put him on edge.

I thought about asking him if he'd come in to get a sleeping pill last night, or whether he was in my room to see if I was okay. I didn't. I pushed away from the wall and searched the area above my head.

"Was it Elodie?" I asked.

Stellan crossed his arms over his chest. "Was what Elodie?"

I took a break from squinting up at the bas-relief on the arch above. It didn't have the symbol from my locket on it and didn't seem to be of the Fates, which were the two clue markers we'd seen so far.

I motioned in the direction Jack had gone. "Whatever happened between the two of you to make you hate each other, when it's obvious you used to be close. It sounds like you both had a thing for her at some point, and now he thinks you're trying to steal *me*."

Stellan's arms dropped to his side, and with that one gesture, he looked tired. "No," he said. "We *all* used to be close. Me and Elodie—we liked each other, but it wasn't . . . We were young. Our bedrooms were on the same hallway." He shrugged like, *what else do you expect?* "And she and Jack, after that . . . they dated for a while."

I was momentarily distracted from the artwork.

"We worked more closely with the Saxons just a few years back. Jack and I were together a lot because of Fitz, and the two of us and Elodie . . . we were friends—us and Luc, too. Jack was practically my younger brother."

I tried to picture what the two of them must have been like when they actually liked each other. And—Jack and Elodie, *together*? I knew from the truth-or-dare game that they'd kissed, but wow.

I'd been quiet long enough that Stellan left me behind. I followed him inside the arch, where there were carved lists of names that must have been soldiers. Column after column, with some of the names underlined.

"So what happened—" I cut off. Something the tour guide with a group next to us said had just sparked something. "Did she say the underlined names are the soldiers who died in battle?"

Stellan shrugged, and leaned over to the tour group and asked someone on the periphery. The lady nodded.

"'Those who gave all hold the key,'" I said. "What if the password is one of the names?"

Stellan squinted up at the names, then down at the bracelet on my arm. I took it off and rotated the tarnished gold rungs inside it.

"I suppose we can try them all," Stellan said.

I scanned the names. "Not all. Only the five-letter ones." I pulled the bracelet off my arm and spun the five bands to spell the first underlined name. When nothing happened, we kept going down the column. *Damas. Binot. Penne.*

Halfway down this side of the arch when my eyes were starting to cross, Stellan took the bracelet.

I read off the next name. Then I said, "So if he used to be like your brother, what happened?"

Stellan spun the bracelet to another password. "We were starting to cook up this crazy scheme where the three of us would work together under Fitz. Be some kind of special Circle-wide Keepers or something, and have Elodie do it, too." He shrugged self-consciously when he saw me raise my eyebrows. "Before this new round of Order attacks, things were easier in the Circle. We were idealistic. But then Oliver Saxon happened."

"The oldest Saxon brother." The brother I'd never know. I remembered how Jack shut down when I asked about him.

Stellan nodded. "He was less than a year older than Lydia and Cole. You know how siblings born in the same year are called Irish twins? They called themselves Irish triplets."

"So . . ." I did the math. "Just a few months younger than me." I was starting to put the time line together. My father must have gotten married and started his family right after my mom left.

Stellan nodded. "It was a routine event. One of Jack's first as a solo Keeper. It was just a freak accident, they said. A car plowed into the crowd. Killed four people. Oliver was one of them."

I went cold all over. "Oh my God."

"There was nothing Jack could have done. He saw it coming maybe half a second before everyone else and tried to push Oliver out of the way, but he only succeeded in landing himself in the hospital, too. He's never forgiven himself."

I shook my head. "*Was* it an accident? Or was it the Order?"

"We never knew. There were rumors, but the Order never claimed responsibility."

"What does that have to do with him being mad at you?"

"Elodie and I were there, too, with Luc. Some things happened, and Jack blamed himself for being distracted . . . When he got out of the hospital, nothing was ever the same."

"That's why he's so overprotective," I said to myself.

"The Saxons kept him on, when there was speculation he'd be . . . well. You can guess. Oliver was his responsibility that day. The firstborn son of the family, lost under his watch. But Saxon—your father—he didn't blame Jack."

"And that's why Jack feels so indebted to them," I said quietly.

I felt a surge of affection for my father, for forgiving the accident. And for Lydia for still accepting Jack.

"That, and—" Stellan said, but stopped abruptly.

"What?"

"Nothing. Forget it."

"What?" I snatched the bracelet out of his hand. "You have to tell me now."

He actually looked uncomfortable. Stellan never looked uncomfortable. "It's not—it's going to seem like I'm trying to make him sound bad, but I'm not. I don't think you really want to know."

He reached for the bracelet again, and I held it away. "Tell me."

He sighed. "The day Oliver was killed, Jack kissed Lydia Saxon. He said it was just the once. She initiated it—I think she's always liked him. But it was at that event, and I saw it happen, and so did Elodie, who he was with at the time. It was the kind of stupid drama that sometimes happened when we were younger and had less responsibility, but we were all upset and preoccupied . . . and then this terrible thing happened."

I let Stellan take the bracelet back out of my hand. On the other side of the monument, I could see Jack and Elodie, pointing up at a fresco.

That *was* awful. But also . . . Jack was upset about me being friendly with Stellan, when he'd kissed everyone I knew? And *Lydia*, of all people?

I followed Stellan blindly around the other side of the arch. This was stupid. What Jack did in the past didn't matter. Yes, Lydia kind of looked like me. And okay, that meant when Jack had first realized I was a Saxon, he wasn't just seeing some girl. He was seeing a different version of a girl he'd already had a thing with.

"I told you you didn't want to know," Stellan said, still turning the letters on the bracelet.

I snatched it out of his hand and looked up at the next column. "The next name is Gudin," I said. "No wait, we've already tried that one."

"No we haven't," Stellan said.

I pointed. "Oh. I saw it over there, but it wasn't underlined."

I twisted the bracelet into *Gudin*. The second I clicked the *N* into place, a *pop* sounded from the bracelet, so loud I nearly dropped it and a couple elderly tourists shot us an alarmed glance. Where the inside of the bracelet had been smooth, the whole word—*Gudin*—was now raised half a centimeter above the rest.

I looked up at Stellan, and my shock was mirrored in his blue eyes. He pulled me out of the crowd and into a shaded corner, where we sat on the low ledge jutting out from the arch, hunched over the bracelet in my lap. "It actually did something." I turned the bracelet over and over in my hands. "This is it. This is *right*."

Stellan took the bracelet gingerly and inspected the now-raised portion. "What does it mean? The rest of the letters don't seem to spell anything, and I still can't see whether there's anything inside it."

I grabbed his arm, and he held out the bracelet so I could see, too. Under the raised portion was a thin line of what looked like topaz, but he was right—we twisted and pulled on it, but this was as far as we could get it open.

"We can figure out what it means later, but it's something. We actually *found* something."

"We actually found something." Stellan's eyes were shining. I realized I was clinging to his arm like a life preserver, and let go. Jack and Elodie appeared at the far side of the arch, and I jumped up and waved to them, any animosity forgotten for a moment as we showed them what we'd found.

"Do you think it's the same password for both?" I said, breathless.

"No way of knowing," Elodie said. "Maybe write down all the other underlined names?"

I immediately pulled out paper and started scribbling. "No," I said. "Not underlined. Twins. The bracelets are twins, and that name, Gudin—there's another Gudin over there. Look for names that repeat."

"Here," Jack said after a few minutes. "This one has a first initial. Maybe that means there are two."

I wrote the name down: *Boyer,* and glanced over the rest.

One second, Jack looked triumphant, and the next, he was staring over my shoulder and his smile blinked off like the power had gone out.

I turned, and my whole body went hot, then cold.

Standing behind us was my sister.

CHAPTER 20

Stellan shoved the bracelet in his pocket. Cole stepped into view, too, and then the twins were striding toward us. Lydia waved.

My heart was racing. It was too late. There was no way they hadn't spotted Stellan and Elodie.

And then, a flash of movement behind them, and this time I was sure. It was the same blue hat I'd seen earlier. The person turned so I could finally see his face—and my heart dropped to my feet.

The person wearing the blue baseball cap was Scarface.

Suddenly, explaining away Stellan and Elodie's presence didn't matter as much.

"Lydia!" I rushed toward my siblings, grabbing both of them by the wrists and dragging them around the corner. "Cole! We have to get out of here."

Jack had already seen, and whispered to Stellan and Elodie, who both had hands on whatever weapons they had hidden.

For a second, I thought about confronting Scarface, even though we had the passwords and would soon have the second bracelet. This could be my chance—if I wasn't worried about him hurting my siblings.

I didn't have much time to consider it. Jack was shielding me and the twins, bundling us to the stairs under the traffic circle and to our waiting car on the other side.

"What are you doing?" Cole grumbled.

"Just go," I urged him. "Trust me. I'll tell you in the car."

I glanced back for Stellan and Elodie, who were now loping down the tunnel. "We lost him," Stellan said.

"Just get in the car," I answered.

We all piled inside. "Go," I said to the driver. "Anywhere. Away."

When the car started moving down the Champs-Élysées, I slumped back against the seat with a sigh. "Get off the main road," I said, and the driver turned off. No one seemed to follow us. My heart was slamming against my rib cage.

"What were you two doing there?" Jack demanded.

"What were *you* doing there?" Lydia countered.

"Who are they?" Cole said, pointing to the passenger seat, where Elodie sat on Stellan's lap.

"Stellan Korolev," Lydia said. "Dauphin Keeper. And"—she looked Elodie up and down—"Elodie Fontaine. Dauphin maid," she said, like none of us were even here. She turned back to me. "Your friend Luc was nearly *killed* earlier. If none of the other attacks convinced you to help us stop the Order, that should. You need to come back with us right now."

"I—what?" My head was swimming. Had the twins tracked me down because of what happened to Luc? "That guy at the Arc de Triomphe was Order. How did they track us?"

I pulled my shoulders out from between Jack and Lydia to swivel and peer behind us. We were skirting the river now, and seemed to be alone. "I think we lost him. Just drive us a little farther—"

"Unnecessary," Cole said under his breath. He was crammed

against the door on the other side of the car, with Lydia next to me and Jack on my other side.

"What do you mean, unnecessary?" I said. "He was *right* behind you. He's been following us—we have to get out of here."

Cole smirked out the window. "Yes. I'm very scared."

Elodie swiveled to stare at him.

Stellan groaned. "*Merde,* El. That's your knee somewhere I don't want your knee."

She ignored him. "What's your problem?" she said to Cole. "What do you mean by that?"

"Cole," Lydia said under her breath.

"What do you think I mean?" Cole said, then to Lydia, "If we have to keep our *sister* around, I'm tired of her being so stupid. I know you want to tell her, too. We weren't even careful today. And the rest of them don't matter. Look, the Dauphin maid knows already."

"She didn't, but now she does." Lydia smacked him. "You idiot. I didn't want to have to clean this up."

"Clean what up?" I said. "What are you talking about?"

And then I saw a look on Elodie's usually calm, bored face I'd never seen before. Pure, unadulterated terror.

"Stop the car," she said to the driver. She was already pulling on the door handle, fumbling with the lock, even though we were still moving, her limbs tangled with Stellan's. "Get out. *Dépêchez-vous!* Avery, Jack, get *out!*"

I was so busy wondering if she'd lost her mind that I didn't see Cole pull a gun until it was pointed at the back of the driver's head. "No," he said. "Don't stop. Lock the doors. You, girl. Hands in the air."

The driver went white and sped back up, and Elodie's hands came up gradually.

"What's going on?" I scrambled away from the twins, onto Jack's lap, and I could feel his heart thudding against my back as he pulled me against him protectively. "Lydia? What's—"

"You too, Keeper," Cole said. His gun was swinging lazily between all of us, so close in the car's small backseat, he could have pressed it to my forehead. "Hands up. Bishop, too."

Jack slowly took his hands off my waist and put them in the air.

"What the hell, Cole?" I said.

"They didn't care that the Order was there." Elodie's voice shook. "They showed up *at the same time.*"

I suddenly had the urge to put my hands over my ears.

"Put it together faster, sister," Cole said, his voice mean and cold.

I felt Jack's chest tense against my back. "No," he whispered. Stellan turned, the shock mirrored in his eyes. And Cole's smirk and Cole's gun and it all hit me like a tidal wave and I was drowning.

All the time we'd spent talking, Lydia teaching me about the Circle, acting like she'd understood. *We should have a secret signal in case you need anything. This one's hot; you'll like him.*

"Yes," Cole said, almost like he was bored, explaining something obvious to a child. "The person you call *Scarface* is ours. All of them are."

I couldn't breathe.

Lydia had been quiet, but now she sat forward, pleading. "Avery, just listen. You were planning to give whatever you found to someone you thought was *Order*. Of course we had to watch you."

"But that means—" I couldn't seem to finish a thought. Every bit of tension I'd interpreted as normal family drama. The Saxons' insistence that *they* would help find my mom. Their deadline for my marriage into the Circle, so conveniently aligned with the Order's deadline. My vision narrowed to just my sister's eyes, so much like mine.

"None of it was real," I whispered.

"It was real," Lydia insisted. "It *is* real. I *want* a sister. I'm the one who convinced Cole and father to give you the chance to do what's best for our family."

"But you never wanted to be one of us," Cole broke in.

I was choking on the words. "You're—you're the 'Order,'" I stammered. "It's *all* been you?"

In the front seat, Elodie sucked in a strangled breath.

And then a new realization dawned. "You have my mom." I lunged toward the twins, my voice shifting into a snarl. "Where is she?"

A gun, cold at my temple. Lydia swatted it away. "Cole, *no*. We're not shooting Avery. Pay attention to the rest of them, though, or they might do something they'll regret." Lydia held me at arm's length, back against Jack. "Your mother is safe."

"It's you killing all the Circle members, too?" Elodie demanded. "Did you attack Luc today?"

"We didn't *hurt* him," Lydia said. "It was a little nudge to remind you who has the upper hand."

Stellan and Elodie both surged forward, like they'd strangle her with their bare hands.

Cole waved his gun, and they stopped.

"You killed all those boys!" I yelled. "How could you do that? Why?"

How was it *possible*? I thought of the fear in the eyes of every Circle member I'd met recently. The hatred. That kind of reaction was for something truly horrifying. Not for little Lydia Saxon and the rest of my family.

"*You* made Eli Abraham kill himself."

"It had to be done." She shrugged, and in that tiny gesture, I saw exactly how it was possible. She'd *giggled* at Eli while he performed for us. Flirted with him like she was just a normal girl. But that same *normal girl* had done all this.

"You did it all yourselves?" I asked. None of us had bothered to put on a seat belt, and Jack and I both grabbed a handhold when we turned sharply. "Or did my—our—" I shuddered. "Did Alistair help, too?"

Cole scowled. "Haven't you heard of plausible deniability? We have the same goals, but he's too soft for most of our plans—if it were up to him, we'd be as weak as the rest of them."

"He's wanted you locked up and safe the whole time," Lydia said, sounding exasperated. "He'll be happy for an excuse to do it now."

I knew I sounded pathetic when I said, "You're supposed to be the good guys."

Lydia shook her head. "There *are* no good guys, Avery. Did you not understand that the Dauphins—your little *friends* here—were trying to enslave you? And the Mikados and the Rajeshes—if you knew more about the Circle, you'd get why we couldn't let you marry into those families. It's for your own good. And ours."

"Are you saying that you killed those guys so I wouldn't choose them?" My voice had gotten shrill. "Who *are* you?"

She frowned. "Who says killing a few people to get the whole Circle not only more powerful but *better* is wrong? We're more right than *anyone*."

"It's got to be done," Cole cut in. "Our oldest brother died. My father's older brother died. It was the Circle's fault, for being so soft. The only way for us to ensure our family's survival is to rule them all."

"We have the purple-eyed girl," Lydia took over. "It's *fate*. If the rest of them see that the killing spree stops once our family fulfills the mandate, there's no way they won't take us as their leaders. And maybe we'll have the tomb on top of it."

Manifest Destiny, I remembered. Fate. Disgust ripped through me.

"We have no choice." Lydia looked me in the eye, and I could see that she believed what she was saying with every ounce of her being. "Sometimes you have to do things you don't want to for the greater good. And it's not that I don't respect them." She yanked up her shirt and pointed at the tattoo of the flower half-covered in petals. "I'll always remember them, just like the rest of the Circle will. Martyrs."

Close up, I could tell that some of the petals were more raw and new than others. "Each petal is someone you killed," I whispered.

Jack leaned over my shoulder, staring at Lydia's rib cage, shell-shocked.

"You—" Stellan broke off in a string of Russian.

"Just kill him," Lydia commanded, pulling her shirt back down. "He's heard too much. Kill the maid, too."

"No!" I cried. "I'll—" Oh God, what could I do? "I've heard it all, too. *I'll* tell someone. And you won't kill me. Just let them go and they won't say anything."

Cole didn't lower the gun. I couldn't just sit back and watch more people I cared about get hurt. There was only one way this could end.

"I'll come with you," I said, "if you let them go."

"Avery, no." Elodie's eyes were on Cole's gun, calculating.

"We're not leaving you," Stellan growled.

"Yes, you are." Stellan had pocketed the bracelet the second we saw Lydia and Cole at the Arc de Triomphe. They'd keep it safe and I'd go with the Saxons to look for my mom, then try to escape. "Go," I said. "Cole, let them out."

Cole's violet eyes flashed angrily. After what seemed like ages, Lydia pulled on his arm, dropping his gun. "We'll get to them later," Lydia said, and told the driver to stop.

Stellan's eyes met mine, and he shook his head. I shifted my gaze to Elodie. "Go," I mouthed. She reached behind them and opened the car door. "You too," I urged Jack, trying to shift off his lap.

"You know I'm not leaving," he said. I did know.

The second Elodie shut the door, we were driving away.

"Mom!" I screamed, for what must have been the hundredth time in the hours since we'd arrived at the Saxons' Paris residence. Guards had stashed me in a windowless room full of TVs, then locked the door behind me. It was unlikely my mom was here—they probably had her in London—but just in case, I'd screamed so much my voice sounded like I'd spent years chain-smoking.

Someone pounded at the door. "I told you she's not here. Shut up."

I kicked the door and paced across the room, waiting. For my father? For Lydia? I pulled on the short piece of hair at the back of my neck. Last time I'd been captured by one of the Circle families, my hair had been the only casualty. But this was my own family. The loss of them alone was already more than I could handle.

On cue, footsteps came, and the lock turned. My father slipped inside, and my first thought was relief that it wasn't Lydia. I never wanted to see my sister again. My second thought was that this felt a thousand times worse that I could have imagined.

My father pushed some buttons on a remote, making every TV in the room spring to life. Each screen showed my own stricken face as I frantically, futilely, pressed my palm over the wound in Takumi Mikado's chest.

"You're a hero now," my father said, setting down the remote on a desk at the edge of the room. All around us, there was the moment Eli looked up and drew a gun. Then there was me, and the first family of Japan, shocked, terrorized. Over and over again. "You came so close to saving Mikado's life."

I tore my eyes away from the screens. "No I didn't."

"In our narrative, you did. You're the girl who could have run away but tried valiantly to save the victim."

I looked at the news broadcast with new eyes. "How could you do this?"

"You only need to watch a few minutes of the news to see the answer to that question. They're *all* looking to us. You're world famous. And now the Circle wants you twice as much." Alistair tidied papers on the desk, setting the stack down with finality. "When I was younger, I believed the families of the Circle could be allies, not enemies. My father and my brother felt the same way, and look where it got them. But I came to see it differently, and your sister understands better than I ever did at her age. People like us aren't meant to be cogs in a machine. Sooner or later, one family is going to take charge, and it has to be us. You'll come to understand."

He reached out to put an arm around me, and I shook him off violently. "I will *never* understand this. And do you really not think the rest of the Circle will find out?"

My father sat in the swiveling desk chair, looking tired again. "I'd hoped you would come around on your own. But if that's not going to happen . . ."

It was hot and stuffy in the room, but my whole body went cold. "You said you loved my mom," I choked out.

My father planted both hands on the desktop and looked right at me. "I don't *want* this, Avery. I don't want it any more than you do."

But he would still threaten her to get me to cooperate, and after everything else I'd found out about the Saxons, I had no doubt he'd follow through. "I'll find the tomb for you," I said desperately. "We have clues. We're so close."

My father tapped his fingers on the pile of papers.

"I'll marry whoever you want if you let her go. Just let her go." I leaned on the desk, too, so I was face-to-face with my father. "Please."

He sank into his desk chair. "I wish I could believe you, but we both know you'd run the moment we released your mother."

"So what are you going to do?" My throat knotted like the design on my locket, as though the thirteen loops were tightening around my neck. "Lock me up with her? Kill us both? You can't do that. We *are* getting closer to the tomb, and if you hurt her, you'll never find out what we know and I'll never agree to be your little princess."

My father rested his chin in his hand and gazed past my shoulder, at a portrait of a man hanging on the wall. The man had my eyes, too. And as he looked at him, there was something in my father's gaze that gave me hope.

I stepped into his line of sight. "Please. Alistair. Father—*Dad*. If you ever loved my mom—if you ever cared about *me*, even a little bit—let me earn my mom's freedom. Worst case scenario, we'll be out of your lives forever and you can go on ruling the Circle with whatever's in the tomb. Just give me a chance."

My father's mouth drew into a hard line, then he sighed heavily. "Okay. Yes. Get us the tomb, and we'll release your mother."

Relief made my knees buckle, and I fell into a chair facing the desk.

"I trust you'll smooth over any vicious rumors your Keeper friends might start about us as well," he said.

"I'll do anything." It came out in a rush. "Just don't hurt her. And please, release Jack. It's not his fault—"

My father sighed. "Avery—" Someone knocked on the door. My father stood, buttoning his coat, and opened it a crack.

"It's Lucien Dauphin, sir," the guard said. "Something about a ludicrous new rumor involving your son and daughter. He came to offer his family's help. Trying to make amends for that wedding stunt, if you ask me."

No. That couldn't be true. Stellan and Elodie and Luc wouldn't be stupid enough to try to rescue me. Would they? I desperately wished the Saxons hadn't confiscated my phone.

A walkie-talkie crackled. "They say he's out front."

"One of you, stay by the door," my father snapped. "The rest, come with me."

He glanced at me. "We'll finish this conversation later." He shut and locked the door behind him. The voices retreated.

No no no. I searched the room again for a way out. No windows, not so much as an air duct.

And then I heard a bump from the hallway, as if something had fallen against the door.

A light knock.

"Avery?" a voice whispered. "Are you in there?"

Elodie.

CHAPTER 21

"I'm here," I called as loud as I dared. "I can't get out. The guards have the keys."

A few seconds later, jingling, and then the door swung open. Elodie held a huge key ring, and Stellan was a few steps away, dragging a crumpled guard away from the door. He grabbed a gun and a knife from the guard's belt.

I shoved past Elodie and scanned the hall for more guards. "What are you guys doing here? They'll kill you."

"If we left you here, they'd kill Jackie and lock you up," Elodie said. "We weren't going to let Luc help, but he insisted."

"I don't think they'll hurt him *at* the Saxons' home," Stellan said over his shoulder, "but he won't hold them off for long."

Elodie peered behind me. "Where's Jack?"

"I don't know."

Elodie cursed and pocketed the key ring. "I'll find him. You get out."

I nodded, but paused. They still had my mom. I grabbed the notepad on Alistair's desk and scribbled, *I'll find the tomb for you. Don't hurt her.*

"Come *on*," Stellan said. "What are you doing?" I tossed the note back on the desk and turned just in time to see the guard rising up, a heavy chair in his hands arcing toward Stellan's head.

"Watch out!" I screamed, and Stellan ducked, but not fast enough. The chair's front leg cracked into his skull, and he stumbled to one knee.

The guard popped to standing and grabbed me, hauling me off down the hall. My legs dragged and I flailed, kicking back at his knee. "Let me go!" I screamed.

The guard clamped a hand over my mouth.

I found skin and ground my teeth together as hard as I could, until I tasted the metallic tang of blood.

He yelled and dropped me in a heap, cradling his hand, a mix of shock and contempt blazing in his eyes. "You little bitch—"

He didn't get to finish. Stellan came up behind him and put a gun to his head.

"Don't—" I said, and at the last second, Stellan took his finger off the trigger and smacked the side of the guard's head with the butt of the gun. The guard fell next to me, and I saw two phones with blue rubberized cases sticking out of his pocket. My untraceable phone, and Jack's, too. I grabbed them and stuffed them into the bag across my chest, and Stellan hauled me to my feet. I spat the remnants of blood out of my mouth, wiping my tongue like I could get rid of the whole idea.

"Your head," I said. Blood matted Stellan's blond hair.

"It's fine." He shook the cobwebs from what was obviously a pretty bad head injury, then pointed his gun down the hall. We were alone.

We hurried to a door, and it opened to a pitch-black stairwell.

Stellan grabbed my hand, and I felt slick blood across his palm. "Are you sure you're okay?" I said.

"Yes. Go."

I clung to Stellan with one hand and the banister with the other, only stumbling once as we made our way down three flights of dark stairs until we were on level ground again. "There's got to be a door," Stellan whispered, and we felt the walls with our free hands, all smooth, no handles or doorjambs.

Suddenly, a door burst open in the wall. Someone held a flashlight, and I made out the glint of a gun. And a person. Scarface.

I didn't think. I didn't consider the gun. I let go of Stellan, wheeled around, and kneed Scarface as hard as I could in the crotch.

Yes, Stellan was right that guys had good reflexes when it came to that, but I had the element of surprise. Scarface fell to one knee, gasping in pain, his gun flying off into the dark.

"That was for killing Fitzpatrick Emerson," I said. "And for kidnapping my mom. Where is she?"

Scarface panted. "I don't know where your damn mother is. Not here."

I was inclined to believe him. I wasn't sure he could be in that much pain and come up with a good lie at the same time.

"I've already called for backup," he said, nodding at Stellan's gun. "You kill me, they'll still be down here before you can get away."

I looked up at the side of the chateau, where Elodie and Jack might be right now. "Call them off," I said.

Scarface just laughed.

Stellan jammed the gun into his head. "We'll take our chances."

"Wait." Suddenly, I had another idea. It was risky, in a lot of ways. But so was having either or both of us captured again.

"No," I said, trying to sound convincing. "He's going to call them off."

Scarface raised an eyebrow up at me.

"The Saxons are not the right side to end up on," I said. I was starting to understand. In the Circle, loyalty goes family first, with the Circle not far behind, but I represented a whole lot more power than the Saxons did.

A frown quirked Scarface's long, dark scar downward. "I know who you are. You belong to the Saxons."

"I don't belong to anybody," I said. "I'm giving you a choice because I think you're smart. We could work together."

Shouts came from the floors above. "Call them off now and let us go," I said, "and when I'm in power, you'll be beside me."

Scarface's eyes flickered between us. "You're going to take over by *yourself*? Without the Saxons?"

"I'm not on the Saxons' side anymore."

Scarface considered my answer. And then he got to his knees.

I tensed, but he bowed, hands across his forehead, palms to me, hands crossed, so they shadowed his face in the flashlight beam. I recognized the posture: at the wedding at Notre-Dame, after I'd revealed myself, the people had done the same thing, pledging their loyalty to me.

I gaped down at him, then at Stellan. I let out a jagged breath. "Okay. Call them off."

Scarface pulled a walkie-talkie out of his belt and barked into it, "No one at the back stairs. Try the east wing."

It had actually worked. "Okay. Um. Stay with Lydia and pretend you're still working for her. Try to keep the guards away while we escape. Luc Dauphin—make sure he gets out safely. And don't let the Saxons do anything to my mother. That's the most important thing."

Scarface nodded. I started toward the door, but he didn't get off his knees.

Stellan stopped me. "You'll have to accept him officially," he said quietly. "Otherwise he's not really yours."

I glanced at the door, outside, freedom. "What do you mean?"

"It's usually done at the ceremony when we get our tattoos." The frown on Stellan's face told me he wasn't sure about this idea. "The tattoo is the symbol of who you're loyal to."

A sacred Circle ceremony. We didn't have time. It wasn't like I could give him a new tattoo, anyway. My hand flew to my necklace, twisting, and then it stopped. The knot symbol, with thirteen loops.

"Where's your tattoo?" I asked Scarface. Without standing or even looking up, he pulled down the back of his collar. There was a compass tattoo there, which had been inked over an old tattoo. I couldn't quite tell, but it could have been an olive branch.

It didn't matter. I unhooked my necklace. "Lighter?" I asked Stellan. He dug it out of his pocket. I flicked it and dangled my necklace in the flame. The orange light glinted off the gold.

"Are you sure you trust him enough to do this?" Stellan said. "It's a big deal."

"I don't care as long as he lets us go," I breathed in his ear. It wasn't like we ever had to see Scarface again if something went wrong.

When I thought it would be hot enough, I tried to grasp the necklace between my thumb and finger, and hissed.

"I'll do it," Stellan said. I shook my head. He might not burn, but it still hurt him. He took a tissue from his pocket and gripped the necklace.

"Tell me where you want it," he said.

But that didn't feel right. "Together," I said. "Above the compass." I put my hand over Stellan's. Together, we pressed the hot necklace into the end of the olive branch. Scarface twitched, and I responded by pressing harder. I wanted it to hurt. For my mom. For Mr. Emerson.

Stellan pulled our hands away, revealing an angry red welt. I hoped it would be enough for us to escape.

Scarface touched his neck, then put his hands to his forehead again.

Despite Scarface's calling them off, a door opened in the stairwell far above.

"Go," I said to Stellan. We shoved through the outer door as footsteps pounded down the stairs.

Scarface leaped up. He intercepted the pair of guards. "They're getting away," one of them said.

And then Scarface unceremoniously slit both their throats.

A strangled gasp escaped my throat. "I didn't mean kill *everybody*!"

The door was closing. I clawed at it, keeping it open. "Don't kill anyone you don't have to!" I yelled.

Stellan grabbed my arm and pulled me away. "Nothing you can do."

I felt sick. With one last glance back, I stumbled after him, letting the door slam.

"You know what our tattoos mean, right?" Stellan said. "Loyalty to the death. He's given that to you now. If they'd seen him letting us escape, he'd be the one killed."

My necklace was still dangling from my wrist. My hands were shaking so hard I couldn't fasten it, and Stellan reached around my neck and did it for me. His white shirt, at my eye level, was stained such a dark red that it looked black in the dim light.

"Is it like stabbing the meat?" I whispered. "Like once you keep seeing people die over and over, it gets easier?"

"No." He dropped the necklace on my chest. It was bloody and still warm. "It never gets easier."

Stellan rested a hand on my shoulder, and I let out a shaky breath. For a second, I thought he was trying to console me, but I realized he was swaying. I caught him around the waist. "Concussion," he said, leaning into me. "I think. Not feeling good. Should probably sit."

I blocked out everything else. We weren't out of the woods yet.

"Do you know where Elodie was going to look for Jack?" I said.

"No." Stellan stumbled a little, and I held him up.

I looked at the chateau. It was four stories tall, all windows. I had absolutely no clue where Jack might be. I hadn't been letting myself worry about him, but now it washed over me. What they'd do to a Keeper who'd gone behind their backs.

Still, they would have kept him alive long enough to interrogate him. And Elodie would find him. Right? And then another thought, just as dark. If they offered him what they'd offered me—side with them and live—could Jack have chosen the people he'd been loyal to all his life?

The question was answered with a crash. A second-story window halfway down the building shattered in a rain of sparkle in the moonlight.

Two people leaned out of the window. Jack and Elodie. I ran toward them, pulling Stellan with me. He tripped over his own feet and came down hard on one of my toes, and I realized his eyes were sliding closed.

I hissed and elbowed him in the side to wake him up. "You have to walk." He mumbled something in Russian. The head injury was way worse than I'd realized, or maybe he'd lost too much blood, but he was heavy, and slipping.

I half dragged him toward the window, where Elodie was dangling from the sill and ready to drop into the hedge below. Just as she fell and jumped up, Jack climbed out after her, and then the lights flicked back on in the house. A shadow entered the room where Jack was hanging.

The guard who'd been outside my room earlier appeared in the window, shouting back over his shoulder. He saw us first, then Jack. He raised his gun.

Something silver swished through the air. Elodie's knife hit the guard in the shoulder, but not before he squeezed the trigger. Jack managed to swing his body in toward the wall, and the bullet missed him, but he lost his grip, and then he was falling, crashing headlong into the brush below.

I threw Stellan's limp form onto Elodie and rushed to the hedge. Jack was sitting up, dazed. "I'm all right," he said, holding his shoulder.

"*Allons-y*," Elodie called, and I hauled Jack to his feet as shouts came from overhead. Jack took Stellan's other side, and we hurried to a car hidden behind the chateau. Elodie jumped in the driver's seat, and we sped away.

CHAPTER 22

Earlier in the day, we'd reserved train tickets to Cannes under fake names. Elodie took Stellan into one of our two first-class suites to do some first aid on his head, and Jack and I trudged silently into the other, exhausted and lost in thought now that the adrenaline was wearing off. The suite was small but elegant, all the walls dark wood, with just a few feet of space on either side of a double bed made up in maroon brocade, and a lone armchair in a small sitting area by the bathroom door. Fresh yellow carnations brightened the space on both bedside tables.

I didn't know how it was possible that the rest of the world was just going on like normal. I felt like nothing would ever be okay again.

Jack came up behind me and surveyed the platform, then yanked the heavy curtains shut. I kept staring at them like I could still see out.

"Elodie thinks we need to tell the whole Circle what they're doing," Jack said.

I turned from the window. I figured this would come up. "Not until we get my mom back." I told him what Alistair had said, and he nodded. "Assuming Alistair keeps his end of the bargain," I went on. "Do you think he will?"

Jack's eyes looked hollow. "Until today, I would have said yes." I recognized his expression. I was sure it was mirrored on my face. Shock. Helplessness. Anger. Doubt. Neither of us had any idea what they were capable of. "Now, I can only say that I hope so."

I hoped so, too. I wouldn't have left if I didn't think he would, but honestly, what did I know?

Jack's normally rugged face looked drawn. "I'm so sorry," he said. "Lydia is a lot of things, and Alistair's not perfect, but I never would have thought . . ."

"I know." I fiddled with the bracelet. I'd gotten it back from Elodie on the way to the station, and it felt weird on my arm with its newly raised inset. "At least there's one upside to all this," I said. "It's not the Order out to get us after all. We don't have to worry about them anymore."

Jack laced his hands behind his head. "I can't believe none of this has been them."

"I know. I wonder what the *real* Order's been up to this whole time."

Jack fiddled with the end of the curtains. "Avery. This is no longer worth it. Any of this. After we get the bracelet, we do whatever we have to do to trade it for your mom, and then we get out. Together. Forget what anyone else thinks."

I looked up. "You'd leave the Circle for good?"

"You wouldn't? You don't want this. You don't care about the Circle."

"But *you* do." I'd wondered whether he'd actually leave with me if that was what I chose to do. I realized now that, deep down, I hadn't believed he would.

Jack palmed his forearm, running his thumb over his compass tattoo. "I thought I did. I cared about the Saxons. I thought staying

with them, with the Circle, was the right thing to do. And now—"
He shook his head. "Now I feel like the right thing is to get as far
from this mess as possible."

Did he ever think the *right thing to do* might not be so simple?

The thought surprised me. Because, honestly, I should agree. I
should want even less to do with the Circle now. My father was willing to swap my freedom for the tomb, and now Jack was saying he'd
come with me. I no longer had to consider how I felt about leaving
my newfound family. I should be ecstatic.

But that wasn't what was going on inside me right now. Of course
there was part of me that *wanted* to run away, but there was another
part of me that felt like I had the whole Circle on my shoulders
now. Like I could *earn* that hopeful look they kept giving me: Dev's
people, and Takumi's. Even Scarface.

That I could be thinking anything like this hadn't even crossed
Jack's mind. For good reason—it was crazy. I thought of Stellan's
words in the apartment in Montmartre. There was no leader of the
Circle, but the closest thing to it was me. Us.

And besides, if Jack and I did run away together, what would that
mean? Would we be pledging to be together forever? Yes, I cared
about him—a lot—but when I looked at it that way, it was a big
commitment.

The knot inside me felt too tight, on the verge of snapping.

I still hadn't answered, and I didn't know what I was supposed to
say. I just smiled and wished I felt it as much as I should. "I'm going
to go clean up."

When I came back after washing dirt and traces of Stellan's blood
off me, Jack was sitting on the bed. He was shirtless, inspecting his
right shoulder in a mirror on the far wall.

He started to pull his shirt back on, but grimaced.

"Don't," I said. "What is it?" I dropped my towel on the bed and came around in front of him, taking the shirt from his hand. I touched the darkening bruise across his shoulder, and he jerked away.

"The fall from the window. Landed right on my shoulder. I'll fix it up tomorrow."

I ran my fingers over his cool skin. Now that I felt a bit more settled, there was something else I had to say, something I'd been pushing out of my mind since seeing Lydia at the Arc de Triomphe. Something I *really* had to know if I was considering running away with Jack. The train jolted. We were moving. I paced to the window and pulled the curtain aside to look out as we slowly left the station behind.

I didn't want to ask, but I couldn't not. "How did Lydia and Cole know where we were today?"

There was a pause. "I don't know."

The knot tightened even more. It was hanging in the air, implicit, but I had to say it. "Did you tell them?"

He let out a long breath. "No."

I rested my forehead against the cool glass with a thump. Thank God. I don't know what I would have done if it had turned out that he'd . . . I shook my head.

"I guess they have sophisticated tracking equipment," I thought out loud. "We told them we were going to Paris. They must have figured it out somehow. And Scarface—oh." I stood up straight. I hadn't told Jack about that part yet. I watched the Paris suburbs go by out the window as I told him the short version of my encounter with Scarface. Branding him with my necklace. The killing of the other guards. How he'd pledged his loyalty to me. I felt strangely detached talking about it.

The bed springs squeaked, and I felt Jack come up behind me. "I'm so sorry. You shouldn't have to deal with something like that—"

"Yes, I should." I twisted to face him. "This is my fight as much as anyone else's. More, really. You can't protect me from everything. Okay?"

Jack put his good arm around me. He smelled like sweat and blood. I leaned into his cool bare chest. "Okay," he said.

The door creaked open, and Stellan poked his head in. "Oops, I'm interrupting," he said. "You should really learn to lock the door."

"You're not interrupting." I slipped out from under Jack's arm. "Is your head okay?" He looked a lot better than he had earlier.

Stellan nodded. He didn't have a shirt on, either, and wore pajama pants that were a good deal too small for him.

"Are those *Elodie's*?" I said.

Stellan pouted. He actually pouted. "My clothes, they have blood all over." His accent was much thicker than usual. "She said I could not sit on the bed unless—" He indicated the pants, and I fought an inappropriate laugh. He surveyed Jack. "Shoulder's dislocated."

Jack nodded.

"His shoulder, it dislocates if you look at it wrong," Stellan said to me. A nostalgic smile brightened his face. Far more lighthearted than he should look after tonight. And definitely woozy.

"Are you drunk?" I said, crawling onto the bed.

Another inappropriately dreamy smile. "Concussion. Pain medication. Too *much* pain medication? But they are not working yet. Are they working yet?" He touched his head and winced as if remembering how much it hurt, and then looked up again like he was surprised to find himself in the room. His eyes focused back on Jack. "Lie down," he ordered, gesturing to the bed.

Jack frowned. "I'll take care of it tomorrow. Or Avery can help me."

Stellan sniffed. "You know she's not strong enough. And that's . . . *Ça va faire mal toute la nuit* unless you fix it," he said.

From where I sat leaning against the headboard, I watched, surprised, as Jack sighed and lay back gingerly. And I was even more surprised when Stellan climbed on the bed, too, and leaned over him.

"The usual?" he said.

Jack nodded, grimacing as Stellan's slim fingers prodded his skin. Then Stellan planted one knee on Jack's chest, and Jack held out his right arm, squeezing his eyes shut.

The scene was so odd, I had to wonder for a second whether I was hallucinating. Interesting, I thought clinically, that *this* is what my brain conjured up under stress.

With his palm at Jack's collarbone, Stellan wrenched hard on his elbow.

Jack tried to stifle a groan. His shoulder moved in an odd, sickening way, and he was breathing hard as Stellan set his arm back down by his side and pressed both palms to his shoulder again, then nodded.

"You're welcome," he said. He climbed off Jack and leaned heavily next to me.

I stared as Jack sat up, rubbing his collarbone.

"His shoulder. The bone, it—" Stellan made an exploding gesture with his hands. "I have to—" He gestured the other direction, putting his hands back together.

"Pop his shoulder back in?" I said.

Stellan pointed at me. "Yes. Done it many times."

"You used to be better at it," Jack said through clenched teeth.

"You used to be tougher," Stellan said cheerfully. He leaned his head back against the headboard. "Tired. But cannot go to sleep. The concussion."

Jack surveyed him warily. "Can you go back to Elodie's room now?"

Stellan opened one eye. "She wants to talk. The bracelet. Heist. I do not want to talk. *You* go talk."

A giggle tried to bubble up in my throat, even though there was nothing funny about any of it. Not quite knowing what else to do, I patted the spot on the other side of me, gesturing for Jack to sit. I wasn't going to kick the painkiller-drunk guy with a head injury out into the hall of a moving train right now.

Stellan grabbed the remote and clicked on the ancient TV bolted to the corner of the cabin. As far as I could tell, it was on a French infomercial selling a blender, and the marketers seemed entirely too excited about it.

After a second's hesitation, Jack crawled up the bed on my other side. I saw him glance at Stellan over my head, but all he did was settle back against the headboard. After a second, he took my hand, firmly, like a proclamation. I was surprised at first, but I let it stay. And the three of us sat there, shoulder to shoulder to shoulder, me and these two boys who turned out to be just about all I had left in the world.

CHAPTER 23

A short time later, Stellan's eyes were at half-mast and falling.

I elbowed him gently in the side. "Wake up."

He blinked hard and muttered something in Russian.

"You're supposed to stay awake," I said, but I wasn't really paying attention. I was watching the news that had come on after the blender infomercial. Every story was still about Eli Abraham, and me holding a dying Takumi Mikado. And my father sitting next to me, Lydia one seat down, both frozen, eyes wide like they had no idea what was going on. A small, disbelieving laugh escaped my lips. They were such *liars*.

My hand clenched Jack's, but he didn't respond. I looked down to see his head loll into the bookcase next to the bed, his face slack and, if not quite peaceful, at least more relaxed in the flickering blue of the TV. I dislodged my hand gently from his, and he kept sleeping.

"He's always been able to sleep so well." There was more than a hint of jealousy in Stellan's voice. "Would be nice. But I wish right now I could lie down with him."

I took a deep breath. "You guys snuggling *would* be cute," I said.

"But really, don't fall asleep yet, okay? I don't want you dying on my watch."

He leaned against me, his head heavy on top of mine, his skin warm against my bare arm. "Keep me awake, then," he murmured. "Tell me stories."

I shoved him gently, and when he gave me a woozy grin, I noticed red running down his forehead. I reached across and handed him a tissue from the bedside table. "I thought Elodie bandaged your head."

The TV was casting a dim blue flicker over Jack's sleeping form. Now they were talking about Prime Minister Mikado, and the anguish on his and his wife's faces made me clench my teeth. I couldn't think about this anymore tonight.

Stellan was dabbing ineffectually at his head.

"You're going to bleed on my bed," I said crossly. "Get up. Bathroom."

I took one last glance back at the news and then followed Stellan. He stood squinting at his head in the mirror. He leaned closer, trying to see the wound, and smacked his forehead right into the glass.

"Ow," he said, indignant, like the mirror had come out and hit him.

I stopped in the doorway. He was so *tall*. His head nearly brushed the train's low ceilings. Tall and intimidating and carved like a statue of a beautiful half-naked Viking prince, and here he was in this tiny train bathroom, with blood running down his forehead, in ladies' pajama pants and with a pout like an angry toddler's. I ducked my head to conceal another inappropriate giggle.

Stellan rubbed his eye with the back of one hand. "What?" he said petulantly, and I bit down hard on my lip. What was wrong with me? I threw a hand over my mouth, but a snort escaped, and all of a sudden, the giggles that had been trying to come out for the last hour burst the floodgate and I was hysterical.

"You look . . . ridiculous," I forced out, and it was high-pitched and desperate, and all of a sudden, I was sure I was about to come fully unhinged. "It's all . . . Everything is ridiculous."

Stellan's pout turned into concern, and confusion. He reached for me.

"No." I stepped out of his grasp. If he tried to hug me or say something reassuring, I would cry. If I cried, I wouldn't stop. "Sit," I ordered.

I pulled a little stool from the vanity, still giggling a little. Stellan sat, his head flopped down until his chin rested on his chest. I inspected his head, where only the top layer of his blond hair was clean, and the mat of blood beneath it hadn't been touched.

I started laughing again, hard enough that I hiccuped. "Elodie did a *horrible* job," I gasped. "What is wrong with her?"

Stellan raised an eyebrow. I took two rasping breaths and shoved it all down. Compartmentalizing. I'd been doing it all night, and I could keep doing it.

"You need to wash it the rest of the way tonight, or it'll never heal right," I said.

Stellan eyed me warily, but used my shoulder to stand up, gesturing to the shower stall.

"I don't know if you should do it yourself." In this state, I was afraid he'd kill himself in the train-sized shower. Or at the very least, not be gentle enough with the wound and rip it open again.

A woozy but wicked grin spread across his face. "Does that mean you're getting in *with* me? I never thought you'd take me up on that rain check, but I won't say no . . ."

"We'll wash it in the *sink*. Sit."

I ran warm water in the basin and swished in some orange-scented shampoo from the shower, and he leaned back until his long torso was taking up half the bathroom. I rolled up one of the puffy white towels and wedged it under the back of his neck. He winced almost imperceptibly, like if he'd had his wits about him he would have been able to suppress it.

"What?" I said. "Did you hurt your shoulder, too?"

He shook his head.

"What is with you guys?" I said. "If you have a broken collarbone or something and you just haven't *mentioned* it . . ."

"It's nothing," he said, but the lie wasn't convincing.

I crossed my arms over my chest. Finally, he took a deep breath, then touched the scars snaking up his neck. Those strange, trans-lucent scars, all up his back and twisting like ghostly vines over the tops of his shoulders and around the sides of his throat.

"Your scars hurt?" I said. "Did you do something to them?"

He shook his head slowly, staring up at the ceiling. "Always," he said, so softly I almost couldn't hear.

It took me a second to understand what he meant. When I did, my breath caught. Of their own accord, my fingers reached out to the same scar he was touching. "The scars *always* hurt?" I said.

He nodded.

I traced the scar down his neck and across his shoulder, at the lesions pearlescent against my own white skin. I didn't know what to say.

Stellan's fingers brushed my hand.

"It's fine," he said. "I'm used to it."

The heat at the back of my eyes built up again. What this world did to people. What it'd done to this boy whose life had been far harder than mine, looking up at me with a mix of emotions in his face I wasn't sure I understood. Wasn't sure I *wanted* to understand. The fact that, despite it all, there was something in me that was telling the truth when I told Jack I didn't want to run.

"Lean back," I said, and splashed the warm water over his hair. Fighting the tightness in my throat left my words clipped, too cheerful. "I hurt my head like this once," I chirped. "I was leaning over, and had left an upper cabinet open, and stood up right into the corner. Blood everywhere! It was disgusting. My mom washed it out. She always knew exactly—" I drew a ragged breath, full of tears that had been building all day that I wouldn't, couldn't let fall. "That's how I know what to do. We'll work the blood out of your hair first to get to the cut and then—and then—" My voice cracked. No more words would come out around the lump in my throat. "And then—"

I stopped when I felt Stellan's hand close around my leg.

"And then, um, we'll sterilize the cut," I continued, my voice high, reedy. "Head wounds bleed a lot, but it'll heal quickly enough if you don't mess with it and then you'll—then you'll—"

Stellan stroked my knee with his thumb, calmly, firmly. Whatever had been building up for so long—the knot pulling tight, my sanity stretching thin—I felt the moment it snapped.

Once the first tear fell, it was a floodgate.

No laughing this time, just silent, steady tears, dripping salty into my mouth for what felt like a long time. The cloying orange shampoo scent, the buzz of the fluorescent light over the sink, the *clack clack clack* of the train tracks. The water sloshed in the basin as Stellan tilted his head up, and I could feel him looking at me.

I took a deep breath, full of the soothing, steady strokes of his thumb on the knee of my jeans and their inherent promise that I wasn't alone but that he wasn't going to force me to talk about it. The last almost-sob died in my throat.

"And then you'll be okay." I blinked the tears away, my vision cleared, and I realized that Stellan's head was still resting heavy in my hands, my fingers still twisted in his hair, blond streaked with red, making shaky ripples in the reddening water.

I disentangled them and wiped the mascara from my face with the back of my hand, then put a little more shampoo in the water and swished it around. Stellan didn't let go of my leg, and I didn't move away.

"That's not normal, about the scars," I said, like the last few minutes hadn't happened. My voice was stronger now. "Scars are supposed to be dead tissue."

He opened his eyes. "Nothing about not burning like a regular human being is normal," he said. "But no, I don't suppose scars should hurt seven years after the fact. I think in some way I always knew there was something . . . off about that. Maybe that's why I never told anyone."

"Nobody else knows?" I said quietly.

He shook his head. My eyes traced the scars again as I thought of everything he must have to do daily that would hurt. I let out a breath through pursed lips before leaning back over the sink, trying to find a position where I didn't have to drape myself across his chest. "Are you okay like this?"

He rested the hand not on my knee on his stomach. "Surprisingly comfortable."

"I'm going to try to be gentle, but tell me if it hurts." I worked the blood out of his hair, trying not to pull on the wound itself. I wasn't sure how well the painkillers were working. After a minute, a small, blissed-out smile came over his face, so I was pretty sure he was okay. I wiped a bead of bloody water off his forehead and gave him a nudge. "You have to stay awake."

"Feels nice, though," he murmured. "Feels *really* nice."

"Have you never had someone do this?"

His eyes slit open and he quirked a *what do you think?* eyebrow.

"I fell asleep once getting my hair washed at the salon," I confessed, trying to keep him conscious. "It was right after one of our moves, and I was really stressed and hardly sleeping. My mom took us to get haircuts and pedicures, and I passed out with my head in the sink and my feet in some lady's hands. My mom convinced them to let me sleep for an *hour*. I woke up with the worst crick in my neck."

Stellan smiled, but I could tell he was fading when his hand dropped from my leg. I tugged on his earlobe. "Hey. Wake up. Let me look at your pupils."

"Mmm," he sighed, but he opened his eyes. His pupils didn't look too dilated, which I was pretty sure was good. He was quiet for a minute, then said, "That guy. The one who—is *yours* now. With the scar on his cheek."

I paused, my hands in the floating blond halo of his hair, which, just for a second, reminded me so much of being underwater that my lungs ached. "Scarface. That's what I call him."

"He looked like someone, but I couldn't remember who. And now I do. An Emir Keeper. Rocco. He was terminated two years ago. For—"

"Having a thing with a family member."

Stellan nodded, and his head bobbed in my hands. "Besides the scar, he looks just like him, and I could have sworn he had an olive branch tattooed under the compass. Did you see that?"

I nodded. "That's impossible, though, right? That Keeper is dead."

I didn't know what it meant, but I didn't want to think about any of it. The train jolted, splashing a little water out of the sink.

"Sorry to bring it up," Stellan said, seeing straight through me as always. "We don't have to talk about it."

"It's fine," I said shortly, but we fell into silence while I kept up the slow task of getting out the blood without making it worse. A short time later, I glanced down to make sure Stellan wasn't asleep and found him watching me openly.

"What?" I said.

"You're pretty."

I rolled my eyes, and not just because right now, with mascara smeared under my eyes and my nose red from crying, I knew I was about as far from *pretty* as I could get. "Stop it."

"Stop what?"

"You know exactly what."

"It's not an offensive thing to say."

"No, it's not *offensive*. It's just . . ." Something about his disoriented state made me feel more open, too, like in the little bubble of tonight, I could say things I wouldn't otherwise say. "You realize there's no reason for you to say stuff like that, right? I get your schtick."

His face screwed up in confusion. "What's *schtick*?"

"It means I know very well that I'm just a prize to everybody in this game, and you're no different. So yeah, I know you flirt with me for the same reason every Circle family we meet wines and dines me. And it's not going to work. So . . . stop it." I felt myself flush.

There was a long beat of silence. His head was clean enough, and I held his hair up and pulled the drain plug.

"I don't think you know anything," he mumbled, letting his eyes close again as I turned on the tap and ran warm water over his head. "You always think you're right. But you're not. You are not always right."

My heart gave a strangled twist. We were quiet for a second.

"You know," he said, "when I first met you . . ." He opened one eye, and the twist spread to my stomach as I remembered Jack, on the Dauphins' balcony, admitting that he liked me as much as I liked him, all along. It started just like this. Don't say it, my mind whispered. I'm not sure I can handle this. *Don't*—

"When I first met you," Stellan said again, sleepily, "I thought you were an idiot."

His eyes slipped back closed, and the breath whooshed out of my lungs.

"Who gets on a plane with a stranger who just pulled a knife on her?" he said. "What is *wrong* with you? I could have been a serial killer."

I half sniffed, half laughed, because he was right. He let me move his head back and forth under the faucet stream.

"But that stupid, naive girl I thought you were would have gotten herself killed off a long time ago," he finally said, his voice fading. "Or at least she would have screamed and run the other way. You're not that much of an idiot after all."

I paused, surprised, and turned off the tap. It took me a second to look back down at him, and when I did, he'd fallen asleep.

I let him sleep for a second while I got the first-aid kit from the cabinet. I couldn't figure out a good way to keep a bandage on his head, so I just sprayed some antibacterial stuff on the wound and nudged him with my knee. He blinked, looking around like he'd not only forgotten the conversation we'd just been having, but like he'd forgotten where he was, too.

"Now we figure out how to keep you awake for a few more hours," I said wearily, handing him a towel for his head.

He made a face, but followed me into our suite, where Jack was sleeping soundly on the far side of the bed, a pillow pulled over his head. I planted myself in the middle again, and Stellan climbed in next to me. I watched Jack's back rise and fall with his breath. As I watched, he twitched, mumbling something in his sleep. I put a hand on his shoulder and he relaxed, and we sat that way, swaying with the train, while Stellan flipped channels until he found what looked like *Family Feud* in French. We turned the sound on to just a whisper, and over the bump and rattle of the tracks, Stellan murmured translations of the winning answers to favorite snacks for a football match and vacation spots for retirees, and the fact that 53 percent of participants said French women started to dye their hair at age forty . . .

I woke up slowly, and immediately wanted to go back to sleep. I was absurdly cozy, pressed against a warm, broad chest, and the shaft of light when I half opened one eye told me it was still early. For the first time in a long time, though, I actually felt rested. I started to shift to look at my watch, but the arms around me pulled me back in tight. "Mmm, no," he protested sleepily in my ear. "Comfortable." And it was; the kind of comfortable where you'd be happy to stay in that semiconscious state forever. I nuzzled back into his arms.

And then all of a sudden, I was fully awake. That was not the soft British accent I might expect to hear first thing in the morning. My eyes fluttered open. It definitely wasn't Jack, because Jack was asleep facing me, our fingers inches away from touching, like we'd been holding hands and they'd come apart in the night.

Suddenly, everything from the day and night before came rushing back.

I bolted upright, blinking the sleep out of my eyes, my contacts sticky and dry. "You fell asleep," I whispered to Stellan.

He blinked, too, barely awake, looking as surprised as I was at the indent in the blankets where I'd just been curled against his chest. "Apparently *we* fell asleep."

I looked guiltily at Jack. Last thing I remembered, we were watching game shows and my hand was on his back.

"Lucky for you, I'm not dead. You're not very good at babysitting." A small smile pulled at Stellan's lips. "Pretty great at cuddling, though."

"Shh," I hissed. I felt my face heat up and shot another glance at Jack. His dark brows drew down, and his mouth twitched like he was talking to someone in a dream. Without making eye contact, I whispered, "I'm going to—" I gestured with my head and made my way into the hall outside our room.

It was later than I thought. The sun had already risen, and I made my way to the space between the cars, where there were large windows on the doors. We were speeding past a vineyard, and a white-washed stone house sat on the top of a rise behind it, and then a field of sunflowers, bright yellow, stretched as far as I could see.

I pulled my hair back into a ponytail, brushing through the tangles with my fingers. I wasn't sure whether it was a step forward or a step back that I'd been able to sleep at all after yesterday. What's more, I think I'd slept the whole night straight through. I couldn't remember the last time that happened.

So I'd just have to sleep sandwiched between them for the rest of my life. *That* wasn't horribly weird and wrong or anything.

A few minutes later, I turned around to footsteps. Stellan was wearing his own clothes again, slim jeans and a T-shirt, dark enough to not show dried blood. I felt myself blush again, thinking about how much of the night I must have spent with his arms wrapped around me. I wondered how we'd ended up that way, whether one of us did it accidentally or whether we just migrated together while we slept, our unconscious minds giving in to the need to hold somebody. He paused when he noticed me, and I wondered if he was thinking the same thing.

He reached around me and hauled open the sliding door.

"Are you allowed to do that?" I backed up a few feet as the wind whipped past, like it could drag me right out the door. The sunflower fields had given way to a ravine, and the train sped along the edge of a cliff.

"Probably not." Stellan tested his weight on one of the handholds at the door of the train, leaning out over the tracks so the wind pulled at his clothes, then leaned back in and lit a cigarette. He let a curl of smoke out of the corner of his mouth, and the breeze rushing past caught it and left not even a wisp.

I made a face at the cigarette, anyway, and he made a face back.

"You seem better," I said. He was back to his old self, not soft and fuzzy around the edges like he'd been last night. "Have you checked on your head?"

He held his cigarette out the door and leaned over for me to look at it. I only had to part his hair and take a cursory glance to realize the cut was much smaller than it had been last night. "It's healing *really* quickly. Weirdly quickly."

He pushed his hair back into place. "Maybe it's the magic skin thing. I guess I have always healed quickly. Never thought much about it."

I would have been interested to know more about the "magic skin thing" if we had time. Maybe in the future. *If* Stellan was in my future at all, I reminded myself. In just a couple days, I'd know. We'd have the second bracelet, and hopefully have the way to the tomb. If all went well, I'd trade it to Alistair for my mom, and then . . . well, then I'd decide. Whether to stay and be part of the world's most powerful secret society, or to get off the grid and make plans to stay off forever.

I leaned against the wall and played with my necklace. When I let go, my hands were smudged with black soot. I inspected the locket, and realized there was dust coming out of the holes in the pattern. I clicked it open.

The picture inside must have gone up in flames when we heated the necklace, because now, it was nothing but ash. I only had time to draw in a surprised breath before the wind rushing by whipped the delicate pieces of my old life into the air as easily as it had the cigarette smoke.

I blinked at the empty locket for a second, then closed it slowly.

"What was in it?" Stellan said after a second.

"A picture of my mom." I wiped the last of the ash from the design and clenched the locket in my fist, against my heart.

Stellan stood quietly for a second, then stubbed out his cigarette and sat down on the top step, folding his long legs into the small space. He patted the step next to him.

I stayed a distance back. "Open train door, sheer cliff face, no thanks."

He curled his lip. "Really? After everything else you've been through, you're scared of *this*?"

I had to admit, the breeze *did* kind of feel nice. I tried to ignore the plunge into the ravine and sat down next to him carefully, though I made sure to keep the hand that wasn't clutching my necklace on the doorjamb.

"See?" Stellan said. "Perfectly safe."

I snorted. No, it wasn't.

Stellan rested his elbows on his knees, and we gazed out at the rocky crags of the cliff, which soon turned to fields again, then the outskirts of a city. If the train was on time, we'd be in Cannes soon. I stood up, brushing off my jeans.

Stellan stood, too, and followed me back to our compartment.

I slid open the door. Jack was, remarkably, still asleep. I put a finger to my lips.

"We don't need to be quiet. He's had *plenty* of sleep," Stellan said. He flopped on his stomach across Jack's side of the bed. "This is how I used to wake him up when we were younger. He'll appreciate it." He pulled up the ankle of Jack's pants and yanked on his leg hairs. Jack sat straight up.

His alarm faded to annoyance when he saw Stellan. "Are you twelve years old?"

Stellan rolled off the bed, looking surprisingly chipper for someone in the aftermath of a concussion.

The speakers overhead crackled to life. There was an announcement in French, then in English. We were about to arrive in Cannes.

"I'll wake Elodie," Stellan said.

Jack ran both hands through his hair. He watched Stellan leave, then found me, perched at the end of the bed. "Good morning," he said.

The greeting sounded awkward. Less like *good morning* and more like other things. *Sorry I fell asleep and left you playing nurse.* Wondering what I thought about the conversation we'd had last night, about leaving together. Maybe a little something he'd never say out loud about the three of us sleeping in the same bed.

Or maybe the awkwardness was just me.

"Good morning." I grabbed the remote from where we must have kicked it in the night and was about to turn off a morning news program and talk to him when I realized my own face was on TV again.

It was the video of me and Takumi Mikado, but this one turned quickly to a still of me, and then a frowning reporter. I turned it up. "What are they saying?"

Jack listened for a second, then glanced at me, alarmed. "They're saying the girl some people were calling a hero is wanted for questioning in the attack."

A dark pit formed in my stomach. "Alistair is trying to turn the Circle against me so it makes sense if I disappear. So it looks like they got rid of me instead of me running away." *You're the hero in our narrative,* he'd said. He could make me the villain just as easily.

But I still had to be out in public to find the twin bracelet. Alistair must not have considered that. "They're going to make me the most wanted person in the world. We're not going to be able to do anything."

The door slid open, and I tensed, already paranoid. How many people on this train had seen this news broadcast? How many people in Cannes?

But Elodie and Stellan slipped inside and slid the door shut behind them. "Turn on—oh. You've already seen."

"We've already seen."

"Well"—Elodie held out a wide-brimmed hat and sunglasses— "we're going to be in Cannes in about ten minutes. Let's try not to get you arrested."

CHAPTER 24

Colette had a car waiting for us at the train station. We kept as low a profile as we could until we were inside—besides anyone who might recognize me, there was still the question of how the Saxons had tracked us to the Arc de Triomphe. Elodie had done a thorough check of our electronics and found no bugs or tracking devices, but even she admitted that the Circle had technology she might not know about.

Cannes was no sleepy seaside town. We got caught in traffic on a street with palm trees running down the center, bordering the ocean. There was hardly an inch of bare sand showing between the bright umbrellas and beach towels, and an overly bronzed, heavyset man wearing only a Speedo lumbered in front of us through the stopped traffic.

"So this is the French Riviera," I said.

Elodie pointed to a white hotel with navy turrets that dominated the skyline along the beachfront. "The Dauphins usually stay at the Carlton, but we'll be at Colette's private villa. She's still a little camera-shy."

That was far better for us. I'm sure there were dozens of Circle members here. For that matter, the Saxons themselves might be attending the festival. If they were, we'd really have to get to the bracelet before they noticed. They knew what it looked like.

On the right ahead, I saw the source of the traffic jam. A swarming crowd of people pushed out into the road, and as we got closer, I saw a banner that must be two stories high itself, proclaiming this to be the site of the *Festival de Cannes.* A flash of red leading up the stairs in front of it was surrounded by photographers in sun hats sitting cross-legged on the ground, cameras in their laps.

"The official opening ceremony is tomorrow, as you know," Elodie said. "But the red carpet's tonight. The photographers wait all day to get a good spot."

The traffic cleared when we got past the festival, and we sped the rest of the way to Colette's villa, which was on a cliff at the far end of the city. It was cream with black shutters, looking over a reflecting pool lined by palms and manicured hedges. Before we could get out of the car, Colette ran down the front steps while the driver got Elodie's bag out of the trunk. She was the only one of us who'd brought luggage, so Colette was getting a nearby department store to send the rest of us some essentials.

The tall hedges hid the villa from the surroundings, and I relaxed for the first time since we saw the news this morning.

"Lucien told me what happened," Colette said, sweeping me into a hug and then kissing Jack on the cheek and throwing her arms around Elodie. "Are you okay? Are you all okay?"

"Besides a few minor injuries," Stellan said. Colette tucked herself against his side, but he just squeezed her shoulder and let go.

I watched her back as she led Elodie and Jack into the villa, and remembered what Stellan had said on the boat. *You use whatever tools you have.*

"You did the same thing to me," I said. His hands in my hair on the plane, taking out my bobby pins, just hours after we met. The inappropriate remarks, directed straight at my overactive blushing mechanism.

He saw me watching Colette and seemed to understand. "I thought you'd be an easy target."

We climbed the wide sandstone steps. "I think I knew it. I knew you wouldn't hurt me. That's why I got on the plane with you."

Stellan opened the door. "What if you'd been wrong?"

I ducked through ahead of him. "I wasn't."

Inside, we found everyone in a sitting room walled by glass, making it look like the room was made of the palm trees and vines outside. I took a seat next to Jack on the sofa, and he slipped an arm around my shoulders. He was taking the assertion that he no longer cared what anyone thought seriously. Elodie noticed and raised an eyebrow in our direction. I ignored her.

She cleared her throat. "As you all know, the bracelet we're here to get is going to be on display at the opening ceremony of the festival tomorrow, and that will be our best—and maybe our only—chance to steal it. So we'll need to be prepared."

I looked around at all the nodding faces. We were becoming a well-oiled machine.

"Here's the plan," Elodie said. "Before the main event tomorrow, there's a red-carpet photo call tonight. Colette and I will recon there. We'll figure out where the bracelet is located, and get a sense of what kind of security there is on it. Tomorrow night, Colette goes to the opening ceremony. When the time's right, she'll signal me, and I'll trip the electricity, which should kill security on the display boxes for a good forty-five seconds before backup generators kick in. Stellan will be with Colette, acting like a bodyguard, and when the lights go out, he'll grab the bracelet and replace it with this one, which Colette found at a thrift shop earlier." She held up a passably similar piece of gold costume jewelry. "And then everyone gets the hell out as fast as they can."

Everyone nodded, except me. "So what's my job?"

"You and Jack make us piña coladas so we can celebrate when we get back." Elodie spread her hands with a flourish. "Listen. You are the single most recognizable person in the world of the Circle right now, and a fugitive outside it. If anyone saw you, it could complicate things. And you," she said to Jack, "are not as recognizable, but there are quite a few Circle members who think you're a traitor and would gladly take your head off, which would really screw up the whole plan. You'll need to stay out of sight, too."

I started to protest, but Jack chimed in. "You're right. We'll stay here."

I bristled and pulled out from under his arm, but then I gave up. "Fine. I'm not going to screw up the plan just because I want to be part of it. I think not using us is silly, but okay. What else?"

"That's it. For now, we lie low and get ready for a heist."

CHAPTER 25

When everyone had dispersed to choose bedrooms, Jack followed me outside through arched French doors and onto a back patio dotted with topiaries and lounge chairs. I wandered to a fountain, where a jumping marble fish sprayed water out of its mouth and into a pond below. Jack stopped beside me, hands in his pockets.

"Sorry about that in there," he said. "Knee-jerk reaction. I should have let you argue with Elodie if you wanted. I would rather have you stay here, but . . ."

I frowned and tucked my hair behind my ears. "I just think it's better to have all of us close in case something goes wrong. But if you all think the risk of me being recognized is too much, then I guess I should just believe you."

Overhead, a pair of birds called to each other, and I leaned against the railing around the fountain and looked up at the surrounding mansions.

We stood in silence for a few seconds, lost in our own thoughts. Finally, Jack held out his arm. I laid my cheek against his chest, and he rested his chin on top of my head. "You know I'd do anything for you, right?" he said. I could feel the words as much as I could hear them. "I don't care how often we don't agree. You can argue with me all day, and I'd still—"

He cut off abruptly, and his hand, which had been tracing small circles on my lower back, stilled. I tensed, staring into his shirt. He'd still what?

"I'd still do what's right for you," he finished. He rubbed my back again. "I always will."

I thought about the part of Jack's past he hadn't told me about. How helpless he must have felt about Oliver Saxon's death; how if it were me, I'd do anything I could to not feel like that again. "I know," I whispered.

He ran his hands up my arms and then pulled away. "Wait here a minute," he said.

He loped across the garden to a bush heavy with pink roses. He plucked one and ran back, offering it to me. "Tonight, when Colette and Elodie are out doing reconnaissance, let me take you out. A proper date. We'll have to go somewhere far away from the action, where no one will recognize us, and it won't be anything fancy, but—"

I was sure I looked skeptical. Really, now? Of all times?

"I'm serious. We never got to go on the date I asked you on in Minnesota. I meant it then, and I mean it a thousand times more now, and everything's such a mess I don't know that there's anything holding us back anymore. Avery West, may I take you on a date?"

I took the rose. This would be good for us. Get things back to normal, if there was such a thing anymore. "Okay. Yes."

I jumped when a door opened on a balcony at one of the houses next door. A woman swept outside in a red bikini. She was wearing a wide-brimmed white hat, but her long, wild, curly hair and thick winged eyeliner was instantly recognizable. Miranda Cruz, who had won the Best Actress Oscar last year. She leaned out over the balcony, looked around, and saw us looking at her. I ducked back behind Jack, just in case.

On cue, Elodie opened the patio door and gestured for us to come in. "I was looking for you," she said. "What part of *everyone here will recognize you* didn't you understand? Don't go outside. For two days. Even you can handle that."

I followed her back into the crisp air-conditioning. "I didn't go from being the Saxons' prisoner to being yours. I'll wear sunglasses or something, but I'm not hiding inside. In fact, why don't I just wear sunglasses and hide out near the festival tomorrow so I can at least be backup? I've been checking the news. All they're saying is that I might be questioned. It's not like they've put out a most-wanted bulletin. Random locals aren't even going to notice me."

"Like sunglasses are going to do anything—" Elodie protested.

"We could disguise her," Colette said. "I do it all the time. Sunglasses aren't enough, but you can get away with a lot by changing your hair and clothes. I'll wear a wig and a huge coat, and I almost don't even need the glasses. It's like people don't see my face when the rest of me isn't what they were expecting."

"So that's what I'll do," I said. I looked down at my long, wavy dark hair falling over my shoulder. "I'll cut my hair."

"She said a *wig*," Elodie said. "The dramatics are unnecessary. Though you do have a lot of hair, and fitting it under a wig . . ."

I touched the piece of hair that had been cut at the wedding. It brushed my collarbone.

"Could use it as an excuse to do something fun," Colette said with a sad smile. "Cut it off to that length. Dye it pink."

I started to laugh, but stopped. "Not a bad idea. I could go hipster.

Get me some pink streaks, some big glasses . . . This cut piece looks ridiculous, anyway. I've been meaning to do *something* with it." I turned to Elodie. "Will you do it?"

When Elodie got back from the drugstore with hair dye, we left the boys and Colette in the main room and shut ourselves in the marble bathroom.

"Time to make you hip. Though that'll take more than just a haircut," Elodie said, tossing a pair of scissors and a box of hair dye on the counter.

I took one last look at myself in the gilded mirror and pulled at the ends of my long hair, then sat on the toilet seat. "Is there anything the rest of us can do while you're at the red-carpet thing tonight?"

Elodie pulled a brush through my hair. "Sit here and be useless."

I bit down hard on my lip. "Why don't you like me?"

She smirked.

"I'm serious. I keep trying to be nice to you, and you still hate me. I just want to make sure you're not going to shave my head right now."

Elodie snagged a knot, and I flinched. "I don't hate you. I think this whole thing's obnoxious, and I kind of wish you'd never come into our lives. But I don't hate you."

"Um, okay. Thanks," I said, not hiding the sarcasm.

She gave an exaggerated sigh. "It's a *compliment*. I think you're handling it okay. I hope you don't hurt him, though. Jackie. He's . . . good. Both of them are."

Oh. So that was what the renewed animosity was about. I thought she'd looked at us all funny on the train this morning. "I thought we agreed we weren't going to talk about this. Weird relationship stuff not conducive to serious clue following, remember?"

"Funny, you say that, but you keep leading both of them on, anyway."

I turned so quickly, the brush yanked on my hair. "Ow. I'm not leading anyone on. I had a thing with Jack. *Have* a thing. Whatever. It's complicated. End of conversation."

"But you want to know what Stellan's tongue tastes like."

"Elodie!" I whipped around again, this time to the door to make sure no one had heard. I hissed through my teeth when the brush caught again, and I ripped it out of her hand and disentangled it myself.

"Am I wrong, though?" She took back the brush and clipped the top layer of hair tight against my head.

"Just drop it, okay?"

Mercifully, Elodie shrugged and gave the short piece of hair a tug. "You're sure about this? You have such *glamoreux* hair. Short hair feels different."

I shook my head a little and felt my hair tickling my skin. I'd worn it long since our first move. I'd never dyed it, never done anything. Was this crazy? Maybe. Was I sure? No. I glanced up at Elodie's blunt bob.

She saw me looking and touched her own hair. "Exactly. You don't want to be like me."

"I was actually just thinking I like yours," I said. I'd spent so much time fighting, stubbornly clinging to the idea of having everything how it used to be, when maybe I should be adapting. Adjusting my hair around what had happened rather than trying to cover up the part I'd lost. I inwardly rolled my eyes at the obvious cheesy metaphor there, but I said, "I want it cut. Do it."

She pursed her lips, studying me like she wasn't sure if I was telling the truth. "Okay."

Still, I held my breath when she pulled my hair taut for the first cut. That distinctive sound of scissors snipping was followed by the whisper of a lock falling to the bathroom floor. It was so much longer than I thought the cut part would be. It lay there on the tile, curled in a spiral. It hit like a punch. "Oh God," I whispered.

"Too late now," Elodie said.

"I know." I watched the second lock fall. And the third.

Soon, Elodie stood in front of me, evening out the hair brushing my collarbones. I touched the freshly snipped ends, and they swung freely.

Elodie took down the clip with the next layer of hair. I swallowed hard.

"I don't hate you, either. Just so you know," I said, trying to distract myself.

She pulled a strand of hair between her fingers. "I know." By the time she took down the top section, my head felt ten pounds lighter.

Finally, she ruffled my hair and smoothed it back from my face. My eyes were still shut tight, and I felt her arrange locks over my ears, then grab my chin and tilt my face up. "Open," she said.

I did, and Elodie's face was inches from mine. She actually smiled, and took my face between her palms. "Stop looking like someone died, or I'm not going to do the pink."

I pasted on a smile that felt fake even to me, and she snorted but grabbed the box of dye. Then she looked me up and down and wrinkled her nose. "Please tell me those aren't the same clothes you had on when we left Greece."

"I haven't exactly had time to go shopping." I touched my hair, trying to sneak a peek over my shoulder into the mirror.

"No! Don't look." Elodie jumped in front of me and pointed at the partition at the end of the room that hid the shower stall. "Your hair needs to be wet, anyway. Shower, and I'll have Colette bring clean clothes, then we'll do the dye."

Almost an hour later, I was showered, my hair was dyed, and Elodie produced a blow-dryer. She kept me facing away from the mirror, and I could feel her twirling my waves around her fingers. When she was done, she actually smiled. "Approved. You can look."

I stood and smoothed the black sheath dress Colette had brought. She and I weren't anywhere near the same size, but the dress was drapey, so it didn't matter.

I took a centering breath and turned around.

I didn't know what I was expecting, but it wasn't this.

Elodie had cut my hair in a long blunt bob that fell to my shoulders. I'd wondered if the short hair would make me look younger, but I looked more sophisticated. Older, in a good way. Without the length of the hair pulling down, my cheekbones stood out more, and my eyes looked bigger, but somehow more proportional at the same time. I looked like me, but not.

And the color. If pink hair could ever look natural, this looked natural. It was bright—it was incredibly bright. It wasn't just pink, it was magenta. But all the pink chunks were on the under layer, and Elodie had woven them in so they peeked through the curls on top. At first you only got a glimpse, but if I tossed my hair or turned my head quickly, it was a flash of neon.

"I love it," I said. "I *love* it. You're a genius."

"I'm going to remember you said that and use it as blackmail," Elodie said, but she looked pleased.

"I don't look like me." I did, but still different enough to walk down the hall at Lakehaven High without anybody recognizing me. "This will work."

"We'll have to put you in baggy clothes, probably, make you look bigger, but it's a start."

I nodded. "Anything. I'll do anything."

Between the hair and the dress, I looked so . . . together. Capable. Confident.

"Thank you," I said. "I couldn't have—thank you."

"You're not going to hug me, are you?" Elodie took a step back.

I felt a real smile creeping across my face. "I won't hug you. But thank you. I like it."

"Well," she said, opening the bathroom door, "now we've wasted half the afternoon, so hopefully it was worth it."

We headed down the stairs. Colette intercepted us in the hall and clapped her hands excitedly, then took my arm and led me into the living room. "What mischief have you all been up to while we've been gone?" Elodie said.

Neither of the boys answered. They peered around her, trying to catch a glimpse of me.

When they did, Jack's mouth dropped open. I don't think he'd believed I'd actually do it. Stellan looked just as shocked. All of a sudden, I felt far more self-conscious than I had a minute ago. Colette flipped the ends of my hair, and I chewed my lip. "Do you like it?" I asked Jack.

"Yes! Yes. Absolutely. Looks brilliant," he said, snapping out of it. "Pink hair, then. That'll make a good disguise."

"You don't like it."

"Don't be such an old person," Elodie said. "She looks fabulous. S, tell her she looks fabulous."

"Fabulous," Stellan echoed, but he barely glanced at me as he toed the ground with one boot.

"Well, *I* like it," I said with as much confidence as I could muster.

This was about being able to leave the house without getting recognized, not about looking pretty. And I *did* like it.

"You look great," Jack jumped in again. "I just—it's so . . . different. I—"

Elodie frowned at him and threw her arm around my shoulders and led me to the front window.

"I hate them," Elodie whispered in my ear. "I've hooked up with both of them, and they were both terrible."

I hiccuped out an appalled laugh.

Elodie made a face. "Okay, that's a lie. It's a complete lie. But I hate them, anyway."

I glanced over my shoulder. "That was the worst pep talk I've ever heard," I whispered.

"It doesn't matter what they think," she said. "Every gay boy in Cannes will want to touch your hair."

I touched my forehead to her shoulder.

"Too much like a hug," she said, pulling away. "And now, Lettie," she said, grabbing Colette's arm, "it's our turn. Surveillance time in less than four hours."

CHAPTER 26

Later, Elodie and Colette were getting ready and Stellan had gone out somewhere. I wandered into the kitchen. I kind of wished we were going after the bracelet tonight. I understood why tomorrow was a better idea, but I was starting to get antsy. At least I had the date with Jack to look forward to. I wondered what we'd do. Idly, I picked up my phone from the counter.

There was a text.

I don't appreciate you not answering me.

Lydia Saxon.

My whole body went cold. But Lydia didn't even know about my untraceable phone—or if she did, it wasn't untraceable anymore.

I started to shout for Jack. We had to get out or the Saxons would find us—had already found us.

And then I saw my phone sitting just where I'd left it earlier, in the sparkling white dining room, on top of my bag.

The phone I was holding wasn't mine.

It was Jack's.

I couldn't help it. I scrolled through his texts. There was a whole series of them.

I sat down hard in one of the Lucite chairs at the dining room table. All I could do was blink at the words on the screen, forming sentences that shouldn't make sense.

The whole dining room wall was doors, and Jack entered through one of them. Between the doors were floor-to-ceiling mirrors, with the same on the wall behind my back, and the uncertain smile on his face reflected back and forth, back and forth, into infinity. "Hi," he said. "I'm sorry I reacted to the hair like that. I was just surprised."

I squeezed the phone in my hands. "Of course." My voice was hollow. "Of course you'd be surprised that I'd want to do anything you don't agree with."

"Avery," he said. "I'm sorry. You look beautiful with any—What's wrong?"

I held up the phone. "I was checking texts. I thought it was mine."

He looked confused for just a second, and then his face fell a thousand times over, taking the whole room with it. I pushed the phone across the table.

"Avery—"

"That *is* how they knew what we were doing in Paris," I said calmly.

Jack sat down hard opposite me. "God. No. This isn't—"

"Isn't what it looks like? Then what is it? Because it looks like you've been telling my sister everything. And lying to all of us about it."

He spread his hands on the glass-topped table. I held my breath. Maybe there was another explanation.

"I was keeping you safe," he said, and everything inside me shattered.

"That was *not* your choice to make."

"Lydia promised she'd send people to watch out for you, without getting in our way," Jack went on.

I held up my hand, pieces clicking together in my head. "Every time I thought I saw somebody watching us, and you pretended it was nothing—*all* those were Saxon people?"

"It was the only way," he pleaded.

It *hurt*. My chest actually hurt, enough that I couldn't help grasping at the front of my shirt. It was like my insides had exploded into a million shards.

"I had no idea what she was really doing," Jack said. "I found out when you did. I would never have—"

"Just stop." I looked out the doors, past white columns and hedges cut into an archway down to the drive. "Do the Saxons know we're here?"

"Absolutely not. I haven't been in contact with her since yesterday, and she's never been able to trace this phone. You have to understand, Avery. Your father wouldn't have let you go to Greece if they didn't have security on you. They wouldn't have let us go to Paris alone yesterday."

I should have known it was all too easy.

"And they actually have been working on the clues—"

"You told them about the *clues*? All of them?" I rested my head in my hands. "Were you in contact with her even before we decided to go to them in the first place?"

"Do you really think we could have stayed hidden in Paris as long as we did? They would have tracked you down. And that way they could have security on our apartment—"

I made a sound like I was choking. "And you've been doing all this with Lydia."

Jack's hands clenched into fists, leaving streaks of his fingers on the glass. "I thought she was on our side. We all wanted to stop the

Order—and Lydia knew you needed space. She didn't want you to feel like you were being watched—"

"But I was!" I jumped up, tamping down the pain with indignation, because that was a little bit easier. This was *humiliating*. I couldn't believe I hadn't seen it. "Did it have to be Lydia, of all people? Besides being a Saxon, she's a girl you've had a thing with."

Jack's head snapped up.

"Stellan told me, since he's the only one who tells me anything anymore. I don't care that you have a history with other girls, but I do care about you lying. After all this *family member and the help* stuff? And God." I ran my hands through my newly short hair. "*Lydia?* She *looks* like me. She's *me,* but a Saxon."

Jack was shaking his head. "Which you're *not.* That's the whole point. I mean, you are, but not in the important ways. You two are nothing alike."

I shoved the chair in hard enough that it almost toppled over. "But this whole time you've been saying *we* shouldn't be together while you went behind my back to *her.*"

"To keep you safe! And you've been going behind *my* back talking to Stellan about things you should be asking me about."

"That is not the same thing." I heard footsteps cross the floor above us and tried to lower my voice. This was bad enough without Elodie and Colette listening. "This isn't about Stellan."

"It's not? You haven't been picking fights with me lately because of him?"

"If anything, *you're* fighting with *me* because of him." I felt like I could punch something. "Can we leave Stellan out of it? This is about you doing exactly what I asked you not to do. You were the only thing in the world I trusted. You had a *choice.* You could have chosen me."

Jack stood, leaning across the table. "I did have a choice. Between doing what you wanted or keeping you alive. Do you know how many times I wished I could be selfish enough to choose *us*?" He pushed away, and the vase of peonies in the center of the table wobbled. "Remember what I told you on the balcony that night after the ball at the Dauphins'? It's *all* been for you."

My fingernails grated the back of the chair and I glimpsed myself in the endless mirrors. I looked crazed. "You should leave before the others find out whose side you're really on."

Jack shook his head. His hands were white-knuckled on the tabletop. "I am on *your* side, Avery! I made a different choice than you would have, because I *care* about you."

"And I'm saying you shouldn't." I grabbed my bag and started out the front of the house. "You shouldn't care about me anymore. Whatever it is we've been doing here—it's over. We're over."

"Be careful," Jack called from behind me after a second, his voice strained. "The hair doesn't make you invisible. Stay hidden, and—"

I ground to a halt at the lacquered front door. "I told you to stop! Stop trying to protect me!"

Jack's boots sounded on the tile, and then he turned the corner. "Avery! You can break up with me, but I can't not care about you."

"It's not breaking up if we were never together in the first place," I said, and slammed the door behind me.

I wasn't crying. I was cried out. But my heart felt like it was about to explode, and I couldn't sit still. I stomped down the residential street and sat at a bus stop, the cold metal of the lonely bench seeping through Colette's dress and into my legs.

I was a mess. What was I doing? Even though it was getting dark, I put my sunglasses on and kept my head down, hoping I looked enough like a random punk kid that no one would give me a second glance. I was pretty sure I believed that Jack hadn't told the Saxons we were here, but I couldn't be certain. And the Circle had eyes everywhere.

I clutched at my bag in my lap like it was my last lifeline. For the first time in my life, I actually belonged somewhere, and yet I kept losing everyone I cared about. Mr. Emerson. My mom. Lydia and my father. Jack.

At least the Dauphins were upfront about it when they snatched me and tried to marry me off to Luc.

I didn't know what to do. I wasn't going back to the villa, but I had nowhere else to go. Without really thinking about it, I felt around in my bag for my phone.

I typed *where are you* and hit send.

I was already walking when the answer came back.

CHAPTER 27

At the bottom of the hill, a pedestrian walkway ran along the shore, dotted with cafes and restaurants and bars. I bypassed one that had dozens of cheerful yellow tables on the sidewalk and, glancing at my phone to confirm the address, pulled open a nondescript maroon door. Inside it was small and dark and warm and *red*—every bulb in the hanging chandeliers seemed to be crimson, and it gave the small bar the air of an elegant but dingy brothel.

I pushed my way between a couple laughing groups of kids a little older than me. Stellan was leaning at the other end of the bar, chatting to the bartender and another guy. I stomped up next to him and took whatever he was drinking out of his hand and took a big gulp, frowning when it turned out to be espresso.

"Hi?" he said, and I ignored the eyebrow raise at his companions, who quietly left us alone.

I put his cup back on the bar with more of a bang than I needed to. "What are you doing here?" I said.

"I wanted coffee."

I looked around. "In a bar?"

One side of his mouth quirked up. "I thought you'd be glad I'd come here rather than having Colette make it for me."

"I don't care what you do with Colette. Why does everyone seem to think . . ." I almost said it out loud, but stopped myself in time. Why does everyone think you're *mine*? I leaned on the bar, running my hands over my hair. Such a mess. I was such a mess. What was I even doing here?

Stellan looked over my shoulder toward the door. "Should I ask where your boyfriend-slash-bodyguard is?"

"I don't care, as long as it's not here." I tried as hard as I could to make the not-caring part true.

Stellan raised an eyebrow.

"He was telling the Saxons what we were doing the whole time. To keep me *safe*, supposedly."

Stellan's whole body tensed. "Did he tell them we're *here*?"

"He says he hasn't talked to them since we found out what they've been doing. I think he's telling the truth."

Stellan raised a finger and two glasses of something clear appeared in front of us. I choked mine down without asking what it was and signaled for another before the bartender had a chance to turn around again.

It was only then that the taste hit me, and I gagged. "That's disgusting."

"Vodka," he answered.

"Do people actually like drinking that?" The next round arrived and I tried to down it again, but a reflex kept it far away from my mouth. I just held it, swirling.

Stellan cleared his throat. The dim light deepened the hollows under his eyes. "So you and Jack . . ."

"Can we not?"

He nodded and took a sip of his own drink.

In about thirty seconds, my stomach started to feel warm. In another minute, it spread to my head, and in another, I felt a little floaty. Finally, I looked around. Despite the vampire lighting, the bar was cozy and friendly, like everyone here had known one another for years. It wasn't the kind of neighborhood bar you saw in the US, with old grizzly men getting wasted on Bud Light. We were the only ones here taking shots of liquor. Most of the patrons were drinking espresso or sipping wine.

"Done," I said into my drink.

Stellan raised his eyebrows.

"Me and Jack. Finished. Over. Whatever we were before, we are now nothing."

I waited to feel pain wash over me, but the sharpest edges had dulled. I deliberately didn't look up to see Stellan's reaction. Behind us was a makeshift dance floor, and a guy was doing a completely inappropriate robot to the sultry French music coming from the speakers. My head felt even fuzzier.

We sipped our drinks in a companionable quiet for a few minutes while I calmed down even more. I liked that about Stellan. He didn't have to fill all the silences.

I leaned on my elbow and watched him watch the rest of the bar. His hair still looked blond in the strange light, though his skin glowed red. He had saved my life in Greece. He'd been pretty good at saving my sanity since then. I wondered what he was thinking right now. He was probably making fun of me in his head. He was probably berating Jack.

And . . . I watched the rest of the bar watch him. One girl and two boys did the most obvious double takes I'd ever seen after noticing him, and then they looked at me with this mix of fascination and jealousy.

Stellan waved his hand in front of my face, and I realized he'd caught me staring at him.

I giggled a little. My drink didn't taste as bad as it had before. "Bottoms up," I said, and clinked my glass against his before draining the rest of it with a minimum of gagging.

Stellan raised one eyebrow. "Easy there, party girl. We have things to do tomorrow. Important things."

I ignored him. Now I understood why people drank. All I'd thought about in the past few minutes was how pretty the boy standing next to me was. A couple more, and I could forget everything that had happened tonight. And the past few days. And actually, for a long time. "More," I said.

Stellan ordered two more drinks in French, but I understood a few words now, and I knew he'd gotten mine with soda. "I'm not *drunk.*"

"I like this shirt. I don't want to clean vomit off it later."

I elbowed him in the side, then did a quick pirouette. My bag didn't quite keep up. It smacked into the bar with a thud, but I kept spinning. "See?" I said over my shoulder. "Not drunk, or I couldn't do that."

"Yes, and you absolutely would have done that sober," Stellan said wryly. I stopped abruptly and stared at his hand, which was suddenly on my waist, steadying me.

I watched him notice, too, then remove it, slowly. I climbed onto one of two just-vacated bar stools. When he sat next to me, I said, "Do you even like the Dauphins? Except for Luc, you don't seem to care about them nearly as much as Jack cared about the Saxons."

"Where did that come from?"

I shrugged.

Stellan's knee hit mine as he sat at the stool next to me. "I do what I have to do for myself. And my sister."

I remembered seeing him at the ball, talking to Madame Dauphin. "You always do what they tell you, though. Madame Dauphin had you spying on me when we first met. And you did it."

"Yes. I had to. That's the point of this job."

My feet reached out, legs barely long enough to hit the footrest under the bar. "You almost seemed afraid of Madame Dauphin. You're not afraid of anyone." The words came out before I could stop them.

"She's . . . hard on me. I can't do anything wrong around her."

"She doesn't like you?"

He smirked. "Something like that."

I gestured for him to go on, and at first it seemed like he wouldn't, but then he took a gulp of his drink. "Okay. A year or so ago, I may have . . . I misjudged a situation."

I shook my head, not sure what he was trying to say.

"It's always been in my best interests to stay on her good side. She's always liked me. Until that point, I didn't realize just how *much*."

It took a few seconds longer than it should have for me to understand. I twisted my bar stool to gape at him. "Wait. Madame Dauphin tried to . . . ?" It sounded like a bad soap opera.

Stellan swirled the splash of vodka left in his glass, and I had a horrifying thought. "Did you?"

"No. But maybe I should have. Now she does everything in her power to make things hard for me. Before, I was in line to take a position that would let me travel to Russia to see my sister a few times a year. Then . . . I wasn't. Which is another reason the thirteenth thing could be helpful. The tomb. Whatever we find."

I swiveled back forward. "That's why you want to find it so much. Leverage."

"That's one reason."

"There's more?"

"There's always more." He spun his glass on the bar. "A few years ago, I found out that the Order had set the fire that killed my family."

I stilled. "I thought it was an accident."

"It wasn't."

"Leverage *and* revenge," I said. I thought I could see right through him like he could through me, but I was wrong. "I didn't know. You didn't tell me."

"You didn't ask the right questions." He finally glanced over. "I didn't lie to you."

"I know. I don't think you've ever really lied to me. Surprisingly."

The look on his face was almost a smile. "Nice to know you think so highly of me."

I reached out to shove him, tipping off my own bar stool in the process and practically landing in his lap. He grabbed my hand to steady me. We both paused, his heart beating under my palm.

"I feel like such an idiot for trusting them," I said. The filter on my mouth had been turned off, and my tongue felt clumsy, like it wasn't keeping up with my brain. "The Saxons only wanted what I could do for them. And Jack . . ."

Stellan's chest rose and fell with a deep breath. He never smelled like cologne. He smelled like something else, like pinpricks of light in the dark. Like *boy*. "It's seductive, being wanted," he said. "It makes us less careful."

I looked his long fingers, holding my hand against his chest, and thought of Jack, trusting the Saxons blindly because they acted like they cared about him. Lydia, talking about how it was appealing, being part of something bigger than yourself. She used that very fact to coax the whole Circle into believing the Order were their enemies.

"And it's seductive *wanting*," Stellan went on, slowly setting my hand back on the bar. "It feels good. And it feels terrible at the same time."

"I don't want anything," I said quietly, pulling myself upright.

The bartender came by, but Stellan motioned him away. "I don't think you actually felt safe when you got on that plane with me. You just *wanted* so much that you were willing to do anything. You wanted this family, this life you could have."

I thought of that first morning, in the car on the way to Prada, when I didn't yet realize quite how far my life had been turned upside down. *Toska*, Stellan had said. *Something's missing, and you ache for it, down to your bones.*

I ran my finger through the condensation on my glass.

"That's how I know you're lying when you say you don't want anything. Being someone who *wants* that much—it doesn't just go away, as much as you try to suppress it. You just hope you can eventually realize what it is you're missing."

"What do *you* want, then?" I said into my drink. "What do you *ache* for?"

He smiled an enigmatic little smile that made me stare at his mouth for a moment too long. "You remember that."

"Of course I do." I gathered my hair away from my face, surprised for a second not to have enough of it to twist into a bun. I let go of it, and it fell back over my shoulders.

Stellan pulled one of the strands of pink.

I batted his hand away. "I know, you don't like it."

"Oh, I like it," he said.

I rolled my eyes and inspected the ends of one of the pink strands. "You don't have to lie. It was pretty obvious that you hated it, and it's okay. I don't care."

He gave a small laugh. "No, I just wasn't stupid enough to say what I thought out loud in front of your sort-of boyfriend."

I raised my eyebrows.

"*Kuklachka*, I think you look . . ." He broke into a string of French. I didn't know what the words meant, but his tone, and the way his eyes flicked over me when he said it—fast enough that it could have been an accident, but slow enough that my skin tingled—made me have to look away.

"Didn't I tell you to stop flirting with me?" I said.

I could hear a smile when he said, "Then suffice it to say I like it."

I pulled my hair back for real this time, quickly, into a messy ponytail.

"Why is it . . . ," I said, the words bouncing like helium balloons. "Why are you sometimes like, my best friend or something? And then sometimes I think you hate me?"

He got very still and watched us in the mirror behind the bar. "I'm sometimes your best friend?"

I found us in the mirror, too. After a few seconds, I pulled a few strands of the pink hair around my face.

"*Kuklachka*." I could feel Stellan looking down at me, then so quietly I barely heard him, "I never hate you."

Something warm that had nothing to do with the drink settled in my chest, and I peered at his sunburst tattoo. *Light in the dark.*

I reached up and traced it with one finger. It was hot over the ink, like it really was the sun burning into his upper back. Then his scars, cool and smooth like marble veins over the warm skin.

And then I noticed he was looking at me in a really odd way.

"Sorry." I pulled away. "I—did that hurt?"

He blinked. "No."

When the next round came, I took a sip and wrinkled my nose. "Doesn't taste right," I said. I grabbed his and took a sip, and the bitter alcohol taste wasn't missing in his. "Hey," I said. "Get me a real one."

"No." He took his drink back and put it out of my reach. That only meant I had to lean all the way across his lap to get at it. The invisible bubble of normal personal space had officially shrunk to nothing.

I sat back up with a triumphant "Ha!" but he snatched the glass away again before I could get a drink.

I pouted. My head was so warm, dreamy light as marshmallow cream. At some point, we'd shifted enough so our feet were touching on the footrest under the bar.

I paused, then moved my foot a little. It was enough to signal to him this was a person he was touching and not a chair leg, and to do the least awkward thing and move away. He didn't. I sat straight again, and even though I could tell my leg would fall asleep pretty soon in this position, I didn't move, either.

At the opposite end of the bar, a couple had started kissing. In the past few minutes, they'd nearly crossed the line into not-appropriate-in-public. "Kiss," I said, drawing out the *s* sound.

"Hmm?" It was a little dreamy, a little unfocused, and I realized that he wasn't perfectly sober, either.

"Kiss. I never thought about it before. Isn't it a strange word? Such a *cute* word. Like the combination of bliss and . . . kitten. Kissssss."

We both watched the couple. His hand crept under her shirt. She nearly knocked their wine off the bar. My foot pressed a little harder into Stellan's. His pressed a little harder back. "Kitten . . . bliss?" he said.

Except now I was watching *him*. He turned and caught me.

"All I'm saying," I said, flustered, "is there's got to be another word for kissing like *that*."

Stellan smiled; his teeth grazed his lower lip, pulling it into his mouth. Our feet still didn't move. "Time for you to sober up," he said. "I'm ordering you coffee."

"Like *you're* sober." I shoved him again, hard enough that I nearly knocked him off his stool.

He grabbed both my wrists with one hand. "More sober than you. *You're* making a scene."

I wrenched one hand away and clapped it over his mouth. He turned back to me, eyes dancing. "Shush," I said.

"Mrmph," he mumbled, warm breath behind my hand. I pulled away an inch. "Bet you cannot go ten seconds without laughing," he said from behind my hand, and propped an elbow on the bar facing me.

I dropped my hand and mirrored him. "Go."

My mouth twitched for a few seconds, trying to giggle. His eyes danced merrily, the inner ring of gold especially bright in the dark. But slowly, the laughter left him.

I was on the very edge of my bar stool. We were facing each other more than we were facing forward now. Our knees, which had already been touching, pressed together purposefully. I felt my lips part.

"Stop it," he breathed, his voice even lower than usual, accent a little thicker.

"Stop what?"

"You know exactly what," he said, mockingly. My earlier words in his mouth.

I glanced down at our legs, back up. After a second, I said, "Why?"

Neither of us moved. "*Kuklachka*," he said. "You never answered me. What do you want?"

I exhaled. I didn't know if it was the fight with Jack, or the vodka, or the music and the dark. Or if all that was only allowing me to feel what I'd been trying not to feel for so long. All I knew was that the knot in my chest was starting to come undone in his hands.

"Do you remember the rest of the meaning of *toska*?" he said. "Sometimes you want something you think you shouldn't." There was less than a foot of space between our faces. "You're not even sure you understand it." I could see the pulse pounding at his throat. "But not having it feels like you can't breathe." For the first time, I noticed my breathing. How shallow it was, how quick.

He leaned even closer. "You want to find the tomb for more than blackmail. You like the idea of all that power. Of having control over your life."

I couldn't see anything in the world but his face.

"You even want the power we could have together," he went on. "Then you wouldn't be alone. You *liked* it when *we* said something and people listened."

I swallowed. He looked at my mouth.

"I think you're even starting to care about the Circle. To want to be part of them. You *want* to be wanted. Say it. I want to hear you say it out loud."

I licked my lips, my mouth suddenly dry. My body wasn't my own. My voice wasn't my own. I *didn't* want it in the way some of the Circle did. I didn't care about money, fame, ruling the world. But the rest of it . . . An hour ago, I would have denied it all. Now . . . "I want it," I whispered. Stellan was still watching me, rapt. "I want all of that."

It was so wrong to feel those things. To feel absolutely anything over and above wanting to save my mom. I couldn't believe I'd just said it out loud. But I felt light. Free.

A smile flickered across Stellan's face. His pupils looked huge in the low light. "What else?"

A thrill shivered through me, hitting low in my stomach. A minuscule shift, and one of his knees slipped between mine. He looked down at it. I did, too.

"Little doll, is there something else you want?" he murmured.

I stared into his eyes. It was only a moment, but the moment dragged back as far as I could remember, like we had never been anywhere but here, suspended precariously between yes and no, between *want* and *don't*.

I felt terrified. I felt powerful. I felt bold.

I nodded.

CHAPTER 28

Stellan stared at me for a beat. Two. Then he stood, abruptly enough that I pitched off my bar stool. He caught me, tossed a handful of euros on the bar, then took my hand and led me outside.

We made it almost to the bottom of the steps.

He turned abruptly, leaving me standing one step higher; he gathered his fingers in my dress and pulled me against him.

There was a second of hesitation, of skin touching skin, a cold nose on a warm cheek, lips almost brushing, so close, and are we really—

I stood on my tiptoes and pressed my lips to his.

It was all the encouragement he needed. Sparks shot from my lips through the tingling tips of my toes. His hand was firm on the back of my neck, lifting my face to his, and the rest of the world fell away.

I'd half expected, after so much buildup, for kissing him to be disappointing.

I was wrong.

He pulled away a few inches, eyes wide. "Oh," I breathed, and it said a million other things that would make me blush to say them out loud. His lips curved into a smile, and then I couldn't see the smile anymore, just feel it, and then there was nothing else.

I realized now that I'd thought about this before, even if I'd tried not to. I'd imagined it would be the almost violence of lips and breath and hands that would burn so hot, it'd flame out as quickly as it had started; that we'd just have to do it once and get it out of our systems.

I hadn't imagined this: the feeling that, even though he had far more experience than I did, he was just as captivated as I was by how our lips took no time at all to get used to each other, the echo of our muffled breaths, the fact that it was chilly outside, but between our faces, it was nothing but soft and warm. I hadn't imagined, though maybe I should have, that this would be the physical manifestation of that way he had always looked at me, since the day we met, like he could tell what was going on inside me so well it was almost uncomfortable. I'd never been kissed by someone who knew what I wanted before I did—exactly when to run his hands through my hair, when to cup my face like it was something precious.

It was deliberate, sweet, frantic at the same time, tinged with vodka and lime and *not* the taste of cigarettes, and I wondered very briefly whether that was for my benefit and then that thought was lost, too, because everything was lost except for the small, pleading noise I made when his mouth broke away from mine.

"*Kuklachka,*" he murmured. "Little doll."

Little doll. That's exactly what I didn't want, wasn't it? To be anyone's plaything in this game.

I forced myself to push him back, hands on his chest. "Do you just want what I can do for you," I whispered, "or do you actually want me?"

I expected him to say whatever it took to keep kissing me, but a look deeper than I would have imagined passed over his face. He licked his lips, and I couldn't help but glance at them. His eyes darkened. "Both," he said, like he'd just realized it himself.

"I thought I wasn't your type," I whispered, remembering the conversation he and Jack had on the boat.

A soft laugh. "You're not." His hands were on my waist, fingers spread on my rib cage like piano keys. "Who's spying now?"

I shrugged, tired of apologizing, then pulled his face back down to mine and didn't let go again.

I didn't know where we were. Who we were. We were on a street for a few minutes, I think. Against a statue in the middle of the sidewalk. Then pressed into a rough stone wall, my feet dangling a foot off the ground, my back clanging against the metal gate of a storefront, closed for the night.

And then things started to look familiar, but I didn't care, and then up a driveway, and I think we went up some stairs, and doors and more doors, and then we very definitely opened the door to a bedroom.

I pulled away with a gasp. "Are we back at Colette's?"

He nodded. His shirt was half untucked, hair everywhere. He must have been staying in a different wing than I was, and thankfully, no one else was around.

I looked inside the room. One soft bedside lamp. Books on the coffee table. Stellan—oh my God, seriously, really, *Stellan,* after everything? I flashed briefly to another set of lips on mine, a kiss that felt so different than this did, a clench in my chest just at the thought— but no, it was Stellan now, in the doorway, waiting. I almost expected the look on his face to be triumph, like it was when I'd asked him to teach me to fight. But there was no hint of smugness.

There was a normal amount of beautiful a person should be allowed to look, then there was him. Was it possible he was actually more attractive all flushed and wild like this, or had I made myself block him out so thoroughly, I'd just forgotten?

"Yes." I took his hand. The door shut behind us. "Okay."

The next time I opened my eyes, I was sitting on the windowsill, Stellan's chest pressed between my knees. We'd been kissing for what had to be hours, but could have been minutes, and with a kiss like this, it was no surprise when I found myself, by some instinct rather than any particular decision, groping for the buttons of his shirt. My fingers felt clumsy, strange. The first button popped open. The second.

He pulled back, breathing hard, watching my hands undress him. His shirt fell off one shoulder, exposing the pattern of his translucent scars, beautiful, glowing in the low light.

A tiny knot of nerves blossomed in my stomach. I knew exactly where this was going if I didn't stop. It wasn't too late to button his shirt back up and keep this as the sweet kind of kiss. The *kitten-bliss* kind of kiss.

But did I *want* to?

Stellan's hand closed on my leg, just at the hem of my skirt. He looked up at me, the same hesitation shining in his eyes.

I must have paused, because just as smoothly, with nothing more than a tender kiss at my jaw, his hand moved back to my waist, wrapped around my back. Safe.

And we were kissing again, just kissing.

The nervous butterflies in my stomach flapped, but he had misunderstood. That pause, the irregular pattering of my heart against my ribs—it wasn't a bad kind of nervous.

I pulled back, just in inch. Just enough for him to take my face in his hands, for his eyes to wonder what I was doing.

I pulled the collar of his shirt through my fingers—then undid one more button.

Really? his eyes said.

His mouth didn't have time to repeat it before mine was on it again. Telling him please, don't think, don't ask, don't talk, for once, don't make me agonize and decide and wonder whether I'm doing the right thing. Just *do*.

The kiss wasn't quite so sweet after that. A while later, another of his buttons undone. Two. His shirt halfway off now.

I glanced toward the crisp white sheets on the bed across the room. So did he. I started to undo another button.

He stopped me, both our hands rising and falling with his uneven breaths.

"Avery, wait," he said. The use of my real name was jarring, and my gaze snapped up. He gently brushed away a strand of my hair that had gotten caught in my mouth, tucking it behind my ear. "Have you ever . . . ?"

I'm sure he already knew the answer. I shook my head. "It doesn't matter," I said, and kissed him again.

After a second, though, he stopped, lips in my hair. "Are you sure?"

"I'm sure," I said, and punctuated it with another long kiss.

"Really sure?" he breathed.

"Really sure." My fingers fumbled with his final button.

"Okay," he sputtered against my mouth. "Wait. Stop. I can't. You can't."

My eyes flew open. "What? Why?"

He sighed like it hurt him physically, and stepped out of my arms, cursing, colorfully, under his breath. "*Kuklachka.*" He perched on the arm of the couch, burying his face in his elbow. "You've had too much to drink. We both have. I just want to make sure—I don't think we should—I don't want to be something you regret."

It hung over us like a wet blanket, and I shivered, despite the heat of my skin. "I won't—"

"Just so you know, this is far more difficult than I'm making it look. Give me a second, okay?" He turned away from me, and I sat, staring. He was serious. And that was incredibly embarrassing.

My skin was hot all over, and then cold. My mind cleared all at once and the real world rushed back.

I jumped up and headed to the door.

The couch creaked behind me. "No, wait." Stellan caught up with me at the door, blocking my way out. "I want you to stay. I just need to be able to think clearly. Okay?"

I pulled away. No. Not okay. It was the same as always. He was just like everyone else in my life, thinking they knew what was right for me better than I did.

"Move, please," I said, not looking him in the eyes.

He ran both hands through his hair. "Avery . . ."

We both jumped when the door slammed open from the outside.

"*Merde,*" Elodie said, breathless, wearing a black evening gown and heavy eye makeup, her bleached hair slicked back from her face in a headband. "There you are. Why weren't you answering your mobile—"

She finally noticed me.

I couldn't imagine what I looked like right now. Stellan was hastily buttoning his shirt. Elodie pursed her lips, and under the humiliation of being rejected was the twinge of knowing I'd just done exactly what she'd said I was going to, and I'd promised I wouldn't.

"Ah," she said. "Of course. Well, sorry to interrupt, but there's a small, tiny, actually very important problem."

CHAPTER 29

When I got to the dining room, Elodie and Colette stood around the table, Elodie in her black dress and Colette in a gossamer white gown that looked like she was wearing the most glamorous bubbles I'd ever seen.

I kept my face down and fell into a chair. My whole body felt prickly, uncomfortable. My head wouldn't stop spinning.

I'd stopped by the bathroom on the way down and tried to comb some of the tangles out of my hair, but I knew I looked as undone as I felt. My eyes were bright, my cheeks breathlessly pink no matter how much water I splashed on them, my dress wrinkled and crushed.

Stellan looked just as obvious as I did. When he sat up straight, I saw that he'd buttoned his shirt crookedly. Colette caught me looking at him, and I saw her eyes flick over both of us. She leaned over and whispered something in his ear, and he hurriedly fixed his buttons, then stole a glance at me that I didn't return.

"Where's Jack?" Colette said.

I rubbed my face. I told them the shortened version, ending with the fact that I'd told him to get out, and it appeared that he had.

"Unfortunately, that's a small problem compared to what I just learned," Elodie said. "We were about to head out to the red-carpet event when we found out that there's been another attack. Something bigger this time. A bomb exploded at the Emir family's compound. It killed their younger son."

"What the hell?" I pulled at a handful of my hair. "Why are they still doing this?"

"Terrorism," Elodie said calmly. "It's exactly how Lydia explained it. The Circle will hail the Saxons as heroes when the mandate is fulfilled and the Order disappears. They're escalating the attacks to stack the final outcome."

"The second we get my mom, we tell somebody," I said. "We *have* to stop them."

"Then we'd better hurry and find this bracelet. At this rate, they're going to kill half the Circle." At the sound of Stellan's voice, a sense memory came on so strong, it nearly knocked me over. Head pleasantly warm, leaning over his lap to grab his drink. Almost falling off my bar stool, my hand pressed to his chest.

"I know." I couldn't look at him. I told myself the renewed flush in my cheeks was just embarrassment at getting drunk and losing control, but the spark and sizzle in every bit of my skin that had touched his said something different.

Elodie stood up. "That brings us to tonight," she said. "The bomb was the last straw. They're canceling the rest of the film festival for security concerns. The red carpet tonight is already in full swing, but it'll be the only event."

"Which means," I said, "tonight is our only chance to steal the bracelet."

We were already late, so Stellan and I rushed to put on our formal attire. The plan had changed. Since we were now going to have to sneak inside to get the bracelet, we'd need all the distraction we could get. Suddenly, me being recognized had gone from a potential disaster to a necessity. I'd draw the eyes of all the Circle members on the red carpet, plus any regular guests and security who had watched the news in the past couple days, and hopefully no one would notice Elodie creeping in a back door to trip the electricity and steal the bracelet herself. Stellan would be with me and Colette, making sure nobody actually tried to hurt me.

"I'll do it as quickly as I can," Elodie was saying. She adjusted a strap on Colette's dress. "I don't want you out there for long. And when the lights come back on, you'll carry on like nothing has happened besides an alarming moment of old wiring plunging the party into a temporary and unremarkable darkness, then you'll say your good nights and get out before Avery actually gets arrested. And if you do get arrested . . . we'll cross that bridge when we come to it."

"That's fine," I said. Colette nodded, too. Stellan was tying his bow tie in the mirror above the bar. When he noticed me watching over the top of the little mirror I was using to put on lipstick, his finger snagged on the end of his tie. Both ends flopped to his chest.

"Hopefully we'll be long gone before they know the bracelet is missing," Elodie finished.

"It seems too . . . simple," I thought out loud.

"The best plans are." Elodie slipped into five-inch heels. "When you see a theft in the movies that revolves around bumping into just the right person at the exact right second to steal a key so someone can hang from the air-conditioning vent and unlock a padlock, you have to know it's unlikely to work. What happens if the guy with the key has bad prawns and spends the whole night in the bathroom and we can't find him?"

"All right," I said. I put my own shoes on. I was wearing a dress of

Elodie's that hit me at midcalf, all intricate gold beadwork from the torso through the slim pencil skirt.

"In fact . . ." Elodie gestured with her red-orange lipstick at me, then at Stellan. "The most complicated part of this plan is that you two have to be a team. After what I saw earlier, I'm wondering if you can handle that."

Colette's eyes got wide. Stellan started to defend us, but I got there first. "Drop it, Elodie. Yes. We've got it under control."

She just shrugged.

"Okay. We're all set except—" I looked around automatically for Jack. The obvious hole in our crew lanced pain through my gut again. "We're all set. Let's do this."

CHAPTER 30

The red carpet had been going on for at least two hours by the time we got there. Our driver wound his way through the paparazzi, and there were so many flashbulbs popping ahead, they could have been strobe lights. Bleachers full of fans waving and yelling and wielding their own cameras lined the opposite side of the road. The red carpet began where we were getting out of the car, then flowed up a set of stairs, where a dozen people, most of whom I recognized, stood smiling and waving.

"That's the cast of Alejandro Ruiz's new movie," Colette said, leaning past me to look out the window. "I was supposed to talk to him on the carpet. I almost forgot this is actual business."

Elodie nodded. "Colette, you get out first, I'll come with you, and Avery, you get out a couple minutes later. Try to draw the whole crowd so nobody sees me sneak around back."

"I know," I said, peering out into the mass of people.

As soon as the car door opened, I was blinded by even more camera flashes. Colette, perfectly poised and practiced, smiled and waved and took the driver's hand to step out of the car. Elodie followed and shut the door behind her, plunging Stellan and me back into darkness.

Colette turned into *Colette LeGrand, A-lister* immediately, posing and winking at cameras and giving cheek kisses to actors who, a few months ago, I would have freaked out about being this close to.

"People should notice me pretty quickly," I said to Stellan. Since we *wanted* everyone to recognize me, I'd pinned my hair up, only pulling dark strands around my face. I'd also replaced my brown contacts with the clear ones. "But we should find someone in the Circle to talk to, anyway, and they'll make a big enough deal to draw even more of a crowd."

Stellan looked out over my shoulder. "There," he said, gesturing to a middle-aged couple talking with a group off to the side of the carpet. "Cousins of the Fredericks. She's a huge gossip."

I nodded, and a silence more awkward than it usually was between us filled the car.

"Avery—" Stellan said. He was cut off by the door opening. We both jumped, and Elodie poked her head in.

"We have to go through metal detectors." She pulled a gun out of her bag and dumped it on the seat, then turned to Stellan. "Maybe you should stay here, just in case we need the weapons."

He shook his head. "I'm not leaving Avery and Colette alone out there."

Elodie pursed her lips and looked over her shoulder. "I don't like this," she said, but slammed the door and hurried back to Colette.

Stellan removed his own gun from his tuxedo jacket and set it next to Elodie's. "They'll be here in the car if we need them," he said, like he was trying to convince himself, and then we were quiet for a few seconds until he took an anticipatory breath.

I spoke before he could say anything. "It's okay. You really don't have to explain." My breath fogged the car window. "You don't have to pretend you care."

He took my arm, turned me roughly to face him. "*That's* what you think? I stopped it *because* I care." He dropped my arm, scowling, and I fixated on the cuffs of his white shirt at the wrists of his tuxedo jacket.

I looked out the opposite window, at lines of limousines and the sea of flashbulbs from tourists' cameras. This was feeling uncomfortably like my fight with Jack. "I remember *someone* telling me that caring doesn't get you anywhere in the Circle."

"You're misquoting me. I said being *nice* doesn't get you anywhere. It's different. But I do care, which is why I didn't want . . ." He huffed out a frustrated breath. Colette and Elodie were halfway down the carpet now. "I drank too much, too, and I wasn't thinking straight. I shouldn't have pushed you and now you're angry."

"You didn't push me—" I could tell I was blushing furiously. I couldn't believe we were *talking* about this. And talking about it now, of all times. Elodie glanced back at the car. "Is it time for us to get out?"

"Probably," he said. He reached past me to the door handle.

"I'm angry because you're just as bad as everybody else," I blurted out. "You're entitled to feel however you want, but I don't need to be protected from making what *you* think is a bad choice. It wasn't your choice. It was mine."

Stellan stiffened, leaning halfway across my lap. The door opened, leaving Stellan's arm floating in midair. The driver held out a hand for me, and I took it.

Cameras turned in our direction. Stellan stepped out of the car, buttoning his tuxedo jacket and grinning at the cameras. His hair was pushed away from his face, and he looked polished and comfortable and like he belonged here. Anyone who didn't recognize me would think *he* was famous and I was a random plus-one.

He offered me his arm. I took it. "Smile," he said, the stiffness contrasting with his own confident grin. "Pretend you belong, and they'll believe you do. That's half the game."

I smiled. I waved. I saw a few people notice me, then do a double take. Then whisper.

I kept my hand firmly in the crook of Stellan's elbow as we made our way toward the couple he'd said were Circle.

Out of the corner of my eye, I saw him lean in closer. "Listen." He smiled at a camera whose owner had run across the carpet to pause in front of us, and when it was gone, he lowered his voice even more. "I know your choices being taken away is your favorite point of moral outrage right now, but it's not that simple. I'm pretty sure what we were about to do takes *two* people. That makes it my decision as much as yours. And I don't feel comfortable taking advantage of a girl who was drunk and upset and otherwise not thinking clearly. And yes," he said stiffly, when I tried to get a word in, "*taking advantage* is what it's called when a guy has to get a girl drunk for her to look in his direction. Okay?"

"I wasn't—"I glanced over my shoulder and smiled mechanically. A lady in an emerald-green dress was talking to a security guard, and they were both looking my way.

We were approaching the Fredericks. Wait, I wanted to say. How does that mean you feel about this? How does that mean *I* feel about this? *Was* it just because I was drunk and upset? If it was, would I still, right now, be thinking about what would have happened if we hadn't stopped?

At least one thing was certain, though. My hand tightened

around his arm, and I kept a bland smile on my face as I whispered, "I knew exactly what I was doing. There was no taking advantage."

Stellan blinked down at me. "In that case, I don't know whether you were doing it to make him mad, or to make yourself feel better, or you actually just had too much to drink . . ." Stellan leaned closer and sparks shot through me. "But if you're upset because you think I didn't want to, you should know that's not true. Really not true."

Flashbulbs went off in my eyes, and then the Fredericks turned.

"Mr. Frederick," Stellan said, slipping right back into his role. "Mrs. Frederick."

They looked annoyed at being interrupted until they saw me. Mrs. Frederick's hand fluttered to her chest. Mr. Frederick said hasty good-byes to the knot of guests they'd been talking to. The security guard I'd seen earlier had a walkie-talkie to his mouth.

My pulse was racing, my arm still clamped in Stellan's. Elodie and Colette were still on the steps. *Anytime now,* I thought in Elodie's direction.

Before I knew what was happening, there was a crowd around us, hanging on my every word as I answered the Fredericks' questions.

Yes, I am American, even though I'm part of the Saxon family. I grew up in the US. No, I didn't know Eli Abraham before that night. It is horrible, yes.

Despite what the news was reporting, most of the group—who were likely all Circle, I realized—were looking at me like I was the second coming. They didn't seem too ready to turn over one of their own, even if she was a wanted criminal. It was the guests on the periphery who hung back like they thought I might be hiding a gun in my tiny beaded bag.

I glanced again at Colette and Elodie, now standing near the front doors. Colette gave me a small nod—and then approached the security guard patrolling the side of the building and pointed to me.

The guard squinted, frowning.

Behind them, Elodie slipped around to the back of the building.

I squeezed Stellan's arm, and he touched my hand in acknowledgment. Phase one complete. He leaned down and whispered in my ear, "The only security I've seen are the ones standing at the front doors and a few more at the sides. They've let a couple people in, probably for the bathroom, so Elodie won't seem too suspicious, but if the guards start to go inside, I'll signal and we'll make an even bigger scene. For now just keep on with this."

I nodded and tried my best to stay engaged in conversations as I waited nervously for the lights to go out. The security guards here probably didn't have the authority to arrest me themselves, but they could have called the police, so I kept listening for sirens in the distance.

And then a car did pull up at the end of the red carpet, but it wasn't the cops. Lydia Saxon got out, followed by her brother.

Stellan saw them at the same time I did, and grabbed my hand, pulling me away. It was too late. My sister's gaze zoomed in on me the second she stepped out of the car, and a chill ran through me like lightning. "I thought they weren't in town," Stellan said.

"Jack said he didn't tell them we were here," I replied. But they could have showed up of their own accord.

"They can't do anything to you in front of all these people," Stellan said.

I nodded. The twins were making a beeline for us, bypassing the photographers calling for them to take a photo. They were a striking pair: Lydia's hair slicked back in a sleek, modern ponytail that grazed the top of her strapless red dress, and Cole's matching dark hair and olive skin topped off with a red bow tie and his usual smirk.

"Avery. So lovely to see you here." Lydia leaned in to kiss me on the cheek, and raised an imperious eyebrow when she saw my hand still caught in Stellan's. I pulled it away and took both her hands in mine, partly to make sure she wasn't hiding any weapons.

"I didn't realize you'd be at the festival," I said. I'd *hoped* that even if they realized I was here they'd leave me alone since I'd promised Alistair the tomb. They must not trust me at all.

"Last-minute decision," Cole cut in. The top of his head only reached Stellan's shoulder, but he looked up at him with a sneer. "We didn't realize you'd be here, either. With the help."

They didn't realize I'd be here? The cameras flashed like a swarm of fireflies in the night.

The Fredericks asked Cole a question, and he turned away to talk to them, but Lydia stayed right next to me. "I can't wait to hear all about what you've been doing in Cannes," she said with that sparkling smile that had tricked me into believing she cared.

I glanced up at the theater. What was Elodie doing? Could she not find the electricity?

"Avery." Colette came up beside me, her gaze cutting to Lydia. "There's a director I'd like you to meet. Come with me for a second?"

I nodded, grateful. Maybe I could hide until—

The lights cut off. *Finally.*

There were stray giggles, like there always seemed to be when darkness fell unexpectedly. And one sharp intake of breath from close by.

I felt Lydia clamp a surprisingly strong hand around my wrist. "Avery, get out of here," she whispered.

"What?"

"It's not safe for us to be here right now." Lydia's whisper was no longer calm. "The electricity wasn't supposed to—just go."

A chill came over me. "What did you do?" I pictured the milling crowds, and then the attack at the Emirs'. Lydia and Cole didn't come to find me, and they didn't come to walk the red carpet.

Stellan was already pulling me and Colette away from the building and the crowd.

Lydia followed us. "Take your Keeper boyfriend if you want. I won't say anything. Just get out of here."

"Are these people going to get hurt?" Stellan said, low enough that no one else could hear us under the low hum of voices. My eyes had started to adjust to the dark, and I saw that he had Lydia's wrist, just like she had mine.

Lydia tried to pull away. Cole was headed toward us. "I can't be sure it'll go off when the power comes back, but it might. If anyone's too close . . ."

"You set a bomb? Here?" Stellan said just as I said, "Elodie. Call her. Now."

Stellan grabbed his phone with the hand not holding my sister.

"We have to get everyone out of here," I said.

I opened my mouth to scream, but Lydia silenced me. "Are you sure you want to do that?"

The scream died on my lips. They still had my mom, and I couldn't be sure Lydia was on the same page as Alistair.

Stellan muttered something into the phone in French, urgent.

"Lydia, these people will *die*," I pleaded.

"It wasn't meant to go off until later," she answered, glancing back at the building. "When everyone was out. We'd grab the bracelet and no one would know."

Of course they knew the bracelet was here. It had probably been the last thing Jack told them before he found out what they were really doing. "I don't care," I said. "We have to evacuate—"

"No! We can't say anything or it'll be obvious we knew about it." Lydia looked surprisingly panicked.

I shook my hand out of hers. I'd let too many innocent people die already. If my mom was here, I'm sure she would agree it was worth the risk.

I took a deep breath and screamed, "Fire!" It was obvious there was no fire, but I kept yelling. Murmurs went up through the crowd. "Everybody get away from the building!" I screamed. Someone else in the crowd caught the panic and screamed, too, and that was it. A couple people started running, and then the crowd stampeded toward us. I yanked Stellan and Colette to the side, behind a car, away from the crush of bodies. The lights above the red carpet flicked back on.

The screams grew louder for a second as the crowd blinked away the brightness—and then they were drowned out by an explosion that rocked the red carpet.

CHAPTER 31

I flung my hands over my head. Stellan threw himself across me and Colette, and the explosion blasted out with a roar and the smell of unnaturally chemical smoke and heat condensed into one gust, like an industrial oven had just been opened. Bits of debris pelted my exposed skin. Overhead, there were mini explosions as the spotlights shattered, and I pulled my head from Stellan's chest in time to see tiny shards of glass fall in a rain of glitter.

Stellan had my shoulders. He was mouthing something I couldn't hear. "What?" I said, and I couldn't hear myself, either. The only sound in my ears was a ringing like a low bell. "Are you okay?" he mouthed. I nodded. "Are you?" Bits of glass made his hair sparkle, and he had a scrape across his left cheek. "I'm fine," he said, and I heard it this time, as if from far away. Colette sat up slowly, and nodded when I asked her the same question.

I stood up. There was a beat of complete stillness, the whole red carpet frozen in place, like we'd been turned to stone. Beat. Mr. Frederick, slumped against a wall, glasses askew, holding his head. Beat. Miranda Cruz, the actress, blood running down her face and onto her white dress. Beat. A photographer crouched over his camera shattered on the ground, staring at the smoke from inside the building. Beat. I searched for Lydia—and she was gone. So was Cole.

And then everyone was running. Stellan and I fought the tide toward the building.

The closer we got to the theater, the more people we saw stumbling away or collapsed on the carpet, bloodied but alive. Thank God the event wasn't inside. Stellan shoved open the door we'd seen Elodie go through, and thick dark smoke billowed out.

I choked, coughing into my elbow. "Elodie!" I screamed through the coughs.

A man in a tuxedo staggered out, his face in his elbow, followed by a security guard helping a woman walk.

"Is there anyone else?" I yelled. They didn't even seem to hear me.

The smoke cleared enough to see flames licking up a wall inside. Stellan shuddered—I knew he didn't like fire—but he said, "I'm going in. Stay here."

Before I could protest, he took a deep breath and darted inside, and even though praying wasn't usually my thing, I prayed that the fire-retardant skin we thought he had would keep him safe. And then I ran to another door and yanked at it until I was convinced it was locked. Around the far side was an unlocked door, but it was too dangerous to contemplate going inside. I screamed for Elodie and then propped it open with a loose brick just in case and ran back around the front.

Colette was waiting at the top of the stairs, people starting to gather around her. "Stellan!" I screamed in the open door. "Elodie!"

There was a flash of movement from behind the wall of smoke.

Figures appeared. As I watched, one of them fell.

I couldn't just watch anymore. I pulled the neckline of my dress up to my face and darted inside. Stellan had his arm under Elodie, pulling her along, both of them stumbling. I grabbed Elodie from him. "Come on!" I screamed, and it sent me into a coughing fit.

From nowhere, arms reached over me, pulling Elodie to her feet. I stood up, wracked with coughs.

Jack?

He pulled off his jacket and threw it to me. "Put it over your face," he said, then picked Elodie up and pushed me along in front of him, shoving me into a set of arms it took me a second to realize were Luc's. Luc grabbed Stellan around the waist, too, and the three of us burst through the door.

The air was so cold and fresh, it burned my throat. Jack set Elodie down and rested his hands on his knees, breathing deep gulps of air. Elodie blinked her eyes open, choking, dazed. Stellan dropped to his knees, coughing.

I looked at Jack, my eyes burning so much, it was hard to see. "How did you know what was going on?"

Jack shook his head. "I didn't. I was bringing you something. I've been working on it since we first found out about the Saxons. I told her to wait in the car. It's too dangerous—"

A flash of blond hair flew through the crowd, and I really had to be hallucinating this time, because there was no way I was seeing this face here, now.

And then my mother swept me into her arms.

CHAPTER 32

Sirens descended on the theater from all directions. Elodie, her whole body covered in a layer of dark soot, hauled herself up and gestured to the rest of us to follow her.

I barely noticed. My mom and I had sunk to the steps, where the red carpet was now ashy gray. I couldn't stop staring at her, like if I did, she might disappear. She was so thin and pale. She had a healing cut over one eye, and her hair was tangled and flat.

I was torn between wanting to kill Lydia and Cole for what they'd done, and wanting to throw myself into her arms and cry.

Like she'd read my mind, she pulled me to her. The stiff sleeves of my gown poked into her chest, but she just hugged me tighter. "We have to go," she whispered. "While they're distracted."

I could see it. Me and my mom, jumping in a cab, crossing a border or two before we slowed down. Doing our best to leave the Circle behind forever without a word of good-bye. Despite everything I'd said earlier—even though it had all been *true*—having my mom here in front of me and knowing I could get her to safety for good nearly changed my mind.

But then I saw Stellan, draping a handkerchief over an ugly, blistering burn that covered the back of his hand.

Jack, sweaty and smeared with ash, his jacket still around my shoulders.

Elodie, clutching a small black purse across her body like it contained a treasure. I had a feeling it did.

And Lydia and Cole, nowhere to be seen. They must have gotten away before anyone could link them to the bombing.

"I can't go yet," I said to my mom.

She took my face in her hands. She looked resigned. "I had a feeling you might say that. Let's go do what needs to be done."

I gestured to everyone else, and we slipped away through the crowd.

We looked for our car, but the driver must have taken off after the bomb exploded. Since we'd arrived late, he was probably one of the only ones to get out before gridlock shut down the street. Unfortunately, he'd taken all our weapons with him, and we had nowhere to go.

So now, we holed up in a tiny cafe on the beach a couple blocks away. Luc had shoved handfuls of euros at the girls at the counter and told them to get out.

I made my way to Jack, who was dead-bolting the cafe door. "Thank you," I said to his back. "My mom. I—" There weren't enough words to say what I wanted to say. I'd broken up with him, stormed out, and spent the rest of the evening in the arms of his ex-best friend. And he—the guy who could never break the rules—had spent that time breaking ties with the only family he'd ever had, all to save the person who mattered most to *me*.

He jiggled the doorknob—locked—and turned to me.

"Thank you so much," I said again.

He nodded and stuffed his hands in his pockets. "I'm sorry," he said. "I'm really so sorry."

I pulled at the sooty hem of my gown. "I know." I couldn't say I forgave him, because I didn't. I plucked my locket off my chest and squeezed it.

Jack's gaze dropped to my feet, and I could see him deflate, but he hid it quickly. "You should thank Rocco—Scarface—next time you see him. He's the one who actually broke her out and sent her here with Luc. I just told him what to do."

I never, in a million years, would have thought I'd have the urge to hug Scarface. And he was more loyal than I'd expected. I'd have to remember that.

I turned back to my mom. Colette had wrapped a shawl around her shoulders, being just as much a mom to my mother as she was to the rest of us. I squeezed beside my mom in a large armchair, and she took my hand and didn't let go.

Jack glanced out the front window, then sat next to Colette on the couch beside us, their sooty clothes staining the worn taupe upholstery gray. Stellan and Elodie sat on our other side, and Luc was at a rickety cafe table across the circle.

"So?" I said.

Elodie held up the bracelet she'd found inside the theater. It *was* a twin, almost exactly. I took the original off my arm, and handed it to her, too.

"The password to the second one is Boyer," I said. "We hope."

Elodie twisted the rungs on the bracelet, and we heard the pop as a portion of it rose up, just like it had on the other one. We let out a collective sigh, but the relief was short-lived. "What now?" Elodie said. "The clues said to unlock it, and we unlocked it. What are we missing?"

"I wonder if there's more to the riddles," Colette said. "Can you say the clues again?"

"The first clue was 'One step closer to unlocking the secret through a union forged in blood.' And then there was the one about the priestesses at Delphi. Then what it says on that bracelet . . ." Luc trailed off and Elodie took over, reading from the bracelet in her hand.

"'Only through the union will my twin and I reveal the dark secret we keep in our hearts.' And the other one talks about 'My twin and I will reveal all, only to the true.'"

"Then there's the mandate," Stellan reminded us. "'Through their union, the birthright of the Diadochi is uncovered.'" He looked up at me. "'Their fates mapped together become the fate of the Circle.'"

Elodie set the bracelets on the coffee table in front of her and rested her elbows on her knees. She'd wiped some of the soot off her face, and now it was eerily striped. "I keep coming back to fate mapping," she said. "'A union forged in blood.' 'Their fates mapped together.' So . . . the union *creates* something that finishes unlocking these bracelets. It has something to do with blood, we're pretty sure. But *physically*, what—"

From behind me, there was an explosion. We all jumped out of our seats, and I realized the lock on the front door had just been shot out.

The door swung open, and in came my brother and sister.

CHAPTER 33

I threw myself in front of my mom. Jack had his gun out already. Stellan reached for where his would be, and cursed to himself when he remembered it was gone with the car. They both paused when they saw that Lydia and Cole had guns already trained on us.

"Don't look so shocked," Lydia said, then turned to me. "I know Father trusts you, and I *want* to, but . . . That dress made it especially easy to plant a tracker."

I stiffened and searched the beadwork frantically until I felt my mom pluck something off my back, near my shoulder blade. A tiny black disc. Lydia shrugged a nonapology, then pointed her gun at Jack. "Jack Bishop, put that gun on the floor."

Jack hesitated, but set his gun down.

Cole gestured at my mom. "How did she get out? I told you we should have killed her."

"If you *touch* her—" I said, but my mom squeezed my hand hard.

"Don't antagonize him," she whispered. Cole didn't look amused.

"Why don't we all have a brainstorming session," Lydia said. She stood a safe distance away so she could shoot anyone who tried to tackle her. "I heard a little, but let me be sure I have this right. Something about these bracelets is still locked, the union is what will open them, and that union appears to have something to do with blood."

I looked at the door and saw Stellan do the same. He gave a tiny shake of his head. We could try to make a run for it, but the twins would kill someone before we got there.

"We're not telling you anything," I said.

"Hmm," Cole mused. "Whose head do they least want to see a hole in?" He spun around lazily, pausing on me, then Colette, but stopping on Luc. "The Dauphin heir. Of course."

Elodie drew a sharp breath, and Stellan got halfway off the couch.

"No no," Cole said, pushing his gun against Luc's skull. Stellan sat back.

"Now," Lydia said. Both bracelets sat on the coffee table between us. Lydia leaned in and picked one up.

Suddenly, there was a knife whipping through the air over her head.

Cole dodged, and the knife grazed his shoulder, then clattered to the ground with a strange hollow clunk. Plastic, and Elodie's. She must have had it strapped to her somewhere, able to get through the metal detector.

In the second it took me to process it, Elodie was already lunging off the couch toward Luc. And then there was a gunshot, and she was thrown back onto a cafe table.

I screamed. Stellan and Colette and Jack all jumped up.

"Sit!" Lydia yelled. "Or I'll hit something more vital next time."

Elodie struggled to sit up, clutching the bleeding side of her torso. She was alive. Stellan started toward her.

"Stay," Lydia said.

"She'll bleed out." Stellan perched at the edge of his couch. "Let me bandage it."

"She should have thought of that before trying to kill my brother," Lydia spat. "If you tell us everything you know quickly, then I'll consider letting you help her."

"No," Elodie choked with a grimace. "Don't tell them."

"As the maid has already determined," Lydia continued, like nothing had happened. She was still holding a bracelet in one hand and her gun in the other. "Blood is the key to this lock. What we need to know is how that works." None of us said anything. "First of all, how could there be a *union* of blood? There's the obvious, which I'm sure you've already discussed. A child."

Jack shot Lydia a look so full of hatred, even I shivered. "There's no way that could work."

Lydia raised her eyebrows. Clearly he'd never talked back to her before. "It's true it's a little outside our time range, but let's run with it for now. If that did turn out to be correct, what would it mean, scientifically?"

Still, none of us said anything, even though we *had* had some ideas.

Elodie's face was turning pale, and she took an unsteady breath. Suddenly, Luc sat forward. "A baby's DNA is the combination of its parents'," he said.

"Luc, don't help them," Elodie grunted.

"I'm not letting you die, El," he said, then continued, "If the parents are some special thing themselves, the combination of their blood could be something else entirely."

We were all gaping at him. It wasn't that I thought Luc was stupid, but I also hadn't thought he'd been paying much attention to the technical details, and here he was parroting theories Elodie had been putting together for days.

My siblings didn't seem as impressed. "So you're saying the DNA in a baby's blood could *unlock* some kind of latch built into this bracelet? A human biological substance could change a nonhuman substance significantly enough to alter it?" Cole said skeptically. "So we have Avery make a baby with whoever the One is, wait nine months, extract its DNA, inject said DNA into these bracelets, and poof! We have four pieces of ugly jewelry instead of two?"

"Interesting theory," Lydia said.

Cole curled his lip. "Let's just smash the things."

"If we smash them, we damage whatever's inside," Lydia said witheringly.

"Now you know as much as we do," I said. Elodie was trying to keep pressure on her wound, but I could tell she was fading. Stellan was poised on the edge of the couch like it was killing him not to run to her. "Let us help her, please."

Lydia shook her head. "Even if the baby hypothesis is true, it doesn't help our cause at the moment. You must have other theories."

"We don't," Jack said. "We're not lying, Lydia. We thought the passwords would unlock the bracelets, but they've only done it halfway."

I wrapped my locket around my fingers nervously and frowned when my fingers came away bloody. One of the cuts on my chest from the explosion must still be bleeding.

I started to wipe it off on my dress—but then stared at the finger. Wait.

Blood. What if this were far simpler than we were making it?

I pressed my lips together.

"What?" Lydia demanded. Of course she'd seen that.

I let my hands fall by my sides. "Nothing."

Lydia came behind me, keeping her gun moving between all of us. "How much longer do you think the maid can hold out?"

Stellan growled low in his throat, and Colette let out a tiny sob. Elodie's eyes were slipping closed.

"Or maybe I'll maim one of the Keepers," Lydia continued. "You're far too fond of both of them, anyway." She glanced at Jack, then at Stellan. I saw her eyes land on the burn on his hand. The handkerchief had slipped off it, and it was already far less red; almost healed. Lydia squinted at it, but there was no way she could realize what it meant.

I tasted bile in the back of my throat. "I was just going to say . . ." I stalled.

Lydia peered over my shoulder. "Blood," she said, running her fingers across my collarbone. Damn. She must have seen me look at it. "Blood has DNA. That's what you're thinking, isn't it? Like combining blood instead of waiting for a baby."

Elodie forced one eye open. "Not the same," she said, her voice weak. "Mixing people's blood together like you're making a cocktail doesn't combine DNA."

"We're guessing here," Lydia said. "Who's to say this isn't the right guess?"

"So we take Avery's blood, and that of the One, mix them together, and inject *that* into the bracelet. I suppose that does cut nine months out of the equation, which is a plus, but it still sounds absurd," Cole said.

"But easy enough to try," Lydia countered. She pointed to Luc. "He's as likely to be the One as any of them."

Cole grabbed Luc's forearm and dragged a knife across it, then passed it to Lydia. Luc sagged back against the couch, wide-eyed. Lydia leaned over me and swiped more blood from my chest. She wiped Luc's blood onto her thumb, rubbed her fingers together, and coated the raised part of the bracelet in her hand.

Even though the rest of us knew nothing that united Luc and me would work, we all watched the bracelet. I watched Cole and Lydia. Maybe while they were distracted, we could overpower them. But they didn't drop their guard.

After a few seconds, as the bracelet just sat there, doing nothing, we all relaxed again.

"It's not him," Lydia said softly. "You all knew that wouldn't work." She went perfectly still for a moment, then dragged the knife deeper across my chest. I gasped, clutching at the stinging cut, and felt hot blood ooze out through my fingers. My mom pulled me close.

Lydia whirled around. Stellan was still on the edge of the next couch over, just a couple feet away. Before I even understood what she was thinking, she slashed out at his forearm with the same knife and wiped the blade in her hand, mixing his blood with mine.

"No," I choked, pulling out of my mom's grasp. Next to me, the rolled-up sleeve of Stellan's shirt was turning crimson. He watched Lydia, mesmerized, as she picked up the other bracelet. She slapped her bloody palm inside it, staining the gold red.

For a second, nothing happened.

And then Napoleon's twin bracelet started to smoke.

CHAPTER 34

"The blood is melting it." Lydia set the bracelet on the coffee table. "Or heating it. Or something. It's a lock. I was *right*."

I felt a hand come around mine, and slipped my bloody fingers through Stellan's. Drops of crimson from our clasped hands fell onto the cafe's worn hardwood floors. We couldn't have been sure before, but there it was: the union was us. Our very own map of fates was real. Stellan was part of the thirteenth bloodline, and even if it wasn't getting married, we, together, meant something.

And apparently, it was far more than symbolic power.

Lydia whirled. "It is him. I *knew* it. When we first walked in, I was surprised he wasn't worse off than that tiny little burn—and just since we've been sitting here, it's healed the rest of the way, hasn't it?"

She was right—as I looked closer, I could see that where the burn had been, there was nothing more than new pink skin, pearlescent like the rest of Stellan's scars.

"How is that possible?" Cole snapped.

"I knew Avery wouldn't get so attached to some nobody Keeper just because he's pretty," Lydia went on, almost proudly.

Stellan let go of my hand.

"This has to do with the thirteen thing that keeps getting mentioned, doesn't it?" Lydia said.

On the coffee table, the bracelet was still smoking.

"But if the thirteenth thing is a person . . . ," Lydia continued. "It means . . . a thirteenth *family* of the Circle?"

"But there were twelve Diadochi," Cole said, contempt and suspicion in equal measure evident in his voice.

"And Alexander." Understanding dawned on Lydia's face. "That's the thirteenth family, isn't it? Everyone thinks he had no heir, but what if he did?"

"But—" Cole sputtered. "But that means—the mandate says—he's the One?"

"Anyone from that bloodline." Lydia perched on a floral ottoman, her gun still in her hand. Despite everything, I was impressed she was putting it all together so quickly. "That's it, isn't it?"

"But the bloodline of the One is—they're supposed to rule over—" Cole pointed the gun at Stellan.

Lydia jumped between them. "That means he's important. We *need* him."

Grimacing, Cole turned back to Luc.

And then there was a popping noise. The gold bracelet snapped into two.

We all gaped at it. Lydia reached for it with her bloody hand, but Elodie said weakly, "No! You don't want to destroy whatever's inside."

Lydia handed the bracelet to Jack. "Open it."

He took it, but put it behind his back. "We got you this far. Let us help Elodie."

Lydia sighed. "Fine."

Stellan leaped up and was laying Elodie on the couch and putting pressure on her wound in seconds.

"Now open it," Lydia said to Jack. "And, Cole, keep an eye on the maid."

"Give me the other gun," Cole said, gesturing to where they'd made Jack lay his on the floor. Lydia handed it to him, and he kept his own trained on Luc, and Jack's on the rest of us.

"Hurry up," Lydia said.

Jack met my eyes. What else could we do? He tugged gently, and it came apart.

Jack glanced up at the rest of us, then pulled a folded piece of paper out of the bracelet, and very carefully straightened and unfolded it.

The paper was only a couple inches wide, and three times that length. I could tell it was about to crumble in Jack's hands. He squinted at the tiny writing.

"Read it," Lydia said. "Need I remind you that we could just kill you all and take the bracelets now that they're open? I don't know why I'm being so nice, but you may as well take advantage of it."

I knew why. She still hoped that somehow, after everything she'd done, that I'd still want to be one of them. She knew I wouldn't if she killed my friends. As crazy as Lydia was, she actually cared about her family.

"Read the scroll," Cole demanded. "I'm tired of the stalling."

Jack looked around at all of us, then cleared his throat. "It's in French. At the top it says, *Transcription of writings discovered in the tomb of Alexander the Great, in his own city, within the thirteenth at the center of twelve. This is the treasure for which I'd searched half my life. There is more—a remedy—but I fear it will only make matters worse, so that I left buried. I warn you out of duty to the Circle. Were this to fall into enemy hands, it would mean nothing but ruin.* It's signed *Napoleon Bonaparte, 1801.*"

We glanced at each other, confused. That made it sound like Napoleon was going to *tell* us what he found in the tomb, not where the tomb actually was.

"Is that all?" Lydia said.

Jack shook his head and read, "*Dearest Helena, I hope you are safe and have not discovered this too late to rid the—traitors . . . no, usurpers,*" he said. "*Rid the usurpers of their power and take back what is rightfully yours.*" We all stole confused looks at one another. Usurpers? "*Since the moment you were born,*" Jack continued, "*I knew I'd do anything to protect you the way I couldn't protect my son, the ruler of the world as far as you can see, or his son after him—your father.*"

Lydia drew in a sharp breath. "My son," she murmured. "And his son after him. The person writing this is—"

"Olympias," Elodie croaked. Stellan was tying the arms of his tuxedo shirt around her torso. "Alexander the Great's mother."

"Alexander's son died young, though," I thought out loud.

"He was a teenager," Jack said. "Not necessarily too young to have a child."

"That's who she's writing to," I breathed. "That child. Helena. Olympias's great-granddaughter."

We all got quiet, and Jack kept reading. "*After they stole my son's dynasty, the Diadochi wished to be linked in such a way that they'd be truly blood. Brothers.*"

"Stole?" I said.

"And *usurpers,*" Stellan agreed. "Keep going."

"*But they had underestimated a woman for the last time. The Order of Olympias and I—*"

"The Order," Lydia whispered. "Do you think—"

"Yes," Colette said shortly. "It has to be."

Jack started again. "*The Order of Olympias and I linked them as*" they demanded, but they could not know I'd planted the seed of their destruction."

Goose bumps rose on my arms, and we all looked at one another silently. There was no denying it now. Olympias wasn't talking about the Diadochi as Alexander's chosen heirs, as the Circle always believed. She was talking about them as thieves—of power, of *her* line's birthright as kings.

Jack held up the scroll. "That's all on this one."

Everyone looked at the other bracelet, then at me and Stellan. He had just finished wrapping Elodie up, and now sat in just a white T-shirt. Lydia jumped up from the ottoman, unceremoniously wiped more blood from his arm, then my chest, and swiped it onto the lock on the second bracelet. Minutes later, we pulled out the second scroll, and Jack started reading again.

"*All you'll need to fulfill the Diadochi's destiny is a female of the line. Be sure she has the violet eyes—that will ensure she has enough of the blood, in the correct configuration.*" Jack looked up at me before he continued. "*Her blood, together with yours, will create*"—his voice wavered—"*will create a plague.*"

"A *plague?*" Stellan said. Cole laughed, harsh and ugly. Everyone else just looked stunned.

"Keep reading," I said.

"*Repeat the Bacchic rites performed when they were linked, with the united blood in their cups. Only the barest drop of the virus is necessary, and the kingdom shall be yours, to the ends of the world.*"

We were all quiet for a long moment. Finally, Elodie broke the silence. "The curse of Olympias," she murmured. Her eyes were closed, but it was a huge relief that she was with it enough to understand what was going on. "I've heard of it. I never thought . . ."

"Does that mean *this* was the weapon in the tomb?" said Cole. "I thought it was supposed to be a weapon against the Order."

Lydia curled her lip at him. "You still care about the Order? According to this, the Order were ineffectual even two thousand years ago. *This* has to be what the mandate meant the whole time. We thought it meant the Order because it was talking about the *greatest enemies*. But it's the Circle who have always been one another's enemies."

Next to me, my mom shuddered.

"Were you guys listening?" I said. "Anyone in the Circle could get this virus if they ingested our blood. *You* wouldn't even be immune."

"Nobody lick Avery or Stellan," Elodie said weakly. I gawked at my bloodied hands, which had suddenly turned into weapons.

Lydia looked at her own hands, too, holding them farther away from her body. "Napoleon said on that scroll that there's a remedy in the tomb. We can still find it. And if not, we'll figure it out. Modern medicine has plenty on whatever scientific advances this woman thought she discovered."

Cole cut her off. "So all we need is to mix their blood and have someone drink it?"

"Not even drink it," Lydia said. "From the sound of this, it'd take just a drop. We might not even have to infect anyone. Just the fact that we have this . . ." I could see the wheels turning in her head. "I don't know what we can do with it, but we can do *something*."

"Not without our blood, you can't," Stellan piped up.

Lydia looked down at her hands again, and at the knife on the ottoman, and I could see in that second what she was thinking.

"We have to wash it off where it's already mixed," I said under my breath. "Off of us, and Lydia."

Jack heard me, and was nodding. We both glanced at Cole, who still had his own gun trained on Luc, and Jack's on us. If we tried to run . . .

"Get ready," Jack said.

"For what?" I whispered, but before I could put it together, Jack took a deep breath and vaulted out of his chair.

Cole pointed the gun at him calmly.

"Jack!" I screamed.

Cole pulled the trigger.

The gun clicked hollowly.

Cole frowned and pulled the trigger once more—one more ineffectual click—and then Jack tackled him. Cole's second gun went off, shooting through a crystal chandelier overhead and into the roof, sending bits of plaster raining down.

"Cole!" Lydia screamed, pointing her own gun in their direction, but obviously afraid to shoot at the writhing mass of arms and legs.

I snatched Lydia's knife off the ottoman and had it at her side before she could cross the circle of chairs to her brother. "Don't move."

She was still for a second, then twisted, trying to knock my knife away. I remembered all my lessons this time. I swung the knife out of her reach and swiped her legs out from under her with one foot. She fell on the ottoman, and I held her down with one knee.

And then Stellan was beside me, wrenching Lydia's gun out of her hand.

Across from us, Luc had thrown himself into the fray, and together, he and Jack ripped away Cole's gun. Jack clocked Cole in the temple with the butt of it, and Cole slumped to the ground.

Lydia shrieked.

Then Jack picked up his own gun from where Cole had dropped

it on the couch. He crossed to where he'd been sitting earlier, and retrieved the clip of bullets from under the overstuffed chair and clicked them back into the gun. He must have taken it out before he set down the gun in the first place. But if it hadn't worked, and Cole had pointed the loaded gun at him instead . . .

I let out a shaky breath, my heart still pounding like a bass drum in my ears.

"Cole! Let me see if he's okay!" Lydia writhed, trying to break free.

"He'll be fine." I shoved her back down and turned to Stellan. "We'll lock them up, but first we have to get the blood off her and us."

Stellan threw her over his shoulder. "Colette," he said as we rushed out of the cafe. "Get Elodie to an ambulance."

My mom was on our heels. "What can I do?" she said.

"Go with Colette and Elodie," I said. She hesitated, but the farther I could get her away from danger, the better I'd feel. "Please."

She finally nodded, kissed me on the head, and ran back. We continued away from the cafe.

Lydia was screaming obscenities. "Is there a fountain?" I yelled over her.

"We'd just be contaminating that water."

I looked around frantically. "The beach. That'd have to dilute it enough."

We darted out into the sand, and I kicked off my heels. Within seconds, we were plunging into the freezing water, pushing against the waves crashing on the shore, the salt stinging my cuts and my gold dress waterlogged and heavy and dragging on me in a way that made me flash back to Greece. I pushed down the panic and heaved the knife as far as I could out to sea—hopefully it would sink before it cut some unsuspecting tourist, but even that would be less dangerous than having it covered in our blood. Stellan threw Lydia into the surf, and I grabbed her, blinking salt water out of my eyes and rubbing at the traces of our blood on her hands.

"Just stop it," she spat. We were about the same size, but she was strong, and it was only the crashing waves that put us on equal footing. "You think you're so good. You think you're not like us. You are. You just don't know it yet."

A wave crashed higher, water spraying into my face. "Lydia—"

My sister's hair stuck to her face in dark tendrils. "Wait until you have something you care enough about to fight for it. Then you'll do whatever you have to. Then you'll understand."

She looked at Stellan, washing off his own hands and arms in the waves, his white shirt glowing in the almost-full moon, and then wrenched away from me and threw herself into the sea. Stellan caught her with a sweep of his arm and held her, kicking.

I ducked under, scrubbing at myself. "Am I clean?" I held out my arms to let Stellan look at my neck, my chest, my arms in the moonlight. We both ignored my struggling sister under his arm.

"You're still bleeding, but I think the mixed blood is gone."

The waves pushed us back into shore, and Stellan dumped Lydia in the sand. She scrambled to her feet, tripping over her sodden formal gown. "Where's Cole?" she demanded, and then we all saw Jack and Luc standing over a crumpled form in the sand.

Lydia ran toward them. "Cole!" she screamed. She threw herself into the sand beside her brother, who was still bleeding from his head.

"He'll be fine, Lydia. Stop screaming," I said, and grabbed Jack's arm. "We have to get them out of here. Take them someplace where we can hold them until we figure out what to do."

Before he could answer, a group of cars screeched to a halt on the street above, and at least a dozen people piled out.

Jack cursed. "Saxon security."

My mouth went dry. The men were sprinting toward the beach.

"Here!" Lydia screamed. "Hurry!"

Stellan pulled out Cole's gun and faced the oncoming wave of people.

"No!" I said. "Everybody run. There are too many of them. Luc! Go!"

Jack nodded. Stellan pointed his gun down at the twins.

"No!" I said. "Don't."

"Why not?" he growled. "We can't let them go. They're going to release a *plague*."

Lydia put her hands up. "We won't," she sobbed. "We're not stupid. Put down the gun, and we'll wait until our security gets here and talk—"

"You don't believe her, do you?" Stellan didn't drop his gun.

I didn't. But . . . "They don't have our blood. And they're still—" I cut off. *They're still my family,* I finished in my head. It sounded crazy, after everything, but it was true. "Please don't," I said out loud.

Jack reached around me and grabbed Stellan's wrist. "Kill them, and the guards will kill you."

"Please," I begged.

Stellan's jaw clenched, but he finally dropped his arm. And then the three of us, plus Luc, were running. I looked back to see Lydia watching us silently. We held each other's eyes for a few seconds, and then the dark swallowed her.

CHAPTER 35

A couple days later, we were back in Paris.

I woke up in the bedroom of the apartment Jack and I had shared in Montmartre. My mom, who had been sleeping next to me, was already in the shower.

I stuck my head out into the living room. Jack was asleep on the couch. I watched him for a few seconds, the rise and fall of his hand on his stomach, his shirt pulled up a few inches, exposing the strange scars on his side that I still didn't know the meaning of. His dark hair, long enough now to be a little wavy, spread over the pillow.

He hadn't said anything more about our breakup, and I hadn't, either. I truly thought I'd lost him forever, and now I wasn't so sure. He trusted too blindly, too deeply, but so did I. I always thought I couldn't let anyone in, but it wasn't true. Over and over, I'd ripped my heart out and handed it to anyone who wanted me. I was finally internalizing that no one was worthy of that kind of blind trust, not even Jack. But maybe that didn't have to mean all or nothing.

Stellan hadn't brought up that night again, either, but there was no doubt that things were different between us. We knew now that the union didn't mean we had to marry each other, but that suddenly didn't seem like a big deal. I'd finally realized what a steady presence he was in my life. He didn't trust anyone, but I had finally realized I could trust him—and maybe more than that.

For just a second, I let myself imagine a conversation I might have had someday with Lydia, if circumstances were different. A real sister talk, about love and lust and loss and confusion and how a person's supposed to understand it all. How I suddenly felt even more confused, and even more alone.

But maybe *alone* wasn't the worst thing. Maybe what I needed right now was to learn to trust *myself.*

I shut the bedroom door.

Stellan, Elodie, and Luc had convinced the Dauphins they just happened to be at Cannes when everything happened, and they were back in Paris, Elodie's bullet wound starting to heal.

Last night, Colette had called us. Though the rest of Cannes had been canceled, Paris Fashion Week was just beginning. Madame Dauphin had gotten it postponed once, while she'd been pregnant, and she wasn't going to push it back again. They were just going to step up security and move forward, and Colette's friend and distant Dauphin cousin Emilia Deschamps was walking in the first show.

Through her, Colette had just learned that Lydia and Cole Saxon would be there as honored guests.

We'd tried to contact Lydia a few times since Cannes, but she hadn't answered. Neither had my father. They didn't have my blood and Stellan's, but they knew about the virus, and that was bad enough. Without me fulfilling the mandate, and without any other gain in power from the tomb, I wasn't sure what they'd do with that knowledge.

So we were going to confront them at the Fashion Week show. They wouldn't be expecting us, and we'd be ready to handle anything they might do. I hoped I could reason with them, and we could come to some semblance of a truce, especially because I still wasn't sure what I was going to do about the Circle. I was so recognizable now, it'd be hard to disappear. And even with my mom back, with it no longer a hypothetical, I wasn't sure I wanted to.

I put on the clothes Colette had sent over—a black beaded mini-dress, a military-inspired jacket, and chunky heels from the new collection we were seeing today. Then Jack and I—and my mom, who'd been with me every second since we'd gotten her back—made our way from Montmartre down to the Carrousel du Louvre, the mall right under the museum.

Colette and Luc met us out front, and Luc led us through mobs of paparazzi yelling not just Colette's name, but mine, too. The news had stopped reporting me as a suspect in Takumi's death, but that didn't stop the Circle from speculating about both that and Cannes. And it didn't stop the media and the world from realizing that the girl in the middle of the Eli Abraham tragedy was at the Cannes bombing and was also Colette LeGrand's new best friend.

Circle or not, *everyone* loved intrigue, especially when it involved famous people. And now the scandalous famous person was me.

We bypassed hordes of extremely thin girls in extremely strange clothing and made our way down the hall. Elie Saab. Miu Miu. Alexander McQueen. Chanel.

Colette led us to Emilia's show. There were probably only a hundred or so people here, but it was a tiny room, crowded and buzzing. We had seats in the front row, and I watched for my siblings.

Stellan and Jack were posted at the back of the room. If the twins made any attempt to kidnap me or Stellan or steal our blood, they'd be taken down in a second.

But Lydia and Cole never showed up, and soon an electronic beat boomed out of the speakers in the ceiling, and a whole line of models in tweed pantsuits, or mirrored jackets with nothing under them, or boxy cocktail dresses like mine started parading down the catwalk. People lined both sides of the runway, snapping photos on their phones and taking notes and crowding in from the back to get a better look.

I watched the clothes, but I mostly watched the people. Making sure nothing happened. Wondering where the Saxons were.

After a bit, the line of models ended, and the last of them came to the end of the catwalk, made a sharp turn, and strutted back up, stopping along the back of the stage. A white-haired man with sunglasses stood in the center, waving. Behind him, a mob of women dressed in black passed out glasses of champagne—to him, to the models, to the people in the first few rows of the crowd, including us.

The white-haired man spoke to the crowd in French. They laughed, and then he switched to English. "And I'd like to extend a special welcome to our honored guest. Cole Saxon, your family's support has been invaluable to our brand this year."

Cole appeared from backstage, smiling his smarmy fake smile. So *that's* where they were. But Lydia wasn't with him. I glanced to the back of the room and saw that Jack and Stellan had both noticed, too.

As one, the whole crowd raised their glasses of champagne in a toast, and I sipped mine without tasting it.

I didn't really want to negotiate with Cole. Lydia was the mastermind—it was her we needed to talk to. Or my father. But if creepy Cole was all we had—

And then a glass shattered, and a woman screamed.

I crouched low and yanked my mom and Colette down next to me. Jack and Stellan both rushed forward, along with people who must have been bodyguards for other guests.

One of the models at the front of the room gasped and screamed again, even louder. It took me a second to understand what she was looking at. Another model was on her knees. She was clutching at her throat, and as I watched, she looked up, bloody tears seeping from her eyes. She coughed twice more, violently, collapsed, and went still.

The whole room stared in shocked silence.

Two models down from her, another girl cried out, and when she took her hands from her eyes, there were streaks of crimson down her cheeks.

I met Stellan's horrified gaze, then Jack's. Elodie screeched to a halt behind them, her shirt loose to accommodate her bandages.

I didn't know how Cole had done it, but I knew what this had to be.

The virus.

The music kept playing, a wild electronic remix, and then it seemed to hit everyone at once. People screamed, jumping out of their chairs. A champagne flute shattered at my feet, spraying my legs with sticky liquid and bits of glass.

Someone a few seats down from me coughed and convulsed, her eyes the very definition of bloodshot, and then she collapsed—right into Jack and Stellan, who were pushing through the crowd in my direction. The white-haired man himself touched his face, then took off his sunglasses. Red tears were streaming down his cheeks.

I found Cole, making his way toward the door in the midst of the chaos. There was more than satisfaction on his face. There was pure, horrifying elation. Between us, half a dozen people lay dead or dying, some of them with frantic loved ones sobbing over them.

"You guys!" I screamed, but Jack and Stellan were laying the dead girl on the floor and couldn't hear me through the terrified shrieks of the crowd.

I pushed toward Cole myself. "What did you do?" I screamed.

Cole raised the champagne glass he was still holding, a manic grin stretching across his face.

I suddenly understood. I looked back at Luc and Colette, Circle members, frozen with glasses of champagne still in their hands. "It's poisoned," I yelled. Cole must have kept a little of our blood somehow, and a little was all it took.

Cole was disappearing out the door. "Jack!" I screamed again. "Stellan!" I didn't have a weapon on me, but somebody had to catch him. I even looked around for the injured Elodie. Finding none of them in the tidal wave of bodies, I was about to run after Cole myself when his eyes got wide. He grinned like he'd just seen something delightful.

I didn't really want to see what made him that happy, but I had to look.

There were plenty of people Cole could have been looking at, but my eyes found her immediately. My mother doubled over in a hacking cough.

Still, it took me a second to understand.

And then my whole world came apart.

"Mom!" I forgot all about Cole, and tripped over my own feet sprinting to her. I reached her just in time to catch her as she fell to her knees, coughing. She looked up, and red tears were forming in the corners of her eyes.

"Mom!" I screamed. "No! No no no!"

Just like with every other person who'd been infected, bloody tears started down her cheeks. It had taken a little longer, but there they were. Her eyes went wide, and she reached up to my face and tried to say something that ended in a choking cough. Then she went limp.

"No!" I shrieked again. I shook her. "Mom!"

Jack pushed me roughly out of the way and felt for a pulse. "CPR," he said, and compressed her chest. I leaned over her, breathing into her lungs. My own mouth filled with the taste of her blood, my eyes with tears. Chest compressions, frantic. Another breath. More compressions, for minutes, hours, a lifetime. I could tell people were gathered around me, but I didn't care.

"Mom!" I sobbed.

Colette dropped to her knees, taking my mom's hand, staring at her soft, now-blank face. "I thought she wasn't Circle."

"She's not!" I gave her another hysterical breath. "This shouldn't be happening! Maybe it's not the virus. Maybe it's something else. Call an ambulance!" I wiped the blood off my mother's face. "She's hurt. We have to stop the bleeding. She needs to go to the hospital. Call somebody!"

Hands came around mine, stopping them. "*Kuklachka,*" Stellan said gently. "She's gone."

"No. No! She just needs help. She's going to be okay." I looked around frantically. "Help! Somebody—"

Jack put two fingers to my mom's neck, waited a few seconds—then shook his head. With two gentle fingers, he closed her eyes.

It was like he'd opened mine.

I blinked a few times and realized what I was seeing. My mother. Lying there, motionless. Like every other person affected by this virus around the room. Not hurt. Dead.

I was exploding.

My heart, my brain, my insides exploded in a shower of red and blood and gore. Like a gunshot to Mr. Emerson's head. Like the blood all over my mom's face. Like flashbulbs and glass and billows of thick dark smoke. It exploded, expanded, took up every part of me. The world was ending. And I was screaming, screaming, so loud I couldn't hear myself, so loud it wasn't real, the world wasn't real, I wasn't real.

And then it all fell around me, hardened. Lava congealed into rock.

I stood up. Slowly, carefully, I took off my blood-covered studded jacket, leaving the remarkably clean dress underneath. I laid it over my mom's face—and then I turned around and walked away.

I vaguely heard voices, vaguely realized I'd been stopped, vaguely realized people were touching me. Someone was wrapping something around my shoulders. Someone else was cleaning my face with a napkin. They were talking, quietly. *What does it mean if she wasn't Circle? She must be and we just didn't know. Did anyone see where Cole went? No.*

The voices faded from my head.

My mom was gone. Mr. Emerson was gone. My own family had killed them.

No.

Stellan had been right back in Paris, in the very beginning. The Saxons were my blood, and I couldn't change that. But they weren't my family.

"Where's Stellan?" I heard my own voice say.

He was right next to me. Jack was on my other side, and they both looked worried.

I could not possibly care less.

I turned to Stellan. "I'm going to stop them from doing this to anyone else. *We're* going to stop them."

Jack took my hand gently. "Avery—" I shook him off.

"She's right," Elodie said. "The virus works. And now they know it."

"There's a cure in the tomb," Luc piped up. "We have to find it. We have to *stop* them."

"No one else in the Circle can know about this," Jack said. "Lydia and Cole are bad enough. If some of the families got wind of it, they'd be after Lydia and Cole for revenge, and who knows how it could escalate?"

I heard them, and I didn't hear them. I still heard the screaming, muted. It could be me. I might always be screaming now.

"No." I heard my own voice over the screaming, hollow. My eyes slowly focused, like I was moving through water. "We tell them."

Everyone stopped, looked at me sideways.

"We tell everyone exactly what the Saxons have been doing, and what they have the potential to do now. We should have told them the second we found out."

"It'll be World War Three," Jack said.

"If we don't tell them, it could be the Black Death all over again," Stellan countered.

"Some families will take their side, even knowing what they've done," said Luc.

"And some *won't* take their side. Some will want to choose another option." Elodie's voice cut through the din. They all looked at me. And at Stellan.

"Fine," I said.

They all looked at one another again. A soothing hand on my back, caressing my hair. Colette.

Elodie took my arm, and then her face was close to mine, forcing me to look at her. "Listen. I know this is a very bad time. But we need you here with us, and to understand what we're talking about. Can you do that, for just a little bit?"

I shook off the hands holding on to me, holding me up like I might fall over, trying to hold me together in one piece. "I know what I'm saying."

"But that would mean—"

"I know what it means." It meant the Circle wouldn't accept what we said without some reassurances. More and more, I'd come to realize the most powerful people in the world just wanted someone to follow as much as anyone did. And I had to give it to them. Alistair's voice back at their dinner table in London echoed through my head. *As much as the mandate is about finding the tomb, it's also about politics. And power. It's about a united Circle, defeating all its enemies.*

They'd have to be united behind me. Stellan had dropped into a folding chair, his head in his hands.

United behind *us.*

Someone shrieked from the hallway. Madame Dauphin dashed into the room, tears running down her cheeks.

Luc took a glance at me, then held out his arms to her. "*Maman.*"

Monsieur Dauphin followed, his broad shoulders filling the doorway. Behind him were guards, some of whom I remembered as Dauphin security. And behind them, the Fredericks from Cannes and some other familiar faces. More Circle. They came warily into the now-quiet room, surveying the damage.

"What was this? Lucien?" Monsieur Dauphin stalked into the room. I realized vaguely I should be afraid, remembering the last time I was near him, at Notre-Dame, while he was trying to force me into marriage.

Instead, I just glared at him. At all of them.

"Lucien," Monsieur Dauphin repeated, and then he turned to Colette, the only other acceptable choice among our motley crew of staff and traitors. "I asked what happened here."

Before Luc could speak, I did, from behind him. "The same people who have been killing your sons now have a biological weapon that could decimate the Circle. These are the results of a very small-scale experiment."

The crowd whispered.

I felt a hand on my shoulder, a heart pounding against my back. Stellan's hand slipped into mine. We stood in front of the people who had run his life for the past decade, and I could tell in a hollow way that he needed to hold on to me, so I let him.

But for once, I didn't need him. Or Jack, on the other side of me. Or anyone. I knew suddenly, unquestionably, that I would never be afraid again. Not of the virus, not of my siblings, not of Stellan's hand in mine and what it meant. The worst had happened. There was nothing else to be afraid of.

Monsieur Dauphin barked something in French, to Luc again. Luc looked back at us, and I nodded. He squared his shoulders. "What she's telling you is that the Order didn't do this," he said. "And they haven't been behind the assassinations, either."

Confusion shot through the group.

"Your enemy has never been the Order," I said over the whispers. "It's the Saxon family."

There was a moment of complete silence, and then the whispers turned into loud protests. I kept talking over them. "They are behind this, and the rest of the murders. And yes, I am part of their bloodline—but I'm not one of them. I'm telling you this now because I can't let this happen."

The chatter was turning angry. Jack stepped up protectively on one side of us, Elodie on the other. Luc and Colette stood out front.

Colette held up a hand. "There's more. We've discovered who the One is."

The group went quiet.

"And no"—Luc turned back to his father, his voice stronger—"it's not me. It's not any of the Circle."

He and Colette moved aside, and he gestured behind him. "It's a lost thirteenth bloodline. Alexander the Great's own bloodline."

Stellan and I were suddenly exposed, our friends flanking us. Stellan's hand squeezed mine tight enough to hurt, and it felt good.

I watched the Dauphins and everyone around them as they finally saw where our fingers intertwined, and shock dawned on their faces.

"It's true," Luc said.

"And you'd better get used to it," Colette piped up, "because they've already fulfilled the mandate. And we're all behind them."

Madame Dauphin's eyes narrowed, disbelieving.

Elodie stepped forward, meeting her gaze with no hesitation. "I no longer belong to you."

Monsieur Dauphin's big hands clenched at his sides. "And the Saxon Keeper?"

We all looked at Jack. "I'm not a Saxon Keeper anymore." He nodded at me and Stellan, then raised his head high. "I'm theirs."

Stellan's hand clenched in mine. The closest thing he had to a brother, and the guy who, until a few days ago, I thought I could be falling in love with, had just pledged himself, his life, to the two of us. Madame Dauphin's hand fluttered to her chest. The rest of them whispered.

I blinked, hollow, and stared down Monsieur Dauphin until he looked away first. The rest of the Circle members, crowded behind him, murmured excitedly.

"All of you stop." It came out of my mouth unbidden. The chatter stopped like a light switch had been flipped. "This isn't a *game*. It's not fun gossip." The cold, hard voice didn't sound like me. I caught a glimpse of myself in a mirror at the end of the runway. I still looked tiny next to Stellan, but together, the two of us and our friends surrounding us formed a wall that, from this angle, looked impenetrable. I stood in the very center, blood still decorating my face like war paint, my dress dark, heavy, like glittering armor.

The whole group was holding its breath, waiting for me to finish.

"We're going to stop them." I took one more look at my mother, at the small body on the floor, covered by an ugly couture jacket.

I'd always had a shell I could put on when I needed it. It had just never been so unbreakable. I let it form the rest of the way around me, straightening my spine, strengthening my voice, crushing any errant emotion that might still be pulsing through me until I felt blissfully, completely empty. Everything looked the same, and everything had changed.

I didn't have to consider what to say next. It was like I'd always known. "We've fulfilled the mandate. We've found what you've been looking for from the tomb." Now they just stared. "You'll do exactly what we say to stop the Saxons from hurting anyone else." The twins' faces flashed through my head. "And then I'm going to kill them."

And I would. And the Circle would help me, because I was their new leader. Stellan and I were. They were ours, as surely as if I'd branded them with the thirteen loops of my necklace. Elodie had been right earlier—some of the families would side with the Saxons. It could be World War III, and I'd be at the front lines. But there was nothing else to do.

Luc gave me a tiny nod over his shoulder and turned back to his parents, to the Circle. "You heard her. But in case that wasn't entirely clear, may I present to you Avery West and Stellan Korolev. The One, and the girl with the purple eyes, united. The new thirteenth family of the Circle of Twelve."

ACKNOWLEDGMENTS

The journey to a finished book can seem as long (and sometimes treacherous) (but fun nevertheless!) as Avery's globe-trotting adventures, and there are a lot of people who helped make this voyage a good one.

The first and biggest thanks go to my editorial team: editor Arianne Lewin and assistant editor Katherine Perkins, the only people in the world who have read all eight billion iterations of this book (sorry, guys!). Ari, you ripped the book to pieces more times than I can count and helped me put it back together into what it was always meant to be. Katherine, you always have just the right genius insight when I've hit a wall I don't think I can get through. Without you two, Avery (and I!) never would have made it this far, and I appreciate you more than I could possibly say.

To the rest of the Penguin team: fab publicity and marketing folks Lauren Donovan, Anna Jarzab, and the rest of that hardworking crew; Theresa Evangelista for a second gorgeous cover; and everyone else who helped get the book out in the world—I am so lucky to be part of the Penguin family.

To my agent, Claudia Ballard, for your continued championing of this series. And to the rest of WME, including the talented film/ TV and foreign rights departments, and especially Anna DeRoy, Erin Conroy, and Laura Bonner.

As a new author, you hear a lot about how stressful the year you debut and write book two in a series can be. Thank you to all the people who made it a lot more fun, especially:

To Dahlia Adler Fisch, who continues to be the best and smartest sounding board, advice-giver, friend, and human. I'm not sure what I'd do without you. To Sofia Embid—this is what happens when you see someone and think, *I want to be friends with her.* And then, a year of wine and books and ridiculous adventures later, you are, and it's the best. To all the amazingly talented 2015 debuts. To my favorite sister wife, Kim Liggett. To Penguin Teen on Tour! (Rachel Hawkins, Jessica Khoury, Morgan Rhodes, and Seth Fishman) for more fun than I thought it was possible to have on a book tour. To my brothers, family, and friends (Brenda Drake and the ABQ writer crew! My wonderful YA book club! Lovely online friends!), who manage to maintain enthusiasm for this crazy book-writing thing I'm doing. To my in-laws, Chuck and Sara—the crew aren't on a sailboat in this book, but a yacht is close enough, right? And to my parents, Jill and Dave, who think I can do anything, even when I'm not so sure. I'm pretty sure you'd be proud even if I just wrote down the alphabet a few thousand times, but it means a lot anyway.

A huge thank-you to everyone who read my book this year, and especially all the readers who obsess about Avery and Jack and Stellan as much as I do. You know who you are—I've met you and talked to you via e-mail and Twitter and Instagram and seen your edits on

Tumblr, and I am so impressed by your creativity and awed by your love of this series. I don't care what other authors say—*my* readers are the best.

Most of all, always, to Andrew. You put up with me, make me feel better, make me a better person. My husband is the best husband there is.

CONTINUE ON FOR A PEEK AT HOW
THE CONSPIRACY CONTINUES . . .

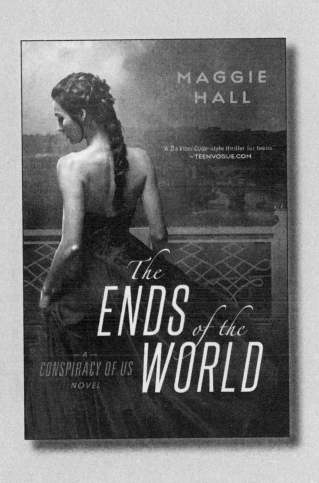

Stellan and I stood in a courtyard outside the Old City, waiting to be called in to the initiation ceremony. The plan was to watch for the box, and if it looked like what we needed, do something to pause this ceremony before it actually went through.

Above, palm trees rustled against the cream stone. We'd been to Jerusalem once before, when the Saxons were considering marrying me off to Daniel Melech, but I hadn't seen much of it that day.

For some reason, I had expected the city to be stuck in time, all old stone and desert and prayer, but I was wrong. It was also modern and clean and bustling. As I looked out the window on our car ride here, people crowded around bus stops, and bikes and cars shared the streets. Blue-and-white Israeli flags waved against a cloudless sky, and a riot of multicolored flowers peeked over balconies.

Jack had told me a little about the city's history the last time we came here. Jerusalem was one of the oldest continuously inhabited cities in the world. There had been so much devastation here—wars, natural disasters, being conquered over and over. And yet it had survived it all, on this same spot, a city of great importance to three major religions and to so many cultures through history. A melting pot and a highly contested land, a bustling modern metropolis and an ancient stronghold all in one. None of us were fans of the Melech family, but their city was a different story. If things were different, I'd want to spend time here.

Now, I brushed those thoughts aside. The last thing I needed was to get sentimental about another city, especially considering what else we'd seen on the way here.

Just around the corner from where we'd stopped the car, I'd seen a group of girls about my age, wearing military uniforms and eating Popsicles in front of a coffee shop. They all held machine guns strapped across their chests as casually as I'd hold a backpack. Nearby, another group of girls in headscarves and jeans leaned against a 50% OFF SALE sign, looking at their phones. Down the street, a group of little boys played soccer.

The worrisome part was that at least half of each group was wearing white surgical masks.

When Cole had slipped the virus into champagne glasses in Paris, a dozen people had died. The world outside the Circle had quickly embraced various theories: it was a deadly new flu, or something in the air. Some even got it right and called it a biological weapon. What they didn't know was that from this, at least, they were safe: the virus only affected Circle members.

The fact that this meant my mother was somehow related to the Circle and hadn't told me was something I hadn't been able to think about yet. What we did have to think about was that, despite the fact that there had only been the one incident, the alarm was spreading all over the globe. We could only hope that if we prevented the Saxons from releasing it further, it would die down eventually.

I realized I was clutching my phone hard enough my fingers had gone white. I shook them out then turned on the phone, looking at news sites. *Mystery Virus Airborne?* one said. *Deaths in Paris Under Investigation.*

I flipped to another tab: the online version of Napoleon's *Oraculum.* The Book of Fate.

Napoleon had found the Oraculum in a different royal tomb in Egypt, and had consulted it to make important decisions. At first we'd thought he might have used it to hide a clue, but as far as we could tell, the book had nothing to do with Alexander or Olympias's curse. I sometimes still looked at it anyway. In this online version, you chose one of the questions, selected one of the groups of stars below, read the answer. One of the questions caught my eye: *Shall I be successful in my present undertaking?*

I brushed a fingertip over one of the star groups at random, and it took me to an answer:

Choose not the path of fear, but that of love.

"Cryptic," Stellan said. I turned to find him looking over my shoulder. "If our political strategy consists of consulting an ancient Greek Magic 8 Ball, I think we need a new plan."

I clicked off the page and flipped him off.

"That's not very ladylike behavior for someone who's about to become a Circle queen."

"If I didn't know better, I'd think you were looking *forward* to this," I said. "I suppose you have gotten exactly what you wanted the whole time. Us together. The girl and the One. The only thing you're not getting is the marriage consummation. Sorry."

"Yes, that's too bad," he said wistfully. "I do prefer all my romantic encounters to be forced by awkward, tragic circumstance and witnessed by hostile strangers." He plucked at the fabric over his chest.

"Maybe I'm just here for the outfit."

Stellan and I looked ready for a cult initiation. Our thin white shifts hung loosely from our shoulders to our bare feet. No matter how much attitude Stellan gave it, his bare ankles made him look uncomfortable as he shifted from foot to foot. I could see the two tattoos on his back through the thin fabric, and also the outlines of his scars. They snaked over his bare shoulders and partway down his arms.

Stellan's "magic skin" was what had allowed him to survive the fire that left those scars. ("Stop calling it magic," Elodie would admonish every time we said the word. "It's highly advanced science we don't understand. Olympias was a genius.") The scars were how we had discovered what Stellan really was. The Circle's thirteenth bloodline—Alexander the Great's own line. The part of the mandate that said *The One walks through fire and isn't burned* was not metaphorical after all.

If the Circle knew the virus came from our blood, they might capture or kill us—either because they were afraid we could be a weapon, or because they wanted to use us as one. So since we couldn't tell them what the *union* really produced, Stellan's scars were how we'd proven our identity.

"The Great modification," the Circle had named it. It had long been rumored that Alexander was not a normal human, that something allowed him to never lose a battle, and to come back from injuries and illnesses that killed thousands of others.

I shuffled my feet on the rough pavement under my own shift. "The virgin sacrifice robes are a little cliché."

"It's cliché because every secret society in the world has taken their cues from the Circle for thousands of years, whether they realize it or not," he said, peering over my head. "To answer your question, no. As you already know, I don't want to become more of a Circle puppet than we already are. Maybe we get inside, see this box, and pull a fire alarm before we have to pledge ourselves to the world's worst people forever. But if not," he said, nudging me exaggeratedly with an elbow, "at least it'll be some comfort that if you can't put a bullet in the Saxons' heads, you can take the Circle from them and ruin their lives, right?"

He wasn't entirely wrong. But he was doing it again: trying to draw me out, trying to be friends. "No one's watching now," I said coolly. "We don't have to pretend to be a happy little couple. Save it for inside."

I wondered what was taking so long. We'd arrived half an hour ago and had been walked through the basics of the ceremony. They'd welcome us, we'd accept. We'd pledge our loyalty. We'd get the tattoos that signified our commitment to the Circle.

Jack and Elodie were pacing at the gate, making sure no unsuspecting tourists wandered in. Occasionally, I saw Jack glance back at us with something besides a Keeper's responsibility on his face.

Despite the fact that he'd nearly gotten us killed reporting on me to the Saxons for what he thought was my own good, and despite the fact that I hadn't forgotten how it felt to learn he'd been lying to me, I trusted that Jack was on our side now. He had promised his loyalty to us, and if nothing else, I knew he'd honor that. He didn't know how not to.

That didn't mean it wasn't awkward. Especially at times like now, or last night, when I could see him deliberately overlook Stellan's hand resting on my back, how I reached up to whisper in his ear. With everything else going on, that unresolved tension was the last thing I wanted to deal with, which was why I hadn't. The boy I'd cared so much about until he broke my trust and my heart. The one who was my "destiny," who I'd had this purely chemical, completely unwanted attraction to until we'd finally given in to it after too many drinks.

And then my mother had died. And then nothing mattered.

I turned when Elodie's boots clicked across the courtyard. She and Jack didn't have to wear the ceremonial robes, so she was in her usual black top and black pants. Her platinum-blond hair was as sleek as usual, but at her hairline, there was an odd patch of what could have been darker hair. I'd never seen Elodie with even a hint of grown-out roots. These really were different times. "They're ready for you. Give me your phones. They'll go in the car with everything else."

There were no weapons allowed inside Circle ceremonies. Stellan had given his up easily enough to make me remember he was just about as deadly without them. I wasn't. I could feel my little knife strapped to my thigh. I hadn't gone anywhere without it since my mom died, and I wasn't about to start now. Elodie was taking just one thing in: a slim bag strapped across her back with Alexander's bone inside, just in case.

When she'd stashed our things away, Elodie led us forward, and Stellan stiffly offered me his arm. I felt the rustling of the thin linen shift against my legs as I walked, the late afternoon breeze flapping its hem.

Elodie took her place on one side of us, Jack on the other. I felt Stellan draw me just a little closer, the ropes of muscles in his forearm tight and tense under my palm. When the four of us were alone, there might be uncomfortable moments. But here, even I had to admit it was us against the world.

With Stellan and me leading the way, we took the steps down

into the darkened cave to candle flames flickering low, and a sea of people in black.

A low chant started at the center of the group, and it moved outward until it filled the chamber. We stopped to acknowledge each person, both bowing low and raising our hands to our foreheads like a prayer. Each person responded with a modified version of the gesture, their raised hands opening before us into a sign of acceptance. Arjun Rajesh smiled. The Fredericks and the Mikados nodded formally. When we reached Luc and his father, Hugo Dauphin, Luc bowed deeply, but Monsieur Dauphin hesitated. He used to have both of us under his thumb: Stellan had been his Keeper, and the Dauphins had once tried to kidnap me and marry me off to Luc. But finally, he raised his hands, too. I felt Stellan tense just a little, and then I felt him stand straighter.

Despite everything, goose bumps rose on my arms, just like they had when the Melechs had obeyed our order last night. We were standing at the center of a group more powerful and dangerous and ancient than I could have imagined existed until recently, and they were accepting us as equals and more. *It's seductive being wanted*, Stellan had said once. He wasn't wrong. We both felt it. We both liked it.

I could tell as both our heads swiveled, searching for the next clue, that we were both still hoping it wouldn't be our lives.

As we passed, the Circle members pulled up the necklines of their black robes into heavy hoods, forming a shadowy knot that enveloped us more and more thickly as we approached the center of the cavern.

Above the crowd, on one of the walls, a symbol was etched. *Our* symbol—the symbol of the new thirteenth family. There had never been a question what it would be. I touched the locket around my neck that bore the same symbol. The thirteen-loop knot. I'd had this locket nearly my whole life, since I found it in my mom's things when I was little. I wasn't sure where the symbol had come from, but I knew it had been instrumental in the quest that had led to where we were now. Our mentor, Fitz, had used it to signify clues he wanted us to pay attention to, and before him, so had Napoleon. And now, if we did finish this ceremony, we would all be tattooed with it.

"This ritual is one the Circle hasn't performed in thousands of years," said the man who must be the master of ceremonies.

I looked around the cave. It was so dark, I couldn't see anything beyond the assembled Circle members. Did someone have the box, or could it be hidden in here?

". . . brings together the full Circle once again as we welcome back to the fold a line that has been lost for as long as we can remember," the man was saying. "The acceptance of the new thirteenth family is an important step in our growth as a Circle. I now present to you the candidates for the new thirteenth family of the Circle of Twelve. The Korolev family."

I felt Stellan look down at me. We were taking my symbol, so we were taking his name. It only seemed fair.

Behind the mass of Circle members, I could see Keepers standing against the far wall. Jack and Elodie, though, were near us. I met Elodie's eyes for a second, and she gave the smallest shake of her head. She hadn't seen anything, either.

"Repeat my words," the moderator said, translating into English after a long speech I couldn't understand. "I pledge fealty to my brothers, and may nothing come between us, to my death." We repeated the words. "I pledge to do no harm to my own, or risk losing my life. My blood, my family, my brothers, stronger as one than apart. The thirteen as one, a world ruled by blood."

"By blood," came a murmur from the group.

From all corners of the room, bells tolled, their light tinging reverberating off the walls. The chanting started up again, low, the bass to the bells' soprano, and then the crowd parted to reveal a fire that had just been lit. I was startled for a moment that they'd let smoke touch this ancient place, but this was the Circle. Of course they would.

The moderator threw a handful of something into the fire and it flared high, blinding me and releasing the pungent scent of herbs. I felt Stellan wince. Fire was one of the only things in the world he was afraid of.

The moderator called something in a language I didn't know, and a smaller group of people stepped forward, holding knives.

"A baptism by flame unites the lines," the moderator said. This was the last part of the ceremony before the tattoos. I felt a tug in my gut. Were we really going through with this?

"Rule by blood!" the moderator announced.

"By blood," the crowd murmured again.

Sergei Vasilyev came forward. He sliced a line across his forearm and let the blood drip into the fire as the flames tried to lick at his skin. Then the moderator handed him something.

It was a small box, its lid hinged open. "This same blood, combined as one, will make the Circle complete," he proclaimed. Combining blood. That sounded as familiar as the box itself.

Mr. Vasilyev let another drop of blood fall into the box, and handed it off to his right. The next Circle family head, and the next, all the way down the line, did the same. The fire crackled, growing as if fueled by the offerings.

I had my eyes planted firmly on the box. Stellan pressed closer, his hand over mine at his elbow. He'd seen, too, and by the look in their eyes, so had Jack and Elodie. It might be the same replica box we'd seen last night. It was the same size and shape. But it looked— different, somehow.

The chanting grew louder. Stellan and I were each handed a knife of our own. By unspoken agreement, we stepped away from each other. The chanting grew frenzied as I came to the edge of the fire. The heat was like a wall this close. I put the tip of the knife to the forearm farthest from Stellan, and drew the blade across my skin. I felt a bead of sweat drip down my chest. I held my arm over the fire, as far in as I could reach, and watched the dark droplets sizzle as they fell.

I stepped back. The box was placed in my hands.

I knew immediately that, though it looked just like the one we'd seen last night, it was not the same. This was far older, like the one at the Melechs' was a toy. I held my arm over it, and let my blood drip inside onto wood already stained red.

And then I saw it. Etched into the back wall of the box was our symbol.

If anyone had spotted it, they might have assumed it had been specially engraved for today. But this carving was not new. I looked up. Stellan's eyes were burning into me like he was trying to read my mind. I tilted the box so he could see, and then glanced back at Jack and Elodie and let my eyes widen a fraction.

The moderator cleared his throat and gestured Stellan forward. The chanting continued.

Stellan stepped to the fire, letting his blood drip. He rejoined me, and I reluctantly handed him the box. Once we finished this, the ceremony would be all but done.

I could see the same thoughts swirl behind Stellan's eyes. He took the box. His blood dripped inside. The bells chimed like a chorus of heartbeats. Row after row, the Circle members got to their knees.

That's when Elodie screamed.

I jumped so hard, I almost knocked the box out of Stellan's hands. The chanting cut off abruptly.

"Run!" she yelled, pointing. "They're coming for us!"

It didn't matter that she was pointing at nothing. It didn't matter that it didn't make sense. This was her version of pulling a fire alarm, and it worked. Keepers were rushing to their families, hustling them toward the exit. People screamed, threw back the hoods on their robes.

"Get to the exit!" Elodie yelled. She grabbed the back of my robe, and Stellan's, and shoved us in the opposite direction. I saw what she was looking at. There were a couple of passageways off the back of the cavern. We were still holding the box. We'd take it and find another way out, pretending we'd gotten lost in the chaos.

I clung to Stellan's arm as we disappeared into the dark mouth of the tunnel. "I don't think there's any way out this way," I whispered.

We squinted into the box. The flames from the main cavern were the only light we had. I heard Elodie's voice, and Jack's, still ushering everyone out. "Look," I said. "The symbol is etched into some kind of metal strip that goes all the way around—"

And then there was a bang so loud, it sounded like the world above us had imploded.